A SONG I USED TO KNOW

GENALEA BARKER

IMMORTAL WORKS
SALT LAKE CITY

Immortal Works LLC
1505 Glenrose Drive
Salt Lake City, Utah 84104
Tel: (385) 202-0116

© 2023 Genalea Barker
genalea.wordpress.com

Cover Art by Lenore Stutznegger
lenorestutz.com

This book is a work of fiction. Names, characters, businesses, organizations, places, events and incidents either are the product of the author's imagination or are used fictitiously. Any resemblance to actual persons, living or dead, events, or locales is entirely coincidental.

ISBN 978-1-953491-69-5 (Paperback)
ASIN B0CNNBLBGN (Kindle)

For my parents, who are still adorable and in love after nearly 50 years.

And of course, for Brett. Our story might not be harrowing, but it's ours and I love it.

CHAPTER
1

Most of my life has been about survival—keep my head down, stay afloat, get by. But here I am, staring at my road not taken, with a second chance to make it happen. Robert Frost made the whole *two roads* scenario seem romantic and glamorous. I just feel like I'm having a panic attack. Or a stroke.

I wipe my clammy hands on my jeans, watching students file into the classroom—the very classroom I'd be in right now if I could just get my feet to *move*.

Why won't my feet move?

This is a terrible idea, that's why.

It would've been a better idea two years ago, back when I still had basic social skills and a sliver of courage. Why did I wait so long to do this?

Survival, Stevie. Remember?

Right. I guess it tracks I'd put college on hold after Uncle Gene died. I had bills to pay. Groceries to buy. But I had dreams once, too. Goals. Maybe they were juvenile, but they were mine. I need something to be mine again. Even if it's fifteen credits at East Washington College paid for exclusively by financial aid, not a full-ride scholarship to Stanford based on talent and merit. That dream was swallowed by Gene's diagnosis. Rotted by his cancer.

This is fine, Stevie. You're. Just. Fine.

Except I'm not. I'm frozen, much like the day Gene collapsed onto the pavement, and I just watched, useless as my brain devolved into mush and the world turned upside down.

I know how to calm my nerves; I've done it a million times before.

But do I really want to be known as the weird girl who hums to herself from day one?

Screw it.

I close my eyes, humming the same tune I've had stuck in my head since I was a child. Something my mother sang to me, haunting and beautiful in a minor key. Sadly, I've never been able to remember the words. They died with her.

Three rounds of my wordless tune and a deep breath later, I find a seat at a table only moments before a lanky, middle-aged professor takes his place at the podium.

He's midway through introductions when someone slips into the seat beside me—a girl with damp auburn hair sticking to her forehead as beads of sweat drip down her face. She's out of breath and near tears. Quietly, I ask if she's alright. She nods, chewing her lips, lids blinking over her emerald eyes.

Wasting little time on pleasantries, the professor passes around questionnaires and instructs us to interview our table mates.

My partner takes the initiative of sliding the paper in front of her and removing a notebook and pen from her bag. I want to ask if she's alright again, but my conversational skills are rusty at best. Instead, I follow her example, taking out my supplies.

She asks the first question on the pre-printed lists. "Are you native to Spokane, or did you move here for school?"

"Born and raised."

"Me too." We both scribble on our papers.

"That's kind of a weird question, don't you think? I mean, who moves to Spokane to attend a junior college?"

"Probably no one," she says, her features softening. "So why choose EWC?"

"It was kind of my only realistic option."

She squints, perhaps pondering my answer, then moves on. How old am I? Which semester of school am I in? My answers pique her interest. If I'm twenty-one, why am I just starting out? Have I been working? Traveling?

I could tell her my legal guardian and only family in the world became ill just after I graduated high school, and I took a detour from college, instead spending a year watching him die slowly. That it drained the ambition and nearly the life out of me. That I've spent the last two years working at Credit Zen—the least *zen* workplace in the world—talking to people only behind the safety of a phone and computer screen. That last spring, when they offered me my third promotion, I went home and applied for EWC and filled out FAFSA forms because I realized if I didn't, I might very well die working in a smelly cubicle in a hellhole call center.

"It was finally the right time."

She jots my ambiguous answers in her neon notebook and licks her lips.

"Are you sure you're alright?" I ask.

She bobs her head but quickly transitions to shaking it. She's definitely going to cry.

Oh no.

Forget *comforting* someone; can I even remember how to talk to people? Without a script staring at me?

"I think it's supposed to get easier," I manage. "You know, the whole finding your rhythm thing."

"I hope so. I mean, I was so certain I could do this. So eager to prove to my parents I *could* handle this. But it's only the first day, and I'm already a hot mess."

"Everyone's a mess on the first day," I say, attempting to console her.

"Not my level of mess." A lonely tear slides down her ivory cheek. She wipes her face with the back of her hand. "You know, I spent most of the last year building houses in Ecuador. You'd think I'd be able to manage a couple college classes. But I've already gotten a parking ticket." She lowers her voice to whisper-scream. "My parents are gonna kill me."

Oh geez. How many times have I heard that one?

I got a C in Algebra, my parents are gonna kill me.

I broke my phone, my parents are gonna kill me.

If I'm out past my curfew again, my parents will kill me.

All these years, I've never responded with, "At least you've got parents." Sometimes I wanted to. I mean, I can't remember the sound of my parents' voices. What I wouldn't give to hear them scolding me for a mistake.

I find a clean but slightly wadded tissue from my backpack and hand it over. "Ecuador, huh? Tell me about that?" Maybe she just needs a distraction.

She sniffs, wiping her eyes then nose with the tissue. "I got my GED when I was sixteen—homeschool kid. I didn't feel like starting college yet, but I also didn't feel like working the cash register somewhere. You know?"

I nod, even though I don't know. *Choice* wasn't something I had a lot of experience with. Especially not in recent years.

"I went with my church group on two different missions. Four months each. They were awesome experiences, and I'm glad I went, but I'm struggling to adjust back. It's hard to explain but it's like I'm coming out of a safety bubble."

That, I could understand a little better. In my own way.

"Change takes time," I say. It's all I've got for now.

She nods. "Thanks for being nice. I needed a friend today."

The sound of *friend* sends a trickle of warmth through my veins. "I did too. What's your name, by the way?"

"Merrin."

"I love that."

A timid smile forms on her lips.

"I'm Stevie."

"Stevie?"

"Technically, it's Stephanie. But I don't remember the last time anyone called me that."

She laughs. "I get it. I have five siblings, and I think maybe two of us regularly go by our full given name. Most of the time, it's nicknames."

"Five?"

She rolls her eyes. "We're not *ultra*-religious or anything."

"No, I wasn't thinking that. I promise." How different her life must be. I might like to have a sister or brother. Maybe not *five*. But...someone.

Merrin takes a breath, releasing what's left of her tension, and shoves the used tissue into her pocket.

"Next question?" she asks. I nod. "What is your favorite brand of toilet paper?"

I snatch the list from her, snorting. "That's not seriously a question, is it?"

"Nah. Just curious." She offers me a deliberately creepy wink.

"You and I, Merrin. We're gonna get along just swell."

I NEVER KNEW three classes could exhaust me so thoroughly, but despite the utter fatigue, this first day feels like a rite of passage, and I can't shake the feeling I might be doing the right thing. That my encounter with Merrin was a good omen, and I might not die alone and miserable. Such hopeful, promising thoughts, I can hardly stand it.

With thirty minutes to spare before my work-study shift at the on-campus daycare begins, I sit on a bench and eat my sad, bland peanut butter sandwich. Last time I went grocery shopping they only had name-brand jelly, and I'm not the kind of person who spends an extra two dollars for name-brand jelly. I wish I could be. Even if I *had* the budget for it, I'm not sure I could get over that mental block. Growing up poor messes with your ability to splurge, even if that *splurge* is a matter of pennies.

Credit Zen paid okay, but they wouldn't work around my school schedule. It was a relief, honestly. Like I was being given permission to move on. Granted, I'm still questioning my sanity over quitting a full-time job to enroll in a junior college and take a part-time work-study position. I'm not typically one to veer from feet-firmly-planted scenarios. Once I forced myself to leap, though, things just kind of *worked out.*

I thought it was a joke at first. The universe pulling me in close, waiting for me to let my guard down right before it slapped me in the face. But that hasn't happened.

Yet.

My stomach teased by cheap bread and peanut butter—just enough to make me feel hungrier—I unlock my bike and pedal to Bright Beginnings for my first shift.

Margorie, the director and possible angel who gave me the job based on nothing but my promise of competency and experience providing end-of-life care for Uncle Gene, greets me at the front door.

"The first day is crazy," she says. "I've got about fifty fires to put out, so I hope you like being thrown in the deep end."

Like it? No. Used to it? Hell yeah.

Before I answer, a young woman about my age comes jogging down the hall, calling, "Sorry, Marge, but I can't find the hair nets." We make brief eye contact, and she smiles.

"In the cabinet above the stove," Margorie says, then gestures to the other girl and me. "Scarlett, Stevie. Stevie, Scarlett." We nod at each other, and Scarlett jogs away.

Margorie points to the preschool room. "You met Jill when you interviewed, right?" I nod. "Great. Follow her lead, help her however she needs, keep the tiny humans alive. Got it?"

"Keep the tiny humans alive," I repeat.

She pats me on the shoulder. "Atta girl." After a quick adjustment of her pink-rimmed glasses, she smooths her silver bob, then returns to her office to answer the phone.

"Bright Beginnings, this is Marge." She looks up from her desk and gives me a final thumbs up. I salute and turn for the pre-k room.

I'm not sure exactly what I'm expecting when I open the door, but fifteen toddlers simultaneously shooting me hopeful grins that immediately fade into disappointed pouts wasn't quite it. A few begin crying for their parents.

Oooooh.

"First day," Jill calls from somewhere amidst the sea of toddler tears. "They'll adjust."

And they do. Most forgive me for being "Miss Stevie" ("Miss *Stebie*" if they can't quite pronounce their *V*s yet) and not their parent, and we stumble into a haphazard rhythm. Messy and chaotic as this job may be, I already love it.

After a few hours hanging with these kids—answering their questions, helping them tie their shoes, singing silly songs with them —there's a swelling inside my heart I *think* might be pride. Or hope. As a bonus, they serve the kids an afternoon snack, and *I get to eat, too*! Salvation in the form of yogurt and graham crackers.

By the end of the day, I'm certain starting school was the right choice, even if it means a little extra struggle financially. At least the house is secure.

My pitiful, gloomy house.

The longer I live here alone, the more I hate it. This place used to *almost* feel like home—a safe space. Back before Gene got sick. But now? Now it's hard to imagine coming home to a worse sight at the end of my day.

It's little more than a depressing shrine—a reminder of all the people I've lost. All the dreams I left behind. I could sell it, but where would I go? An overpriced apartment building somewhere? *If* I could even find one that would accept me on my wages and non-existent credit history.

So, I keep the house, night after night, sleeping on a mattress on the living room floor, surrounded by stacks of second-hand books and CDs. Aside from the coffee table and old stereo, there isn't much else to speak of. I sold uneccesary appliances and any furniture that was in good condition, hauled everything reeking of cigarette smoke to the side of the road, and bid farewell.

Now it just reeks of solitude. Or maybe that's the empty refrigerator.

I grab an old family portrait from the mantel, brushing my thumb against those long-ago faces. Happy young parents who thought they had a lifetime ahead of them with the bright-eyed, honey-haired toddler in their arms. "Hey guys," I whisper. I hold my parents to my chest, sinking to my mattress.

I roll onto my side, clutching my picture in one hand and selecting a CD with the other—I need the company. I've consumed music like oxygen over the years, hopeful I'd find out my nameless lullaby was real. Each time I grabbed a stack of discards from the library or hit up a garage sale, I imagined that melody miraculously bursting from the speakers, gifting me a long-lost treasure. But a dozen years, thousands of hours, and countless genres later, the song remains an enigma.

I asked Uncle Gene at least a hundred times if he remembered the lyrics, but he never obliged.

"Sing me Mommy's song," I'd beg.

"Hush, Stevie."

Always the same. *Be quiet, Stevie. Stop asking, Stevie. Give it up, Stevie.*

Even on his deathbed, Uncle Gene swore it was all a false memory I conjured in my despair.

"I've never heard it before. Let me sleep, Stevie. I'm tired."

I can't blame the guy. If I'd been him, I probably would've resented me, too.

I don't remember much about the night of the accident, but I found an old newspaper clipping once.

Icy road conditions.

Drowsiness a probable factor.

My car seat ejected before our sedan rolled down an embankment, killing my parents, leaving me the sole survivor.

Miracle.

Lucky.

Blessed.

I'm not sure who was *luckier*, me or Uncle Gene. Sure, I woke up in a hospital room to find out my parents were dead, but Gene was thrown in front of a filial bus at the same moment he lost his only sister.

Before he became my parent, Uncle Gene adored me; I have a few pictures to prove it. But that was the beautiful before, when he was still a carefree, sometimes babysitter. Before my father's carelessness left me behind. Afterward, the hope drained out of him. He tried his best to love me, but he could never bury the past.

Then along came cancer. Even if trying to beat cancer wasn't akin to capturing the wind in a net, I don't think he would've had the resolve to fight it. Once that diagnosis came, he willingly succumbed. What was left to live for, except a child he resented, who'd given up everything to care for him while he slowly slipped away?

I start the stereo and roll back onto the mattress as music bounces off the barren walls of my house. With a deep breath, I tell myself, "I can do this," even though I'm not sure I can. Hugging the picture back to my chest, I absorb the music and the memory of my parents' love, letting the world fall away.

CHAPTER
2

Growing up, most of my friendships were on the surface. Strictly shallow end. We hung out at school, hardly ever outside it. People don't exactly line up around the block to be besties with the poor girl, especially not the one who lives with her grouchy uncle.

So when Merrin continues striking up conversations, asking me questions like she's genuinely interested in me, it's hard to accept she might actually mean it. At first, I worry I'm her adopted pet. Pitiable. A too-thin, mangy dog afraid of people, roaming in back alleys searching for scraps. A stray Merrin simply wants to feed and take home as a project.

But the more I'm around her, the quieter those cynical voices in my head become. When I begin actively participating in our conversations rather than being a silent partner, pieces of my former personality resurface.

Between consistent interactions with the animated and occasionally overzealous Merrin, and my daily shift with rambunctious toddlers, all those parts of me I've let wither and wane start uncoiling, creeping back toward the light. I'm a living person again, not merely a ghost of my former self.

Merrin lends me a validity I haven't known I needed. And the daycare kids? Well...

Bright Beginnings gives me *purpose*.

I use my knowledge of music to bring light and silliness into the classroom. The kids love how I seem to have a song for literally every occasion (even if sometimes, I fudge the lyrics a bit—they don't need to know). It becomes a game to them—testing me with random words or names to see if I can come up with a song to fit.

Jill, the head teacher, is on board with this most of the time, except when the class gets a little too riled up. On the whole, I think she at least appreciates my enthusiasm.

Scarlett, another work-study student, spends most of her shift in the kitchen but occasionally floats between classrooms. We're in the same place often enough that we graduate from *acquaintances* to *friends* without much effort.

After years of seclusion, I have *two* friends and a routine beyond waking up, existing in a constant state of disillusionment, and sleeping. I'm no longer stifled by predictability, which is as wonderful as it is occasionally terrifying. I'm still not used to people striking up conversations, so when Merrin jumps into my line of sight as I'm locking up my bike, I nearly fall backward.

"Have you finished your 'How To' speech yet?" she asks.

"Murphy!" I gasp, my hand to my heart.

"Wow, you're jumpy," she says. "Who's Murphy?"

After a calming breath, I ask, "Ever heard of Murphy's Law?"

She knits her brow. "Anything that can go wrong, will?" I nod. "I still don't get it."

I laugh, then start toward the building. She walks in step with me, and it's strange how this provides a sense of comfort and familiarity.

"It's nothing," I say. How can I explain a bizarre coping mechanism like blaming all the garbage parts of my life on Murphy's Law and using it as an expletive? I settle on changing the subject. "I haven't even started my speech yet. What about you?"

"No, but I've finally settled on a topic."

"Which is?"

"How to properly apply eyeliner. Everyone does it wrong. Drives me crazy." She tucks her hair behind her ear, sighing as though the thought of educating the world on this subject exhausts her.

"Did you wear a lot of eyeliner building houses?" I tease.

She rams her shoulder into mine. "Look, I'm not shallow or

anything. Or maybe I am. I just think anything worth doing is worth doing *right*. If you're gonna spend time at the mirror applying makeup, you should at least know what you're doing."

"And this is why I don't even bother."

"Well, your skin is flawless, can't say I blame you. I'd go au naturel every day if I looked like you."

I wish I were the kind of person who could say thank you right now, but compliments are so foreign to me. I swallow and stare at the ground as we approach the classroom.

"Hey, you wanna get together this weekend?" Merrin asks. "Help each other with our speeches? I could use an audience to practice on besides my parents."

I take too long to respond, and her whole body deflates as she takes a seat at our table.

"Good idea," I say, sitting next to her. "I could use the practice. Public speaking is not my forte."

She laughs. "Mine, either. Part of why I'm in this class, if I'm being honest."

I side-eye her. This girl has never shied away from conversation with me, but she's admitting to taking Speech 101 on purpose? Not as some course requirement?

"You seem pretty confident," I say.

"I'm not," she says, shaking her head. "You're just easy to talk to."

Again, I don't know how to respond. It's never occurred to me Merrin might need someone like me as much as I need someone like her. It's never occurred to me I could be a benefit to *anyone*, really.

"You in the dorms?" she asks. "We could hang there. I mean, you're welcome to come to my house, but my parents are...well, *parents*."

I huff a quiet laugh. "So long as your parents don't think it's weird a twenty-something is randomly popping by to hang with their teenage daughter?"

She scoffs. "Well, rude. I'm almost eighteen. But please. Nothing fazes my mom. Youngest of six, remember? She's too tired to be surprised."

We're about a minute from class starting, so I pull out my ancient, second-hand cell phone Gene bought me as a graduation present, the intention being I'd have a way to call him when I went off to California. Merrin eyes the relic with deep concern.

"Hey," I say, "it may not be pretty, but it's what we're working with. Just put your number in there, and we'll hash out the details later."

SINCE GENE'S DIAGNOSIS, I've let myself slip into extreme seclusion. Everything imploded right after graduation. *Right* after. We were supposed to go out to eat. Commemorate the big day and all I'd accomplished—Valedictorian and a full scholarship to Stanford between music and academics. Graduation day marked the first time he ever said he was proud of me. Well, he alluded to it. Close enough.

"You did it, kid. And you did it well. Let's celebrate."

I think I said thank you, but I don't remember. The only thing on my mind was the graduation party. Oblivious to how pale Gene looked under the orange sunset, I yammered on, reminding him I would be leaving with my friends that night, not returning until morning. When he collapsed, I was so dumbstruck I hardly had the sense to call for help.

He refused treatment for the cancer, claiming he was too old—a lie—and the disease was too strong. Arguing with Gene never yielded positive results, so I granted his wish, postponing college to care for him until cancer eventually did claim him, almost a year later. No one could have guessed it would have played out so long. The doctors assured Gene if he did nothing, he'd be lucky to have three months. Gene took care of his "arrangements" about five minutes after we left the hospital.

"It won't be long now," he told me. "But you'll get along well without me. I know I've been hard on you, Stevie Rae, but it's made you tough. And you're smart, too. You keep it up. Don't take no crap from nobody, and you'll be fine."

It was the second time he tried to tell me he was proud. The last, too.

He gradually disappeared until he was unrecognizable. Awkward as our relationship was, as much as he resented me, he was all I had left in the world. Letting him go felt like saying goodbye to a part of myself. Like there was barely anything left of me.

My shallow-end, surface friends were a year deep into their college experiences and had forgotten about me completely for all I knew. I was alone, newly left in charge of a house, no clue what I was doing. Nothing changed for two years, not even with my job—it was strictly a source of survival, not a social outlet.

So, while making a single, sincere friend might barely warrant a mention for some people, it's a breakthrough for me. A championship trophy to cling to.

†

Merrin's house is situated in a quiet cul-de-sac. Lovely, but somehow intimidating, the autumn *Welcome* wreath on the door notwithstanding.

Before I even knock, the door flies open, and I'm face to face with a smiling Merrin. "You made it!" she says, grabbing my wrist. She pulls me through the door and slams it behind me.

"So, this Stevie is real, is she?" an unknown voice calls with skepticism.

"You're hilarious, mother." Merrin rolls her eyes and—still holding my wrist—leads me into the living room where her mom sits, knitting. "Mom, Stevie. Stevie, Mom." She points back and forth as she introduces us.

Their living room is such a stark contrast to mine, it stops me in my tracks. There's a huge sectional and two recliners. A TV mounted above a fireplace and built-in shelves on either side. Framed family pictures on the mantel and hanging on walls. The room smells like vanilla and leather.

Wearing a nervous grin, I wave my hand once at Merrin's mom. "Hi, um—"

"Call me Nancy," she says, taking her eyes off her work and offering me a warm smile. Her hands adjust, revealing her project—a yellow baby bootie. "So, Merrin, she looks too mature and sensible to be hanging around you. What lie did you tell to get her over here?"

"That I'd pay her."

"It's true," I interject. "And I need the scratch."

"Alright then," Nancy says, "you two enjoy your business transaction."

"Dirty," Merrin whispers.

"Watch it," her mother half-heartedly warns before Merrin leads me away.

"Your mom seems...normal."

"Yeah, she's pretty chill. Benefit to being the youngest, I guess. She used to be fairly uptight and strict, but now..." She shrugs. "Meh."

Merrin opens the door to her room, and I have to wait for my eyes to adjust to the brightness. Shades of orange, pink, and green adorn her walls, with bedding to match. Reading my face, she sighs.

"Yeah. I know. My parents immediately regretted their decision to let me choose the colors. It was my birthday present a few years back, and my dad says it *stays* this way until I move out. Something about 'living with the consequences of my actions' or whatever."

I laugh. "Hey, own it. You like bright things. Nothing wrong with that." Though it begs the question why she seems to like me so much.

"It's more that I love color. I've never been able to pick a favorite."

"I get it. I'm that way with music. I couldn't pick a favorite genre, let alone a favorite song."

"Yes! You get it."

We situate ourselves on Merrin's bed with our notebooks. "So," I say, "I was thinking maybe for my topic—"

"Hey, what are you doing next weekend?" she asks.

I know we're the only two people in her room, and I know she's talking to me, but still, I look from side to side. "Me?"

She laughs. "Duh, you."

"Nothing. Why?"

"It's my birthday. Wanna drive to Coeur d'Alene with me? Go to Silverwood? Ride all the roller coasters and flirt with all the boys and eat all the salted pretzels?"

"Um, wow. I'm not... I mean, I don't think..."

"It's my treat. Well, my parents' treat. It's what I asked for this year. Admission for me and a friend."

I cock my brow. "Are you sure you don't want to take someone you've known longer than five minutes? I mean, you can't even be sure I'm not a serial killer yet."

She twists her lips and lifts a shoulder. "It's a risk I'm willing to take."

I want to say something, but I'm too busy trying to tame my smile and utter shock.

"What do you say?" she asks. "You like roller coasters?"

"I've never been on one," I admit, cringing. "I'll probably puke."

She tilts her head from side to side. "Don't worry. I'll hold your hair back."

On the verge of tears, I find a pen and open to a blank page in my notebook. If I speak, I'll cry. Instead, I draw a heart with a smiley face on it and show it to her.

She grins, nodding. "Yeah. You make my heart happy, too."

CHAPTER
3

There was a time when the turn of the seasons meant only a change in scenery. Autumn brought with it vibrant color, a sense of letting go, whimsical pumpkin décor on front porches. Now, this mid-October shift in temperature fills me with a deep, aching sense of dread.

The mattress on my living room floor isn't just some random quirk of mine. To regulate the temperature of my living space, afford heat in the coldest months, and stay cool in the summer, I closed up the bedrooms. The windows are ancient, single-pane jokes. Might as well be cling wrap. Luckily, in the fall of my senior year, a brutal storm sent a branch through the front window. Insurance covered a new one.

But even huddled in that living room, I'm not sure I can last the winter on work-study wages.

The wind picks up as I pedal to Bright Beginnings, weaving through the tree branches. Each howl an accumulating list of worries.

Heat.

New shoes.

Groceries.

Property taxes.

Heeeeaaaat.

The anxiety weighs me down. By the time I lock up my bike, I feel three inches shorter and a hundred pounds heavier. My phone buzzes, and I open up the text from Merrin—a selfie we took at Silverwood.

Forgot to send you this one! It's my favorite.

It's a good picture. A great picture, actually. But even those smiling faces on my screen don't lighten my load. Lacking the enthusiasm for a proper reply, I shove my phone in my back pocket and slump toward the building, head drooping, grumbling inwardly.

Buck up, Stevie. Deep breaths. Don't cry, don't cry, don't cry. Never let them see you down. Deep br— Something cold and hard knocks me off my feet, cutting off my inner monologue.

"Murphy!"

I lose my footing, falling backward onto the ground, my phone crunching on impact. *Lovely. One more thing I can't afford.*

"Sorry!" calls a deep voice.

I dust myself off. "My fault. I wasn't looking."

"Neither was I. I just swung the door open. I'm so sorry." A tan hand appears in front of my face, and I accept it, awkwardly maneuvering my legs and feet to stand back up.

"Thanks," I say, brushing tiny pebbles off my palms before looking up to meet my assailant—a tall stranger clutching a few pieces of yellow paper. Probably just a dad dropping his kid off for the afternoon, though I've never seen him before. And I would have noticed him—all that dark, curly hair. So thick and long enough to tuck behind his ears.

"You're not hurt?" He seems concerned, though hurried and distant.

"Nope. Thanks for the hand up."

He holds the door open for me, and I give him a small wave as I pass, mumbling to myself. "I hate this day."

Margorie hollers at me from her office the moment I step into the building. "Promising new post on the bulletin board, Stevie, if you're looking for a little extra cash."

With a quick "Thanks," I rush to the bulletin. A yellow paper—same color as the hurried stranger's—posted in the middle catches my attention. I rip it from the corkboard and read as I walk back outside, not wanting to waste any time. Key phrases spring me into action.

Babysitter needed, Evenings, Three-year-old boy, 4:45-10 p.m. weekdays.

"Excuse me!" I call without thinking. "Wait! Sir!"

No my gosh, Stevie. What are you doing?

But I keep running toward this complete stranger standing beside his Subaru, one leg already propped inside.

"Hi," I breathe, halting.

"Hi?" He brings both feet back to solid ground and folds his arms across his chest.

"Is this your flyer?" I hold the creased paper in front of him as I catch my breath.

"Yes," he answers, slow and inquisitive. *Almost* amused.

"I beg your pardon. This is rudely presumptuous of me, but I'd like the job." I pause, wincing. "Yeah, listening to myself just now was embarrassing. Regardless, I stand by it."

He touches his tongue to his tooth, and I can't help admiring the shape of his mouth. "No retractions?"

"Nope. I'm doubling down."

"Well, by all means, state your case. You've got two minutes." He looks at his watch, completely serious.

"Oh, wow. Okay." I blow out a quick puff of air. "Well, for starters, I work *here*. The preschool room mainly, three and four-year-olds. I love it—really. And the kids seem to like me. I could work the hours you listed without any conflicts, ever. I had to pass a criminal background check to work here, I'm fingerprinted, current on my vaccines, and I just did my CPR cert at the end of September. So, I've got that going for me." I pause to take a breath. "I swear I'm not a crazy person." Except I am, and he knows it. No job for Stevie. I consider turning and walking away in shame without waiting for a reply.

"How long have you worked here?"

Ah-ha! Hope!

"It's my first semester here." He sighs. *Dang it.* I hurry on. "I mean, I have a resume with my other work experience and references, but I was a customer service rep at a call center, not necessarily helpful when caring for toddlers. Unless you count remaining calm while dealing with unreasonable people." He snickers, and I panic. "Oh gosh, that wasn't intended as an insult toward your kid."

"No, no. I get it. They don't call them threenagers for nothing." His grin widens, and my heart flip-flops.

Lord, give me strength. That mouth.

I clear my throat. "Yeah. I got cursed at a lot in customer service, but nothing like since I started working here."

"Really? Like what."

"Oh, some I wouldn't repeat. My favorite this week was 'damn teacher.'"

"Let me guess. You enforced the rules?"

"Precisely. A grievous offense. I'm the worst."

"Sounds like it." But he says this with a smile. "Do you have your resume on you?"

"Right. Yes." I dig through my bag for a spare resume. I printed several back in August for work-study interviews but only ever needed one for Marge. I've never taken them out of my backpack. They have, however, slipped from the sheet protector I originally put them in. They're torn, crumpled, and unsalvageable.

"Never mind," I sigh, defeated. "It's toast. Sorry. Not really professional of me, is it?" Tacked on top of the fact that I've already acted like a raving lunatic.

He offers a sympathetic frown. "I was in college once too. Don't sweat it."

"I can print out a new one," I say, half-smiling, half-wincing.

He nods, pondering a moment, glancing around the parking lot at nothing in particular. A gust of wind blows curly locks in his face. As he swipes them away, I can't help but notice the lack of a wedding ring on his finger.

"When do you get off?" he asks.

I shake off my intrusive focus on his features. "Quarter after four."

"Why don't you come by and meet Daniel—my son—after you get off? We'll see how you two get along."

"Perfect." He gives me his address and directions. "I'll see you again soon then, Mr.—"

"Shepard."

I glance down at the paper I'm holding, and of course, right in front of me in bold letters:

Contact Mason Shepard.

"Ha! Right there all along. Sorry about that."

He squints, like it's silly of me to apologize. It probably is, but I'm giddy. This guy is giving me a chance even though I ran after him with my arms flailing like a crazed pigeon.

"Well," I say, taking a calming breath. "I have to get inside. Thank you for your time. Sorry if I held you up." Now I've apologized twice. But I walk away like nothing awkward just happened and start my shift.

So suave, Stevie. So suave.

Mr. Shepard's directions take me to an upscale neighborhood about two miles from EWC; roughly halfway between campus and my house. Really the perfect location, considering my mode of transportation. Easy enough to bike or walk. So long as I've got a working flashlight and pepper spray, I'll be fine. *If* I get the job.

His house is large but not ostentatious. It almost looks out of place in this neighborhood, like it belongs on a few acres in the middle of nowhere. There's a large front porch with a wooden swing, a detached two-car garage, and a basketball hoop in the driveway. All that's missing is a white-picket fence. Much like Merrin's house, and in total contrast to mine, this looks like a *home*.

I hesitate on the sidewalk a moment before approaching the house, pulling my bike alongside me. A nervous energy buzzes through me, and I miss my kickstand twice before getting it right. I feel underdressed and windblown as I make the final steps toward his door. My jeans are frayed at the heel and thin at the knees. My faded navy tee has a crusty patch from a kid—several, in fact—spilling milk on me at snack time an hour ago, and my hair is disheveled per usual. Fantastic. I knock anyway.

The door opens before I can reach up to tuck stray hairs behind my ears, but I paint on a smile. Mr. Shepard greets me with a blank expression. Tall, dark, handsome to my eyes—from his well-groomed beard to the Chuck Taylors on his feet—I have to force myself not to gawk at my potential employer.

"Mr. Shepard. Hi."

"You look out of breath," is his reply.

I can work with it. "I rode my bike."

"Oh." He peeks outside at my once yellow bike, now washed out by the sun, then steps aside. "Come in."

I take time to wipe my feet on the *Welcome* mat.

"So, forgive me," he says. "I never asked your name. But when I called Margorie and described the, um, *petite* girl with a unique vernacular, she said, 'Sounds like Stevie.'"

I laugh, not just because he's afraid to call me short, but because he legitimately never asked my name, and I never offered. And *still*, he agreed to give me a shot. Either this is my lucky day, or I'm about to become a headline and a cautionary tale. Again.

What would the papers say this time?

We don't blame her; he was cute.

"Well, one, you can say *short*. It's not secret. Or offensive. Unless you're about to start quoting a certain Randy Newman song. Second, yes. I'm Stevie. No wires crossed."

He clamps his lips as if trying to hide a smile, then coughs.

"How old are you, Stevie, if I might ask?"

"Twenty-one."

"That's good." I raise an eyebrow. "I just mean I wanted someone a little more mature than an eighteen-year-old fresh from the shelter of mom and dad. I was eighteen once and—well, that's all I meant."

"Understood." A sweaty lock of hair slides off my forehead and into my eye. I slick it back, attempting to tuck it into my ponytail.

Mr. Shepard draws in a sharp breath. "Oh, gosh. I'm so sorry," he says.

"For what?"

"The bruise. Your forehead."

"Oh. I hadn't noticed." Though now that I'm touching it, it's definitely tender.

"I feel awful."

I wave a dismissive hand. "It's nothing. I'll live."

He shakes his head, a subtle grin playing on his lips. "Well, then. I guess you should meet the little man." He gestures, and I follow him out of the entryway and up the stairs. "He's in the playroom with his grandma. She's been watching him for me, but as much as she will *never* admit it, it's too much for her. She's tired, and she misses her quiet evenings at home with my dad."

I nod, holding in all the personal questions arising.

The tinkering of toys and giggles of innocence drift down the hall, growing louder as we approach the playroom. Mr. Shepard's mother, slightly round and gray, sits on the floor with little Daniel in her lap.

Daniel has his father's dark hair but with shorter, tighter curls. Darling. His little voice, which can't quite enunciate properly, is easily the sweetest sound I've ever heard. He holds two cars in his lap, one larger than the other, detailing the adventures of Daddy Car and Baby Car. Mr. Shepard and I hesitate at the door to listen, but as soon as Daniel notices us standing there, he pauses.

"Who's that?" he asks, big, blue eyes on me.

"Daniel, this is Stevie. Stevie, that's my Danny Boy. And my mother, Miranda."

"Hi, Daniel." I kneel, eye level with him. "Is it alright if I come in and sit down?"

He squints, twisting his lips as he ponders. "Mmmm, okay."

I take a seat on the floor and cross my legs. "I liked your story. What do the cars do next?"

"Dey go to da hopipal."

I speak enough *toddler* to decipher. "Why'd they go to the hospital? What happened?"

"Daddy Car got huwt."

"Bummer! Did the doctors get him all fixed up?"

"Dey gabe him a shot. Den, he got all stwong, and he could climb da walls, and he was Spidoman!"

"Hold up. Plot twist. This was an origin story?" He laughs at my enthusiasm. "I did *not* see that coming. Very crafty, little man."

He extends his little hand toward me, and I reach for it. He leaves the comfort of his grandma's lap and sits in mine. I keep my calm while inwardly cheering. I'm *crushing* this interview, and toddlers are notoriously judgmental.

"Did you seed my Spidoman costume?" Daniel asks, holding one of my hands in both of his, examining it.

"You have a Spiderman costume?" I increase my excitement to match his. He looks at me then, flashing a smile that showcases one perfect dimple. Only one. "No way."

He nods. "Uh-huh. I hab *all* kinds of supohewo costumes."

"Really? You're so lucky. I don't have *any* superhero costumes. Is Spiderman your favorite?"

"Yeah!"

"He's my favorite, too!"

He tugs his shoulders to his ears, beaming. "I love to be Spidoman. He goes like dis!" Jumping up, he shows off his web-slinging stance.

"Whoa. You did that *just* like him. Are you sure your name isn't really Peter Parker?"

He returns to my lap, throwing his head back in a laugh, his hands coming up to cover his toothy grin. I never knew I could swoon over a child. But this kid? I don't understand it, but he already has my heart. If he says *jump*, I'll build a trampoline.

"My name isn't Peto Parko!" he says when his giggles subside. "I'm Danol Mason Shepowd."

"My mistake," I concede. "You want to hear a secret?" He nods. I bring my tone low and secretive. "My last name really *is* Parker."

His eyes widen. "Can you stay and play supohewoes wif me today?"

"Danny Boy," Mason interrupts from the doorway, "maybe Stevie can play Superhero another day. Right now, I need to talk to her for a minute. Would you like Stevie to come back and play with you again?"

"Yes, please."

Oh, my heart.

"Why don't you take Grandma downstairs and help her with dinner, alright?"

"Okay!"

Daniel follows Miranda out of the room. "Gramma Randa, we could have cookies for dinner?"

Miranda tousles his hair. "If you can make cookies out of spaghetti, sure."

"He's a clever kid," I observe. "Polite, too."

"Clever?" Mason says. "Absolutely. Polite? Some of the time."

"Regardless, his vocabulary and comprehension are rather amazing."

"Yeah, he's smart." He ponders a minute, like he's simply thinking about how much he loves his life. Lucky guy. "He's a good kid. But he's had a bit of a tantrum regression lately."

"Gotcha."

"I'm sure it's just an adjustment period and he'll be fine, but it's been brutal."

I wince. "I imagine."

"It's always something. Every time you think you're settling into a routine...turns out you're wrong." I nod, unsure how to respond as a non-parent. Eventually, he sighs, continuing, "Look, I'm impressed. The interaction you two just shared was... I mean, he seems to *really* like you."

"The feeling is mutual," I say. "He's adorable."

"I hear that a lot."

"Well, you would."

He laughs, shaking his head. "You understood him so well."

"Toddlers are my jam."

"Well, I spoke at length with Margorie, then with your supervising teacher. Jill?"

"Yes. Jill."

"They had infinitely wonderful things to say about you. Jill says you implemented a music curriculum in her classroom?"

I cough a restrained laugh. "It's generous of her to put it that way. I'm just a classroom aide. But yes, I started doing short music lessons with the kids a couple times a week."

"Like what? Singing?"

"We sing. Sometimes we use egg shakers or mini tambourines to practice keeping a steady rhythm. Basic stuff. Sometimes we'll put things to music to help kids remember important things like how to spell their names or their phone numbers. Nothing advanced, but it's fun."

His lip twitches, deep brown eyes scanning my face. "That's... They can't possibly pay you enough for that as a work-study."

"That's not the kids' fault."

He studies me a little longer. I can't tell if I've impressed him or he's passing judgment. It's quiet for a few moments. Almost awkward but not quite.

Mesmerized by his features once again, my thoughts come out like word vomit. "I thought brown eyes were dominant."

Good golly, Stevie Rae.

"What?" he asks, then he huffs a quick laugh. "Oh, yeah. Danny's a mutant or something. I don't know." Mason Shepard waves a flippant hand, either not noticing or not caring that I've been studying his eyes.

"Well," he says, "I need to be getting to work soon, and I'm getting an oddly strong gut feeling about this. I'm going to trust it and pray I'm not wrong. When can you start?"

"Monday?" *Is this really happening?*

"Do you cook at all?"

"Yes." *This can't be happening.*

"Most days, I'll have dinner taken care of before I go. Something already in the oven, or at least ready for it. But there will be the rare day when you'll need to assemble a meal."

"Not a problem at all." *I think this is really happening!*

"You're welcome to eat with him, of course. If the weather permits, he likes to go to the park down the street. He goes to bed between seven-thirty and eight. Beforehand he gets a small snack, then it's PJs, brush teeth, a story, and off to bed. Sound like something you can handle?"

"Absolutely."

"Once he's in bed, you can do your homework or watch TV or whatever—keep it PG-13, please, in case he sneaks down. And no guests."

"No guests. No smut," I say.

He fights off a laugh, then clears his throat. "Do you smoke? Drink? Because that's all well and good so long as you're not doing it on my property when you're looking after my son."

"Mr. Shepard, I don't drink." Who could afford it, seriously? "And my uncle—who was considered a 'light smoker'—died of lung cancer. I would never touch a cigarette. I don't do any drugs. I don't swear. Well, okay, that's a lie." He lets a chuckle escape, then bites down on his lips. "Let's just say I keep it G-rated around kids."

"Good." He nods, a hint of amusement in his eyes. Then, more seriously, he says, "I'm sorry about your uncle."

I reply with a weak, "Yeah," stunned at the realization I've said it aloud—something I've never done. *Uncle Gene is dead.* Now it's escaped so swiftly, my brain is struggling to catch up.

When he brings up wages, I refrain from choking. He's offering to pay twice what I was expecting. No more adding water to the last bits of my shampoo to make it last longer. No more involuntarily losing weight because I'm struggling to afford food.

This man is a godsend, and more attractive the longer I look at him. The curls tucked behind his ears, the kempt beard, the sleeves of his flannel shirt rolled up to his elbows. Strap a guitar to him, and he'll be ready for an Open Mic Night. Does he play guitar? If he plays guitar, I'm doomed. It doesn't make sense I'm still attracted to musicians after what the last one put me through, but even if I don't *trust* them, I still like to look. Further proof of my damage, I guess.

Following him down the stairs, I convey my gratitude. "Mr. Shepard, thank you so much."

"Mason. You can call me Mason."

"Noted." I hesitate at the front door. "So, I'll see you Monday afternoon?"

"Yes."

"Not to push my luck, but why?" He stares while I gather my thoughts. "Back at Bright Beginnings, after I chased you down like a lunatic, why did you stand calmly and listen to me babble on? Was it a train wreck situation?"

"Honestly, I felt awful for ramming the door into your face. Listening was the least I could do."

"Ah, so it was pity."

He shakes his head, smiling. "Maybe it started like that. Then you used phrases like 'I beg your pardon' completely unironically.

You seemed quick and...*funny*. I thought it was worth hearing you out. Afterward, it was a gut feeling."

"Well. Okay then." I stare for a few more seconds before shaking it off. "Thanks again, Mr. Shepard."

"Mason," he corrects.

"Right. Sorry." I look beyond him then and holler a goodbye to Daniel.

"Bye, lady!" he shouts back.

I'm laughing when I step back into the autumn air.

"Nice bike," is Mason's final goodbye before he closes the door.

I thank the empty space in front of me before I turn on my heel and open my mouth in a silent scream.

This is happening!

I dance all the way to my bike, fueled by the rhythm of my elated heart.

CHAPTER
4

I sit with my knees pulled to my chest atop Merrin's queen-sized bed, detailing my moment of complete insanity that led to a second job. An assortment of snacks surrounds us as she takes my hair from my messy, sweaty ponytail and gently begins brushing out tangles. I can't remember a time when anyone did this for me; it's a strange and soothing pleasure.

"I'd be lying if I said I wasn't a little sad about this," she says. "But if it's what you want to do, then I'm happy for you."

The job isn't so much a *want* as a *need*. But I like how Merrin doesn't know me as the poor girl everyone knew me as in grade school, so I don't correct her.

"We'll still have plenty of time to hang out," I say. "We can get together every single weekend if you want."

"You promise?"

"Merrin, you're my best friend. I promise."

"Yeah?"

"Yes. Also, I love coming over here. Your house always smells good. You couldn't get rid of me if you tried."

She laughs, separating my hair into sections and weaving them together. "You know, I never appreciated how good the house smelled until I came back from my first trip to Ecuador. I had a whole new appreciation for a lot of things, to be honest."

"I bet." I understand this. I never appreciated how simple my life was until Gene started declining and couldn't work or handle the bills anymore.

Merrin pats my back. "There. All done."

"Thank you. I'm sure it looks amazing."

"Nothing exciting. Four-strand braid. You've got great hair. You need a trim, though."

I laugh, scooting away from her and relaxing against her headboard. "I didn't even know there was such a thing as a four-strand braid. I can barely manage a three-strand."

"I could teach you. And I could take care of those split ends, too."

I side-eye her. "I'm okay, thanks."

She holds her hands up defensively. "I'm good. I swear. It's what I want to do."

"Cosmetology?"

"Yeah. I've wanted it for a long time, actually. But it's...scary. You're either good enough to make a living, or you're not. There's really no in-between. And a lot of it hinges on how you connect with people, not just your talent. And I *suck* at connecting with people."

I narrow my gaze.

"I told you, I'm not sure why things are easy with you. But I'm not like this with most people. I clam up and stumble all over the place. Hence, speech."

"Are you taking anything else?"

"Chemistry."

"Why Chemistry?"

"Because it's fascinating."

I nod, pulling my lips taut. "Alright, then."

"Plus, my parents agreed to pay for my kit if I took a couple college classes first. And those things are pricey."

"Hard to pass that up," I agree.

"Exactly. Besides, it's been really good for me."

"Well, clearly. You met *me*." I bat my lashes.

She sticks her tongue out, then laughs. "Exactly. I met you."

My FIRST DAY with Daniel is long, exhausting, and absolutely wonderful. He tests all of my limits—and my sanity—but is quick to hug or cuddle me just as I'm on the verge of sending him to a time-out. Adorability is his superpower, and I'm a sucker for it.

With his favorite "train book!" read twice, and his stars and planets projection nightlight on, I tuck him between his soft blue sheets with his stuffed brachiosaurus, Herman, and quietly leave his room.

I clean our dinner mess, tidy up any toys strewn about, and make my way through the house, surveying my surroundings.

I'm already acquainted with the kitchen—custom white cabinets, butcher-block countertops, and newer appliances (almost too advanced for my know-how). I know almost every toy in Daniel's planes, trains, and automobiles themed playroom. I've foraged his closet to find the *right* superhero jammies. But as for the rest of the house, I haven't had time to notice it.

It's a large, open space. Free of clutter. A handful of framed family pictures adorn the walls. It's easy to spot Mason's dad; they're essentially the same person, thirty years or so apart. And the guy who looks like a masculine version of "Gramma Randa" is likely Mason's brother. He appears to have a wife and daughters of his own. But no pictures of anyone who might be Daniel's mother. Not out in the open for my eyes, anyway.

Not that it's my business—I rarely divulge information about my life to anyone. Why should I expect to know the intimate details of anyone else? Still, I'm curious.

There are two sizeable living areas. One is well-used, just off the kitchen. Large sectional and recliners. A massive TV and more gaming consoles than I knew existed. The other room is off the entryway and has a gorgeous white baby grand. Seeing that piano makes my fingers itch; I haven't played in years. It also serves as a reminder of young, naïve Stevie, who thought an offer of free piano lessons from a fellow choir nerd truly meant *free* piano lessons. I'm not sure what would happen if I sat down at those ivories now, even five years later.

The space also boasts an expansive collection of vinyl and a sound system which probably costs more than my entire house. Rather sexy, honestly. Mason Shepard might be the only person I've ever met with a larger music collection than mine.

I settle into a pillowy recliner in the living room with my homework once I've toured the house. When I hear the front door, I gather my things and meet Mason in the entryway.

Despite his heavy footfalls and the dark circles around his eyes, there's a contentment behind his sagging smile.

"How was the first day?" he asks.

"Busy but wonderful. We had a great time."

"Glad to hear it." A thought seems to occur to him, and he snaps his fingers, wide-eyed. "Oh! Stevie."

"Yes?"

"There was some info I wanted to get from you before you go."

I set down my backpack.

"What do you need?"

"You know, basic contact information. Since I never did get your resume." *Whoops.* "Friday was kind of a whirlwind, and I forgot to ask," he rushes, graciously assuming some of the blame.

"*Well,*" I start, contorting my face. "I can give you my number, but I'm afraid it won't do you any good right now."

"How's that?"

"You remember the, uh, *incident* on Friday?" I open a small pocket of my backpack where I tucked the shattered mess after the collision and pull out my now unusable phone.

He winces. "Oh no."

"Yeah," I sigh, staring at the crumbling screen and exposed innards.

He covers his mouth, attempting to muffle a laugh. "I've never seen a phone so thoroughly broken."

"Right?"

"I'm so sorry."

"It's okay. It was cheap to begin with and used when I got it. I've known for a while now it was not long for this world."

He's *trying* to frown, but his face isn't cooperating.

"Anyway, I won't be answering that number any time soon. It wasn't on a plan or anything, just a no-contract antique."

"Please, let me replace it. It was my fault."

"No. It was an accident. I promise I'll replace it as soon as I can. Give me a couple weeks to set the money aside. Until then, you can always leave a message at Bright Beginnings if you need to reach me for anything. Change of schedule, whatever." I pull a folded, crumpled syllabus and a pen from my backpack. I scribble on the blank side of the paper and pass it over.

"Here's the rest of my info, though. Just in case."

"Stephanie Renae Parker," he reads, amused.

"Yeah. You probably didn't need to know my full name. No one even calls me that. My parents called me Stevie Rae for short. It stuck." *Stop rambling, Stevie.*

"Like Stevie Ray Vaughan. Not that you're old enough to know who he is."

I smirk. "Hey, don't insult me. *Pride and Joy* is iconic. Though, if I had to choose a bluesy-inspired, old white guy to listen to—based *solely* on musicality—I'd play Eric Clapton or Jeff Healey over Vaughan."

He stares open-mouthed, the tip of his tongue pressed against his top canine. I shift my weight from side to side, *waiting*.

Eventually, he clears his throat. "Um, so, I noticed you're on your bike again." I nod. "I do have a truck in the garage, and in case—heaven forbid—there's an emergency, you could use that. There's a car seat in there for Danny. You have a license, right? How's your driving record?"

I nod. "Have a license. Record's clean." It helps I haven't driven in over two years.

"Now, I mean *emergencies*—" he starts.

"Hospital. Four-hour shoe sales. Got it." That provokes a grin. Maybe because of the state of my shoes—holes forming along the sides, the soles starting to detach. Duct tape is in their near future.

"Right." He shakes his head as he opens the door for me. "Goodnight, Stevie."

As I walk past him, I can't help but notice the smell of sandalwood rising from his skin. It triggers a memory, and my stomach turns. I book it out of there, drawing in a large gasp of fresh night air.

"Anoder song! Please! Again!"

"Daniel, this is the last one."

"Yes. Just one mow."

"After this song, I'm walking out that door, and you're going to sleep. Understood?"

With a nod, Daniel drops back to his pillow, closing his eyes and hugging Herman to his chest.

Usually, I get away with one or two lullabies at bedtime. Tonight, he's demanding extra since I've explained I won't be back until Monday. He doesn't quite grasp the concept of a weekend yet and feels "tomorrow and the next day" is too long to go without a "Stebie Song."

I finish with another round of the Spiderman theme song. Something I researched specifically for him. I'd only known the first two lines—like everyone else on the planet—but went down a black hole of YouTube videos on campus earlier this week to learn the rest.

"Stebie?"

"Yes, Daniel?"

"Maybe you could just do one mow."

"Goodnight, Daniel."

He pouts but doesn't argue. I tousle his curly hair one final time before leaving his room.

"Homework or TV?" I debate aloud. "Homework...TV?" I can get all my homework done and have a free weekend, or I can take advantage of having a TV to watch. The internal argument lasts so long I settle on neither, pulling out *Dead Souls* from my backpack instead. I've had it since high school but never read it. Actually, I've started it twice, but all the Russian names are so hard to follow I gave up both times.

Engrossed in Chichikov's absurd journey, I don't hear Mason come home or his footsteps as he enters the room.

"*Dead Souls*, huh?"

"Murphy!" I gasp. The book lurches out of my hands; I nearly throw it *at* him.

"Sorry. I didn't mean to scare you."

"A bit late," I say, breathless.

He stifles a laugh, setting down his messenger bag.

"Yes. *Dead Souls*," I answer, having composed myself.

"Great book."

"If you can follow the insane plot and Russian names."

He folds his arms across his chest. "Yeah, I'll give you that. It took me a few tries to get all the way through it."

"This is my third and final attempt. If I can't get it this time, I'll accept my mediocrity and give up."

He smirks. "You know, we have furniture. You don't have to read on the floor."

I'm so used to the floor I haven't even noticed. "Oh. Right. You have," I pause, "very plush carpet." *Nope. Not weird at all.*

I stand, and too late, he offers me his hand. He stutters as he draws back.

"So..." He tries to cover up the awkward silence. "You know the Spiderman theme song, huh?"

"I do now," I deadpan.

"He says you sing to him every night."

"That's okay, right?"

He frowns as if to ask what kind of world I grew up in that I have to ask. "Of course, it's okay."

"You never know. You could be one of those anti-lullaby households."

"This isn't the town from *Footloose*." He rubs his temples. "Sorry, all my pop-culture references are a million years old. You probably don't even—"

"*Ahem*," I say, holding up a finger. "First of all, I'm insulted. Again. Second, they were anti-*dancing* in *Footloose*. Which I hope you're not against either because Daniel and I boogie down. We also worship Kevin Bacon and his rage dancing. The shrine goes up next week."

Mason's laugh comes out more of a snort. "Yeah," he says, "Danny showed me his moonwalk."

"Amazing, right? The kid's got better rhythm than I do."

"I'm glad you two get on so well. I worried it would be a disaster." I'm not sure if this should offend me. "I didn't think *you* would be a disaster, Stevie," he rushes. "I meant, well, not many strangers come into our lives. We're pretty secluded. I worried going back to work outside the house would throw off our rather delicate balance."

"You worked from home until now?"

"Since Danny was about a year old, yeah." His expression changes. There's a sudden pain—a darkness—reflected in his eyes. "I could have kept working from home. Maybe I should have. But it feels good, getting out of the house regularly. Interacting with other adults. That probably sounds terrible."

"No. Mr. Shepard, it doesn't. I don't have kids, but I understand seclusion and how difficult it can be."

"Please, call me Mason."

"Mason," I correct. The smile he slides me does strange things to my impulse control. I suddenly want to touch his arm or run my fingers through his thick, wavy hair. Then I remember the sandalwood on his skin, and I taste bile. Being in the room with this man is an internal roller coaster. "I should go." A statement directed more at myself than at him.

He stops me before I'm out the door. "Am I seeing things, or is your bike light *taped* on?"

"Perhaps?" I shrug, twisting my lips.

"That really isn't safe, Stevie."

"Red Green does it all the time."

"Who's Red Green?"

"Ha!" I cackle. "Spoken like someone who had more than three channels and a library card growing up."

He squints, unamused. "What?"

"And you thought *your* pop-culture references were outdated," I mumble. "Never mind. Look, I've never had a legit fixture for the light, and it's worked just fine for me the last two years." He looks about to protest, so I rob him of the opportunity. With a little too much enthusiasm, I say, "You two enjoy your weekend."

He sighs in defeat and hands over my week's pay.

While assessing whether I need another layer of duct tape around my light, I feel someone peering at me from behind the window, but when I look, I only see the curtain waving.

CHAPTER 5

"So, tell me more about Mason. You didn't give me any details last time." Merrin sits cross-legged on the floor of her bedroom, chemistry book in her lap, though I get the feeling it's mainly for aesthetic at this point; she's been relentlessly chatty.

I, on the other hand, am desperately trying to maintain focus on my biology textbook. "He's nice. And he seems to like music and books as much as I do, which I thought was impossible."

"Ooooh," she coos. "Tell me more."

I side-eye her. "*And,*" I intone, "he pays me to watch his kid. It's a non-starter. I don't want to do anything to jeopardize my job."

Not only do I need the money, but for the first time ever, I'm realizing work doesn't *have* to be solely for survival. It can be fulfilling. It can be *enjoyable.* I never saw Gene happy about work, but he did what he had to for us. I *hated* the call center, but I did it to keep the house and eat. Bright Beginnings? It's fun, but financial aid only allows me so many hours a week. Watching Daniel, though? I love it, *and* it pays well. I bought beyond the bare necessities at the grocery store yesterday for the first time in *months.*

"Well," Merrin sighs, "I guess I can't fault you for that."

"Thanks for your approval. Now, it's getting late, and I really need to finish reviewing this chapter. There's a quiz tomorrow."

"So, you're not interested in Mason?" I shake my head. "Are you seeing anyone else?"

"I'm not seeing anyone else," I assure her. "Now, can I study? I'm shooting for straight As this semester."

"Why? Overachiever? Are you even interested in biology?"

I glare at her. "Actually, science isn't my thing. At all. But I have no idea what I want to do with my life, so Gen Ed it is. And no, I'm not an overachiever by nature, but there's a $500 scholarship with my name on it next semester if *all* I do is maintain a 4.0. There. Happy now?" With my eyes back on my book, I inhale. Where was I? Mitosis?

"I think I'm in love." She delivers this information casually, as though she's said, "I think I should try bangs."

I close my textbook, exhaling. "Oh, really?"

"With Luke." She smiles, innocent and sweet.

"Who's Luke?"

"From speech class! Luke." I shake my head, blank. "Super cute? Sits behind us? Luke!"

"Okay?"

"I bumped into him a few times last week around campus. He bought me lunch."

"And?"

"And I think I love him. He's so cute. He's smart and funny. But he's twenty."

"Which is *barely* older than you."

"Yeah, but old enough my parents might be...*hesitant* to let me go out with him. I still live here, so they still make the rules to an extent."

I twist my lips. "I see."

"So, say Luke has a friend..."

"Merrin," I say, low and accusatory. All the prodding is beginning to make sense.

"And the two of them wanted to take us out on a double date..."

"What have you done, Merrin?"

"Nothing yet. I wanted to gauge how open you might be to this particular hypothetical situation. Make sure you were legitimately single and not interested in a certain someone else."

"I *am* single, but I can run my own romantic life. Or lack thereof."

"Just keep an open mind, Stevie. Please." She clasps her hands in front of her chest like a prayer. "If you go, my mom might relax enough to see me as an adult and trust me a bit. You know?"

My lips trill over a heavy sigh. "I'll *try* to keep an open mind," I say. "Now, can I *please* focus?"

"Oh, come on. You've been *reviewing* that chapter for an hour. I'm sure you'll ace your quiz. Besides, this is *love* we're talking about. It trumps all."

I love Merrin, and I adore Scarlett. But something I'm noticing in all my conversations with them—neither one understands I can't afford to mess around. I don't have the option of building houses in Ecuador on my parent's dime or dumbing around EWC for four years just to *try everything* like Scarlett has. While I envy their cavalier attitude, I can't afford it.

"Stevie," Merrin pleads. "This is *important*."

I twist my lips. "Love? Already, huh?"

"Definitely. Maybe. You think he could be my first kiss?"

No my gosh. The girl hasn't even been *kissed*.

"You mean in all that time building houses, you never had a thing with...*anyone*?"

"Trust me, those boys wouldn't have known how to come onto me if I'd jumped out in front of them naked."

I sputter a laugh. "Well, did you even try?"

"Ha! No. Thought about it a couple times. There was this one guy...*oof*. So gorgeous. But clueless as they come."

"Nice house, nobody home."

"Exactly."

"Well, I hope—for your sake—Luke is different. But also, if he disrespects you even *once*, I've read many murder mysteries, and I promise you, they'll never find his body."

"Man, I love having a best friend."

I smile. "Me too."

MY INSECURITY IS a weakness of which I'm well-aware. It's not like I set out to be this way, or like I haven't tried to pep talk myself out of it. But between my parents, all my public-school *friends*, and Uncle Gene, everyone I've ever cared about has vanished from my life one way or another.

Merrin gushing over a boy is a completely normal development, and I'm happy for her. But that intrusive voice in my head keeps asking, *what if she forgets about you now?*

Scarlett is the next closest thing I have to a friend, and I found out today she plans on transferring to Walla Walla next semester to finish her bachelors. So there goes *that* connection.

These things are out of my control; worrying about them won't change the outcome, and yet, here I am wallowing when I should be enjoying my time with the happiest four-year-old on the planet. Daniel's birthday was last week, and I think he's still mildly intoxicated from the over-stimulation and the new toys. All I could gift him was a used book, but thankfully he was over the moon. Probably because it's a story about monsters who love underpants.

Buck up, Stevie. Time to be the grown-up.

I root around the Shepard's pantry, considering my options. "Daniel, what'aya say to helping me make some oatmeal scotchies?"

He's running around the kitchen island at top speed. The reason remains unclear.

"What are those?" he asks, not even panting. Oh, to be four.

"Cookies."

My answer halts him in his tracks. "Cookies?"

"Sure. What better way to combat the mid-week slumps, right?"

He turns in circles, chanting, "Coo-kies. Coo-kies. Coo-kies."

Daniel sits on the counter and "helps." By the time we're done, sugar and flour coat nearly every kitchen surface. His giggles and "sneaky" attempts to grab bits of raw batter make it all worth it. I absentmindedly hum as I spoon dough onto a baking sheet.

"What words go with dat song?" Daniel asks me.

Hearing someone else pose this question makes my hands an

instant clammy mess and sends my heart racing. I drop my scoop onto the ground.

"What happened, Stebie? Did you drop it?"

I'm speechless as I pick the scoop up and wash it in the sink.

"If you make a mistake, dat's okay," Daniel says. "But you shouldn't drop stuff. You'll break it."

When I've caught my breath, I manage to tell him, "I don't know what words go with that song, munchkin. Sorry."

"You sing it to me at bedtime."

"No, sweetie. How about I just sing you the cowboy song tonight?"

"Oh! Da cowboy song. Sing da cowboy song." Emotional crisis semi-averted.

I ask their little Echo device to play a classic rock station, and we resume baking.

I keep a smile plastered on my face for that boy's sake all evening, but as soon as he's asleep, I deflate.

I'd already been teetering on the brink of a meltdown, and Daniel's inquiry about the unknown lyrics to *my* song tipped the scales. Something about the way he said it—I saw myself. Heard myself. One innocent question ripped open my past, poured salt on old wounds, and now I feel like burrowing into the ground and being left to die.

I find mind-numbing television and sit on the sectional with a handful of cookies. It's some ridiculous cop show full of punchy one-liners and physical comedy. I can't bring myself to laugh, but I'm at least starting to feel less broken. Until, at the end of the episode, they throw in a dash of drama and happy tears over some long-awaited reunion between a mother and daughter.

Murphy, would this day just give me a break?!

Now I'm crying all over my cookies.

I miss my mom—weird, because I hardly remember her. She's more of a feeling than a person in my memories. Small as the connection is, I've spent most of my life knowing if she were still here, everything would be different. I wouldn't have grown up in that house with that depressed, dissociated man. I wouldn't have been a target later on. The smell of sandalwood might not make my stomach turn. *Sandalwood.*

"What, no Gogol today?" Mason asks, entering the room.

I startle, bringing a hand to my chest. "Murphy!"

"Dang, you're jumpy. What's that all about anyway? *Murphy?*"

I wipe my face, sniffling. "Nothing fascinating."

"What's wrong?" he asks, coming closer.

"I'm fine." I turn off the TV.

"Stevie, you're crying."

"It's, you know, allergies." Because I really can't come up with a better lie.

"Allergic to what? All the pets we don't have?" He sits a few feet away, a determined scowl on his face. "What happened?"

"I'm tired. My eyes are watery." He glowers, unconvinced. "I'm fine, I promise."

Though under the gaze of his guileless eyes, I'm fighting the compulsion to spill the darkest secrets of my soul—my whole life story, down to the tiniest and ugliest of details. Would he fire me for going all crazy and emotional on him when we barely know each other? Would he be sad for me? Would he be bored? Would it matter?

"I made cookies with the munchkin," I say. "Oatmeal scotchies."

He lets out a slow, long breath, reluctantly letting the mystery of the crying girl on his couch remain unsolved. "I thought I smelled something wonderful. Come on. You look like you could use a cookie."

I follow him to the kitchen, not bothering to tell him I've already eaten at least eight of them.

"So, you've survived the first few weeks," he says. "Having regrets?"

"Not one." He cocks his brow. "No. I mean it. Mr. Shepard, you have a great kid. He's uniquely wonderful and absolutely hilarious."

"Please call me Mason," he reiterates with a sigh.

I nod, twisting my lips. "Are you sure it's not too casual to call you by your first name?"

"I don't mind it. But if you have a desperate need to respect your elders or something..."

"Look, ancient references notwithstanding, I'm not convinced you're much older than me. Are you?"

Wearing a sly smile, he nabs a cookie. His first bite still swimming around in his mouth, he lets out a dramatic, "Omagosh!" rolling his eyes. "These are incredible."

"Oh," I wave a dismissive hand, "thanks."

"Seriously, Stevie. Next level." The rest of his cookie disappears in one bite, and he helps himself to another. "Best cookies I've ever had."

A hint of pride radiates as I admit, "It's my mom's recipe." My mind wanders—a vision of my mother working over the kitchen counter, smiling down at me as she offers me a spoon dipped in fresh batter. "She was always baking. I don't remember if she was an exceptional cook, but I remember her making the best treats and desserts." There she is again, singing along with the radio, lifting me up onto the counter to watch as she works. "I have this old recipe box of hers. I've spent countless hours trying them all out. Like if I could perfect them, it might somehow bring a little bit of her back to life."

The vision of Mom fades, a somber Mason Shepard taking her place. My cheeks are wet. *Noooo my gosh.* "I..." My fingers brushed my lips, then my cheeks. "I didn't mean..."

"I didn't know, Stevie. I'm so sorry."

I shake my head, trying to figure out how I carelessly let so much of my life slip out.

"You were young when she died?" he asks.

"I was Daniel's age." Mason offers me a cookie. I accept with a sigh. "Almost exactly Daniel's age, actually." This realization makes me sad in a different way. I chew slowly.

"Can I ask how it happened?"

"We were driving home late," I say without even pausing to consider whether this is the right move. "I'm not sure why. My uncle would never tell me, and I honestly don't remember. I get flashes, you know? Dad smiling as he straps me into a five-point harness. Mom winking back from the front seat. Then, nothing until I wake up in a hospital room. There was a rainbow painted on one of the walls. I stared at that stupid rainbow, waiting for my parents to walk through the door and tell me it was all a mistake. They weren't dead. I wasn't alone."

It's been a common inquiry throughout my life. *How did they die?* I've always kept it short, simple. *Car accident.* Now? I include detail for some unknown reason. Painful to recall detail.

"The story is Dad fell asleep at the wheel, and my parents weren't lucky enough to survive like I was. 'Cause you know, I'm just," deep sigh, "so lucky."

"The uncle you mentioned," Mason says. "The one who died of lung cancer?"

I'm surprised by his recollection. "Yeah, he raised me. Sort of."

He frowns when I add that last part. "You weren't close?"

I roll my neck, exhaling. "It was a rocky relationship. He just... He missed his sister, and I was extra baggage he hadn't planned on being saddled with. Made things complicated. He died two years ago. I think he was rather relieved to go."

"You were so young," Mason whispers. "To go so long without parental support... That has to be difficult. You've obviously borne it well. I'm sure your mother would be proud." I taste an isolated tear on my lip. "And not just of how well you make her cookies."

I laugh, flicking the tear away. "Thank you."

"You should get going."

"Ah," I clear my throat. "Yes, I should."

"That came out wrong," he rushes. "I just meant it's late, and you're on your bike. It's so dark. Not to mention, it's getting cold. You really should consider putting the bike away for the season."

"Not exactly an option."

"You don't have a car?"

"You caught me." I click my tongue and point a finger at him, making light of the whole thing, ignoring the familiar sting of pity his words carry.

"But that'll get dangerous. The ice and snow..." His voice trails off while his eyes hold mine, disapproving.

"I've got studded tires. And if it's ever too tricky to ride, I can walk."

"You'll walk? In the dark? Alone?"

"I've got pepper spray," I say. He rolls his eyes, finding no humor in my *duh!* statement. "Look, I'm used to it. My car broke down beyond repair a couple years ago. I paid some weasel about a week's wages to tell me it was unsalvageable, and that was the end of it. I bought the bike and the *good* tires. No more gas to buy, no more insurance."

"I get that. I do. I'm just a little concerned—"

"Well, don't be," I snap. "I'm not going to stand here defending my decisions to you. You have *no* idea..." I clench and unclench my fists. "Look, I'm not some pathetic little schoolgirl floating aimlessly, in need of saving. I've been on my own for a long time, and I'm doing just fine." Well, maybe *just fine* is stretching it.

Mason stands silent, maybe even ashamed, staring at the floor.

Crap. My gut turns, and not just because I've eaten too many cookies. Regret floods every corner of my conscience.

We stand in semi-awkward silence for a while, neither of us knowing how to mend it. Finally, I bite the bullet, offering a quiet goodnight. He returns the farewell with a faint smile. As I grab my backpack, it takes every ounce of willpower not to full-on sprint out of the house.

CHAPTER
6

Aside from speech class, my midterms are all online, which is how I find myself with three hours of free time on a crisp Friday morning. Leaving the testing center, I'm trying to decide between finding a vacant couch in the Student Union Building and reading or going home and taking a nap, when I bump—literally bump—into Merrin, walking side by side with Luke, both of them rosy-cheeked and smiling.

"Oh, Stevie! I was hoping to see you!" Merrin grabs my hand. "Luke, call me later about tomorrow, okay?"

He tries to downplay his pleasure in the request as he backs away. The two of them hold eye contact for a few moments before Merrin grips my hand harder and starts walking, pulling me along with her.

"He's so cute! Oh my gosh, Stevie! He's so... Oh my gosh!"

"Clearly."

"How much do you love me?"

"Merrin," I grumble. "What did you do?"

"Please just hear me out!" I plant my feet, facing her, signaling for her to continue. "Derek—you know, he sits next to Luke in Speech."

I have no idea who Derek is, but she doesn't seem to care.

"Well, he totally thinks you're hot."

I feign a gag—or maybe it's real. "Hot? Are we in *middle school?*"

Merrin rolls her eyes, undeterred. "Luke and I were thinking we could all double-date tomorrow. Dinner and a scary movie."

"Hot?"

"It'll be fun!"

"*Hot?!*"

"Yeah, hot. So what?"

"Is he thirteen?"

"He's twenty, like Luke."

"Ugh, *Merrin*."

"*Stevie*," she imitates. I let a smile slip. "Come on. I'm the baby. The *baby*. Do you know what that means? It means my mom would rather I die surrounded by cats than go on a single date with a guy who's pushing legal drinking age."

"I thought you said nothing fazed her."

"That was before I told her about Luke. It triggered some overprotective instinct in her or something. She got all weepy and weird."

Though I know Merrin's seeking sympathy for her plight, I'm straining to envision what my mom would have looked like in such a moment. If I confessed a crush to her. Would she ask for details? Play it cool? Become *weepy* and *weird*?

"One double-date," Merrin pleads. "That's all I'm asking. Do this *one* thing for me. I promise, Sunday night, we can steal a bag of the Halloween candy—my mom always buys too much for trick-or-treaters—and watch romcoms or something. A reward, if you will."

She waits a few moments for me to respond, but I'm still processing.

"Look," she says. "Maybe Derek's not the most eloquent guy in the world, but I'm sure he's decent. Why don't you at least give it a chance?"

I chew on my cheek, weighing pros and cons. Worst-case scenario, I get a free meal out of the deal. The chances of enjoying the company of a guy with a limited, juvenile vernacular are slim, but she isn't asking me to be *alone* with him.

She lets out a final pathetic "*Please!*" complete with bulging, heartsick eyes and a pouting lip. While working with children has hardened me against such cunning tactics, I don't *hate* the idea of a date. It's more I don't know if I remember how to do it. I'd been on a couple dates in high school, and while they weren't anything worth writing home over, they'd been moderately enjoyable. Harmlessly flirtatious. I deserve to have that again. Don't I? And I love Merrin. Her, and her emerald eyes, which grow more pitiable by the moment.

I release an exasperated sigh. "You can put away your sad face now."

"Oh, thank you, thank you!" Merrin jumps as she hugs me, forcing me to bounce with her.

"Okay, okay. Calm down, or I'll back out. I swear I will."

"You will not regret this!"

"Pick another phrase," I order, almost certain I will regret this.

"I will owe you big time!"

"Better. Accurate."

"Why don't you stay over tonight? We could help each other get some major homework out of the way and then tomorrow..." She rubs her hands together. "Makeover time! Come on, we'll do facials and paint our nails. I'll do your makeup. It'll be amazing."

"Merrin. I'm not sure I'm in a makeover mood. And your place is a bit far for me to ride tonight."

She shakes her head. "It's admirable—you saving the planet and all. But couldn't you drive tonight? One time? For me?"

"I don't have a car," I mumble.

Her eyes widen. "*Oh.* I didn't realize."

"I'll just come tomorrow—"

"Let me pick you up after work tonight. You get done at ten, right? My dad has a truck. We'll throw your bike in the back, swing by your house and get your clothes."

"That's too much trouble."

"It's really not. You work two jobs, Stevie. I'm sure you're exhausted. Let me do this for you. After all, I owe you a favor, right?"

I laugh. "Many, in fact."

She pulls out her phone. "What's Mason's address?"

"Really, Mer—"

"Stevie, I'm not backing down on this. I don't know about you, but I *need* a girls' night. Tonight. With my best friend. I'm prepared to go to extreme lengths to get it, so you might as well spare yourself the energy of arguing with me." She folds her arms and taps her foot.

She's being obstinate, and yet, it tugs on my heartstrings. "*Fine*," I say, pretending to be annoyed. "You win."

She grins, linking her arm in mine. "I love when I win."

Reluctant to retract the shroud over my unconventional living situation, I pack a bag for Merrin's house before work and haul it with me. One day I'll be ready to show her the wizard behind the curtain —or lack thereof—but not today.

I'm not ashamed of my poverty or my situation in general. But I've learned people treat you differently when they discover you're poor, or orphaned, or live alone with your surly uncle. That you don't have a car or television, and you glean all your entertainment from books and CDs acquired from garage sales, second-hand stores, and library discard piles. Merrin is young, sheltered, and the sincerest friend I've ever had. I don't want her to feel uncomfortable. Or worse, pity me. She's sure to do enough of that when she sees my scant choices for date apparel. I've packed a few tops and my least worn pair of jeans. Hopefully, something is worthy of her discerning eye.

The more I think about the prospect of a *blind date*, the more I want to relocate to a remote cave and disappear from society. I sit on the floor of the darkened classroom full of sleeping children, wishing there was a way I could back out of this without letting Merrin down.

Scarlett enters the room, stepping over children as she comes to sit by me.

"Snack prep over already?" I whisper.

"Yeah. Marge said to hang with you until Jill gets back from break. You look terrible, Stevie."

"Oh, wow. Thank you. Best compliment I've had all week. Nay, all year."

"You look worried," she rephrases, furrowing her brow. "What's wrong?"

I wrinkle my nose, shrugging. "I'm neurotic, but other than that, nothing."

"Well, then I guess we sit here silently on the cold, hard ground, staring into the void, listening to the same instrumental rendition of *Baa, Baa, Black Sheep* on repeat until our ears bleed."

"Okay, Bubbly Becky. Save some incessant optimism for the rest of us, would you? Murphy." She shimmies her shoulders, a cocky grin on her face. "My friend set me up on a weird, semi-blind, double date for tomorrow. It's wigging me out."

"Why? A date would be so good for you."

I squint, frowning.

"No offense, alright," she says. "You just seem...reserved. Like you could afford to live a little."

"And again, thank you."

"I *said* 'no offense.'"

I huff a quiet laugh. "It's not like I'm opposed to dating in general. But I don't know this guy. I have no clue what I'm walking into. He could be *really* good-looking, or he could be a massive jerk, or he could be... It doesn't matter. He's a person, and I'm horrible at meeting new people. No offense, but the only reason you and I eased into a rhythm so quickly is because you're as weird as I am. You just own it better."

She side-eyes me, her mouth gaping.

"What? I *said*, 'no offense.'"

She punches my shoulder, suppressing a laugh.

"Stevie, relax. It's one date. If it's awful, you can always text me. I'll call you in a panic and give you an out."

"I haven't replaced my phone yet," I say. "But thank you. I appreciate that."

"Girl. Still? You're joking, right?"

"It's on the agenda for this weekend. I get paid today." I say it with a giddy undertone, rubbing my palms together.

"Does this dude pay you weekly?"

"Yup."

"Lucky. I don't know why you're still doing work-study when you have that gig. Two jobs? It's excessive."

Spoken like someone who doesn't pay property taxes and city utilities.

When I offer no response, she squeezes my arm. "Hey, sorry. It's not my place. Work as much as you need to. But you should cut loose once in a while, even if it's for a super awkward blind date that ends in disaster. At the very least, it gives you an anecdote to share down the road."

"That's fair." I sigh. "You're right."

"Of course, I am. But we do need to address...this." She waves her hand in a circle.

"You just gestured to all of me."

She cringes. "Yeah."

Ouch.

"Honey, you look like a ghost, all sad and limp. Stand a little straighter. Let your hair hang down. Pluck your eyebrows, brush on some bronzer. You'll be a whole new marvelous you." She takes a deep breath. "Either way, you'll drive this guy bonkers. You're small —short, small, whatever—guys love it. You're like a fun-sized candy bar. They can't get enough of you."

I cock my head, twisting my lips. "I don't think that's accurate. Also, gross."

She shakes her head, rolling her eyes. "Trust me. This will be fun for you, so long as you erase the permanent *eff off* from your face."

I gasp. "I do *not*."

"Well, you kinda do. But I can't blame or judge you. I have big-time RBF."

"RBF?"

She leans in, whispering, "Resting bitch face."

I frown. "Do I have RBF?"

"No. It's more like you're just leery of everyone."

"Oh." Well, that tracks. I'll own it.

Scarlet reaches over and grabs my face, smushing my cheeks.

"How is this helpful?" I ask, her hands impeding my speech.

"It's not," she deadpans before letting go.

She carries on the remainder of nap time, but in the end, all I get out of the whole thing is "pluck your eyebrows."

When I arrive at the Shepards' house later, Daniel flings the front door open moments after I knock. He's talking before I can even see his face. "Stebie! Can we'd make mow cookies today?"

"We'll see, little man." I set my bag down and take Daniel's hand. We walk through the house to the living room, and I plop myself on the couch, pulling him onto my lap. He doesn't stop talking the entire time.

"Today I don't think da park sounds good because it's cold. But I miss my fwends. So maybe we could put on hats and glubs and go. Did you'd know Halloween is Sunday and I'm gonna be Spidoman? I have new boots and a mask! And Stebie?"

"Yes, Danny?"

"You really need to make mow cookies after dinner. Daddy made chicky pot pie!"

"I need to, huh?"

He grabs my cheeks the same way Scarlett had a couple hours ago. "Yes, buddy." Like it's the most important thing in the world. "You need to make dem."

"Daniel," Mason sighs, entering the room. "Let go of Stevie's face. Personal space, buddy. Remember?" Daniel does as his father asks. "Hi, Stevie." Mason stands with his messenger bag slung over his shoulder. A tired smile accompanies his business casual attire. He's shaved and taken several inches off his hair. His curls are tighter now without the weight.

My cheeks flush, thinking of how I snapped at him the other

night. I swallow, offering a nod—a subtle acknowledgment of his presence. How long am I going to act like this around him? Is this just a *forever* thing now?

He stares at me, probably waiting to see if I'll offer anything other than a quiet "Hello, Mason." I could tell him I like his haircut or ask him how his day has been, but my short greeting is all I can muster.

"Alrighty." Mason sighs, kneeling, his gaze shifting to Daniel. "Come give me a hug, monster." Daniel hops off my lap and sprints into his father's arms.

"I love you, Daddy."

"I love you too, buddy." He kisses Daniel and stands back up before the light comes on. "Danny boy! You did it!" Daniel is already running toward the stairs. "I'm not the only one who heard 'love' come out of his mouth? Not 'lub' but 'love.'"

"No. I heard it, too."

"I've been so worried I wasn't focusing enough on his speech these last few months."

"Clearly, he's doing just fine." Personally, it makes me sad. I adore hearing his *V*s come out as *B*s. "You shouldn't worry. He's way ahead of most of the boys I work with at the daycare. I promise, he's thriving. Take a breath."

His eyes hold mine. "Thank you, Stevie." Again, I only nod. "You know, Daniel was right. It's cold. I don't think you should be riding your bike tonight." He gestures to me. "You're not even wearing a proper coat."

My oversized hoodie is entirely sufficient. "Pedaling keeps me warm," I argue.

"You can take the truck home tonight. Bring it back Monday. I don't need it this weekend."

"Wow. It's nice of you to offer. But I—"

"I insist. It's too cold. You'll be miserable."

"It's a generous thought, but my friend is picking me up tonight."

"Oh. Good. I'm glad." We're silent a moment longer before he glances at the wall clock. "Shoot, now I really *do* need to go."

"Well, skedaddle!"

He laughs. "Skedaddle?"

"You heard me," I deadpan.

He shakes his head, muttering, "Yes, ma'am."

Something about the way he says it... Heat rises into my neck and my insides spasm—I don't want to dissect why.

"I'll probably be home early," he says. Then he's gone.

CHAPTER
7

It's only nine when Mason joins me in the family room and falls onto the couch.

"You cut your hair," I acknowledge, putting away my biology homework.

"Yeah, it was time to clean up." He rubs his face where his beard had been. "I was lookin' a little sloppy."

"I don't think *sloppy* is the right word, but this looks nice, too."

He nods, his eyes scanning my face. I can tell there's *something* he wants to say, but nothing comes out. Eventually, he blinks and shakes his head like he's pulling himself back into the present. "It smells amazing in here," he says.

"Oh, right. You had some overripe bananas, so Danny and I made muffins with them. I hope that's okay."

"Absolutely not. I'm appalled."

I roll my eyes. "I *meant* that I hope I didn't overstep. Maybe you had grand plans for those bananas. I don't know your life!"

He laughs.

"I should have asked," I add more sincerely.

"I'll never be angry coming home to muffins," he says. "Or cookies. Or whatever. I'm glad you two have fun while I'm gone. Honestly, you're a saint to let him help in the kitchen. I don't have that kind of patience."

"It's easy to come in and be patient for a few hours a day. This is your entire life. It's different."

He nods. "Fair point."

"It occurs to me now, as I'm wondering why you're home an hour early, I don't even know what it is you do." How had I taken this job knowing so little about this man? Stranger still, he offered me the job knowing so little about me. Maybe we're both idiots.

"You mean, what kind of job allows me to get away with working twenty-five hours a week but still supports my family and pays for private childcare?"

"I was trying to be a little more subtle about it, but yeah. It's drugs, right?"

"Big time. All the drugs."

"Knew it." I shake my head with a *tsk tsk.*

Stifling a laugh, he adjusts in his seat. "Well, to answer the first question, I'm home early because tonight was a test night, and everyone finished quickly, which leads me to answer two. I teach some I.T. courses at Continuing Ed." I tilt my head, squinting, digesting this unexpected detail. "It's not the most glamorous place to work, but I missed teaching, and I didn't want to miss all of Daniel's waking hours or constantly be working when home. Not to mention all the office hours you put in on a traditional campus. This fits the bill. For now."

"Hold up. *Missed* teaching?" He nods. "Are we talking college-level courses?" He nods again. "Meaning Master's Degree?" He stares on, grinning as I put the pieces together. "So you already had your master's and were previously teaching, took a few years off, and went back..." He awaits my next question with raised brows. "How old *are* you?"

"Twenty-nine. I, uh... So, I'm a huge geek. A bit of an overachiever too. Nothing outrageous. I just started college really young. Master's by twenty-two, that sort of thing."

"And you seemed so normal."

He laughs. "Thanks, I guess. Anyway, it gets more embarrassing. My family has...*money*. Therefore, I had money. A fund set aside for college—up to eight years, depending on what I wanted to do." My face goes numb. "But I was awarded enough scholarships that most of it was still just sitting there when I finished up."

"Jackpot," I mumble. He tosses his hands into a good-natured shrug.

"So, when I started feeling burned out from being *Professor Shepard* and a full-time single dad, I switched things up and took a work-from-home network administration job. Took on some random side jobs building or fixing PCs. It's something I've done for friends and family since I was a teenager. Enough people threw my name around that I always had an extra income.

"Long story longer, when I decided to start teaching again, I could afford to take a job I'm overqualified for that doesn't pay exceptionally well. It's not how I planned things out back when I was in college, but it works. And I'll take it."

"I get it."

"Yeah?"

"Well, in a different way, of course. I understand needing to take whatever path you can to get where you need to go. Even if it feels like a detour or a betrayal to your former self."

We sit in comfortable silence for a few moments.

"Well, you got my life story out of me," he teases. "Tell me something about you."

"There's nothing exciting or glamorous to tell," I assure him. "Really, the biggest stuff you already know. Stevie—Orphan." I gesture to myself.

"But that's not *who* you are," he says. Some days, it feels like that's *all* I am. "What are you going to school for?"

"I have *no* idea. I just knew I needed to start doing something with my life again, instead of just what I *had* to do to get by. The CSR job I mentioned?" He nods. "I took it after Gene died because I needed an income. And I hated every minute there. It was awful, but I was also sort of lost and didn't know what else to do. I just kept putting in the hours and earning a paycheck. Turnover was insane, but since I needed the money and kept showing up, they kept *promoting* me, which meant I got all the escalated calls."

"Oof," he breathes, cringing.

"That was my life. Get yelled at by angry people, read from a script, eat, sleep, repeat. About two years in, I sort of woke up. Snapped out of it. Whatever. When I realized I qualified for enough financial aid to cover a full course load at East Washington, I just sort of...jumped. Escaped. However you want to look at it."

"Wow."

"I know. Risky move. I still question my sanity."

"Risky, sure. But also bold. Even if you're just taking Gen Ed classes and don't know where it's headed. You shouldn't have to automatically know what you want to do with your life. Take some time. Figure it out. I say good for you."

"Sounds like you pretty much always knew what you wanted to do. Straight shot to master's by your early twenties? Doesn't sound like a lot of fooling around there."

"Oh, I fooled around plenty. We won't get into that."

His eyes bulge as he says it, and I can't help but laugh.

"I admit, I'm one of the lucky few who knew early on what I wanted to do. But hey, maybe you already know too. Maybe you used to know. Maybe you just forgot."

I stare, speechless. *Maybe I just forgot.* It makes sense. I've lost myself over the last three years. I've forgotten.

"So," he breaks my trance. "I have something for you."

"For me?" He pulls a sleek new phone out of his messenger bag and hands it over. "What's this?" I ask. He cocks his brow. "Okay, clearly, I know what this *is*. But...what is this?"

"It's nothing less than what I owe. I should have gotten it for you much sooner."

It's at least ten steps up from anything I would have bought for myself. Already, it's tucked inside a protective case, a screen guard affixed. He stares as I gradually register what's happening.

"You shouldn't have done this." I click the power button. The screen lights up; he's already charged it for me.

He takes the original packaging out of his bag, placing it between us. "The charger is in there, along with all the network info. I wrote your number down on the front of the manual. It's a no-contract thing. I paid it up for three months. The network has great reviews in this area, but if you don't like it, hopefully, three months is enough time to figure something else out."

"Mason..."

"Stevie, please don't make this into a thing. I'm not being generous here. It was my fault your other one broke, and the guilt was suffocating. Not to mention I hated you not having a phone when you take Daniel anywhere. If there was an emergency...? I'm sorry I waited so long."

"I was going to buy one for myself this weekend. You shouldn't have."

"And yet, I did."

"You should deduct this from my pay." How many weeks will this set me back?

"Can't do it. Won't do it. Just take the damn phone." He clears his throat. "Excuse me. Just take the phone." I open my mouth to protest, but he takes the phone and the box and carefully puts them in my backpack, sealing the gesture.

"Um. Thank you," I manage.

"That wasn't too painful, was it?"

I scowl.

"You're welcome," he revises.

I chew on my lip a moment before changing the subject. "Finished Gogol."

"Really? How did you like it?"

"It was so weird." He laughs. "But great. I mean, I really enjoyed it. It was hilarious in a way no other book has ever been to me. I've read satires before. I've even read—what's the word—societal satires. But buying dead people as a business endeavor? Who comes up with that? Makes you wonder what horrific childhood trauma Gogol endured. He could probably give me a run for my money." I close my eyes, tensing as I realize what I've just said. *Dammit.*

When I look back at Mason, he's somber, but he seems to

somehow know not to pry further into my statement. "Any ideas for your next read?"

Bless him for not dissecting my words.

"I might not be reading anything other than Eric Carle or Dr. Suess for a solid month."

He laughs, and I love the sound of it. I love the fact that I made him laugh even more. But then he yawns, and his arms stretch outward, and I get a whiff of sandalwood. I hate how this person who is so kind and attractive in the best, rough-cut way smells like the worst person I've ever met. Like my worst memory. Like the origin story behind my hesitance to trust anyone. Even someone like Mason Shepard.

"Are you okay?" he asks, his voice gentle, though rattled. He stands from the couch, disappears, and comes back with a box of tissues.

Oh. My. Gosh. When did I start crying?

Mortified, I take a tissue and wipe my eyes and cheeks. "Sorry," I mumble.

"Don't be. Can I help? Did I do or say something—"

"No." I clear my throat. He sits next to me again, but closer. I have to scoot away. He takes my lead and inches back. There's more than confusion behind his chocolate eyes right now. He looks almost...*hurt.* "I'm sorry," I say, shaking my head. "It's not anything you did. And I can't even believe I'm this upset right now. It's so stupid. I'm so stupid."

Mason frowns. "Don't say that."

I release a shaky breath. "I'm going to ask you something I have no right to ask you." He nods, awaiting the rest. It takes me a few tries to say it aloud. "Is there any way you could change your soap?"

With a laugh, he scrunches up his nose. "What?"

"Maybe it's your deodorant. I don't know. Whichever one has sandalwood in it. Would it be a horrendous inconvenience to change it?"

He stops laughing, realizing I'm serious.

"I told you it was stupid," I say.

"No," he says. "Does it remind you of something sad?"

"In a way."

"Your uncle?"

"No. Uncle Gene smelled like cigarettes and coffee. Which, weirdly, I miss."

This disarms him a moment—long enough for a fleeting smile to cross his lips—before he remembers the origin of this conversation.

"Did someone hurt you, Stevie?"

I close my eyes, inhaling and shaking my head. I can't talk about this right now. I grab my backpack and stand. "I think I'll wait outside until my friend picks me up."

At the front door, I try and fail to turn the knob twice. Clasping my shaky hands together, I let my forehead fall against the frame. *Breathe, Stevie. Calm down.*

I hear slow, cautious footsteps behind me. They come closer, then halt, and it sounds like someone is heading up the stairs. When I turn, Mason has perched himself on one of the steps near the landing. His hands are folded in his lap.

"Is this far enough away?" he asks.

"I'm so sorry."

He shakes his head. "Please, don't be. So, tell me. Big plans with this friend tonight?"

Just like that, he's changing the subject and pretending nothing weird just happened. Now I like him even more.

"Not tonight," I say. "My friend, Merrin, she sort of forced me to go on a blind double date with her tomorrow."

"How nice of her," he quips.

"Right? And apparently, it's going to take so long for her to transform me into a socially acceptable version of myself that I have to stay over at her house. I get a feeling the makeover begins at dawn."

Mason cocks his head, creasing his brow. "What's there to makeover?"

I'm unsure how flattered to feel. It's entirely possible he's trying to be nice to the girl who keeps crying on his couch, seemingly unprovoked. We stare at each other in awkward silence until he yawns.

"I'm sorry," he says. "Please don't take that as commentary. It's just been a long week. Guess I'm more tired than I thought."

I wag my thumb behind me. "I'm sure Merrin will be here any minute. I can just wait outside."

"If you would be more comfortable outside, feel free. But please don't for my sake. And let me pay you first."

He stands, pulling out his wallet and counting fresh bills.

I hold my breath as he slowly walks toward me, extending his hand. After I've taken the money, he retreats to the steps.

Normally I don't pay attention, but tonight the bills in my hand feel too thick.

"I think you gave me too much," I say, glancing down. Sure enough, he's overpaid me. I try to hand some of it back.

He holds his hands up. "I don't want it back."

"Please, don't give me handouts because I had a minor meltdown. It's patronizing."

He sighs. "I didn't mean it that way."

"First the phone, now *this*. And don't think I didn't notice you put a new light on my bike. I *like* working for what I have."

He perks up. "Well, your bike was a safety hazard. If your light had fallen off, you could have been run over and killed, and then who would watch my kid? I'm just trying to save myself the trouble of hiring anyone else. The phone, we've already established, was owed. And as for the money, Daniel hasn't thrown a tantrum since your second week here. His attitude and speech are steadily improving. Consider it a tip for a job well done. It has nothing to do with what happened back there." He points behind him, toward the living room.

Despite the ugly memories triggered by his *gifts*, I can't help but relax a little. "Well, the tantrums were easy. After navigating his first few, I realized his motivation wasn't frustration—which is what I see most with kids at work—it was attention. So, the next time he threw a tantrum over having to leave the park and come home, I threw myself down and had one too. After a few seconds, I asked, 'Should we keep this up, or would you like to go home?' He stood up, got into the stroller, and never did it again."

He shakes his head in disbelief. "Genius."

"More like insane! I was mortified. But after using some of the resources at Bright Beginnings and the early childhood textbooks at the library, I decided to give the most out-there method a shot. Figured I had nothing to lose."

"See, who else would do that? No one. Who else would teach him songs like 'Black Hole Sun' in lullaby form?" He cocks his head as I stifle a laugh.

"Hey, the lyrics aren't any more depressing than 'Rock-a-Bye, Baby' or 'You Are My Sunshine.' Change up the key, tweak the tune, and there are a myriad of grunge and rock songs that work at bedtime."

"See! That. That's why I'm thankful every day I ran you over with that door." I stop mid-laugh, realizing he's completely serious. "You weren't my first interview for this position. I advertised online and at a couple of job centers. Five other people interviewed with us before I ever put that flyer up at the daycare. Then you came along. Daniel and I both just knew."

I can't grasp at a reply.

"Take the bonus," he says. "You've more than earned it. Use it on something fun or even frivolous. Treat yourself."

"Something fun, huh?" I ask quietly. He nods. "Oh! Property taxes!" I feign excitement.

"Um. You pay property taxes?"

"I'm pretty sure it's a legal requirement when you own a home," I deadpan.

He stares with his signature open-mouthed curiosity, his tongue pressed against his top canine. Eventually, he clears his throat. "I think a more natural response might have been new shoes or something. But property taxes—if you like—work too."

I bite my lip, not peering at the thick layer of duct tape wrapped around the toes of my shoes, though I know they're likely the reason for his suggestion. "I, uh..." I take a slow breath. "I hope you and Daniel have a fun weekend. Maybe take a picture of him in his costume for me?"

He grins. "I will. I hope you have fun on your date," he offers.

"Oh, I'm sure it will be an epic disaster. I'm terrible in social situations with strangers. You know this. You've *seen* it."

He laughs. "Well, you can't have everything. Has to be a character flaw in there somewhere." The way his dark eyes hold mine. The way his smile stretches across his square jawline. Mason Shepard is swiftly graduating from *attractive* to *sexy as hell*, and it's becoming difficult to be around him, despite the sandalwood.

Before I can say or do anything horrifically stupid, Merrin pulls into the driveway in her dad's truck, and I slip out the front door.

CHAPTER
8

"This is it?" Merrin frowns at my pile of clothes sprawled on her bed.

"Yup. This is it." I sit beside my wardrobe. "Depressing?"

"No. I don't think it's a complete fail. Actually, I think I'm stealing this." She picks a navy top with a subtle floral print from the allotment.

"Go for it." I've worn it twice—graduation and Uncle Gene's funeral. "Keep it if you like." I never want to wear it again.

"Well then, maybe I will. We can swap. I've got a bunch of stuff that would look *amazing* on you."

"No, that's not—"

"Do you think I should pair this with a skirt or jeans?" she asks, holding the top so it drapes in front of her.

"Mer, you're a thousand times more qualified to answer that question. Anything you put together will be absolutely perfect." Merrin exudes a confidence in her fashion I never knew was possible.

"Well," she says, batting her lashes. "Thank you. You'll look fabulous tonight, too. I promise." She turns to her closet and begins sifting through it.

"Well, if anyone could make me presentable, it's you."

She turns back to me, rolling her eyes. "Stop. You're gorgeous. You just need...*updating*."

"Ha!" I snort. "Thanks."

"You're not wrong, though. This is what I do best." She pulls a thick section of clothing from her closet and places it on her bed. "I don't just want to be a cosmetologist; I want to be a personal stylist.

Not a lot of call for that around here, I know. But it's my dream. My sister, Jocelyn, got me interested when I was tiny. She's the expert—been making her own clothes longer than I've been alive."

My eyes widen.

"She's twelve years older," Merrin explains. "But I was always her little buddy, and she passed on what wisdom she could before moving away."

"Where does she live?"

"New York. She works for *Ellis*, but she's gearing up to start her own label."

"Wait? *Ellis*? As in the fancy pants clothing line? How has this not come up before?"

"I didn't think you'd know what I was talking about."

Ouch! "Well, now, that was just unnecessary."

"What?" she asks, wide-eyed.

"I know I don't have the appearance of someone who thinks twice about their fashion choices, but I am human, Merrin. You don't have to own a giraffe to know they exist."

"Well, sor-ry. Anyway, the point is: Josie's a genius."

"You miss her?"

"Yeah," she sighs. "For whatever reason, we were really close when I was little. Jo and Mo."

"Mo? How precious."

"She calls me that. And *only* she calls me that." She glares to drive the point home. "Anyway, all this time she's been gone, she's done her best to keep me up to date, keep me interested. She sends me clothes, shoes, accessories. Everything." She pulls an entire drawer out of her dresser, sets it on her bed, and starts piecing together outfits. "Trust me, I'll send you off on this date looking like you stepped off the runway."

Watching her hands mold masterpieces from separates, I don't doubt her.

"How do you feel about a dress?" she asks.

"In general, I'm not opposed. For a blind date?" I twist my lips. "Can't we just keep it casual?"

"There is such a thing as a casual dress, Stevie! Live a little. I have this adorable wrap dress that would look *amazing* on you."

"If I ever make it to a second date, I'll consider it."

"*Fine-ah.* Here. Be *casual.*" She throws a pair of dark-washed jeans in my lap. They still have a price tag on them. I choke.

"Merrin, I can't wear a pair of two-hundred-dollar jeans. They'll kick me out of them."

She cuts the price tag off. "There. Problem solved." I don't move. "Oh, just try them on. Josie sent me those last year, and they don't fit over my hips. They're wasting away in here." I stare, stone-faced. "I don't concern myself with how she comes by this stuff. Neither should you."

"What does *that* mean?"

"She didn't *steal* them! I just mean, she trades with other designers sometimes. Or takes on a side job for a little under-the-table payment. Like killer jeans she can send to her baby sister."

Hesitantly, I step into them. I assume they won't fit, which will shut her up, but they slide over my thighs and hips effortlessly.

"Told you." Merrin crosses her arms and smirks in victory as I zip and button the jeans, stunned.

They hug me all the way down and look good doing it. "They're a little long," I manage, dry-mouthed.

"A bit, yeah."

"Wow, those are amazing," Nancy says, appearing in the doorway. She puts her hands on her hips, studying me for a moment. "Would heels solve the length issue?"

Merrin claps her hands together. "I have just the ones. You can walk in heels, right?" I nod, though I'm not actually sure. It's been a while.

Merrin makes a thorough mess of her closet but eventually emerges with a pair of gray suede booties with a three-inch heel.

"These you *can't* keep." She sets them at my feet. "You're about a seven, right?"

I slide one foot in with ease, then the other.

"Perfect," Nancy and Merrin say in unison.

I practice walking around the room, hoping to avoid falling on my face in public later.

"Now, Stevie," Nancy says. "What can you tell me about this Luke character?"

"From what I can glean, he's a very nice, well-mannered young man. Also, quite a talented public speaker," I add semi-seriously.

"You'll keep an eye on him?" Despite the playfulness of her tone, there's an urgency behind her eyes.

"Oh, you bet I will. He will be a perfect gentleman, or he'll lose a hand. Or worse."

Nancy smiles. "Good girl. I'm counting on you." I salute, and she winks before leaving the room.

I touch Merrin's arm. "I'm serious, Merrin. If that guy is anything less than completely and utterly respectful—"

"You worry too much, bu—"

"I'm serious, Merrin."

"Stevie! Chill. You do worry too much, *but* I appreciate it. I'm not sure if you've deduced this, but I'm kind of a whoopsie baby."

I sputter a laugh. "Um, okay?"

"I mean, they've never called me that or made me feel it or anything, but there's a five-year gap between my closest brother and me. Everyone else is closer in age, and they've all been out of the house a while. It's really nice to have a sort of big sister around again."

I love the idea of being a big sister, but if I say this out loud, I might cry. Instead, I clear my throat and change the subject.

"Let me see that top on you." I haven't even finished the sentence before Merrin is undressing and redressing, ironically ecstatic to wear my clearance top after she's given me a pair of boutique jeans. She fills it out perfectly. Places where it hung awkwardly on me, it hugs her figure.

"You're stunning."

"Thank you. Now," she says, clapping her hands, "come with me. I have my work cut out for me yet. When was the last time you plucked those eyebrows?"

$$\dagger$$

"I FEEL SO STRANGE," I whine.

"Don't insult me." Merrin tugs a piece of my hair harder than necessary to drive her demand home.

"Ow!"

"Well, hold still and it won't happen again," she barks.

"Okay, okay. Easy, Sweeney Todd."

As much as I'm grateful for Merrin's help in this department, I grow more agitated and exhausted by the moment. She didn't just remove unwanted facial hair—which hurt like hell—and insist on giving me a trim. I've had to field questions I've never thought twice about.

Why aren't your ears pierced, Stevie?

What do you mean you've never had a pedicure?

How do you not know what astringent is?

WHAT DO YOU MEAN YOU DON'T USE DAILY MOISTURIZER?!

The list of things I'm doing wrong is extensive, apparently.

"I can't even believe how amazing you look right now," Merrin whispers. "No wonder you don't wear makeup on the regular. You're just trying not to offend us mere mortals."

"Oh, shuddup," I grumble, uncomfortable with the flattery. "I don't wear makeup because I've never gotten the hang of it." It's mostly the truth. The real truth is I never tried. What's the point when there's no one to show you how?

"Well, I can help you if you like," she says. "I mean, a little basic highlighting is all you need for every day."

"Merrin, I told you, I don't feel the need—"

She holds a mirror in front of my face to silence me. I take it from her, wanting a closer look.

"Told you," she beams.

My reflection is a stranger—not so plain and pale as the girl I'm accustomed to. A subtle but effective application of shadow and liner accentuates her deep blue eyes. Thick, honey waves frame her expertly contoured face.

"Wow." I hand the mirror back to Merrin. "Thank you."

"You're welcome. I told you there wasn't much to it. Just a little color. Nothing wrong with a little color, Stevie."

"I don't remember the last time I wore my hair down."

"I could show you, then you could do it all the time. With all those split ends gone, your hair is very manageable. I swear it's all super simple."

"You've done an amazing job. And I'm grateful. But—"

"Why must you fight it? It's simple self-care, Stevie."

"Mer—"

"Don't you ever miss the days of your mom doing your hair and letting you play with her blush and lipstick? Didn't you always feel so special? So pretty? You should let yourself have that from time to time."

Just tell her. You should tell her. But instead, I stand and walk away.

"I'll get dressed now. Practice in the heels a little more."

Merrin does a final primp at her vanity mirror minutes before the boys are due to arrive.

"You're gorgeous, Mer. All of the time. Stop fidgeting."

Nancy appears in Merrin's room. Again. She's made approximately ten visits in the last five minutes. This time she looks teary. "I need pictures!" She vanishes.

"Is she okay?" I ask.

Merrin rolls her eyes. "I told you she's weird and weepy. I know it's my first date and all, but you'd think she'd be used to this by now."

"But you're the baby," I say.

"But I'm the baby," she agrees. "I'm just glad my dad's not home."

"Where is he?"

"He goes out of town for work sometimes. For the bank."

"Get together, girls!" Nancy reappears with her phone. We stand together. "You're so grown up!" She wipes a tear from her cheek. "My baby is dating! I can't believe this. I'm so old! Stand closer. Perfect. You girls want me to take pictures with your phones?"

"Your camera is better than mine," Merrin says. "Just text them to me. And Stevie hasn't replaced her phone yet."

"Actually," I start, holding up my finger. I run to my backpack, pulling out my new phone. When I unlock it, I find an unread text message. *Mason.* He must have programmed his number in before he gave it to me.

There's a picture of Danny in his costume.

He's been wearing it all day, "practicing," he says. Have fun tonight.

I take a moment to swallow down my smile and the flush in my cheeks before opening the camera function and passing my phone to Nancy.

"I'd love a picture," I say. "Thanks."

"When did you get a new phone?" Merrin's hand is over her heart, a very *clutch-my-pearls* look about her. "Were you ever going to tell me?"

"Shh! It happened kind of suddenly. I'll tell you about it later. Just look happy for the picture." She glares a moment, then cooperates.

Nancy gets us at a few different angles before the doorbell rings. Merrin squeals and shimmies before rushing past her mom toward the front door.

"Keep an eye on my baby girl," Nancy pleads with me.

"Promise." I hug her—it feels like the natural thing to do. "Do you want me to text you updates?" I wave my phone in front of her. "What's your number?"

"No, no." She wipes a finger under her eye. "I'm being silly. She's *eighteen*. It's not like I didn't know this was coming."

I hug her again, and she laughs.

"Bless you, Stevie. I'm so glad she has you. You two just have fun."

I pull back, promising, "I'll get her home safe."

She mouths *thank you* before I join Merrin at the door.

The boys stand on the front porch, Luke holding a solitary yellow rose, and the one I assume is Derek stands behind him. Merrin and Luke both blush as she accepts the rose. It's so annoying it's almost cute. Or is it the other way around?

Merrin takes a long whiff before she sets the flower on a small console table, then we step outside.

"Hi, Stevie." Derek extends his hand. I shake it. "I'm Derek, and I did not bring you a rose. I hope you'll still come out with me."

"I'll give you a chance," I say. "But I expect a giant box of candy at the movies in lieu of flowers."

"Dang," he sighs. "An elaborate bouquet would have been cheaper."

"Choices, Derek. Life is about choices." He smirks and escorts me to the car.

Derek is easy to talk to—easy on the eyes as well—and charming, but I'm still pretty certain when all is said and done, I'll never see him again outside of class.

He has blemish-free skin, pale-blue eyes, and strawberry-blonde hair secured with the appropriate amount of product. His smile reveals teeth so white, I swear they sparkle. He's cute, but he just doesn't *quite* do it for me. I attempt to make the best of it anyway, smiling, chatting, feigning interest even when I'm bored.

Meanwhile, it's obvious Luke and Merrin are each other's type, and they're aching to be alone together. The tension is palpable; it's awkward standing too close to them. I think Merrin has forgotten how to breathe a few times; she's so giddy.

We get to the theater with a little time to spare, so Derek and I send Luke and Merrin to find seats while we collect snacks. It'll give them a few minutes to speak freely to each other, but not long enough I'll feel guilty for letting her out of my sight when I promised Nancy I wouldn't.

"So, you like scary movies?" Derek makes bland conversation while we wait in line.

"No, actually. I hate jump scares, and I can't stand gore."

He pinches his brow. "Then why did you agree to come?"

"Because Merrin asked me to."

He locks eyes with me, a smirk tucked in the corner of his mouth. "So, it had nothing to do with me? Not my striking good looks or delightful personality?"

It's the first sign of a legitimate sense of humor. I decide to test it further.

"Honestly, Derek, I didn't know who you were until tonight."

He claps a hand to his chest. "Well, ouch."

I shrug. "Don't take it too personally."

"Kind of hard not to. I notice you every class. You're pretty much *all* I notice."

A cheap, dim thrill flickers inside me. The way this guy is looking at me, the gravel in his voice—he's coming onto me. I'm just not sure I want it. I'm less sure I can *trust* it.

"I'm glad you came anyway," he says, brushing a stray hair off my cheek. His fingers linger, and I'm surprisingly disinclined to back away.

Another spark of excitement in my belly drives me one step closer to him. It's small and unintentional, but there's no denying that I'm leaning into this—whatever *this* is. He slants further down. *He's going to kiss me. Am I about to let him? I think I am. Do I even like this guy? How could I possibly know? He's a legitimate* stranger.

My internal debate is interrupted when the concession clerk loudly clears his throat.

"What can I get you?" he asks.

Any anticipation left inside me fizzles, relief swooping in to take its place. I'm not ready for this. Not here. Not now.

"I'm going to the bathroom," I announce before bolting out of the lobby, leaving Derek to get snacks by himself.

The end-of-the-date walk to the door has a knot forming in my stomach. He could kiss me. I could let him.

We stroll ahead of Luke and Merrin, leaving them to "chat" in the car for a minute. "I'm glad you came tonight," Derek says. "Despite the lack of roses and everything."

"Well, you at least followed through with the snacks. I'm a sucker for Skittles."

He laughs. "So you had a good time?"

I spend too long debating how to answer this, and he clutches his chest for the second time tonight.

"You're killin' me here, Stevie."

I turn to face him. "I'll make an appearance at your funeral. But without flowers. Because fair is fair."

He shakes his head. "Maybe I'll bring flowers next time," he says.

"Very bold to assume there'll be a next time."

I can't tell if I'm flirting or trying to let him down gently. Maybe it's a very thin line.

His smile softens, and he tilts his head toward mine.

After a loud gulp, I manage a quiet, "Goodnight, Derek." I turn on my heel and walk through the front door, closing it behind me.

CHAPTER
9

Monday morning speech class brings on a resurgence of nervous knots in my stomach. Three days ago, I didn't even know Derek existed. Saturday, between a mediocre dinner and a bad movie, he touched my face in public, leaned in close to kiss me, and was *almost* successful. He would have kissed me on Merrin's front porch if I'd let him.

Why didn't I let him? He's cute enough, can hold a decent conversation, and it wasn't like he was inappropriate or anything. Sure, he was a little full of himself, but he was...*nice?* Not to mention, I haven't been kissed since high school. Though not all of those kisses were sweet. Some I've locked away. Maybe that's why I'm hesitant to let anyone kiss me again. Or maybe it's just that as cute as Derek is, he sets off a red flag in my head. It's subtle but says, *don't go there, Stevie.*

I feel Derek's eyes on me during class but refuse to turn around. Those knots in my stomach want me to. *Hey, let's have a little fun,* they say. *So what if he's not* the guy? *He's a guy, and he's cute.* But I take slow and steady breaths, attempting to internally talk down my hormones. Merrin, on the other hand, glances back at Luke every other minute. They exchanged approximately three thousand texts over the weekend. Her cheeks have been a constant flush, and the only noises to escape her ever-smiling lips have been giggles and sighs.

It's insufferable.

When the professor dismisses class, Merrin gathers her things and gives me a giddy smile that says, *I like you but he's a boy so I'll see you later*, and makes a beeline for Luke. I bolt toward the women's bathroom, unwilling to tempt those less sensible voices in my head. I'm about an inch shy of the door when warm fingers catch my wrist.

"Where's the fire, Stevie?" Those ridiculous knots inside burn. That's where the fire is, in my stupid stomach. Derek turns me toward him. "Not running away from me, are you?"

"Don't give yourself so much credit," I say, overcome by an unfamiliar compulsion to flirt, to be coy. Derek's hand around my wrist isn't helping.

"So you're *not* running away from me?"

"None of your business." His hand slides up to my elbow as we come toe to toe. "We're in the way, you know." I gesture to the bathroom door.

His smile grows mischievous. "Then we should move." He winks. "Walk you to your next class?"

I narrow my gaze, debating the right move. "It's in another building."

"Perfect. More time to visit. Discuss a possible second date."

"*Wow*. I can't tell if I find your confidence admirable or cringey."

He does this subtle jerk with his head. "Come on. We'll hit up a vending machine on the way. I hear you're a sucker for snacks."

That little red flag fades and blurs as I surrender a smile. "Be still my heart. And they say chivalry is dead."

Leaning into our banter, he offers up his elbow—very debonair. I surprise myself by slipping my arm through his and falling into step beside him.

"Well," he says, "I knew after last time I'd need to come armed with more than good looks to impress you."

"I don't need to be *impressed*, Derek."

"Then what do you want, Stevie?"

I shrug. "I'm not sure. What are you offering?"

"I'll be whatever you want me to be." He flashes a grin so charming, my brain glitches. I stare longer than I intend to, all the while that voice in my head repeats *I haven't been kissed since high school.*

Before I know it, we're turning down an unfamiliar hallway instead of making our way toward the exit.

"Um, wrong way," I say, hooking my thumb over my shoulder. When I try to backstep, he shifts, taking me by the wrist again. He quickens his pace and leads me further into unknown territory.

And just like that, Derek is opening a door, guiding me into a small room with a compact, upright piano and a couple of music stands. The walls are covered in soundproofing materials.

Those flutters of excitement turn to stone and drag me down. I think I might vomit.

"I don't want to be in here," I say.

Derek backs me against the door, his fingers trailing my cheek, then my neck. He follows the collar of my shirt down my chest. My heart is racing in all the wrong ways.

"Please don't," I whisper. "Please don't touch me."

He moves his hand away from my chest but doesn't withdraw it completely. He has his other hand braced against the door behind me. Discomfort escalates to panic as memories come in waves. Hot breath on my neck. Hands on my thighs. Lips attacking mine.

"I won't hurt you," Derek says. But that's what that bastard Todd said all those years ago, and it wasn't true then. I doubt it's true now.

Derek keeps leaning in, his lips searching for mine. They land softly on the corner of my mouth, and I tell myself this is different. Derek isn't *Todd.* Derek is genuinely interested in me, and it's just a kiss, and everything is okay, and I don't need to hyperventilate.

I haven't kissed back yet, but Derek is still moving his lips against mine. His hand slides from my shoulder down to my waist, under the hem of my shirt. I draw a sharp inhale and flinch as his fingers inch toward my ribcage.

Snapping out of panic mode, I shove both hands against his chest, and he stumbles backward.

"Don't touch me," I say again, louder.

"Whoa, whoa, whoa. What's the matter?" He steps closer, hands and lips coming for me. "We were having fun, weren't we?"

"This isn't fun for me. Back off."

He tilts his head, raising a brow. "You didn't say please."

These words ignite a different kind of fire in my belly. I throat whack him with a straight and firm hand, then knee him in the groin. He makes choking noises as he doubles over.

"Please," I say, my hands pressed flat against my stomach. Before I grab my backpack, I take a long, deep breath. As I find the doorknob, he speaks—more like croaks—through a sharp gasp.

"What the...? Why?"

"I said *no*, douchebag."

I speed walk to my next class, which I'm already late for, and sit in the back of the classroom, where I retain none of the lesson. It's impossible to hear anything over the thumping inside my head.

It's been five years since I've had to shove someone off of me. I'm grateful I remembered how.

My upbringing was unorthodox and came with a slew of disadvantages. But the bonus to being raised by that grumpy old man was that he never once instilled in me to *look pretty* for the boys. He didn't spew garbage like *if a boy teases you and hurts your feelings, it's just because he likes you.* One thing he'd been right about when he got sick—he *had* been hard on me, but it *did* make me tough.

You don't take no crap from nobody, Stevie.

When Todd came onto me in the music room after school, and I said no, he didn't listen. Only, he was more aggressive about it than Derek was. I had to *fight* Todd off me. I was still crying when Gene came home from work hours later. Technically, because nothing *happened*, we couldn't press charges. Well, we could have, but the police said we'd need a good lawyer, which we couldn't afford. Todd wasn't allowed back on campus, though, and Gene made sure from that moment on, I carried pepper spray and knew how to handle myself.

Little did he know he was preparing me for a not-so-distant

future: living alone as a single woman. Maybe in that regard, *Todd* was the best worst thing that could have happened to me, even if it had spoiled me for the piano. And sandalwood. Maybe it's broken me completely. I'm not sure. All I know is being in that tiny, dark room with a piano and a guy who didn't take *no* for an answer has put me over the edge, and I'm free-falling.

Two classes and a bike ride to Bright Beginnings later, I'm still shaking. The drumming in my head is subsiding, but I'm too jittery to lock up my bike; I can't get the combination knobs to cooperate.

When a hand lands on my shoulder, I jump about three feet and gasp.

"Girl, it's me. Calm down." Scarlett is smiling, laughing. Then, she sees my face and wraps an arm around my shoulder. "Come on," she says, pulling me close.

Inside a small, quiet, unoccupied office, Scarlett guides me into a chair and sits across from me.

"What happened?" she asks.

"We're late. I should get clocked in."

"We're fine. Just take a breath. Tell me what happened."

"Nothing. Nothing happened."

"Babe, you're shaking. Something happened."

"No. Something *could* have happened. But I stuck my knee between his legs and left."

Scarlett's eyes bulge. "I'm getting Marge." She stands and heads for the door. "We're calling campus security."

"No, don't." I put my hand up, waving her back to her seat. "It's not like that. He just...he tried to kiss me when I said no."

She arches a brow.

"I know, I know. That's still not okay. Which is why I clotheslined him and kneed him...you know."

She lets out a low whistle. "Damn, girl. You don't fool around."

"I'm a single woman who lives alone. I can't afford to." She nods, concurring. "It just rattled me." I rub my shaky hands together, focusing on my breathing.

She sits there a moment, not saying anything. Just...existing in the same space with a look of support and understanding. It's enough. "I'll go tell Marge you just need a minute for a family matter or something," she says, then holds my hand in hers and squeezes it. "For the record, I'm really proud of you."

I squeeze back. "Thanks. I'm a little proud of me, too."

When I'm alone, I pull out my phone to text Merrin.

> Before you hear otherwise, Derek is a sleaze and I am not a psycho.

MERRIN

> ?????

> I'll call you after I get Danny to bed tonight. Please don't be alone with Luke until we've talked. I need to know he's better than his friend.

MERRIN

> Stevie, what the H happened?

> You know you can swear with me, right? I'm not your mom or dad.

MERRIN

> Ha! If you were, I'd have said what the heck or what in the world. I wouldn't have left it open to interpretation.

> Fair point. Talk tonight.

After my shift, I'm mostly pulled together. The two-mile ride to Mason and Daniel's helps. Fresh air. Exercise. Deep breaths.

I've already cried in front of Mason. *Twice.* I've snapped at him. Honestly, it's a miracle he hasn't fired me. Time to conceal all my crazy; I need this job.

I roll my neck, ring my hands, and knock. Daniel swings the door open for me and jumps into my arms.

"My Stevie!" he cries.

I close the door behind me and head toward the living room. "How are you today, munchkin?"

"I ate too much candy when Daddy told me not to and I got a tummy ache but den I had a big poop and now I feel better!"

Bless this kid. "Good to know," I say at the same time Mason comes into view. He's standing at the stove, dragging his hands down his face.

"Lovely, Danny Boy," he sighs. "So glad you shared that with Stevie. I'm sure it made her day."

I laugh. "Actually, yeah, it totally did."

Mason stares at me a moment with a lopsided grin before he says, "Hi."

Why is it suddenly a thousand degrees in here? "Hi," I return.

He nods toward the stove. "I was a little late getting the lasagna in the oven. Still needs another thirty minutes."

"We can wait, right Danny?"

Danny pouts his lips. "I guess."

Mason and I laugh, then I kiss Daniel's soft hair and take in a big whiff of his sour apple shampoo. This morning's unpleasantness fades further into the background the longer I'm around this kid.

Mason approaches, eyeing Daniel. "Alright, buddy. Hugs."

Daniel gets a little overeager to leap from my arms into Mason's and nearly falls. I step and adjust to catch him at the same time Mason does. Daniel laughs the whole time, not realizing how close his head was to landing on the hard floor. Or simply not caring.

We wind up in a group huddle, Mason and I each holding a hand to Daniel's back, a few of our fingers overlapping. We don't shift or pull away from each other as his eyes lock with mine.

I draw in a shallow breath, and I'm hit with notes of pine and fresh breezes. No sandalwood.

"You changed it," I whisper, not looking away.

"Of course I did." He says it with such ease and simplicity, and a warmth balloons inside my chest.

I spend another moment or two in stunned silence before I pass Daniel off to his father and turn away, walking toward the living room. I bury my face in my hands, trying to hide the rush of emotions crashing over me in heavy, encompassing waves.

When I hear the exchange of goodbyes and the pitter-patter of feet down the hall and up the stairs, I wait for Mason's steps to fade toward the front door. There's nothing. Bracing myself, I turn back around, peeking through my fingers. He's standing where I left him, wearing an expression caught between a frown and a smile like he doesn't know how to feel right now. Honestly, neither do I, though I seem to be fighting the urge to hug him. In the weeks I've been here, all the kindness he's shown me, all the gestures—the phone, the bike light, the bonus—none of it compares to this.

I pry my hands from my face, clearing my throat. Unable to speak, I mouth *thank you.*

There's a tenderness behind his eyes as he mouths, *you're welcome,* then walks away.

CHAPTER
10

It's been eleven days since the Derek incident, and Luke is still with Merrin. I have to give the guy *some* credit for not running away after I lectured him at length about learning from the mistakes of his douchebag friend. Luke and Derek still share a desk in Speech, which means making occasional eye contact with the moron. His face never has anything nice to say to mine, which I take as no loss whatsoever.

At the end of class, Merrin and I gather our things.

"Hey," she says, "is it cool if I don't walk out with you? I've got a stupid project meeting with my chem lab partner. I don't want to be late."

"Of course. Go. Be amazing. You don't have to ask my permission."

"You sure you're not going to throat punch her if she doesn't?" a snarky Derek interjects, clearly still licking wounds.

Luke scolds his friend for being *an ass.*

Merrin gapes at me in a very *he did* not *just say that* kind of way.

Hoisting my backpack over my shoulder, I sigh. "The difference, Derek, is *she's* not trying to feel me up after I've said no." I whip around and meet his eyes, wide in anger. Or maybe just embarrassment. I haven't been quiet.

Luke snorts as he smacks Derek's arm. "You had that comin', bro."

With a flippant shrug, I saunter out of the classroom, rather impressed with myself. Luke's laughter and Merrin's enthusiastic, "Yas, queen!" follow me down the hall.

I practically skip to my next class, exhilarated after standing up for myself again. And without assaulting anyone, no less. My hair is down today—a rarity—and I run my fingers through it, interlocking my hands at the base of my neck.

Breathe, Stevie. Focus. I still have two more classes to sit through.

Just as my flushed cheeks begin to cool and my heart rate slows to normal, my phone buzzes.

MASON

> Dan and I are out and about for some appointments today. Can we pick you up at BB after your shift? Save you a ride?

His name on my screen brings on a smile I can't tame. All the color flies back into my cheeks. *Play it cool, play it cool.*

> Sounds perfect. Thanks!

I spend the rest of the day kicking myself, worried *perfect* came off as too strong a word.

♪

"Stevie's widing in my twuck." Daniel talks in sing-song as we leave Bright Beginnings.

"I guess I should be grateful he's at least enunciating the *t*," Mason says, "so it doesn't sound like he's cursing you out."

I laugh. "I don't know. I think one day you'll wake up to find him speaking with perfect articulation, and you'll be so depressed you won't know what to do with yourself. Honestly, I miss being *Stebie.*"

"Stevie is widing in my twuck," Daniel sings on repeat.

"You're right," Mason concedes. "I should stop pushing and just... let it be."

At the same time, Daniel and I sing, "let it be, let it be!" I look back at him in his booster seat, smiling as he continues belting the lyrics. He muddles the verses with the chorus to the point the words make no sense, but I don't correct him.

"I guess it makes sense you'd sing him Beatles songs, too," Mason says.

"Well, duh." He side-eyes me with a grin. "But seriously, about the rest of it, you're his dad. It's your choice. And don't let anyone, least of all me, tell you how to do it. I'm just saying there are worse things he could be doing than struggling with his Rs."

Back at the house, I unlatch Daniel's five-point harness while Mason lifts my bike from the bed of his truck. As Danny maneuvers out of his seat and into my arms, he clings to my neck.

"My Stevie smells good," he says.

"Aw. Thanks, buddy."

"You welcome. You look lovely today."

"Oof. You're melting my heart, little man. Lovely? That's the nicest thing anyone has ever called me. Thank you." I kiss his cheek and set him down.

"I told Stevie she's lovely, Daddy," Daniel says, hugging Mason's legs. "It's yo tuwn."

"It's my turn?" Daniel nods, and Mason winks at him. I chew on my lip and start toward the house. Mason's voice stops me. "He's right. You're lovely today. And all the days." I can't tell if he's being facetious or completely serious.

"Um, thanks," I say, barely audible.

"Your hair, it's like...golden. It looks nice down."

I'm unsure how widely to smile or how gracious to be because this is all making my insides mushy and confused. I mumble a "thanks" as I hear Daniel running up to me.

"Stevie," he says, tugging on my pant leg, "I could like some milk in my blue cup."

Bless you, child. It pulls the trigger on the awkward moment, killing it.

I HAVEN'T BEEN WORKING with kids for long, but I know enough to know the rate at which four-year-old Daniel mentions death is over the top. I've spent all evening debating whether to discuss it with Mason, and when he comes home from work, he immediately detects my anxiety.

"What's wrong?" he asks, panicked. "What happened? Is Danny okay?"

"He's fine." I hold my hands up. "Nothing bad happened. No one is hurt. Everything's fine."

He puts a hand to his chest, exhaling.

"Sorry if I scared you," I say.

"What's wrong?"

"I don't want to be indelicate or intrusive, but it's, well..." I take a deep breath. "Daniel seems fixated on death at times. When he plays and tells stories, people always die. Most days, I can brush over it, but tonight...? It was just a little unnerving."

"Oh." Mason plops onto the couch. His face contorts, and his eyes wander like he's solving a puzzle in his head. Something appears to be funny, then immediately depressing.

"I hate to upset you. I just wasn't sure if this was a *thing*, and if there was a specific way you'd like me to handle it...?"

"My—Daniel's mother," Mason whispers. "She... When he was a baby..."

My heart sinks. My knees finally stop shaking, but only because I've gone limp.

"Dan overheard an inappropriate conversation I had with my mom a while ago. It's hard to explain."

"I'm so sorry she passed. That's devastating."

He takes a beat, tugging at his lips before he responds. "She was a complicated person. I made some spiteful comments I shouldn't have that made light of her dying. It stuck with him. I've talked with him about death and tried to let him get all his questions out so we could put it behind us. I've tried to help him understand death is permanent and not a joke. But, well..."

"I'm sorry to pour salt on old wounds."

"No. You didn't. Our appointments today? One of them was for Danny to speak with a counselor."

I lean forward. "Is he okay?"

Mason offers a fleeting smile. "Yeah. He's okay. But there was some discussion about his mom. I'm sure that's why he was a little over the top today."

"Makes sense."

The room falls silent, neither of us knowing where to go from here.

"Well, I should get going," I announce, abruptly standing and grabbing my backpack.

"Stevie, please take the truck. You're going to freeze. I won't need it over the weekend."

"It's not so bad tonight."

"I told you the truck was for 'just in case.' This qualifies as 'just in case.'"

I stare at the ground as I walk toward the front door.

He follows after me. "Why is this complicated? It's cold. You don't have a car. I have two. It's simple math."

"It's not simple for me," I mumble.

"What does that mean?"

I turn around. "I can't explain it. And I don't want to right now. Maybe one day. I just...my independence means something to me. I hate feeling like I owe anyone—"

"I'm not asking for anything in return."

I believe him. Of course, I *believe* him. The man who changed his body wash because I asked, offering zero context. But what happened with Derek ripped my past wide open, and old scars feel too fresh. I'm too vulnerable to accept generosity right now, even from someone so gentle and kind as Mason Shepard.

I manage a half-hearted grin. "Maybe another day. Just not tonight."

"You're stubborn, you know that?"

"I prefer tenacious."

"I know you've always looked out for yourself, but—"

"You wouldn't understand," I snap. "And I'm not in the mood to explain it to you. So please just let me go."

He nods, reaching into his back pocket and pulling out my week's pay.

I stare at his outstretched hand, chewing the insides of my cheeks, unable to comprehend why I want to run away from this man and kiss him at the same time. With shaky, reluctant fingers, I take the money and leave.

I LOVE and hate grocery shopping. It's less stressful now with a second income, but a hint of melancholy lingers. Gene's been gone nearly three years, yet I always find myself in front of the assorted nuts, searching for his favorite trail mix. He hated the kind with the raisins, instead preferring the *indulgent* mix with extra chocolate.

"At this point, you might as well buy a bag of M&Ms," I would say.

"I like the peanuts," he'd argue.

"Then get peanut M&Ms."

"Just put them in the cart, Stevie."

It was such a ridiculous argument, but it always escalated, ending in grunting and eye-rolling. Now, I miss it. I peruse the trail mix options, sighing. Maybe I've been here five minutes. Maybe it's been a few seconds. My phone buzzes—probably Merrin—and I snap out of it.

I stroll down the aisle, tucking my loose hair behind my ears as I go. I'd stood in front of the mirror this morning, brushing it, and all I could hear was, "Your hair...it's golden...it looks nice down." The echo of Mason's words brought on an elated smile, too quickly eclipsed by all the reasons I could never pursue him.

Some girls are at liberty to explore their complicated feelings for an attractive man in a position of power; I am not one of them. Do I sometimes get lost in Mason's eyes to the point I forget to breathe? Sure. Do I sometimes feel like running my hands through his wavy hair and kissing him full on the mouth? Yup. But do I need this job? More than anything.

As much as I wanted to tell him everything yesterday and explain my irrational response to gifts and gestures, I can't help feeling it's safer to keep him at a distance. Or maybe I just *really* care what he thinks, and I don't want him to see me as weak.

I sigh listlessly as I park myself in the breakfast aisle, a half-empty basket hanging from my arm. I like the cereal with the clumps of dried yogurt, and they're out. My mind says, *you're going to buy yogurt, anyway. Just call it a draw.* But it's not the same. They have it in the name-brand version, which costs twice as much as the generic I normally buy. I'm ready to grab for it anyway, to allow myself a tiny splurge, when a grating voice makes my entire body cringe.

"Well, well." Ugh. *Derek.* "Am I allowed to say hello, or will that earn me a right hook?"

"Back off, Derek," I say through clenched teeth.

"Will you even look at me?"

Turning to face him, I watch his smug smirk widen.

"Wasn't so hard, was it?"

"Dude, I don't know what your problem is, but can we not do this right here? Right now?"

"Hey, I'm allowed to buy cereal, too. Growing boys need their Cocoa Puffs."

"Clearly," I sigh, "you're allowed to buy cereal. You're even allowed to say hello. But you don't need to keep rehashing the same garbage every time you see me. Just let it go and move on."

"Dammit, woman, you friggin' got me where it counts. Pretty extreme. Maybe I don't want to let it go. Then you had to embarrass me about it yesterday."

An irritated growl rumbles in my throat. "*I* didn't bring it up yesterday, genius. You did! I'm sorry if that was *embarrassing* for you, but what do you expect when you just poke, poke, *poke?*"

"I went in for a harmless *kiss.*"

"After I asked you to stop. Emphatically." My words come out shrill, louder than seems appropriate for the breakfast aisle of a Grocery Outlet. I breathe slowly through my nose and lower my voice. "Can you just grab your Cocoa Whatevers and go, please?"

"It's okay for you to humiliate me in class, but the grocery store is taking it too far, huh?"

I groan, tightening my fist at my side. "You're repugnant, you know that?"

"And you're a scared little virgin," he shoots back.

I almost drop my basket. "The hell, Derek?" He reaches for my shoulder, and I jerk back.

"See," he says. "I can tell by the way you flinch and pull away."

My whole face burns. "Look, I'm sorry you can't handle rejection or whatever, but I'm two seconds away from emptying an entire canister of pepper spray in your face, you arrogant ass." He rolls his eyes. "Oh, you bet I carry it. Always."

He opens his mouth to speak, but a smooth voice behind me cuts him off.

"There you are. I've been looking everywhere."

My breath catches in my chest as I turn around to see Mason standing there, pushing a cart with Daniel and a few groceries inside it.

Daniel beams at the sight of me, nearly falling out of the cart in his efforts to jump into my arms. Abandoning my basket on the floor, I secure him in a tight hug. He presses his smiling face against my shoulder.

"My Stevie," he whispers.

Mason's eyes pierce mine, asking silently if I'm alright. I offer a subtle nod, and he holds out his car keys. "Why don't you and Daniel head outside? I'll meet you there."

Accepting the keys with trembling fingers, I leave the store with the giggling toddler in my arms.

I let Daniel sit on my lap in the front seat while we wait for Mason. He tells me all about his day, though much of it is clearly fiction. I offer intermittent smiles and single-syllable responses, playing with his curly hair as I listen. I focus entirely on him, not once looking up to see if a certain jerk ever comes through the front doors. When Mason opens the driver's side door, I jump, and a small cry escapes my lips.

"Are you alright?" He places a gentle hand on my arm. I nod, taking in a large breath. "Are you sure?"

"Mmhmm."

"Kay. Give me a second." He unloads his cart into the back while I chew on the insides of my cheeks. I blink back tears, taking long and heavy breaths in through my nose, out through tight lips. *Don't cry. Not here.*

Mason holds up a couple of bags in my line of sight. "Yours," he informs me, then sets them down.

"You shouldn't have, but thank you."

He climbs into the driver's seat and closes the door.

"You guys always shop here?" I ask, my tone so numb and disconnected I hardly recognize my voice.

"Normally on Fridays. But with all our appointments yesterday..."

"I see."

"Stevie?"

"Hm?" I still can't look at him.

"Who *was* that guy?"

"Just some dou—" I stop myself, looking at Daniel, blissfully playing with the zipper of my jacket. Finally, I meet Mason's gaze. "Just some *juice box*," I substitute. Mason squints, his lips tugged into a perplexed frown until he understands I'm swapping out *douchebag*. His features soften, and his shoulders shake as he laughs. Daniel laughs to match him, then stone-faced, asks for a juice box.

"When we get home," Mason says. Then back to me, "I know you hate people swooping in when you're clearly able to handle yourself, but I didn't like the way he was talking to you. Or looking at you. Or breathing or standing."

My cheeks twitch. "I didn't either. Thank you. For swooping in. I wasn't looking forward to having to assault him a second time."

"Wait, *what*?"

I cover Danny's ears, which makes him giggle. "He tried to put his hands where they didn't belong. I said no. He didn't listen. I made him listen." Mason nods, sticking out his bottom lip. "He was the blind date," I add, letting my palms fall away from Daniel's ears.

"Well, clearly, *that* went well."

I laugh. "Yeah. He's a creep."

"What's a creep?" Daniel asks.

Whoops. "Well, like the bad guys Spiderman fights," I improvise.

"Oh. Okay." He nods, returning his attention to my zipper.

"Thank you for being my Spiderman," I whisper to Mason, immediately regretting it. It feels like too much and somehow not enough.

"Anytime." His smile is subtle but sincere. It takes all my inner strength to look away.

Pressing my forehead against Daniel's, I cross my eyes. He makes his own silly face, then laughs with his whole body. I hug him close, taking another calming breath.

"Are you on your bike?" Mason asks. I shake my head. "Walked?" I nod. "I'll drop you home."

Home is the last place I want to go. "Merrin's," I croak.

"Sorry?"

I clear my throat. "Could you take me to Merrin's? Please?"

"Whatever you need. Are you sure you're ready? We can sit here as long as you want."

I allow myself another glance. Mason's curly hair falls over his forehead, and I have to sit on my hand to keep from brushing it back. *Whatever I need, as long as I want?* It's him. I want and need him. But for now, this car and his smile are enough.

CHAPTER
11

It's never taken much for me to cry. Still, it seems a little excessive to be curled up in Merrin's bed, crying into her lap within minutes of my arrival.

I didn't call or text ahead. I just showed up with two random bags of groceries, my lips clamped shut, my chest constricting, holding in the tears until we were safely in her room with the door closed, then I lost it. She doesn't ask questions, just strokes my hair, rubs my back, hands me tissues, and lets me slobber all over her until I fall asleep.

I awake in a darkened room, groggy, my head pounding. Merrin sits beside me, her face illuminated by the glow of her television. John Wayne moves across the screen with his signature hitch in his giddyup.

"Didn't peg you for a fan of The Duke," I croak. She reaches for the remote. "No. Leave it. I like Big Jake. 'Don't call me Daddy,'" I say in the worst John Wayne impersonation ever.

"My grandpa loved westerns," she says. "I used to watch with him. He passed away a couple years ago. I know they're problematic, societally speaking, but watching them makes me feel safe." She looks at me, scrunching her nose. "That probably sounds dumb."

"Not even." I attempt to sit up. My head retaliates, and I flop back down. Merrin touches cool fingers to my forehead.

"I'll be right back. Hang tight."

She brings me water, a cold washcloth, and Tylenol.

"I'm being too much trouble," I say.

"Stop it. Crying gives me a headache, too." Her care is effortless, almost methodical.

"You've done this before."

"Big family, remember? You learn a thing or two. What about you? You never talk about your family."

Her words cut through me. "I don't have one," I say. She squints, her brows crushing together. I point to myself. "My parents died when I was four. My uncle took me in, then died when I was nineteen. He liked westerns, too." I add the last part like I haven't just dropped a bomb on her. "That's why I never invite you over. Why I don't talk about my family. My house is sad and empty and sometimes I am too." I'm crying again.

Merrin lies beside me, wrapping an arm around my middle and burying her face in my hair. "I wish I'd known," she whispers. "I've said some stupid things, Stevie. Some really insensitive things."

"I didn't want you to know." I wipe my face. "I liked having a friend who hadn't seen those sadder parts of me. But that wasn't fair to you."

"Hey, this isn't about me. Don't worry about it." She squeezes me as more tears fall.

I blink at the ceiling, trying to pull myself together.

"I just didn't want to be the friend you pity. You know? I didn't want to feel like a burden to anyone. All my friends back in high school were weird around me. Like, try as I might to fit in, I was still the girl with dead parents who lived with her ornery uncle. It defined me. No one ever wanted to come to my house. I didn't get invited to a lot of social activities. When people found out my feelings were hurt, they'd say things like, 'We didn't want you to feel out of place.' Or, because we were poor, 'We didn't think you'd be able to afford it.' I always felt like an afterthought. I wanted a chance to be normal."

Merrin squeezes me again. "You're not an afterthought, and I don't pity you. You are the furthest thing from a burden I have in my life. Understand?"

I nod but can't respond further. My headache is starting to subside, and I don't want to risk another breakdown.

"Can I stay here tonight?" I ask.

"Of course." Merrin sits up, wiping her face.

"Don't you need to ask your parents?"

"I already did. Mom said yes a little too enthusiastically. I think she wants to adopt you." She slumps, cupping a hand across her mouth. "Oh, gosh. Stevie, I'm sorry. See? There I go saying stupid things."

"Hey, your mom can adopt me any day." Can you legally adopt an adult? I'd be all for it. "You guys have been amazing to me."

She smiles. "It's not hard. You're pretty lovable."

We watch *Big Jake* in silence for a while.

"Listen," Merrin says, "you're under no obligation, but do you want to tell me what happened to make you show up unexpectedly? Not that I don't love having you here."

I give her the abridged summation of events.

"Oh. My. Wow." She lets out a heavy sigh, her lips fluttering over it.

"It just rattled me a bit. I know we were in public and nothing was going to happen. He's just a jerk, not dangerous. Not yet, anyway. Then with the whole Mason swooping in and making me feel like a damsel in distress, it just... I can't really explain why. It's been a strange few months, and I just needed to cry."

"I don't blame you. I'm so glad Mason was there to step in."

"Honestly, so am I. And I love how he just walked up and pulled me away, didn't try to get in the middle of anything. I don't think he even acknowledged Derek. I mean, I didn't ask if he said anything after I left, but I doubt it. He probably just left Derek scratching his head, wondering what happened."

"Ugh. Derek. What a douchenozzle."

I sputter a laugh. "That's a good word for him."

"How's your head?" she asks, frowning at me. "Any better?"

"A bit."

"You should eat."

I nod. "Would be smart."

"Frosting?" she offers with raised brows. I laugh. "Seriously, it's my favorite when I'm sad."

"I'm not sad anymore," I assure her. "Besides, I could use something substantial. I haven't eaten since breakfast."

"Well," she breathes, standing from the bed. "That's unacceptable. I'll go make you a plate."

I reach for her hand. "Wait. Just a second." She sits beside me again. "Thank you."

"I've hardly done anything."

"I knew I could come here. I knew I'd be safe, and someone here would listen to me and care about me. That's *huge*. It's what I've needed but haven't had for a long time. Seriously, Mer. You're the best thing to happen to me."

"Don't make *me* cry."

I squeeze her hand in mine, release it, and wipe moisture from under her eyes.

"I'm the best thing, huh? Better than *Mason*?" She shoots me a teasing grin, and I blush despite my best efforts.

"I can't—I mean, I *don't* think of him that way," I lie.

"Sure." She drags the word out, both of us knowing the truth. "Whatever you say." She stands again to leave but stops at her door to look back at me.

"You were wrong, you know," she says. "You do have a family." Tears well again. "I'm your family now."

"MERRIN, I appreciate the effort, but I'm not buying any of those. I have the ones I want. You will not change my mind."

Merrin has been attempting to introduce me to "Retail Therapy," but not surprisingly, I'm doing it wrong. I've turned down perfume, expensive makeup she'd tried to tell me was "an investment," high heels, and more.

I came to the mall with a single goal in mind: shoes. Only what I need—no frivolity. She keeps handing me more fashionable boots than the ones I've selected. Mine are practical—a sturdy pair of dark brown, waterproof Timberlands with good traction.

"Please just try these ones on." She pushes a pair of zip-up ankle boots my way. "They're much cuter."

"And I would be miserable wearing them. I'd slip and slide all over the place. My feet would be cold and sore by the time I got anywhere. I'm getting these ones." They're already on my feet. My old rags, formerly known as shoes, are ready for the nearest garbage can. "I'm completely sold on them. Personally, I think these are cute. They suit me."

She hangs her head and begins putting back all the shoes she gathered in hopes of changing my mind. "Fine," she grumbles, "have it your way. You are the worst person to shop with."

"Just one of my many character flaws," I sigh. "Deal with it, babe."

"Honestly, it's your worst quality."

"Look, Mer, maybe someday I'll be able to buy a bottle of twenty-five-dollar shampoo just because I feel like it, but today is not that day. If it weren't for my job looking after Daniel, I wouldn't even be able to get new shoes. I'd be wearing *these* through winter." I hold up the shabby shoes before relinquishing them to the garbage bin.

Merrin frowns, then looks at my feet. "I guess in comparison, those *are* cute."

I nudge her shoulder as I pass by on the way to checkout.

For the first time in my life, I went for what I *wanted*, not what was cheapest on the clearance rack. Do I want to gag when the girl behind the counter rings them up? A little. But I walk out of the store feeling like a new woman, and my feet. Feel. Amazing.

"He must pay you well," Merrin says. "You didn't even flinch when you bought those."

"Oh, I screamed on the inside," I assure her. "This is a first for me. But I need good shoes."

"Well, thank you, Mason," she mumbles.

"Yes. Thank you, Mason."

I've tried to put him out of my mind today, but it's impossible. I keep thinking of him coming to my rescue at the grocery store yesterday. Of his dark eyes silently asking if I was alright. How he'd so easily inserted himself for my sake.

"Stevie? Where'd you go?" Merrin waves her hand in front of me.

I smile, snapping out of it. "I'm here."

"Should we eat?" She starts toward the food court and gestures for me to follow.

"Yes. Absolutely." But my brain is so foggy with *what-ifs* that I can't string enough words together to order. Merrin finally tells me to find us a table while she orders for me.

I take the first open seat and flop down, my mind wandering to places I've purposefully blocked off. It's gotten progressively harder the last few weeks since Mason changed soap simply because I asked. And the way he said, *Of course I did*, and kept his hand on mine. Like he might feel something too.

"Stevie? Dude! Where are you?" Merrin appears at the table with a platter of fries and burgers.

"What?"

"I didn't know if you liked cheese on yours, so I got one without."

"I'll eat whatever. Thanks. And I'll pay you back."

"It's nothing. Don't worry about it." She sits down, pushing food in my direction. "You've been out of it since you bought the boots. Regretting your decision?"

I laugh. "No, but nice try."

She takes a bite of her burger, staring at me. "Okay, what is going on with you?" she asks, her mouth still full.

I don't know what's going on with me. How would I explain it to someone else?

After forcing a loud swallow, Merrin asks, "Why are you smiling?"

"Am I smiling?"

She raises an eyebrow. "Stevie." It comes out low, accusatory. "Why are you smiling?"

"It's stupid. Let's just eat." But I have no appetite.

She points a plastic straw at me. "I *will* cut you."

"Geez, Mer."

"Tell me why your face is doing that weird, glowy thing, and we won't have any problems." She stabs her straw into the lid of her cup. "Wouldn't happen to have anything to do with a certain, generous, 'we don't go there because he's off limits' someone, would it?" She wriggles her brows.

I sigh, defeated. "I'm falling for him. Hard. Alright?"

"Gasp!" she teases, bringing her hand to her chest.

"Har-har."

"I'm *stunned*, I tell you. Gobsmacked."

Panic wells. "Wait, am I that much of an open book? Do you think he knows? What if he knows? Merrin!"

"Well, he hasn't fired you. So..."

"That's comforting."

"Maybe you should throw yourself at him. See what happens." She shrugs, wide-eyed, then takes another bite of her burger.

"This isn't funny, Merrin. It's...it's...I hate it here."

She laughs, chewing. I pick up a fry, then put it back.

"You're both adults, Stevie. I don't see the complication here."

Of course, *she* doesn't. Bless her sheltered little heart.

"I need this job, Merrin. I *love* this job. I don't want to throw it away."

"There are other jobs. And if money is tight, I'm sure my parents could—"

"No. I don't want handouts. And there's more to it than that. It's hard to explain."

"I wish you'd try."

I release a heavy sigh. "I love you. You know that, right?"

She smiles. "I do."

"Then trust me when I tell you that one day, you'll be privy to all the weirdest, scariest, most difficult parts of my life. Past and present. All the hard-to-follow anecdotes and messed up family dynamics. But it's going to take time. Okay? I've never had someone in my life like you before. It's wonderful, but it's an adjustment. Just give me time. Please."

She reaches across the table and squeezes my fingers.

"I can do that," she says. "But only because I love you so much. Patience isn't my strong suit."

"Gasp," I say, mimicking her earlier tone. "You don't say."

"Shuddup," she mumbles, throwing a fry at my face before we both descend in a fit of laughter.

CHAPTER
12

Being around Mason used to be a roller coaster, but lately, it all feels like falling. The *grocery incident* only made it worse. Or better. It's hard to tell.

I'd been unable to squeak out anything other than a timid *hello* and *goodbye* when I arrived today, though I've managed to put on a happy face and enjoy my time with Daniel. Once he's in bed, there's nothing left to do but *dwell* and I find myself sinking.

I try and fail to focus on homework or reading. Normally, music proves a solid distraction, but tonight it's just highlighting memories and feelings previously buried but dredged up in recent weeks, thanks to *Derek* and his escapades in that little soundproof practice room.

I force myself through the house, toward the room with the baby grand, and slowly approach the bench. Regret and shame turn in my stomach as I slide into place and stare at the keys. A stairway of ebony and ivory, just waiting for my fingers to dance across it.

Music was the one thing that always made sense to me. The first time an elementary school teacher taught us *Every Good Boy Does Fine* and *A Space for a FACE*, I could read music. No further instruction required.

In middle school, my music teacher favored me. Gave me all the solos, used me as an example. Praised my range. Most of the choir hated me and called me a *brown noser* and a *suck-up*. It never bothered me, though. I was carving my path out of Spokane and into college. I was *surviving*.

Not having a piano at home, I only ever got a chance to practice at school, and there wasn't much opportunity for it. Until...until, until, until.

Todd.

I can give you lessons after school. I'll drive you home.

He said it was for fun. A favor. No charge. He was twenty-something, earning a tiny stipend by accompanying choir every day. Our teacher doted on him. He was one of her former students, and she trusted him, so I thought I could, too. Turns out he was just a sleaze with an affinity for playing piano and duping naïve girls.

You're so talented, Stevie. A natural.

"Stevie?"

It takes me a moment to realize the hand on my shoulder isn't a shadow of my past, and I let out a small yelp as I jump, bumping into the keys and striking an unmelodious chord. By the time I'm off the bench and facing Mason, I feel tears stinging the corners of my eyes.

"Are you okay? I think I said your name five times."

I take a deep breath, shaking out my hands. "Just zoned out, is all. Sorry to get so dramatic." I manage a quick, fake laugh. "Been so long since I played. I guess I just forgot how it works."

He humors me with a weak, lopsided smile. "I don't play nearly as much as I should, either."

"Well, at least you know how, and you're not one of those people with a baby grand *just for show*. Because gross."

"Agreed."

"Look, about Saturday. Mason, I—"

"We don't have to talk about Saturday. If you want to pretend it never happened, it's fine. You don't owe me anything. I'm just glad I was there."

"Me too. But, um..." I scratch my scalp, wrinkling my nose. "How much did you hear?"

"Enough to know the guy was out of line. Should that asshat— uh..." He clears his throat. "Should he ever bother you again, *please* call me. I would love to punch that guy. With my Outback."

"Does anything say *Washington* like death by Subaru?"

He ponders for a moment. "Maybe death by Starbucks."

The gravity of his eyes traps me for a little too long before I can shake it off. Ignoring the warm flutters coursing through my *everything*, I find my backpack and shoes.

"So, you *did* get new shoes," he observes.

"Yeah. Only so many times you can duct tape something together before you just look trashy."

"You weren't trashy. You were eccentric. Whimsical."

I roll my eyes before kneeling to tie my laces. "Said the liar."

His laugh rings out, full and deep, further fueling the nervous energy inside me. I *love* his laugh. Being the one to make him laugh? Even better.

He opens the door for me when I'm ready to leave.

"Are you sure you won't take the truck?"

"Are you ever going to stop asking me?"

"Are you ever going to change your answer?" he counters.

"Entirely possible."

"Said the liar."

I bite my bottom lip, failing to suppress a lovesick grin. After a moment of hovering in the doorway, fiddling with my fingers, I turn to leave.

His quiet "Goodnight, Stevie" breaks through the silence of the sleepy streets, and I swear I hear it ringing in my ears all the way home.

ON FRIDAY, winter kicks in with an inversion and a ten-degree drop in temperature. It's the kind of cold that burns your face and lungs, making you question your decision to live where you do. It's *stupid* cold.

Afraid of crashing on the ice, I walk to classes and Bright Beginnings. I book it out of work as soon as possible, knowing the commute will take longer and not wanting to make Mason late for work.

I'm five minutes down the road when a familiar Outback pulls over and Mason rolls down the window.

"Come on," he says, waving.

Daniel sings my name as I get in the front seat, and Mason takes my hands and holds them up to the heating vent before I've had a chance to buckle in.

"I texted you," Mason says. "Said we'd pick you up today. It's too cold to be out in this, Stevie."

My teeth are chattering, so I don't respond. Mason turns up the heat, then rubs my hands in his.

"Do you not own gloves?"

"I th-think they f-fell out of my pocket yesterday. I c-can't find them."

"Stevie, you should always, *always* wear gloves when it's cold," Daniel calls from the back seat. "Or you get fwostbite and *die*."

I laugh.

Mason rolls his eyes. "Solid science lesson, Danny Boy. Thanks."

"You welcome," Daniel sings.

"Did you not see my text?" Mason asks. "We weren't *that* late. I'd hope you'd trust me to follow through a little better than that."

The shaking having subsided, words come a little easier. "No phones allowed in the classrooms. I knew walking would take time, so I didn't bother to stop and check for messages on the way out. I just...*went*."

He sighs. "I'm so sorry we were late. Our appointment ran long."

"I'm fine."

"You're *frozen*."

"Drive, Daddy. Drive!" Daniel calls. "I need a cheese stick *now*."

Mason releases my hands, looking behind him. "Manners, kiddo. Try that again."

"May I *pah-lease* have a cheese stick befow I pewish?"

I sputter a laugh, bowing forward in my seat.

"Teach him new ways to say *die*, they said," Mason grumbles. "Wonderful."

But soon, he's laughing right along with me. My cheeks ache and tears form as I attempt to gather myself. When I sit up and look at Mason, I almost lose it and start all over. But something in his expression shifts, and it sobers me.

"I can't take this anymore," he says. "You're driving the truck from now on. Through winter, at least. It's not a request."

I glower. "What is it, then? A condition of employment?"

"No. I just mean, as your friend and someone who cares, I'm *begging* you to accept this one thing from me."

"What if you need it for something?" I ask, looking down at my hands.

"Then I'll borrow it back. Or we can switch. Something."

I nod, chewing on my lip.

"I can't pretend to understand why this is so hard for you," he says, "but I'm asking you to trust me."

Those words seep into my soul. *Trust me.*

"Friends, huh?" I mumble.

"Haven't we been?"

With a sigh, I relent. "Okay."

"Okay?"

When I look back at him, he's wearing a hopeful grin. It's adorable, and it makes me smile. "Okay," I repeat.

He checks for traffic before shifting into gear with a heavy breath. "Okay."

"But this inversion won't last—"

"Don't ruin the moment, Stevie."

I bite down on my lips, holding in a laugh.

It's been hours since Mason held my hands to the heat, and I still feel his touch. It was a simple gesture—a kindness, really, and I shouldn't be dwelling on it. But the more time I spend as an accessory in Mason's life, the more I want to mean something to him. The more I long for him to want me and hold me in a way beyond *friendship* and *caring*. It's likely a pointless daydream.

I sit on the floor next to the coffee table and select an Americana music station on my phone. Something mellow and relaxing to get me through this mountain of homework. Distraction. Distraction is good. Granted, it's a little hard to distract myself sitting in the middle of *his* living room, surrounded by the very essence of him. I've read the same page twice now and retained zero information.

You're hopeless, Stevie.

Switching it up, I pull out a notebook and start on a rough draft. It takes me ten minutes to write a single sentence. Somewhere in the middle of the second paragraph, I hear Mason's familiar footsteps in the hall. Pretending to be so focused I don't hear him, I continue scribbling across the page as he enters the room. He addresses me, but I write down a few more disconnected, pointless words before I look up.

"Oh, hi there." *Suave, Stevie. Suave.*

"How was your night? How was the monster?"

"He was perfect per usual." My hand cramps from clutching my pen too hard. I shake it out and stretch my fingers.

"Working too hard?" he asks, collapsing onto the couch. "Which class?"

"It's nothing," I say. "Just a rough draft for American Lit."

He nods. "They make you hand write them? How very nineties."

That's funny. I should laugh, but I'm still too tense. "Just personal preference. I always handwrite to start so I can easily type it up on campus."

"Wait. You don't have a laptop?" I shake my head. "No desktop at home?"

"I did, once. It's long dead now." He frowns. "I'll manage alright a little longer. I've been saving up for one." I gesture to him. "Wouldn't happen to know an I.T. guy, would you? Someone who might be able to steer me in the right direction?"

He laughs lightly. "Maybe. But you realize we have a computer, right? A few of them, in fact. Please, feel free to use whatever you need when you're here. For whatever you need. I don't mind."

"That's generous. Really." I meet his eyes, offering a close-lipped grin.

He shakes his head, knowing full well I have no intention of accepting the offer, waving around his gorgeous smile that does strange things to my heart.

"American Lit?" he asks.

"What?"

"You said American Lit. As a freshman?"

"Yeah, just for fun. My ACT score in English was high enough to test out of 101 and 102."

He nods, smiling. "Yeah, that makes sense."

I put my head down, packing up my books while attempting to hide my blushing cheeks.

"Who is this?" he asks.

"Hmm?"

"Who's singing?"

"Oh!" I fumble for my phone to silence it. "Sorry."

"Don't be."

"*That*," I say, pocketing my phone, "was The Civil Wars. They make the most amazing harmonies, but they tragically broke up. Twice."

"Dang. I hate when that happens."

"Right?" I grow more animated. "It's a legitimate crime against humanity if you ask me. They did a cover of 'Disarm' that's literally the most hauntingly gorgeous thing you've ever heard in your life."

"I'll have to check it out," he offers, smiling.

Tone it down, Stevie.

"I, uh, get excited about music," I say, grounding myself. "It's like...a whole thing. Never mind."

"You shouldn't be embarrassed about that," he says. "It's rather adorable."

My mouth goes dry as a hint of panic rises behind his chocolate eyes like maybe he didn't mean to say that out loud.

After a moment of awkward silence, Mason clears his throat. "Do you have classes at all next week?"

"Nope. You?"

He rakes his hand through his hair. "No. We're off for the week, but I have a favor to ask." I nod, inviting the rest. "Would you be able to come for a few hours Wednesday afternoon? I've got a thing—an appointment—with my parents. It's not kid friendly."

I knit my brow. "Is everything okay?"

He closes his eyes, first with a nod, then a shake of his head. With a sigh, he looks back at me. "It's..." There's a sadness to his features. A darkness. *Pain.*

"You don't have to tell me," I say. "I can be here. What time?"

"Are you sure? You don't have any plans with friends or...?"

"I'm sure. What time?"

"Three. I don't know how long it'll be."

"As long as you and Danny need." I'd do anything for them. I almost say it out loud, but I restrain myself.

He thanks me, handing over my week's pay and the keys to the truck.

The drive home is strange. The truck is warm and smells like linen air freshener with a hint of graham cracker crumbs. I'm grateful, but somehow, it feels like a consolation prize. A stand in for what I really want. *Mason.* All I can think of is the pain etched on his face over whatever appointment he has next week, and how badly I wish I could absorb it for him.

Even more than that, I can't help but think of the way *he* sometimes looks at *me*, like maybe—just *maybe*—he wishes he could do the same for all the things that haunt me.

CHAPTER 13

Merrin's busy all day Wednesday between church commitments and her large family coming into town for Thanksgiving. I have nothing to do but wait around for three o'clock. No more homework. Nothing. I have books to read, sure, but I can't focus on any of them.

Anytime I sit still too long, all I can think about is the way Mason looked when he told me my love of music was adorable and how much he seems to be dreading whatever appointment he has today. These two things play on a loop, leaving room for little else. In the shower this morning, I used body wash in my hair, then shaved an entire leg with the plastic cap still on the razor. I have zero chill.

Bracing myself against a kitchen counter, I scroll through my favorite music stations, settling on the *shuffle all* feature; I lack the necessary patience to make a decision. First up is a Motown station. The Temptations singing "Ain't Too Proud to Beg" brings a fleeting smile to my face. I turn up the volume, set my phone down, then bury my face in my hands and take a deep breath.

They always come in flashes—visions of my mother. Typically brought on by sounds and smells. Music and baking. *Flash.* There she is, at the kitchen counter, a mixing spoon to her mouth like a microphone. Maybe it's a forced, false memory—a desperate attempt from my brain to offer solace amidst my despair. But it seems a likely scene. She was always singing or humming. That much I remember. But the words? Her voice? Those vanished long ago. Like her nameless tune that haunts me, so do these flashes where I can see her smiling face for a mere moment, feel her love and joy for a split second. That's always where they end, offering no legitimate details. Nothing to cling to.

That haunting melody cycles through my mind as I take another deep breath. A phantom touch engulfs me. *Flash.* My mother holding me on her lap, rocking me, singing. I try to pry the words from the memory, but they turn to dust as she opens her mouth.

Another deep breath, and this time it's a smell that hits me. Cinnamon.

Whether real or imagined, it's enough to guide me toward a worthy distraction.

Since I started working for Mason, I've begun filling my fridge and pantry with more than bare necessities. Within a minute of scouring, I assemble everything necessary for sweet dough. I'm kneading before I know it. My phone shuffles between genres, and I hum or sing along, regardless of how well I know or like the song. While the dough rises, I meticulously clean my house, my music blaring in the background.

Between baking and cleaning, a couple hours pass, and I'm sweating through my clothes and have to shower again. Standing in fresh clothes, my hair dripping from its *third* washing of the day—something I'm sure Merrin would disapprove of—I smile at the alluring, aromatic cinnamon rolls resting on my counter. I spread the cream cheese frosting over them while they're still warm, so it softens, filling every nook and cranny.

"Perfect," I say, congratulating myself. But too quickly, my contentment wanes.

There's a batch of twelve beautiful cinnamon rolls staring back at me. But I have no one to share them with.

Defeated, I set an alarm for 2:30 p.m. and crawl into bed, burrowing under my blankets.

WHEN MASON ANSWERS THE DOOR, I pass him a plate of cinnamon rolls.

"I come bearing gifts," I say, trying to sound like I haven't spent the last several hours despondently crying into a pillow.

He accepts the plate with a curious grin, but as he inhales, his head lolls.

"What are you doing to me, Stevie?" he says, sticking his finger into the icing and tasting it. His eyes widen, and he cocks his head. "*What?* You made these?"

I nod, unable to speak.

"Stevie!" A muffled voice cries. I look down as Daniel plows into my legs, a sleeping bag over his head.

"Huh," I say. "When did you guys get a house ghost?"

"A ghost?" Daniel asks, throwing his sleeping bag to the ground. "I'm not a ghost. I'm a supohewo but mine cape is too big."

"Touché."

"To-what?" he asks, puzzled.

Mason and I laugh.

"Never mind," I say, hoisting him onto my hip. He pushes his forehead against mine. I cross my eyes, and he giggles. I live for this giggle.

Daniel and I stay so busy I lose all track of time until my phone starts dinging with notifications. I double check the clock—5:30.

MASON

> This is taking forever. I'm so sorry.

> There's a pizza on the way for dinner.

> I should be another hour, tops.

I send him a picture of Daniel in his dinosaur costume, knocking over the block towers we built.

> He's fine. We're fine. Take your time.

But if you ordered pineapple on that pizza, you're dead to me.

I'm kidding, of course. I grew up poor; put whatever the heck you want on a pizza, I'll eat it. But I like the idea of giving him something to smile about in the midst of whatever is stressing him out. When he sends back several laughing emojis, something flutters under my skin.

There's no way around this. I'm falling for this guy—my *boss*, technically—and I'm not sure how much longer I can hold it in. Though maybe Merrin is right, and I should just go for it. But if I do, and I'm wrong, or it backfires... How much more loss can my heart take? How much do I dare risk it?

After dinner, Daniel and I both start to lag, feeling the effects of hours of play. I start a classic rock station on my phone, and we settle on the couch with a stack of his favorite books. Before I've finished the first one, he's out. He's so comfy and smells so good, I don't want to move him. I reach beside me, palming around my backpack until I pull out *Ender's Game*, my American Lit assignment for Thanksgiving break.

"Nothing Else Matters" starts on my phone as I open my book, balancing it in one hand while my other gently moves up and down Daniel's back.

"Didn't have you pegged for an Orson Scott Card fan."

I startle, dropping my book to the ground. Mason is standing behind the couch, staring down at Daniel and me, a widespread grin on his face.

"Let it be known," he whispers, "that my kid is sleeping to the dulcet tones of Metallica."

"He's got good taste."

I carefully maneuver off the couch, grab a blanket from the back of the recliner, and drape it over Daniel. He stirs, and I place a gentle hand on his head, kissing his temple.

"Sleep tight, munchkin," I whisper.

I gather my things and walk toward the front of the house. I'm fumbling with my phone in the hall when Mason joins me.

"You cast a wide net," he says, "with your music *and* literary tastes."

I laugh, shoving my book in my backpack and zipping it up. "Well, the book is for class, so..." I shrug. "But yeah. I like variety."

"I'm sorry again for running so late. The stupid meeting got out of hand. Then, of course, traffic was a nightmare."

"It's no problem, I swear. Did the meeting go...favorably? At least?"

He chews on his bottom lip, blinking at the ceiling. "Not quite."

My heart hurts for him, even though I have zero context for what's happening. "I wish I could say something useful here," I manage.

His eyes soften, and I think I might melt under his gaze. Damn, he's gorgeous, even when he's being ambiguous.

As I'm hoisting my backpack over my shoulder and Mason is fishing his wallet from his back pocket, a shrill cry comes from the living room.

"Stevie!"

My heart sinks as I rush back to the couch.

"Stevie! Where'd you go?"

"Shh, buddy. I'm here."

I sit on the couch and pull him onto my lap. "You left me alone!" he cries. "I was alone!"

"No, honey. I'm right here. Stevie's right here."

I kiss the top of his head, rocking him back and forth. Mason sits next to us, frowning. He reaches over, rubbing Daniel's back.

"Hey, buddy," he says softly. "You're okay. Sorry you woke up alone."

"I had a bad dream that Stevie went away," he whimpers. I adjust to hold him tighter, and my hand brushes Mason's. I feel it everywhere.

"I'm here," I repeat. "And I'll come back again next week. Okay?"

"Not tomorrow?"

"No, honey. But soon."

"Tomorrow, we go see Gramma Randa and Grampa Wes," Mason says. "Remember? Eat lots of mashed potatoes and yummy pie."

Daniel sniffles. "I don't like pie," he whines, then starts crying again.

"Oh, my love," I coo. "You're so sleepy. Can I tuck you into bed? Would that be better? With your nightlight?"

"And two Stevie Songs?"

I laugh. "You can have as many Stevie Songs as you want, so long as your dad says it's okay."

Mason nods, smiling. I adjust Daniel against my chest and carry him up the stairs with Mason following close behind. Mason pulls back Daniel's sheets, and I situate him on his bed.

Sitting on the edge of the mattress, I brush Daniel's soft black curls with my fingers, watching as his eyes roll to the back of his head and his lids droop.

"So sleepy," I whisper before starting one of Daniel's favorite songs."Castle on a Cloud." When Mason's voice joins mine, smooth and full and beautiful, I suffer a momentary malfunction.

Holy how is this happening? Am I dreaming?

Failing to wrap my head around it completely, I start in on an improvised harmony, letting Mason's strong baritone take the lead. By the end, Daniel's eyes are completely closed, and his chest moves in a steady, gentle rhythm. Quietly, Mason and I slip out of his room and down the stairs.

"Um, so when Daniel said you sang to him..." Mason says, scratching at his scalp. "I had no idea you were so..." Blood rushes to my cheeks as I clamp down on my lips. "Wow."

"Thanks," I manage, then shift the focus back to him. "I'm impressed you knew something from *Les Mis*."

"My mom's favorite musical. Heard it a lot growing up."

"Makes sense. It's a lot of people's favorite."

"But not yours?"

"It's up there, don't get me wrong. I love it. But I also love

Hadestown and *Phantom* and *Dear Evan Hansen* and *Urinetown* and... Look, I couldn't pick a favorite *genre* of music if my life depended on it. Least of all, a favorite musical."

He chuckles, crossing his arms over his chest. "As I said, you cast a wide net. I'm impressed."

"I've spent my life listening to anything and everything. Searching for..." I stop myself, swallow, and continue with an abridged version of the truth. "You remember when I cracked about having three channels and a library card?" He nods. "I wasn't kidding. There was a channel that played old movies, PBS, and a home shopping network. That was about it. Gene watched mostly westerns, which got a little redundant after a while. So, I rented a lot of CDs from the library and read a lot of books."

He nods, like he wants to understand but can't.

"I was also a choir nerd through and through in school. When I decided to try for a vocal scholarship, I really had no choice but to challenge myself and absorb as much as I possibly could."

"You're in school on a vocal scholarship? That's amazing."

"No." I clear my throat. "Not this time. I could have been, though. Stanford." His eyes widen. "Partial vocal scholarship, partial academic. I was nearly gone, possibly never coming back. Then Gene got sick. But looking back, I'm sure they would have chewed me up and spat me out as a music major." Why do I keep *saying things* around him? His mere presence breaks down my barriers, my life spilling out one dramatic short story at a time.

Mason's eyes in slits, his head cocked, he opens his mouth a few times before anything comes out. "You gave up Stanford? Really?"

"What else could I do? He was the only parent I had left." I'm on the defensive, but I don't want to be. Not after that moment we just had where our voices were working in harmony. Damn, I've missed having anyone to sing with. I take a deep breath and gesture to him. "You have a *gorgeous* voice," I say.

"You're being generous, but thank you." His lips curl, and his eyes brighten. "But you... I could listen to you sing all day long."

Heaven help me.

"What other hidden talents do you have?" he asks.

Overwhelmed by the flattery, it takes me a moment to respond. "None that I know of. You seem to have quite a few, though."

He twists his lips, his hand reaching up and tugging at the back of his neck. "You know," he says, "that's the first time Daniel's cried out for anyone other than me. He really loves you."

I shrug, my eyes shifting up and over. "Well, I'm rather loveable."

He huffs a laugh, closing his eyes and shaking his head. I'm unsure what it means, and I'm too afraid to dissect it.

"I should go," I say. "You guys have a good time with your family tomorrow."

"Are you doing anything? You won't be alone, will you?"

"I'll be with the Caraways—Merrin's family. They invited me."

"I'm glad." He walks to the door and opens it. "I'll walk you out. I salted the pavement when I got home, but it's still icy out there."

I grab my bag. "No, that's not—"

"Stevie, please."

There's fatigue behind those words.

Stevie, please.

As though being around me, reasoning with me, all exhausts him.

Swallowing loudly, I nod and let him brace his hand under my elbow as we step into the bitter night air. I hold my breath as he accompanies me to the detached garage. Though there's no need, he keeps hold of me until I'm securely in my seat. He closes the door, patting his hand against the window, mouthing *goodnight*.

It might be a trick of my desperate imagination, but it feels like a solid minute before he breaks eye contact and steps away.

CHAPTER
14

Nancy answers the door wearing a stressed smile. "Happy Thanksgiving," she says.

"And to you," I return, stepping inside. When I remove my coat, Nancy gasps.

"Don't you look lovely!"

"Thank you," I say, flush. I'm wearing one of the three dresses I now own, thanks to Merrin. Still adjusting to my new wardrobe, the compliments always catch me off guard.

"Well, welcome. Welcome to our zoo." Playful squeals carry through the house. "Merrin's in the kitchen. Children are everywhere. Make yourself at home." She peeks through the door before closing it. "I see you finally put the bike away. What's the cool thing to say? Nice wheels?" I laugh. She's adorable. "A truck is a smart choice."

"It's not mine," I say.

Merrin comes into my line of sight and rushes in for a hug. She's been so busy I haven't seen her since the weekend. She squeezes a little too tight to make up for the lost time.

"I'm glad you finally accepted his offer," she whispers in my ear.

Nancy's still looking at me with a quizzical brow.

"It's, um, a company car," I say. "So to speak."

"You get a company car?" The question comes from a stranger, though his resemblance to Merrin gives him away as a brother.

"Stevie, meet my oldest brother, Artie."

I accept Artie's firm handshake.

"I've heard a lot about you, Stevie. My sister's obsessed with you."

"Well, it's mutual. And not creepy at all."

He laughs as Merrin takes my arm.

"Come on. I'll introduce you to everyone." Walking to the living room, Merrin whispers, "My brother Finley brought home a fiancée."

"Good for him."

"Not so much. Dad doesn't think Fin has it together enough to support a family. It's a whole thing. It's been a tense twenty-four hours."

"I'll tread carefully."

"Good plan."

Caraways fill the living room, gabbing and laughing. The patriarch, Max, sits in his chair, a hint—*just* a hint—of contentment about him.

Finley sits in *very* close proximity to his gorgeous, raven-haired fiancée, Carmen. Two of Merrin's sisters are here with their families. The dark and domineering Cecily and her husband, Carlton (annoyingly, their children all have 'C' names), and gentle, fairer skinned, and pregnant Arwin with her quiet, unflinching husband, Noah. The children don't stand still long enough for me to distinguish them from one another.

"Josie, of course, couldn't make it," Merrin says after making introductions.

"Typical," Finley grumbles.

Arwin tsks at him. "We can't expect her to fly in for every single holiday, Fin. She's a very busy girl. And it's a very expensive flight."

"Excuses, excuses," Fin sighs. "She doesn't want to come face everyone now that she's *failed* miserably." Carmen smacks his shoulder. I sense I'm missing an inside joke.

Merrin catches me up as siblings chatter. "Jo just started up her own label."

"That's amazing."

"Yeah, she really is. I'm sure at least one of us is wearing something she designed and made today." Everyone looks at their ensemble, but no one speaks up. Finally, Cecily points to Fin.

"That's one of hers."

Fin tugs at his sweater, puzzled. "No, it isn't. You gave me this, Cece."

"She sent it for Carl. It didn't fit, so I passed it on."

"Dude! You wrapped this and gave it to me for Christmas!"

Cecily waves a dismissive hand. "At least I gave you something."

Eventually, the cry of "Dinner!" hurries everyone into the dining room. I finally meet Artie's wife, Lucy, who's just finished putting her six-month-old down for a nap. I also sort through the youngsters, eight in all, counting the sleeping baby.

Merrin's siblings tease her for this being her first year allowed at the "Grown Up" table, claiming that if it weren't for me, she'd be sitting at the "Kids Table" with her nieces and nephews. I laugh, but Merrin assures me it isn't a joke.

"I wish they were kidding," she mumbles.

"Aww. Poor baby," comes back to her from everyone, almost in unison.

The Caraways are their own culture. I fall in love with the insane volume, the fast-paced conversation, and how *everyone* talks with their hands. I keep expecting a glass to tip over when anyone gets the least bit excited.

"So, Stevie. Not to pry, but... Well, here I go." Cecily talks with her mouth half full. "What's your story? Where's your family?"

"Cece! Manners!" Arwin snaps.

"What? It's a normal question?"

"Yes, but you asked it like a bi—"

"Fin!" Max interrupts.

"Big brat, Dad. Geez. What did you think I was going to say?" Fin looks completely serious, though we all know he's not. His father's face reddens.

I speak quickly, hoping to diffuse the situation. "My family isn't around."

"They move away? You stick around for school?"

"Something like that."

"Where'd they go?" she continues to prod.

"Cece! Stop!" There's a thud under the table as Merrin scolds her sister.

"Ow! *What?* Geez, Mer."

"They passed," I say. "My parents. Almost eighteen years ago. My mother's brother took me in. He died two—it'll be three years ago in April."

Silence falls on the table like bricks. Merrin glares at Cece, who chews her turkey and looks solemnly at her plate.

Nancy gestures toward me. "I'm just glad you're here with us, Stevie. You can consider us your family today and any other day you wish to. That is if we haven't completely terrified you," she adds with a wink.

"Thanks," I say. "I'm glad I'm here, too. Dinner is amazing, by the way. All of it."

"Yeah, Ma. Stellar turkey." Food rolls around in Fin's open mouth as he speaks.

Carmen elbows him, glaring. "Really, Finley. Feign a little dignity, would you?"

"So, have you two love birds set a date yet?" Artie asks.

"Actually, Art, I wanted to ask you," Fin starts.

"No."

"You haven't heard the question!"

"No."

"Man, just hear me out!"

"You can't have your wedding at the farm."

"You have a farm?" I blurt.

"Near Palouse," Lucy clarifies. "The farm I grew up on. Artie and I took over not long after we married."

"Palouse?" I ask. She and Artie both nod. "Wow. Gorgeous landscape." From what I've seen in pictures, anyway.

Artie throws his hands up. "Yes. Thank you. It *is* gorgeous. And it's also a lot of friggin' work. I won't have you turning it into a circus for your wedding, Fin."

"Dude! You're so stuck on yourself. I don't want to get married on your precious land."

"Oh. Good."

"We're doing a church wedding to appease Carmen's parents," Fin says. "We only want your place for the reception."

Artie looks ready to blow steam. "*Fin—*"

"When?" Lucy asks.

"Mid-May," Fin says.

"*This* May?" Max booms. "Are you serious? That's not remotely enough time. You know your mother and I—"

"*Waited a year*," all his children recite in monotonous unison.

"We know, Dad," Fin says, rolling his eyes. "But Cece and Carl were only engaged like...three months. Arwin basically eloped."

"*I* waited a year," Artie says.

"Suck up," Fin grumbles.

With a heavy sigh, Artie relents, "We'll think about it. It would depend on the date."

"I'm sure it'll be fine," Lucy adds. "We're so happy for you two."

Carmen smiles as Fin kisses her temple.

Max clears his throat. "Can we talk about something else now?"

"Maxwell," Nancy intones. "Don't be a spoilsport."

"Nan, I just don't understand it. It's so sudden."

"*Max*, this is hardly the time or place. We have *guests*."

"Dad," Fin interrupts, "I'm sorry we sprung this on you. I know this seems sudden." He puts his arm around Carmen. "But Pop, I expect you really do understand, whether you admit it or not. Sure, you *waited* a year to get married. But whenever you tell that story, you conveniently leave out the part where you proposed to Mom on, what, the second date?"

"Third," Nancy corrects, watching her husband with sheer adoration. Though he tries to keep a stern brow and taunt lips, Max can't help but soften under his wife's gaze. "But it was more a declaration of intent. I didn't officially get a ring until we were three months in. He exuded *some* restraint."

"Look," Fin sighs, "we all know love really isn't as messy as everyone makes it out to be." Ripples of laughter and scoffing make their way around the table.

"I know marriage takes work—duh," he says. "But the falling in love. The *ah-ha* moment where you realize *this is the one*. That doesn't take a decade-long saga of breakups and makeups. Sometimes, you just *know*. And we just...*know*. And yes, we could have waited, but we figured it'd just be a waste of time."

Fin kisses the blushing Carmen once again.

Max closes his eyes, massaging his temples. Everyone holds their breath.

"Nance," he says, resting his elbows on the table and clasping his hands. "It would appear we've raised a bunch of sappy romantics." A wave of light chuckles circles the dining room. With a heavy sigh, Max finishes, "Heaven help you, Finley. You two kids are in for a roller coaster."

"Perfect," Fin says. "I love roller coasters."

Everyone breathes a collective sigh of relief, and light-hearted dinner banter resumes.

I'm smiling, and I'm happy for Fin, though I hardly know him. But a jagged cord of jealousy tightens around my heart. I've had my *ah-ha* moment already. Try as I might to deny it, I've fallen hard for Mason, and waiting for him to come around is excruciating. We have moments where he's flirty and smiles like he adores me, even moments where he says out *loud* I'm *adorable* or I look lovely *all the days*. He seems so often on the cusp of saying or doing so much more, but there's a wall there.

He'll touch me or offer the occasional meaningful look, but that's where it ends. I guess I always hoped when I had that *ah-ha* moment, the other person would have it, too. If Mason has, he's taking his sweet time doing anything about it.

Maybe it's time I bury these feelings. Maybe that's how I survive this and keep breathing.

As MUCH AS I hate the idea of not seeing Daniel *or* Mason for nearly a month, I think it might be good for me. Distance, time, all good things. If my heart had a switch I could just *flip*, that would be easier. But I'll take time and distance.

The semester is over, but Mason's asked me to watch Daniel one last time before my official *break*. Another non-kid-friendly appointment. When I knock on the door, he answers in a full, fitted suit.

Hot damn.

I manage not to say it aloud, but my eyes bulge, and my jaw goes slack as I shove a plate of cookies toward him.

"For us?"

"Lemon crinkle," I say.

He lifts the plastic wrap, inhaling, and his eyes roll to the back of his head. "We don't deserve you," he mutters.

I step inside and follow him toward the kitchen. Danny comes running at me and bounds into my arms.

"My Stevie!"

"Hey, munchkin."

"We get to watch the Owl movie!" he shouts.

I gasp. "Owl movie? That sounds amazing. I can't wait."

"You realize you don't have to feed us, right?" Mason asks, his mouth half-full of cookie crumbs.

I situate Daniel on my shoulders, which makes him giggle and grab onto my head.

"Sometimes, it's wonderful living alone," I admit. "Other times, it's just...*lonely*. Baking is..."

"A distraction," he finishes.

"Exactly. But then I wind up with two loaves of banana bread or nine-by-thirteens of cinnamon rolls or dozens of cookies and no one to share them with. So, I leave some at the daycare when I can, some with the Caraways. Some I share with you guys."

Mason hands Daniel a cookie, and he drops it on my head. We all laugh as I maneuver Daniel to the ground and shoo him to sit at the table with his treat. Mason reaches up and brushes crumbs out of my hair, and I hold my breath.

"Thank you," I whisper when he's done.

He stares a moment before looking away and offering a quiet, "You're welcome."

After clearing my throat, I gesture to his suit. "So, fancy meeting?"

"I need to appear put together. Responsible."

"Nailed it," I say with a nod.

"Are you sure? Or do I just look stuck up and unapproachable?"

Scanning him up and down, I'm at a loss for words. All I can think of is how *great* his butt looks in those pants. *Chill, Stevie.* Yes. Time and distance will be good.

"I'm the worst person to ask for fashion advice," I say. "If you're going for *approachable* or *down-to-earth*, you could ditch the tie and switch the jacket for a pullover? Maybe?" I toss up my hands. Where's Merrin when you need her? "I told you, I'm the worst person to ask."

He looks at the clock on the microwave. "It's too late to worry about it now. I need to run. I rented Danny a movie, and you guys can pop some popcorn. Have fun, alright? I have no idea how long this will take, but there's leftovers in the fridge if I'm not back by dinner."

"Stop worrying," I say, motioning toward the front of the house. "We'll be fine. Now get. Danny and I apparently have a date with some *owls*, if I'm not mistaken."

Mason shakes his head, offering his final goodbyes through an airy laugh.

CHAPTER
15

The Mason who left four hours ago is not the Mason who returns home. There'd been a glimmer of something in him when I arrived with a plate full of cookies. Now, he trudges through the house, loosening his tie as he goes, a black cloud of defeat engulfing him.

"Danny tried to stay up for you, but he crashed about ten minutes ago," I say.

He nods, not saying anything.

"Are you okay?"

"No. Yes. I don't know."

"What's wrong?" I rise from the recliner, taking a step toward him. He looks at me for a moment with his mouth half open as if to speak but doesn't. Eventually, he takes a seat on the couch.

"Do you want me to leave?" I ask. He shakes his head, so I sit on the other end of the couch. "Is there anything I can do?"

"Distract me," he says. "Tell me something good."

"Good?" I ask.

"Or funny. Or ridiculous. Or even sad." There's a plea behind his eyes when he glances at me. "Just...distract me," he repeats softly.

I turn toward him, pulling my legs onto the couch and crossing them in front of me.

"I was about ten when I first learned what Murphy's Law was," I start, "and it resonated with me. It became a sort of coping mechanism, something to blame all the crappy days on. Somewhere I made the conscious decision that from there on out, anything that went wrong was *Murphy's* fault. Anytime someone was cruel at school, or a teacher made insensitive remarks about my *living situation*, or whenever Gene left a permission slip unsigned or forgot my birthday, or I made a new friend just for them to ditch me when they realized I was poor and lived with an 'old grumpy dude,' I just chalked it all up to Murphy's Law and began using it as an expletive. Happy, sad, angry, or otherwise."

Mason's not looking at me, but I can see his lips curling into a subtle grin.

"Hence," I say.

"Murphy," he finishes, then turns toward me. "That's pretty genius for a ten-year-old."

"I grew up fast."

He frowns. "I hate that for you."

I shrug. "It is what it is."

He draws in a sharp breath. "I hate that even more. It's such a cop-out."

"Yeah," I agree. "But unfortunately, sometimes it's true."

He deflates. Probably because I'm right, and whatever is weighing on him right now is one of those horrid instances where it truly *is what it is*, and he feels powerless. I wish I could fix it for him.

"I have something for you," he says, digging in his pocket and pulling out a folded piece of paper. His hand extends toward mine.

"What's this?"

"Read it."

Once it's unfolded, it takes me several moments to process what I'm looking at. A cold weight settles in my chest as I clap my hand over my mouth. He's gifting me the truck. All I have to do is sign, make a trip to the DMV, and the truck could be mine. This isn't real. It can't be.

"Merry Christmas," he says.

I look at him, back at the paper, then back up at him. This happens several times. I can't stop staring, and I can't comprehend it.

"Why?" I manage. "Why would you do this?"

There's an animated eagerness about him. "Because I can, and I want to."

I shake my head, close my eyes, and finally lower my hand. "I can't accept this. It's *beyond* too much."

"It's really not, Stevie," he whispers. "You deserve it all and more."

I place the paper on the couch cushion, still shaking my head. He takes my hand in his, squeezing. With a knife in my throat and my heart pounding between my ears, I meet his gaze.

"I would..." he starts, then sighs. "It would make me so happy if you'd accept this."

"Mason, I can't."

"You *can*," he says, squeezing my hand harder. "I wish I could give you more."

"More than a *vehicle*? Like what? An island? This is *too much*," I repeat, firmer, pulling my hand away.

"It's a *gift*," he argues. "It's meant to be a little extravagant."

"I don't need your extravagance!" I snap, standing. "I don't want handouts. I don't want to be your charity case. I just want to come here and do my job and make a living like everyone else on the planet. Everyone *not* born into privilege and six-figure college funds."

I wince at my insensitive words and harsh tone, fumbling for a *sorry* but coming up empty. Instead, I walk to the front door and start putting on my boots. Mason catches up to me as I'm lacing them.

"You're not a charity case to me, Stevie. And I find it a little insulting you think I view you that way."

Standing, I clench and unclench my fists in midair but ultimately have no response.

"Look," he says. "I get it. You've made it abundantly clear you don't need me, or anyone else for that matter, to step in and save you. I'm not *trying* to save you, Stevie. And accepting a gesture once in a while will not undermine your official title as superhuman, alright? We all get it. You're better, stronger, and more adaptable than *anyone.* Owning the truck won't change any of that. You'll simply be more mobile."

I shake my head. "You don't get it. It would be such a huge gesture. So outrageously generous. I'd never be able to match that. Not now. Maybe not ever."

"I'm not asking for anything in return," he says through an agitated groan.

"I want to believe that. I do. But..." Tears well.

I could just tell him everything. Right here. Right now. I could tell him all of it. But I don't know how.

His face falls as he crosses his arms over his chest. "You want to, but you don't."

I'm not sure if his words wound him or me more.

Tears pool at the corners of my eyes. Mason sighs.

"Just forget about it," he says. "Have a good Christmas, Stevie. I'll see you next month."

"Should I walk?" I ask.

He rubs the bridge of his nose between his forefinger and thumb. "Of *course,* you shouldn't walk." He drops his hand from his face, revealing the tension in his jaw. "Do you really think I'm so petty? Drive the truck. Go home. Grow the hell up. Maybe get over yourself a little bit, because *dammit,* you're exhausting."

His words wreck me, and it takes all my strength to stand tall as a steady stream of hot tears rolls down my cheek.

He flinches.

"Shit, Stevie. I didn't mean—"

I turn on my heel, fling the door open, and storm out. Halfway to the garage, I slip on a patch of ice and land on my back. Lacking the wherewithal to stand, I think I might just lie here a while on the cold hard ground, crying, thinking of all the wrong turns I've made in my life. All the people I miss. All the people who failed me. All the *Murphy's Law* days I chalked up to unfortunate random events rather than cope with the fact that I'd been given a raw, shitty deal. That my dad didn't value his life or mine enough to not drive drowsy.

That Uncle Gene didn't love me enough to function beyond his depression. That Todd saw a target on my back and ruined piano *and* kind gestures for me, and I still haven't figured out how to get past it.

Strong arms hook under my shoulders and pull me to standing.

"Are you okay?" Mason asks.

I whip around, ready to yell at him, to tell him not to touch me. But when I see him standing there, his hair blowing in his face, I lose my voice. We're toe to toe, and I can't remember how to breathe, let alone speak.

How is it possible to feel so much for this man? From the moment I met him, he's been this safe space. Familiar. Like that song I used to know. No matter how much of him I get, there's always more I want. *Need.* Like if I could just grasp that remaining piece of the puzzle, I'd have *everything.*

I can't help but brush his dark, wavy locks off his cheek and let my fingers linger. He leans into my hand and closes his eyes.

"I can't. Stevie, I *can't.*"

It's barely a whisper, but it's enough. He *can't.* So I leave. This time I don't fall. This time I don't cry. I don't even look back. I just drive.

I HAVEN'T CELEBRATED Christmas since Uncle Gene passed. I've been too isolated and numb to notice the season come or go. I worked my shifts at Credit Zen without much acknowledgment of the time of year, though I responded to the occasional "Merry Christmas" or "Happy Holidays" from a co-worker. Dwelling on the season could only bring misery; I spared it wherever possible.

This year, though... This year I'm fully aware of the impending holiday, and my lack of anyone to share it with.

Merrin is in New York with her parents visiting Josie. They haven't shared a Christmas together in several years, so they're taking an extended trip—she won't be back until January. I've been without her for almost a week and still have two more to go. In a short few months, Merrin has become my *person*, and I miss my person.

Since the awkward incident at Mason's four nights ago, I've had nothing to do but sit alone in my drafty house, listening to music and staring at pictures of people I miss. Granted, there's at least a new picture to look at. My Christmas present from Merrin—along with makeup I don't know how to apply properly and salon brand hair products so nice I'm not sure I have the courage to use them—is a framed photo of us at Thanksgiving. We're side by side on a bench in the Caraways' backyard, our faces pink from the cold, our hands folded together in my lap. The shutter clicked just as Merrin leaned her head against my shoulder, both of us mid-laughter. The frame is distressed wood, with the word *sisters* discreetly written in the corner. This is my new prized possession.

But even this perfect picture and the comfort it brings, knowing I have a family again—even if not in the traditional sense—doesn't assuage the loneliness. Without Merrin around, I'm left to wallow in my misery, and losing my ability to power through.

It's noon on Saturday, and I'm still in bed, crying in my flannel pajamas and a too-big, second-hand robe. I want my mom. I want my dad. I even want Uncle Gene.

I want to be blasting music in the kitchen, helping Mom prepare a Christmas meal. Something I never had the privilege of experiencing. Or maybe arguing with my dad over which Christmas tree we should get. I'd settle for sitting across from Gene, eating a Hungry Man microwave dinner, Johnny Cash playing in the background—the *only* music we ever agreed on in our entire coexistence.

Anything other than this debilitating void inside me.

Wiping my face and adorning my slippers, I venture into the kitchen. Rooting through the pantry, I find everything I need to make my mother's magical peanut butter bread. Probably my most revisited recipe of hers.

"It's a Christmas miracle, Mom," I whisper, hoping somewhere she hears me and smiles, maybe even laughs. I long to remember her laugh; I'm sure it was beautiful, just like the pictures of her I treasure.

I pull the corresponding recipe card from the tattered box, even though I know it by heart. Handling the same piece of faded cardstock she once had, seeing her hand-written notes where she tweaked the original measurements. It's like having her in the kitchen with me—almost. I hum that same old nameless tune as I bake, imagining somewhere she's singing along with me. Maybe she's disappointed in me for not remembering the words. Maybe she's just happy I remember her at all.

I've put two loaves in the oven—one with chocolate chips, one without—when it occurs to me I have no one to share them with. I can freeze one of them. Take it to the Caraways when they return from New York. As for the other... Looks like I'm eating peanut butter loaf for breakfast, lunch, and dinner for the foreseeable future.

The kitchen warms from the heat of the oven, filling with a heavenly mix of aromas. I wrap my arms around my middle, overcome by the emptiness inside. In this moment, my life seems purposeless. Heartsick over a man I have no business pursuing, confirmed when I made the *slightest* move—a *hint* of affection—and was met with *I can't*. My only true friend is eighteen, just starting her life, with every potential to outgrow me before long. I make desserts to fill the time and give them away. My most consistent company is the cynical voice in my head and this damned tune I can't remember the words to. I double over, letting another wave of tears consume me.

I'm losing my strength, ready to fall to the floor, when a foreign noise fills the otherwise silent house.

CHAPTER
16

I must be delusional; that couldn't have actually been the doorbell. It's old, practically broken—nothing more than a brief *clang*.

"You're hearing things," I whisper to myself, slowly straightening. "You're delusional."

But it rings again, followed by three rapid knocks.

I shuffle to the front door, my insides in knots. No one ever shows up at my house. Maybe it's those guys who walk around town in full suits, even in summer when it's ninety degrees outside, come to save my soul, or whatever it is they do. Maybe they like peanut butter loaf.

Of all the scenarios running through my mind—missionaries, Jehovah's Witnesses, serial killer, Girl Scouts—I never expect to be startled speechless by the perfectly scruffy and stupidly gorgeous figure of a man on my doorstep.

"Hey," he says.

Aware of my haggard appearance, all the heat rises to my cheeks as I hug my arms around myself. "Um, hi," I manage, taking a few steps back.

He knits his brow. "You're crying. What's wrong?"

"Come in, I guess."

He kicks his feet against the side of the house before stepping inside and closing the door behind him. My sleeves make poor substitutes for tissue, but I do my best to clean my face before meeting his gaze again.

"What's wrong?" he asks again. "Come, sit...down..." His voice fades as he takes notice of his surroundings. "Or not."

I make a grand, sweeping gesture. "Lifestyles of the rich and the famous, eh?"

"Um, were you robbed? Unrelated, what smells so good?"

The obnoxious buzz of my old egg timer summons me to the kitchen. "Not robbed," I say as I walk, "just poor. Want some peanut butter loaf?"

I'm aware of his eyes on me as I slide my hands into oven mitts, pull the loaves from the oven, and place them on a cooling rack.

"Excuse me a moment, would you?" I draw in a sharp breath, then beeline for the bathroom. First, I blow my nose, eliciting horrible sounds no human should ever be subjected to, least of all Mason. I tend to my teeth next, followed by my hair. A little dry shampoo—thank goodness Merrin introduced me to this miracle—a lot of brushing and a simple braid to one side. Splashing water in my face, I mumble to the blotchy, sad girl in the mirror. "A Christmas miracle, huh?" I apply deodorant liberally, put on a bra, and swap my robe for a clean hoodie. "Spoke too soon."

Back in the kitchen, Mason turns in a slow circle, eyes wandering my threadbare home. The sight of me halts him to attention, his boots squeaking against the old linoleum floor.

"What were you expecting?" I ask. "A baby grand and a five-thousand-dollar stereo?"

"No. Wait, what?"

"Nothing, it was a bitter dig at your wealth to try and make myself feel better," I admit.

He suppresses a smile, shaking his head as he pulls off his slouchy knit cap. "How'd it work?" he asks.

"Not so much," I mutter, sliding the warm loaves out of their pans.

"Stevie, I didn't realize..."

"That I was this type of poor? It's not so bad. Not anymore, anyway." I gesture to a cereal box on the counter and the fresh bread on the cooling rack. "But now you know why I chased you down like a lunatic when I saw your flyer. Now I can eat more than one meal a day and pay the heating bill. That job saved me."

He closes his eyes, contorting his face as though I've just hurt him.

"What happened?" he asks, opening his eyes after a lengthy pause.

"What *didn't* happen? I took care of Gene full time near the end. I had no income. He hardly had any. Hospital bills started flooding in from a couple of ER visits and an ambulance ride."

"But those were *his* bills. They couldn't force *you* to pay them."

"Except I was nineteen, and everyone who ever loved me was dead. I had no idea what I was doing. I was scared and confused, living alone in this house. The one blessing was this house *was* free and clear, and there's no inheritance tax in this state. But that's where it ended. His final notices kept filling up the mailbox. Collectors called the house at all hours. I cut the home phone line because the only people calling wanted money I didn't have."

"I can't imagine," he mutters.

"Eventually, I sorted it out. But the medical bills were just a portion of the problem. Have you purchased a casket or a burial plot lately?" He shakes his head. "There was a little money from his life insurance policy and his savings—not nearly enough. Then, of course, he died in April. He'd been gone about a week when the notice came about the property taxes." Mason cringes. "Yeah. That was fun. I knew nothing about homeownership, and he'd been too out of it to say, 'Hey, just a head's up, kiddo...' Instead, I got thrown into the deep end. With boulders attached to my feet." I swallow. "I fancy myself pretty capable, but I wasn't prepared for everything that would happen after Gene died or how ill-equipped I'd be to handle it."

"Stevie, I'm..."

"It's okay. It's what happened, and I can't change the past. It took me some time to find my footing, but I'm getting there. School, jobs I love. I'm out of debt—as far as I know. And I just take it one day, one expense at a time." I draw in a long breath. "I've never said any of this out loud to anyone before."

He rubs the back of his neck. "I wish you'd told me sooner."

"What difference would it have made?"

"I don't know." He twists his lips. "This place has what—two, three bedrooms?"

"Two."

"Did you consider getting a roommate to help with expenses? You're close to EWC and could charge a *lot*."

"Trust me, I considered it. But it terrified me. There are truly odious people on this planet, and no one would have known to come looking for me if I went missing." Mason laughs through a frown. "Anyone could have moved in, trashed the place, and run off. Then where would I be? I thought about selling it—being rid of the constant burden. But...in today's market? I'd be an idiot. I don't have a mortgage. Have you seen rental prices lately?"

"Yeah. Financially, it makes way more sense to stay." He tugs at his bottom lip, then sighs. "I can't imagine what you've been through, Stevie."

I lift a shoulder. "I probably did everything wrong. But I wasn't prepared for all the decisions I'd have to make. Or to become isolated here with Gene while what few friends I had moved away and forgot about me. I knew it would be hard, but I didn't..." My voice catches at the back of my fiery throat. "I just didn't know." I sniffle and wipe my nose with my sleeve. "I've done the best I could. I think."

"From what I can tell, you've done amazing."

"Thanks," I say through a weak grin. The validation provides some solace.

"You still could have told me," he whispers.

"Spoken like someone who's never been sell-the-TV-to-pay-the-water-bill or stealing-toiletries-from-hotel-carts poor. My whole life, anytime anyone got close enough to see me—really *see* me—they pulled away. And the ones who saw me and leaned in... They thought they could manipulate..." I'm starting to cry again, so I clear

my throat and grab a knife. "With or without chocolate chips?"
I ask.

Mason hesitates, concerned eyes searching mine. Eventually, he
sighs. "Are you kidding?"

"Chocolate chips it is. Full disclosure, this isn't cool enough and it
will crumble. But I'm hungry and I don't care." I cut us each a slice
and order him to eat.

Resting his hat on the counter and exchanging it for the warm
bread, he obeys. "Oh. My. Gosh. How is everything you make so
delicious?"

"Real butter. Dark brown sugar. Cocaine."

He cackles, dusting crumbs from his chest. "That'd do it."

"Where's Danny?"

"Playing at a friend's house."

"Ah."

We finish our bread in silence.

"Not that I don't love surprise visitors, especially on days when
I'm in pajamas at an embarrassing hour." I curtsy. "But what exactly
are you doing here?"

He reaches into his back pocket, pulls out an envelope, and sets it
between us on the countertop. "I'm sorry about Tuesday. I *yelled* at
you then didn't pay you. I think I'm officially Scrooge at this point."

I shake my head. "No. You're not. I haven't been fair to you." I
brace myself against the kitchen counter. He does the same, folding
his arms across his chest. "My responses to certain things must seem
irrational. I think maybe I'm defective. But there's more to it than me
just feeling like a charity case and getting defensive. You asked me
once if someone hurt me. They did, though maybe not in the way
you're thinking."

His jaw is set, and there's a stern crease in his brow like he's
preemptively angry about whatever I'm about to tell him.

"That night you found me staring at the piano..." I shake my
head. "I don't even know where to start this." With a sharp breath, I
drag my hands down my face and try again. "The music room was my

salvation at school. It was my shelter. The one place things made sense, and I felt important and qualified for something. You know? We didn't have a piano at home, but I always wanted to learn. I tinkered around when I could, but it's hard to make real progress when you've only got a few minutes here and there.

"When I was sixteen, there was this guy who accompanied the choir. *Todd...*" Saying his name out loud makes me shudder, and I think I might vomit all over my kitchen. I swallow down bile. "He was like twenty, I think. A former student. Everyone loved him. He walked in when I was trying to teach myself a song over lunch break. He said I was a *natural*. Asked where I took lessons. When I said I'd never had lessons but always wanted them, he offered. I turned him down because I couldn't pay him. He said he wouldn't charge me. It'd just be for fun. But again, I turned him down because I didn't have a bike then. We lived almost five miles from the school, and I didn't want to miss the bus. So *then* he said he'd teach me and drive me home."

I chew on my lips, looking at the ground. Mason releases an audible, shaky breath.

"I didn't have a lot of experience with generosity. My life, up to that point, had been mostly disappointments. It seemed like a change of luck, and I wanted to increase my chances of getting accepted into a music program. Plus, he had a nice smile, and he smelled good. Like sandalwood." I look at Mason briefly before looking back at the floor, but he doesn't notice because his eyes are closed, and he's shaking his head.

"Todd started giving me lessons a couple times a week, then driving me home. For a couple of months, it was normal. The most annoying part of this whole saga is he was *actually* a good teacher. I was developing a real skill for it, and he was encouraging and kept bringing me sheet music. Never asked for a dime. But then one day he pulled..." My breaths hitch at the back of my throat, and I tug at my collar before I'm able to finish. "He pulled himself out, and he grabbed my hand..."

Mason tenses beside me—I don't see it, but I can *feel* it.

"I pulled away. Said no. He threw out a fake apology about how we must have gotten *wires crossed*. As far as I knew, I hadn't even hinted at being interested in him—or *that*—but I thought it was an honest, stupid, horny guy mistake. He kept asking me not to say anything because he loved accompanying the choir, and he'd never hurt me. It was all just a *mistake*. So, like a damn idiot, I went back for another lesson a few days later." I wipe my hands under my eyes, blinking up at the ceiling. "I was so stupid."

"Don't say that," Mason whispers.

"He sat next to me on the bench, like always. Gave me a few pointers on the Debussy piece I was trying to master. For a few minutes, I felt validated. Like it truly had just been a misunderstanding. Then he said something about making our arrangement *worth his while*. Next thing I knew, his hands were on me, and his mouth was attacking mine. I fought him off. It took *everything*, but I fought the prick off me and ran.

"I stopped playing and tried to forget. Once my college plans were derailed, and I wasn't constantly in a music room, staring at a piano, it became easier to pretend it never happened. But then, I start watching Danny, and you smell like sandalwood. Then that bastard Derek pulls me into a tiny piano practice room and puts his hands on me when I say no, and it's like a dam burst. *Everything* came back to the surface." I look at Mason again; his eyes are glistening. "That's why I asked you to change your soap. That's why every gesture puts me on edge or makes me snap. Why I'm always so jumpy. It's why when you handed me that piece of paper, even though I've gotten to know you, and I know you meant *only* good by it..."

Mason shakes his head. "I hate what he did to you. That he spoiled those things for you."

"It was years ago..."

"That doesn't make it better or diminish what you went through. Stevie, I wish..." His voice trails off, and he rubs his forehead. "I shouldn't have pressed you. You said no, and I didn't listen. I've been such an ass. I'm so sorry."

"No. You've only ever been generous with me and expected *nothing* in return. It's just that in doing so, you forced me to face some things I've kept locked away for a long time, and I did a terrible job of it."

With a creased brow, he frowns at me. "Could you maybe stop beating yourself up about this? You were *sixteen*."

"I let my guard down," I counter.

"Because you wanted to believe there was good in the world. We all want that, especially when we're young."

We hold each other in a silent stare, and maybe it's because I spent hours crying and my head is fuzzy, but I have no idea the signal he's trying to get across. He reads as clear and consistent as a Picasso painting.

"I feel woozy," I say. "I think I need to sit, if that's alright."

"Of course." He walks with me to the living room, where I plop awkwardly onto my mattress, then excuses himself to use the bathroom.

"How did I get here?" I whisper-scream, throwing myself backward, eyes searching the popcorn ceiling as though it might answer me back. Part of me is mortified Mason knows the *real* life I lead and some of the more gruesome parts of my past. Part of me is relieved. Part of me is just *really* confused.

Looking back on the last couple months, I see so many mixed signals and almost moments, all building to those few precious seconds Tuesday night when he leaned into my hand, then told me he *couldn't*. Not that he didn't *want* to. He *couldn't*.

"So, full disclosure," his smooth voice echoes through my sparse house, "I'm snooping a bit."

"Snoop away," I offer. My hands tugging at my face, I mumble, "What could you possibly find that would make today any more awkward."

"It's only awkward if we let it be," rings out calmly from the hallway. I turn my face into my pillow, mentally smacking myself for not keeping my thoughts silent. A few moments later, he hollers again. "Want me to fix this for you?"

"What?" My unsteady arms and legs manage to coordinate, and I rise to my feet.

"This old camcorder?"

He stands outside the hall closet, where I've stashed a few odds and ends. He's holding an old, broken camcorder with a tape stuck in it.

"Oh, that," I say. "I found it in the top of Gene's closet after he died. No clue what would be on there, seeing as I didn't even know he owned one. He rarely took pictures, forget video."

"I'd guess it's twenty-five years old. Maybe a bit more. You think it was his?"

"I don't know who else's it would have been. No one else ever lived here with us. There were no other tapes with it. I have no clue what's on there or if I even want to know." That last statement feels only half true. "If you think you can fix it, you're welcome to."

"I can't promise anything," he says, "but I'll see what I can do." I nod. "You feeling any better?"

"Hmm?" Oh, right. I'm supposed to be *woozy*. "I'm fine. Just a little lightheaded."

"Here." With a firm arm around my midriff, he leads me back to the mattress. "Sit," he says, and I do. He takes a spot next to me. "So, why the mattress? Out here, I mean?"

"Temperature's easier to regulate out here. The bedroom windows are single-pane." I point to the large window behind me. "That one's newer. Thicker. I keep the rooms closed up and live out here as a desperate budgeting tactic." He nods. "And as for it being on the floor, I *had* a bed frame, but it broke when I tried to move it without fully disassembling it." After I became enraged with it, throwing and knocking about various parts, that is. Grieving is a peculiar process.

"It's so quiet here," he whispers. "It's eerie."

I shrug. "You get used to the quiet."

"Are you here alone for Christmas?"

"Yup." He frowns. "What are you and Dan doing?"

"My family has a cabin. My parents, my brother, his wife, their daughters...we all hole up there a few days with no TV or internet and just...chill."

"Ah, the Stevie Parker experience, but with company."

He squints, laughing. "What?"

I sweep my arm in front of me, smirking. "No TV. No internet."

He hangs his head. "I'm such a jerk."

"I'm *kidding*. It honestly sounds amazing."

"It doesn't suck." He tugs at his bottom lip. "I hate that you're here alone for Christmas. You deserve better."

"You keep using that word. *Deserve*. I don't think I *deserve* things because I'm an orphan." I regret the word choice, as I no longer wish to think of myself as an orphan. Merrin keeps reminding me she's my family now.

"We always want good things for the people we care about, don't we?" I blush. His phone buzzes. "Shoot. I've got to pick up Danny. Are you sure you're alright?"

I feign a smile. "Give him a hug from me."

He stands, but hovers.

"I'll grab your hat," I mumble.

"Oh, right."

I wobble to the kitchen. When I return and hand over his hat, his mouth opens, but nothing comes out. I bid him goodbye at the front door, watching as he makes it to the curb before halting. He turns and jogs back up the walk, slipping and nearly falling on a patch of ice. My fingers clutch the door frame, my lips pulling into a harsh cringe.

"Come with us," he breathes, steadying himself. "Come with us for Christmas."

"What?"

"No one should be alone. *You* shouldn't be alone."

"Mason..." My head relaxes against the doorframe. "That would be more than a little weird, don't you think?"

He scrunches his nose. "Would it, though?"

"Ha!" I shake my head, but he doesn't take any of it back. This is a *legitimate* invite. "I'd feel so intrusive," I add. "Out of place."

"Look, you'd have your own room. You could stay in there the whole time if you want, reading, listening to music, only coming out when you absolutely felt up to it. But if you *wanted* to be around people, you could be. We're not the most impressive crowd, but we have a good time together. I think you could enjoy yourself there, too."

I chew my lip, mulling it over.

"Stevie, we've been friends, haven't we?" I nod, my head moving against the cold, worn wood. "So come with us. As my—our—friend. Be ready to leave Thursday morning. Plan to stay at least three days."

"Mason..."

"Stevie..." He mimics my tone.

With a heavy sigh, I relent, "Thursday morning," then slowly close the door.

CHAPTER
17

I spend the week a jittery mess and text Merrin approximately five hundred times. We're split in our decision of what Mason's invitation means. She's one-hundred-percent sure it's because he's hoping something happens, but I'm unconvinced. Whatever his reasons, and as awkward as it will absolutely be, I'm...*excited?*

I've packed, overthought every choice, unpacked, and repacked my bag three times by the time Mason calls Wednesday.

"Slight hitch," he says, and my heart sinks. "My sister-in-law was put on bedrest this morning after her prenatal checkup."

"Oh, gosh. How far along?"

"Almost eight months."

"Poor woman." I say *poor woman,* but I'm thinking *whyyyy?*

"Daniel and I are heading to my parents to exchange presents, then they're heading to Coeur d'Alene to see Logan and Rachel's crew. I figured adding another toddler to the mix right now wouldn't be helping."

"Oh" is all I can say as I sink onto my mattress.

"Here's the thing," he sighs. "You're still invited to the cabin. But it's totally your call on whether you're comfortable with that."

"Oh," I say again, unable to manage more than a single syllable.

"You can take your time and think about it."

"Stevie!" a small voice cries in the background.

"Hey, Danny. Are you excited for Christmas?"

"You gonna come sledding with me," he says.

"Danny Boy," Mason says softly. "It's still a maybe. Be patient, buddy."

"Don't worry, Stevie," Danny says. "It's kinda scary the first time, but I'll show you how and keep you safe."

"Well," I sigh. "How could I say no to that?"

The line is quiet for a moment. I almost ask if anyone is still there.

"You'll come?" Mason asks.

"I'll come."

It's subtle, but I think I hear a clap or a high five.

"Okay, then," he says. "We'll see you tomorrow."

I unpack everything and start all over again. This time I include the makeup and shampoo Merrin bought me for Christmas, then spend an hour watching eyeliner tutorials.

"Daddy, what's a skank?" Mason about drives off the road, and I strain against my laughter so hard it physically hurts.

With regained composure, Mason asks, "Daniel, where did you hear that word?"

"Gramma Randa told Grampa Wes that if Stevie, if, um, if Stevie, um... Gramma say if Stevie was still coming to the cabin, she's a skank, and you shouldn't want a skank taking care of your baby. But you don't have a baby."

My laughter and smile immediately ceasing, I will the car to turn around and drive me home.

Mason swears under his breath, and I avert my eyes out the window to the snow-covered mountains.

"Stevie," he whispers, "I'm so sorry."

Quietly, I request he take me home, but he shakes his head.

"Danny," he says, "Grandma shouldn't have used that word, and I'm sure she's very sorry. It's a mean word people sometimes call each other if they're confused and upset. I don't ever want to hear you say it again, okay?"

"Okay, Daddy. But why is Gramma Randa comfused at Stevie?"

"Buddy, don't worry about it. It's alright, and we shouldn't think about it anymore."

"Stevie, when do you dig for gold?" I don't have to ask him to repeat the question. Mason and I know exactly which additional phrase Daniel heard from Gramma Randa. "'Cause I never seen any gold."

"Danny Boy, there's no gold," Mason urges. "Grandma made a mistake—that's all." He pulls a tablet from the center console and hands it to me. "Could you find a movie on there for him, please? Otherwise, the next hour might feel like three. Or ten. Or *hell*." He mouths the last part.

I sift through the downloaded content, press play on a Wiggles movie, and pass the tablet back to Daniel. He sings along, hopefully leaving all thoughts of his *confused* Grandma behind him, though she remains clear and present in my mind.

"Mason, maybe this is a mistake," I whisper.

"Don't go there. My mother, she's... Look, she's wrong. And out of line. And I'm sorry. But that's all."

"But maybe this is confusing for him. Don't you ever think he's too attached to me?"

"Stevie, I'm not attached to you, okay," Daniel calls up to me. "I'm in mine seat. I'm strapped in safe!"

"You're absolutely right, sweetie," I say.

"Beep beep! Buckle up!" he sings.

"You're such a smart boy." I offer him a wide grin, then eye Mason, lowering my voice. "I mean, this isn't normal. Is it?"

"So what? Let my mother stew all she wants. You're my friend. I —*we*—care about you. I'm not turning this car around. We're going to the cabin, and we're going to have a Merry Freakin' Christmas, dangit!" He hits his hand against the steering wheel for effect, and we both laugh. "There's nothing wrong with this."

"So," I try. Changing the subject seems like a good idea, but I can't come up with anything else.

"Yeah. So." He frowns. "Again, I'm so sorry. My mom really isn't a horrible person. I wasn't present when Dan overheard those particular phrases, but I will definitely be discussing it with her."

"It's okay." It's not. It hurts. "Let's just forget it."

"Yes. Let's." Though we both know neither of us will forget. At least not yet. Tough as I am, all the things I've been called in my life, *gold-digging skank* will stick with me for a while.

"Did you declare a major for next semester?" Mason asks.

"Not officially."

"But you've made a decision?" he asks. I nod. "You going to take music back up again?"

"Well, yes, but not as a major."

"So, you're becoming a professional pastry chef and opening up a bakery? I'd eat there every single day."

I laugh. "Thanks for the support. But no. Baking is personal for me. It's not something I'm willing to share with the general public."

"Well, to be fair, the general public can be the absolute worst."

"True."

"Okay, so...?"

"I've landed on early childhood education, teaching preschool. I've decided I rather enjoy spending my days with little people."

"Because it makes you feel tall?"

"Ha!" I pause to collect myself. It's a fair dig. "That might be part of it." I punch his shoulder as an afterthought. "Jerk."

"I'm sorry. You're not that short."

"Liar. Daniel will be taller than me in about two years."

"Or two months."

"Hey, now."

He snickers, then composes himself. "Okay, okay. So why—the real reason?"

"At first, it seemed obvious: music teacher. Makes sense, right? And who doesn't love teaching elementary school kids to play the recorder?"

"Ah, Satan's music."

"Indeed."

"But not every school has a thriving music program," he acknowledges. "Or the budget for one at all."

"Yes! Precisely. But enhancing early education with music? Maybe it's delusional to think I'll make some lasting impact. It just feels right, though. Exciting."

"I'm happy for you." He smiles, turning to me a moment before focusing back on the road. "Plan to transfer anywhere exciting to finish your degree?"

"Nah. Early Childhood Ed is one of the few bachelor's programs EWC offers."

"Oh, wow. And you're okay sticking around?"

"Why wouldn't I be?"

He turns a hand up. "I don't know, Stevie. You gave up Stanford for Spokane. I mean, sure, it's a great place to live and all, but don't you ever think about leaving it behind? Trying to get into a bigger school? See more than our little corner of the world?"

I shake my head. "I like it here. I don't feel that ache to leave it all behind like I used to. Who knows? Maybe one day, I'll sell everything I own—which isn't much—and just...travel. Or not. Honestly, if I call Washington and even Spokane *home* the rest of my life, I think I'm okay with it."

He sighs. "I say way to go. You should do what feels right. There's so much pressure to choose careers for the wrong reasons these days, money mostly. It shouldn't have to be about the money."

"Said the rich boy."

"True enough." He tries to suppress a smirk. "In my defense, I didn't choose a major for the money. I was just...lucky."

"Give yourself a little more credit than *lucky*."

"Nah. I just sort of won the lottery. Now, there's an option for you," he teases. "Start buying up tickets. Solid investment."

"Don't gamble. Uncle Gene taught me that."

"He didn't gamble?"

"Oh no, he loved his stupid scratchers and mega tickets. We never won anything—not a penny—but he just kept on buying them.

Sometimes he chose them over milk. I ate a lot of dry cereal growing up." I pause, wishing I could take some of it back. "Despite how it must come off sometimes, Uncle Gene wasn't evil."

"I believe you." He looks over, a sympathetic grin on his lips.

"I mean, we had our issues, and he made some questionable decisions during his worst bouts of depression. But he was a decent parent. He read to me every night when I was little. Not typical children's books either—lots of adventures and westerns." I pause, allowing for a listless sigh. "My love of reading—that all came from him."

"That's not nothing. That's special."

"You noticed the books, right? At the house? Stacked everywhere?" He nods. "He forgot my birthday the first year I lived with him. Felt terrible. So, one day he takes me on this drive and says, 'We're going to a special store where you can pick out as many books as you like.' I was still so young; all I knew was I got to choose a load of books to keep. I didn't care or even notice they were used. When I got older, I realized it was the library's discarded book sale. Take all you want for a donation type of thing. He sometimes got me a present for my birthday or Christmas when he could afford it, but mostly, he took me to that book sale every time it came around." Mention of our little tradition makes me sentimental, weepy even. I watch the snow-topped mountains rise and fall against the skyline, pulling back the tears, pushing them down.

"That's a priceless memory. I'm glad you have that."

I avert the topic before my stupid *feelings* take over. "Enough about me. Back to you, money bags." He releases a quick, sharp laugh. "How did your family come into such grand wealth anyway?"

"Who said it was grand?"

"You did."

"Right. I did that. Well, my grandpa, always a hard worker, got lucky with some investments. Like, Forrest Gump lucky. My dad's an inventor and entrepreneur with enough patents to keep him in comfort, and my mom has an intense eye for investing and planning.

So, a lot of my money is undeserved generational wealth. I can't claim to have earned it."

"So, what you're saying is that you're more loaded than you let on?"

He twists his lips. "Maybe. A little. Why?"

"Nothing. You just seem so normal. Unspoiled. I guess I imagined the wealthy to be delusional. Disgusting."

"And you don't find me disgusting?"

"Not because of your money, anyway."

"You cut me deep, Stevie."

"Yeah, you're bleeding all over the place."

"It's inward, alright."

Is he flirting? I know *I* am, though I'm trying desperately not to, given the toddler in the back seat.

"So, this cabin," I say, shifting the conversation again. "Where is it, exactly?"

"In the middle of nowhere. There are a handful of other cabins in the area, and there's a combination gas station, grocery, and laundromat about five miles down the road, but not much else. And as a matter of fact..." The car slows as we turn a corner. "You see that place on the hill?" He points to a large log house peeking between patches of snow-covered pine trees.

"That's it?"

"Yup. Look, Dan. You see? We're almost there."

Daniel claps his hands, cheering.

"That's your family *cabin*?" I scoff at him. The house more closely resembles an estate. He shrugs. "Well, then."

The Shepards' cabin is large but modestly furnished. There are at least six bedrooms. Mason offers me the largest one with a private bathroom and a king-sized bed. The blankets are soft and smell of lilacs. With a deep inhale, I know I can fall asleep right here and now if I want. That is, until Daniel runs in and jumps on top of me.

"Sledding!" he yells. "Let's go sledding, Stevie! I show you how!"

We play outside for hours, and this is my first truly blissful snow-centered experience since my parents died. I have a few winter memories leading up to that point—the most vivid one being a five-second clip of my mother kneeling to adjust my hat, tugging my gloves on tighter, then kissing my cold nose. Then she disappears, running through the white snow in a pink coat. I have a picture of my mom and me next to a snowman we built and one with my dad where I'm shoving a snowball in his face. Aside from what I can see in those photographs, I can't recall many details. Today is all the more bittersweet because of that.

We stay outside until the sun disappears, a full-bellied moon taking over the night sky. After dinner, Mason goes into "town" for a few groceries and better cell service. Though he claims not to be tired, Daniel falls asleep in my lap before we've settled on which bedtime story to read. Rocking him gently, watching the glow of the fire, quiet Christmas music playing on the stereo, my eyelids grow heavy, and I, too, succumb to the hours of childish play. I dream of fields of undisturbed white snow until a bright sun appears, melting it all away.

When I open my eyes, Mason stands in front of me, looking on, phone in hand. "Sorry. I couldn't pass it up," he whispers, pocketing his phone.

I stretch my legs and reach up to rub my sweaty face. "S'okay. What time is it?"

"About nine," he answers, sitting in the recliner beside mine. "What time did he pass out?"

"About ten seconds after you left." He laughs quietly, reaching over to stroke Daniel's forehead.

"Did you get an update on your sister-in-law?"

He nods, sighing. "Yeah, I talked to Logan for a bit. Everything and everyone is fine. They think the baby might come a little early, but she's far enough along they don't foresee any serious complications. Poor Rachel's just stuck on bedrest until that happens."

"I'm so glad she's okay."

"Me, too. I can't even imagine... They've got three girls. If anything had happened to her..."

I want to reach out and hold his hand, to reassure him. Instead, I pivot the conversation. "Three girls, huh? What about this one?"

"My guess is a boy, but they don't know for sure. They've always chosen to be surprised come delivery."

I cringe. "That sounds like torture."

He laughs, nodding. "I couldn't do it."

I take in the smell of the sweet toddler in my lap and sigh. Daniel stretches and relaxes in my arms. "I should get him to bed," I say, clutching him, preparing to stand.

"I'll get him," Mason insists, carefully lifting Daniel off my lap and carrying him to bed. When he rejoins me, he brings me a blanket to replace the warmth that Daniel had provided. We watch the lulling glow of the fire together, not speaking. It's a contented quiet I'm unfamiliar with.

"It's so peaceful," I say.

"The noise of childhood wearing you thin?"

I bite my lip, smiling. "No. I love the noise. I only meant, growing up, it was quiet almost all the time, but it was...vacant. This is happy quiet."

"Happy quiet?"

"Yes. Happy quiet." I repeat, though I know he's teasing.

"So, you want a life full of quiet, contented moments?"

"No, I want a life full of noise. Lots of noise." He smiles, curious and confused. "I always thought I was content in my solitude. Then I spent Thanksgiving with Merrin's family."

"Happy loud," he says, smirking.

"Exactly. It was beautiful. I want that. And at the end of the day, I want blissful peace, knowing all is well. That everyone is loved and fulfilled."

"I see." He pauses, watching the fire again. I try, but it's difficult to tear my eyes from his features, more striking than ever in the orange glow of the room. He catches me staring, and I hope my blush is mistaken as a response to the heat of the fire. He doesn't seem to read into my stare, though. Instead, he asks, "Do you want kids someday?"

Ignoring the burning in my chest and the lump in my throat, I manage, "I could do with a few. When the time—no. When the person is right."

He creases his brow.

"Maybe it's a juvenile sentiment, but I've always felt the person was more important than the timing. Probably because my parents died so young. I think if we sit around, waiting for the stars to align, we're bound to live in a perpetual state of disappointment."

He offers the hint of a smile before averting his eyes. I've risked so much—put so much out in the open just now—yet he has no discernible response. I clear my throat.

"What about you?" I ask. "Do you think you'll get married? Have more kids?"

He's quiet so long I almost say goodnight and leave. Just as I'm bracing to stand, he speaks.

"I'd like to remarry." This is the first time he's confirmed ever being married to Daniel's mother. "More kids, sure. But I don't know when or *if* that'll happen. I just try to be completely in it right now, you know?"

The conversation dwindles once more, and I focus on the serenity of the fire. Every crackle and hiss.

"About my mom," Mason says after a lull. "I'm truly sorry for what she said."

"You didn't say it. You don't have to keep apologizing."

"So long as you know *I* don't feel that... I mean, I don't think—"

"That I'm a gold-digging skank?" I finish.

He drags his hands down his face. "It sounds so much worse out loud," he says. "No, Stevie. The thought never occurred to me." He looks at me. "*I* invited *you* here. Remember?"

I nod. "And I want to be here," I admit. There's something else I should tell him, but it requires all my courage.

You're a grown woman, Stevie. You can do this.

"I heard you last week," I say. "When you said you couldn't..." I choke on the words. "I heard you. And I'll respect that."

He flinches, closing his eyes. "It's complicated," he sighs.

Translation: *I'm not ready to talk about it yet.*

A sentiment I understand, even if it's cruel and unusual punishment *not* to know what's going on with him. When he opens his eyes again, we lock gazes and just...live in it, unashamedly searching each other's faces. All I discern from him is pain.

A pop of the fire brings us both out of the moment.

"The fire," he starts, standing. "I should feed the fire."

"I'm tired. I think I'll go to bed now."

We say goodnight, and I retire to my thick blankets on my fluffy bed that suddenly seems too big and altogether empty.

CHAPTER
18

Though I awake Christmas Eve morning cocooned in soft, warm blankets, my toes and nose sting with cold. The aroma of coffee means one of two things: Mason is up, the fires are started, and there's a warm place just *waiting* for my frozen rear. Or, they've got a programmable coffee maker here, and Mason set it last night. It's likely the latter, but I risk it anyway.

Following the sound of pops and crackles, my gamble pays off, and I sit on the stone hearth next to the warm, orange blaze. It doesn't occur to me to be embarrassed by my wrinkled pajamas, or the way my hair is flopping around in a messy pile on top of my head, until Mason joins me by the fire.

Didn't think this one through, did you, Stevie?

Running out of the room and reappearing well-groomed might be a bit obvious at this point, though. At least these pajamas are relatively new. No holes or stains.

"How do you take your coffee?" he asks through a yawn.

I peer up at him with a slight grimace. "Will you be offended if I say I *don't* drink coffee?"

He cocks his head, arching a brow. "Why would that offend me?"

"It seems to offend a lot of people. I love the smell, but I think it tastes like burnt punishment."

That makes him laugh, then slide a hand across his mouth, pausing to tug on his bottom lip. "Give me a minute," he says.

Sounds trickle from the kitchen. Water, a kettle, mugs, silverware. I stay perched on the hearth, waiting, processing the fact that I'm here in all my morning glory. The longer I wait, the less I care about what I look (or smell) like; I'm just glad I'm with *him*.

Mason returns with two mugs and passes me one.

"Hot cocoa more your scene?" he asks.

I wrap my hands around the warm mug and inhale. "Yes. Thank you."

"I honestly don't like coffee either. But until now, I thought I was alone in my distaste. Over the years, all my friends and colleagues have acted as though it's some crime against nature."

"Well, we can't have everything. Has to be a flaw in there somewhere." Maybe it's too forward, throwing back words he used on me months ago. I could be giving too much away. But his smirk puts me at ease. We both clear our throats and take long sips of our cocoa.

"I'm sorry it's so cold this morning," he says. "The power went out for a bit last night."

"Oh no. Is Danny warm enough?"

This question seems to give him pause, then make him smile. "He's fine. There's a space heater in his room. Not that he slept there. He came in with me at three a.m. asking for a peanut butter and honey sandwich."

I chuckle. "Of course, he did."

"He wanted to get ready to go sledding, too. Took him a while to settle down. Anyway, when I got up, I moved the heater to my room. Long story longer, he's warm enough. I promise."

"Don't feel like you have to be awake for my sake. I don't need company or anything. If you were up half the night..."

"It's okay. I wanted to get the tree set up anyway. Danny will want to decorate the moment he wakes up, I'm sure."

My giddiness propels itself out of my mouth. "We have a tree? I didn't see a tree."

"We keep a fake one here. You know, with the lights already built in? Takes a lot of the fun out of it, in my opinion."

I laugh. "That's all we ever had—Gene and I. About ten years ago, one of the sections went out, so there was this dead spot right around the middle. Very classy." I pause for a slow breath, a sip of cocoa. "This might sound stupid, but I brought an ornament with me. Can I hang it on your tree, too?"

"That's not stupid. And yes, of course, you can."

After I've showered and put on the *tiniest* bit of makeup, I find Mason in the living room manipulating fake plastic branches to give the tree a fuller appearance. Without asking if he wants my help, I start tweaking and bending branches opposite him. We meet somewhere in the middle, and my breath catches in my chest as he reaches above me. I bite my lip, going about my business, trying to think of anything other than the closeness of him. Then his nose brushes my hair, he inhales, and my heart stops.

He mumbles something under his breath, and I'm almost certain it's, "You smell so good." Then he freezes, maybe to see if I noticed.

This is now the only shampoo and conditioner I will ever use for the rest of my life, even if I have to sell my organs to afford it.

As Mason backs away, I tuck my chin and slump my shoulders, attempting to hide my flushed cheeks.

"Danny will be up any minute," he says. "I'll make us some breakfast. You like pancakes?"

Of course, I like pancakes. I *love* pancakes. But I can't remember anyone ever offering to make them for me.

"Stevie?"

"Hmm?"

"Pancakes?"

"You're perfect," I murmur. Then quickly, "Pancakes. Pancakes are perfect."

WE DECORATE the tree to the sounds of old Christmas albums playing through crackly speakers. The cabin stereo is significantly less sophisticated than the one at Mason's house, and I like how it makes this experience feel more authentic. More akin to what I'm used to.

Outside, the morning sun is muted by clouds so close they kiss the windows, and tiny flurries are just beginning to drift into view. The longer I experience *cabin life*, the deeper I fall in love with it.

"So," Mason asks, snapping me out of my trance. "Any particular reason your face lit up when I mentioned decorating the tree?"

I relinquish the "Baby's First Christmas" ornament I've been clutching for several minutes to an empty branch. The precious keepsake holds a picture of my parents and me when I wasn't quite a year old. Caressing the picture, I sigh.

"It's the first decent memory I have after my parents died." I tug at the ends of my sleeves, burying my hands in the fabric as I sit on the opposite end of the couch from Mason. "As far as I knew, Santa was magic. Grownups always tell you that Santa is magic." I speak quietly, careful not to attract the attention of Daniel, admiring all the ornaments on the glowing tree, singing Jingle Bells to himself over and over again.

"When you're four, you believe it. Or at least you want to. Everyone said if I told him what I wanted and if I was good, he'd get it for me. I heard it in daycare. I heard it on TV. Read it in books. So, I asked Uncle Gene to help me write a letter to Santa. He humored me at first, but when I asked him to write that I wanted Mommy and Daddy back for Christmas, he started crying. 'Santa can't do that, Rae.' Then he cried louder because he remembered I wasn't Rae."

Mason shifts to the edge of his seat, closer observing the ornament. "She was beautiful, your mother," he says.

"She was." I slump back against the cushions. "Eventually, I took Gene's words to heart. Santa couldn't bring back what was gone forever. I was inconsolable. He asked me what else I might like, basically promised me the moon. But I said if Santa couldn't bring me my parents, he probably wasn't even magic enough to know I'd moved, and anything I asked for wouldn't come to me anyway. Gene said if we decorated a tree and put it *right* in the center of that front window and wrote my name on it, Santa would know. That was *my* house. *My* tree. In my four-year-old mind, it made sense."

"Did he really put your name on it?"

I laugh. "Yeah. We—well, *he*—made snowflakes out of coffee filters. My skills with scissors were still pretty limited at that point. But he wrote my name on every single one. And he put them on that flimsy fake tree. We didn't have many traditions together, but every year, without fail, he put aside anything else going on or any ill will between us at the time, and he decorated that tree with me." I wipe a sneaky tear from the corner of my eye. "That old tree fell apart the last Christmas he was alive. Which is appropriate, I guess."

Mason scoots closer to me and puts his hand on my arm. I feel it everywhere, almost like he's lending me some of his strength. "I'm sorry you lost him, too."

"He refused treatment. Did I ever tell you? Said he was ready to go. And I watched him wilt away for almost a year.

"I can't fault him for it, though. If I were him, I probably would have been ready to go, too. He missed her—my mom. She was his world. Their dad ran out not long after my mom was born, then my grandma died when Gene was barely twenty and my mom was twelve. He finished raising her. For years, it was just the two of them. They were so close, and when she died, something inside him just... broke. Then he got stuck with me. How unfair was that? He'd already done more than his fair share raising my mom. No wonder he resented me."

"Regardless of his own trauma, you were a child. You deserved love."

"He was just so lost. I guess he's not anymore. At least, I hope he's not."

"But now you're alone." Mason withdraws his kind touch. It relieves and disappoints me all at once.

I sigh. "But I'm not anymore. I mean, yes, I have no legitimate relatives left. But Merrin, her family, they've sort of claimed me. Which I'm okay with. And I've got...other friends." I slide him a look, and he grins. "Sure, I still get lonely. But doesn't everyone?"

"Yeah," he agrees. "That's fair."

"This is just my phase of life right now, and it's temporary. I've only been back in the world—*really* participating in my life, not just watching it pass by—for a few months. It'll get better." I shake my head, twisting my lips. "When I think of all that time I wasted just...*existing*..."

"Don't go there, Stevie. You did the best you could."

"But given my family history of untimely deaths, you'd think I'd know better than to let life pass me by."

"You didn't. You're living. You've got this."

I meet his gaze, wearing a half-smile. "I hope you're right."

"I usually am," he teases.

I observe the tree as our conversation fizzles. It's perfect; a well-balanced combination of handicrafts, obviously made by children, and more traditional trinkets and keepsakes. The areas of the tree where Daniel hung ornaments are adorably obvious, five or six to each branch.

"You have her name, don't you?" Mason asks after a time.

"Hmm?"

"That day when I teased you for including your middle name... Your mother was Renae, wasn't she?"

I nod. "Yeah. Renae. Rae for short."

"Well, the name was rightfully passed on. You look just like her."

"Thank you," I whisper, trying to hold myself together. How I ache for her.

His hand extends slowly toward my cheek, but he doesn't follow through. Instead, he moves farther away from me and watches the snow falling outside the window.

CHRISTMAS MORNING LOST its childish wonderment for me long ago. I've still enjoyed the holiday as a whole, especially the tree—presents or no presents under it, it's bright and beautiful and calming. The excitement, though, the itch to wake up early Christmas morning? Those sentiments are buried deep in my past.

Christmas morning at the Shepards' cabin, however, is different. I'm eager. Giddy, even. Not for my sake but for Mason and Daniel's. Watching Daniel's eyes light up at his presents and the smile it puts on Mason's face fills me with an enchanting joy. A drug almost, one I could easily overdose on. Yet the sight of such love and bliss also intensifies my longing for my mom and dad, even Gene. I want my family back. And as much as I keep trying to fight it, I want to be part of *this* family, too.

Daniel opens the puzzle and books I bought for him and is thrilled beyond anything I hoped for. He assures me he will "use them every day!" and thanks me with a tight hug and kiss on the cheek.

"I picked a present for you, too, Stevie!" he calls, running back to the tree. He brings me something concealed haphazardly with Spiderman wrapping paper. "I wrapped it mine self!"

"Aw, honey." I pull him in for another hug. "I love it."

"You didn't open it yet," he says, giggling.

"You're the sweetest boy in the world. You know that?"

He sighs. "I know."

I laugh, peering at Mason, who has his hands over his face, laughing along with me.

"Help me open it, munchkin." With gusto, he helps peel back the paper to reveal a board game. It's based on the movie we saw the last time I watched him. The night Mason offered me the truck.

"Now we can play it together!" he cheers.

"It's perfect, Danny." I pull him in for one last tight squeeze before setting him loose to explore all his new things.

Hugging the board game to my chest, I turn toward Mason. "I think this is my favorite gift in the history of ever."

Mason beams. "He really did pick it out by himself, and he *mostly* wrapped it alone. I had to cut the paper and dispense some tape."

"He's such an amazing kid. Seriously. I, uh..." I clear my throat. "I have something for you. It's for both of you, technically. But mostly for you." I snatch his book from under the tree. I ordered it not long after I started working for him—honestly, the easiest splurge I've ever made in my life. I got sucked into an online advertisement for personalized books, and it was too perfect to pass up. I doubt I'd ever have had the courage to give it to him, though, were it not for his invitation to the cabin. *We're friends,* he'd said. *I care about you.* I know he means it, whether he returns my deepening love or not. Whether his *I can't* was because of me or him.

I chew on my lips as he tentatively opens the package. "Oh my gosh. Stevie, this is..." He runs his hand over the cover. *The Adventures of Super Dad and Danny Boy.* Turns out, you really *can* buy almost anything on the internet. I had only prefabricated options for the actual story line. Not a lot of variety. But I was able to customize the illustrations to an extent—the skin tone, hairstyle, and eye color of the main characters. It's not a perfect resemblance, but it's obvious who they're intended to be. Brown eyes and brown curly hair for Super Dad. Baby blues and black curls for Danny Boy. Their costumes are red and blue, an homage to Daniel's favorite superhero.

Mason begins thumbing through the pages. "This is genuinely the coolest thing I've ever seen."

"Hopefully, this serves as a reminder for you. You always seem so worried that you're not doing enough of this or that for him. Like you're so unsure of yourself. I can't imagine the weight you feel every single day, but you *are* his hero. You're literally everything to him. And you're doing a great job. I just want you to remember that."

His eyes hold mine for a long time before he shakes it off. "I don't have the right words. Thank you doesn't feel like enough."

I nod in Daniel's direction. "I don't need words. I get to see his face when you read it to him. That's enough."

And it is.

He calls Daniel over. They read the book together several times in a row, and their evident joy says more than I could ever need.

CHAPTER
19

Daniel falls asleep on the floor in front of the Christmas tree with dried bits of macaroni and cheese around his lips, clutching a die-cast train in each hand. Given he flew out of bed this morning at six and played non-stop with his new toys until lunchtime, it's no surprise.

Mason carries him into bed for a proper nap, and I start cleaning torn bits of wrapping paper and plastic packaging from the floor.

"You don't need to do that," Mason says, returning.

"I know." I don't stop cleaning.

"Stevie, could you look at me for a second?"

I freeze.

"Please?" he says.

Slowly, I straighten. He's clutching a gift box to his chest, wearing a guarded smile.

"Can we sit?" he asks, motioning to the couch.

With a hesitant nod, I do. He sits beside me, placing the box on my lap.

"What's this?"

"I hope it's more acceptable than a truck," he sighs.

A brief, nervous laugh escapes my lips. I haven't even looked at the box; I'm fixated on Mason and the expression on his face I can't quite read. Fear? Hope? Maybe even excitement? It's a heavy look, whatever it is. I have to force my attention away from him and down to the plain, white gift box.

Inching the lid open, I gasp at the sleek, black laptop staring back at me.

"No," I whisper.

"No more hand-written rough drafts," he says.

"Did you..." I examine the laptop, searching for a familiar brand name or logo. "Did you build this?"

"It's partially recycled and refurbished parts I had on hand, but I swear it runs like new. I guarantee my work."

He *built* it. From recycled parts, no less, meaning he's beginning to understand my hesitance toward frivolity, and my disdain for waste.

"Do you like it?" he asks through a guarded smile.

"Mason, I..." I bite my lip, shaking my head. "This is so thoughtful."

He braces himself, probably waiting on a lecture. He's expecting a backlash, and still, he did this for me. Everything he does makes me fall harder, which is equal parts exhilarating and painful. Because while I'm falling, falling, falling, *gone*, I have absolutely no idea how he really feels about me.

"Thank you," I say. "I'm so grateful."

He arches an eyebrow. "Yeah?"

"Yes."

His eyes light up, and he laughs. It's short and sharp. "Phew!"

I scrunch my nose. "Aw. You were nervous."

"Yes. Very. But not just because..." He sighs. Without a word, he opens his hands and nods toward the laptop. I hand it to him. "There's something else—something I want to show you."

He clicks around, then sets the laptop on the ottoman and scoots it close. There's a video file open on the screen, but it's not playing yet.

"Mason, is that...?" A burst of nerves and heat surges through me.

"I couldn't save all of it," he says, "but I got a lot off of there."

My hand flies to my chest as I draw in a sharp breath.

"It wasn't Gene's camera, Stevie." I'm crying already. "It was theirs."

I release my breath slowly through tight lips, trying to steel myself for whatever comes next.

"Merry Christmas, Stevie Rae." He says it through a giddy smile, then presses a key and watches me as the video comes to life.

Her voice. *Her* voice. My mother. I slap my hand over my mouth, muffling the cry that escapes. "Mom," I whisper. "*Mama.*"

She's sitting in a rocker, rubbing her round belly, talking to it. Talking to *me*. She stops when she notices the camera. "Mark, get that thing away from me. What are you doing?"

"We can't wait until she's here to make sure it works, Rae."

"Well, if you'd have just bought one new instead of from a yard sale, for crying out loud."

"Hey, would you rather the camera come from a yard sale or the infant seat? We dream on a budget, babe."

"Just turn it off. No one wants to see this." She hides her face.

"*Everyone* wants to see this." There's so much love in his voice. "You're beautiful, Renae." She is. She's so beautiful.

Next, she's standing hunched slightly with a hand pressed under her bulging belly. She's laughing, though she looks to be in pain. "We can't wait to meet you, baby girl!" she calls. The picture gets muddled as the camera finds my dad's face.

"We're so excited!" he says. "Daddy can't wait to hold you, sweetheart. And teach you to play the guitar. And how to ride a bike. And how to land a right hook."

"Mark!" my mother screeches. "I love you, but I will break that camera across your face. Let's go!"

The screen cuts to Mom in a hospital bed, holding me. Dad sits beside her. They're both red-faced and puffy-eyed. A familiar voice behind the camera introduces the scene.

"Mark and Renae Parker have welcomed little Stephanie into this world—a perfect baby girl. She came out strong, kicking and screaming."

"Singing," my mother corrects. Uncle Gene laughs behind the

camera. My mother kisses the baby. Kisses *me*. "She came into this world singing."

There are bits and pieces of footage spanning what appears to be my first year of life. Short clips, but precious. Every last one. Even the ones where the picture is distorted. I'm full-blown sobbing by the time we reach my first steps.

"Mason..." I turn to him, touching his knee. "Mason, I..." I want to thank him, then go finish my cry privately. Then I hear it. *It.*

My song.

A strange and rather horrible sound escapes my throat as I turn to see the image of my mother rocking me, singing in an exhausted yet perfectly on-key voice.

> *The sun is playing hide and seek*
> *The man in the moon is singing*
> *The crickets play while the birds are away*
> *But Stevie's still not sleeping*
> *Untold wonder awaits you tonight*
> *In that magical land we call dreaming*
> *Maybe you'll fly and set sail to the sky*
> *If only you were sleeping*
> *Stevie is lovely, and Stevie is kind*
> *Stevie is mine for the keeping*
> *Stevie is more than I ever hoped for*
> *But Stevie's still not sleeping*

"Stop it," I screech. "Stop... Stop it." I can't watch any more, if there is any more.

It has words. My song has words. It's *real*, and it's *mine*. She made it up just for me.

The room blurs. My heart races. At some point, I must have quit breathing because now I'm gasping for air. My head grows heavy and droops, falling into my hands.

"Stevie?" Mason's voice is distant and muffled.

I lose control. I *break*. Foreign and shrill cries and gargles spew from my mouth, the spaces between filled with erratic gasps and wheezing.

Mason hugs me to him, rubbing circles on my back, trying to calm me. Every so often, he speaks. Reassuring messages like, "I've got you," or, "You're okay." I don't know how long it is before I attempt to sit up and speak.

"I h-have-have... I have to go." I try to stand.

Mason gently holds my hand. "Stevie, even if we weren't in the middle of nowhere, you can't go anywhere right now. Not like this. Just breathe."

"I can't. I don't. I can't..." I fall against him again, bringing my flannel shirt up to try and cover my face, willing myself to disappear. "Please. I can't..."

"Stevie, it's alright. I've got you."

"It's not alright!" I yell. "It's not."

"*Breathe.*" He holds me tighter.

I keep trying to find a rhythm. Every time I think maybe I'm getting there, another ugly sob escapes, and I start all over again.

"Stevie, I had no idea it would upset you so much. I'm so sorry." Poor Mason, ignorant of the significance of his discovery. He diligently rubs my back, trying to help me find my breathing pattern. How many times must I be the neurotic girl crying on his couch?

"I need...tissues," I finally manage. I have snot all over my sleeve. He leaves and returns with a box. I start blowing my nose, not even caring that it's loud and gross. What dignity do I have left at this point? Next, he brings me water, holding the cup for me while I sip sloppily through a straw.

"You're being," I take another shaky breath, "too nice. You don't... h-have to..."

"What else can I do?" He pushes a wet, tangled lock of hair out of my face. Why does he have to be so perfect? "Stevie, I'm so sorry."

My breathing isn't so labored anymore. My eyes burn, and there's a chaotic drumline where my heart should be, but I can breathe. "You didn't do anything wrong," I croak.

"I never expected it would elicit this. If I'd known..." He shakes his head, still holding my face. I allow myself to rest against his palm, closing my eyes just as he did that night in his driveway. This time, no one says, *I can't*.

"What can I do?" he asks again. His voice is silky. His breath, molten lava against my skin.

All I want is to fall back into his arms and *stay*, letting him shelter me. But what if his current affection is born of pity? Does he feel sorry for the train wreck I've become? *Again*? Or is it possible there truly is more between us, and this isn't a one-sided delusion?

I can't trust it. My head is too fuzzy; I can't trust anything.

"This isn't fair," I whisper, opening my eyes but avoiding his. Slowly, I pull farther away, turning from him and wiping my face with my shirt. Classy. "I keep falling apart in front of you. I can't even *leave* and go break down alone and salvage what little dignity I have left."

"This has nothing to do with dignity, alright? We're miles beyond that. Please, look at me." I can't. "This isn't about your pride right now, it's about *you*. Your wellbeing. You just had a panic attack, Stevie. Whether you want to admit it or not. All I care about right now is that you're okay."

"Well, I'm not," I whisper scream. Desperate to release my rage but aware of a sleeping toddler down the hall. "It's that song. That stupid, wonderful song."

Mason puts his arm around me again, urging me back into him. I cave, resting against his chest, fisting the fabric of his sweater. Finding my voice, keeping my rhythm... It all seems a little easier with his heartbeat reverberating in my ear.

"It's been with me my whole life," I continue. "When they died, I kept the melody, but the words left. It was like they vanished right along with my mother. I asked for help. I *begged*. 'Uncle Gene, do you remember Mommy's song?' 'Shut up, Stevie! She's dead. She doesn't have a song!'"

I pause to let a few necessary sobs out. My anger diminishes, and I feel in control of my voice again.

"I thought I just made it up. I thought, maybe, I was so desperate for a memory to cling to that I made the whole damn thing up. I gave up all hope of remembering the words years ago."

"That must have been torture," he says, his fingers combing through my hair.

"You have no idea... You couldn't have possibly known what that song means," deep breath, "means to me." He encases me in both arms, and I let myself curl up into him like it's the most natural thing in the world. Maybe it is.

"DADDY. Daddy, wake up! Daddy, I'm hungry!"

"I'm up, buddy," Mason whispers. "Just give me a second, ok?"

The gravity of my situation begins to sink in.

I fell asleep. I fell asleep on the couch. Wait, no, I fell asleep on Mason. I had a full-blown panic attack, then fell asleep on him.

I finally gather the courage to open my eyes. Yup, that's Mason's favorite shawl-neck sweater I'm drooling on. *Oh, no.* I sit up, wiping my mouth first, then the goop from my eyes. *Oh, please, no.* I peek at him through my fingers. He sits calmly, smiling. Not embarrassed. Not worried. Just smiling.

"Stevie, are you sick?" Daniel asks, coming to my side. "I like to snuggle Daddy when I'm sick, too."

Oh, dear.

I can't decide whether to laugh or cry, where to look, what to do. Mason keeps his perfect smile.

"Stevie? Stevie? Are you sick?" Daniel starts climbing into my lap.

Mason snatches him up and pulls him close. "Give Stevie some space, buddy."

"Um, hi," I finally manage, my voice scratchy and low.

"Hi," the boys return in unison.

Daniel giggles, and I want to laugh along for his sake, but my foggy, pounding head won't oblige. *Everything* hurts.

"How are you feeling?" Mason asks.

"I'm not sure I can answer that right now."

He nods. "That's fair."

"Daddy, I'm super hungry!" Daniel wails.

What time is it? How long did I sleep sprawled out across Mason like that? Did I snore? *Noooo my gosh. Please, no.* It would be too much. This is already *so* much.

I start to stand, but Mason puts a gentle hand on my arm. "Please, don't rush. I'll fix us something to eat. Okay?"

"Sure."

"Do you need anything? Water? Pain reliever?"

"Time machine?" I murmur. "Invisibility cloak?"

There's an urgency behind his eyes as he slides his hand down my arm, resting it on my knee. "Stop. How much time have you spent scolding yourself for things completely beyond your control?"

His words sober me, and my chest constricts. I swallow, loud and slow.

"When has it *ever* worked? When has it ever made anything better?"

There's a flutter in my stomach as I realize his thumb is ever so subtly caressing the side of my knee. It's small but deliberate. My eyes dart to his as my breaths grow ragged. If I'm not mistaken, there's a yearning behind his deep browns. But there are apologies in them, too. That same *I can't* look. I want to peel back all his layers and figure out exactly what it means.

"Daddy, I'm *super duper* hungry!"

With a twitch of his lips—almost a smile—Mason withdraws his touch, leading Daniel into the kitchen.

I escape to my room and don't come back out. I clean myself up, put on fresh pajamas, and crawl into bed.

Mason knocks on my door and asks if I'm hungry. I pull the covers over my head, holding my breath until his footsteps fade down the hall.

Daniel knocks on my door and asks me to go sledding. I cry silently into my pillow as Mason whispers to him that *Stevie isn't feeling well* and *Let Stevie rest* and *Another time, Danny Boy.*

I hate disappointing that sweet baby, but I'm not any good to him the way I am right now.

Mason knocks on my door long after darkness falls.

"Daniel's asleep. Can we talk?"

I don't answer.

"Stevie?"

Nothing.

"I made you a plate. You should try to eat something."

I'm so hungry it hurts, but I don't say anything.

"I'll just leave it here."

He doesn't speak for a long while, but the hallway light is on, and I can still see the shadow cast by his presence under the bedroom door.

"Stevie, *please.*"

I toss back the covers and shuffle to the door. When I crack it open, he straightens, and his eyes brighten. There's a plate in his hand with some meatloaf, mixed veggies, and mashed potatoes.

"It's not your typical holiday dinner, I know. I told you, we're pretty low-key when we're here."

I don't smile or say thank you as I accept the plate and start closing the door again.

"Stevie, I brought you here to make your Christmas better, and somehow, I think I made it worse. I'm so sorry. I never meant—"

"You didn't do anything wrong," I say. It's flat and callous. He deflates, his eyes sinking to the floor.

"I'm not trying to hurt you, Stevie," he whispers. "That's the last thing I want to do."

I'm not sure where the courage comes from, but I find myself pleading with him in a cracking whisper, "Then *stop* sending me mixed signals."

These words seem to destroy him. He's fading into oblivion before my eyes as he says, barely audible, "You deserve more than I can give you."

"*Deserve.*" There's that word again. I shake my head, chewing on the inside of my cheek. He takes a step back, and I take that as my cue to close the door with a clipped, "Goodnight, Mason."

CHAPTER
20

The next morning, we pack up and leave. It's the tragic end of something, maybe everything, and yet it's somehow also a colossal relief. Nothing ventured, nothing gained, nothing *lost*. I can go home and try to forget every look and touch and almost moment.

As mixed as our signals have been over these last couple months, we've never started anything. We've never officially said the words. Never *I'm falling for you* or even *I like you*. Mason's never promised me anything, and I've never conveyed the depths of my longing. No promises made, nothing broken. So why does the sound of shattering glass echo in my ears every time I look at him?

Irrelevant. This was a non-starter; I knew that from the beginning. If only I'd listened to my own words and never let myself even *hope* for more.

I stare out the window the entire drive back to Spokane, not uttering a word. All I can think about is going home, crawling into bed, and watching those home movies on repeat until I choke on my misery or Merrin comes back to town and distracts me. Whichever comes first.

Mason and Daniel picked me up when we left Thursday, so when Mason misses the turn for my neighborhood and heads toward his own, I look at him. His eyes are focused on the road, and his jaw is set.

"You missed my street," I say.

He jerks his head. Not quite a shake, but enough to say *No, I didn't*. He's driving me to his house on purpose, but I'm not sure why.

We pull into the garage, and I don't unbuckle. He jerks his head again, this one is a little more deliberate; I'm being summoned.

He gets out and unbuckles Daniel from his seat, closing the door behind him.

The two of them are probably in the house by now, and I'm still sitting in the passenger seat, stewing. My phone buzzes.

Please trust me, and come inside.

I'm not sure how I feel about the fact that he said, *please trust me* before he asked me again to come inside, but I think I like it. I think I love it. Except I'm not sure I can trust him after the hot and cold routine he's put me through.

My phone buzzes again.

Stevie, I'm sorry. Please come inside and talk to me.

I lose the battle with myself and go into his house. It's cold, and I don't feel like walking home. When I step inside, he's not waiting by the door, so I move through the house until I find him in the kitchen. He's braced against the counter, his feet crossed at the ankles and his arms folded across his chest. When he sees me, he snaps up.

Looking around, I knit my brow. "Where's Danny?"

With a subtle shake of his head, he answers, "Upstairs playing. I figured the chances of him being preoccupied here were better than sitting in your driveway. And I *really* need to talk to you."

There's an earnestness etched on his face, and I know he's serious. *Something* is eating at him. With a deep, shaky breath, I step farther into the kitchen and sit on a bar stool.

"What is it, Mason?" My voice is tired because my heart is tired.

He shoves his hands in his pockets, taking a few steps closer. "I need..." His voice trails off. He's still stepping closer. Slowly, with the tiniest steps ever known to man. But. He's. Moving. Closer.

I swallow.

"If I'm being honest," he says, "it's more that I have a question I need to ask you."

Another step closer to me. My stomach flip-flops. "Oh-okay."

"It's important," he says, only inches remaining between us. "And

I've been wanting to ask you for a long time." He places his hands on my knees, leaving me breathless. "But it's...a big deal. A big change."

"Yeah?" I stammer, unsure where to look or what to do besides sit there, stupid and limp.

His lips hover over mine so closely I taste his breath. "Like, life-altering."

Don't do this if you don't mean it. Don't do this if you don't mean it. Tell him, Stevie!

"Mason, don't do this if you don't mean it."

He braces himself on the counter, caging me between his arms. "Stevie," he whispers, "I *swear* I mean it," and I know these words will forever be inscribed on my heart.

I mean it.

Cotton-mouthed, I force a loud swallow. "What changed?"

"*Everything*. You've changed everything."

His lips press to mine, and after months of falling, falling, falling, I'm *flying*. My eyes stay open because I need to be sure this is real. I think, *I should pinch myself to be sure*, but I'm so overcome with euphoria I literally can't move. When his lips retreat—ever so slightly —I'm still staring at him, feeling his kiss *everywhere*, struggling to breathe.

He arches a brow. "Stevie?"

I blink. "You said you had a question." It's such a stupid thing to say right now. Why am I ruining this?

But he grins, and his hands move from the countertop to either side of my face. His thumbs stroke my cheeks.

"Go out with me on New Year's Eve?" he asks.

Somehow, I manage to choke on a laugh and snort simultaneously. Very attractive. "Yes," I say.

"Yes?"

"Hell yes."

We connect again, all smiles and anticipation. He lifts me from the bar stool, and I wrap my legs around his waist. With a few deliberate steps, he has me pinned against the fridge.

He can't get close enough, hold me tight enough. Kissing him wipes the slate clean; no one else ever existed before him. The intensity steadily building, Mason moans into my mouth, and I think I'm officially dead now. I've died, and this is Heaven.

Too soon, he stops kissing me and braces his forehead against mine.

"I'm not delusional, then?" I ask, panting.

"Hell no. This? It's been happening for a *while*."

"It certainly has been for *me*."

He clutches me tighter as he steps away from the fridge, setting me down on the countertop. His warm hands push hair out of my face, tucking it behind my ears.

"Yeah?" he asks, "How long?"

"Since the day you ran me over with the door."

He cringes. "I helped you up, too, if you remember."

I bury my face in his neck, kiss it, then pull back. "I remember."

"I've wanted this so long. I just... I didn't know how to tell you. I didn't think it was possible for you to... I thought I would be completely out of line." His hands contour to my neck, and he kisses my cheek. My temple. My forehead. He sighs, I swoon, and we tangle together again. A distant giggle startles me, and I brace my hands against his chest.

"Danny," I say, my lips still touching his. "I don't want him to come down and see us like this."

"Like this?" His voice is husky as he clutches me tighter. Easily succumbing to his charms, I kiss him again—softly—then regain my ground. "I know," he agrees. "I know." He kisses my nose before putting a little distance between us. "For the record, though," he breathes, "that was..."

"I know."

"Best ever."

"Me too."

"Record setting," he finishes. I nod, touching his cheek. He kisses my palm, then holds it to his chest so I can feel his heart pounding.

He traces my lips with the fingers of his free hand. "I shouldn't have waited so long."

"You really shouldn't have," I scold through a laugh and a few tears. So, we kiss again for good measure.

When we part, I push his curly hair back, raking my fingers through it.

"Seriously," I say. "What changed? Why now?"

He sighs, pulling me in for a hug and resting his cheek on the top of my head. A long silence follows as I bury my face in his chest and breathe him in.

"Stevie, I've been waiting..."

"For what?"

"I... I just didn't know how to do this. For starters, you technically work for me, and I didn't want to be *that* guy. I've got a kid, which means dating *anyone* is complicated. Not to mention, I found this whole thing terrifying because I haven't felt this way in...*ever*."

Those words seep into my skin and make me warm all over. I clutch him tighter as he kisses the top of my head.

"The last few days—you and me and Danny at the cabin." He draws in an unsteady breath. "I know I'm not making any sense, and I'm sorry. I just couldn't hold this in any longer."

"So, you brought me here where I couldn't run away to test whether or not this was a good idea?"

He laughs. "Yeah, maybe not the most gentlemanly move. I fought with myself about how to do this the whole drive home. Nothing seemed like the *right way*, so I just acted on impulse."

"I mean, you realize I'm stuck here unless I walk home or you make Danny get *back* in his car seat."

He pulls back, an eyebrow arched and a teasing smirk on his lips. "Maybe I don't *want* you going anywhere."

"I'm not saying I'm eager to leave..."

He gives me a quick kiss, then puts his forehead to mine. "We'll drive you home whenever you want, or I can order a ride share. Whichever."

Daniel comes bounding down the stairs, and Mason steps away.

"You still here, Stevie!" Danny calls, smiling.

"Yes, munchkin. I'm still here."

He runs to me and puts his hands on my knees, peering up at me with those baby blues. "Can we'd play the owl game?"

I look from Danny to Mason, both of them smiling like I'm their favorite person in the world, and my heart feels ready to leap out of my chest.

Squeezing Danny's hand, I say, "We should *absolutely* play the owl game."

I SPEND the rest of the day with my two favorite boys. Somewhere between board games and bedtime, we order pizza for dinner, and Mason holds my hand under the table the entire time. It's such a simple gesture—hand holding. But with the right person, it's *intimate*. Everything between Mason and I feels intimate now. Too much, yet not enough.

While Mason puts Danny to bed, I start unloading the car. We've been so wrapped up in absorbing the newness of this—whatever it is —that we never bothered to grab anything other than that board game. I'm carrying in the last of the luggage when Mason descends the stairs with a resigned smile.

"You did *not* need to do that," he says.

"Well, I needed my stuff anyway."

"You want to head home?"

"*Well*, I've got this amazing new laptop I'm a little excited to familiarize myself with."

He laughs, then swoops me up. "You really like it?"

I grab the back of his neck and kiss him, long and deep.

"So," he says a minute later, "that's a 'yes'?"

Refusing to verbally feed his ego, I kiss him again.

"Can I show you a couple things on it? I found this awesome, user-friendly composing software."

"Composing?" I furrow my brow. "You overestimate my abilities, Mason."

"Nonsense. Where is it?"

I point to the small table in the entryway. He grabs the laptop, then pulls me along behind him into the living room, not letting go until he's situated us on the couch with me on his lap.

He starts explaining all the features, and I've never seen Mason talk about technology like this before. I imagine this is how *I* look when I talk about music. He's fully animated and engaged as he tells me about two-terabyte hard drives and i7 processors and GTX graphics cards. Even more so when he gets to the composing software.

"It's amazing, Stevie. You legit just turn on the mic, set it next to the piano, and play. Or sing. Whichever. It transcribes the sheet music for you."

I bite my lip, and he uses his thumb to gently urge it free. My smile spreads.

"That's better," he whispers, then kisses me. "Look, I know this is complicated for you, and I'm not trying to downplay your *very* legitimate hesitations or force you back into something, but I just thought..." He sighs. "Your previous experience centered around someone teaching you existing notes on a page. But I've heard what you can do with a melody—the way you can transform something rough or edgy into something beautiful. You're like John Paul White and Joy Williams. Only better because you're you."

I gape. "You listened to The Civil Wars?"

"You suggested them. Of course, I did. You conveniently left out their cover of 'Billie Jean.'"

"Genius, right?"

He grins, nodding. "What if this is the door that gets you back in? Creating your own music—nothing that links back to those awful memories?"

There are no words for how much I adore this man. *Love* this man.

"Stevie?"

He says this because I've been staring a while now, just absorbing this moment. This feeling.

I make sure the laptop is moved safely to the coffee table before I turn back to Mason, pressing my lips to his and clutching his hair between my fingers. He slides down on the couch, taking me with him.

Minutes later, scanning my face, he asks, "So you like it?"

I roll my eyes. "Stop fishing for compliments when you've *literally* got a girl on top of you. You *know* I love it—the laptop. The software. All of it." I glance over to the coffee table. The computer screen is still lit up. My focus shifts to a shortcut for the video file Mason showed me yesterday. "All of it," I repeat.

Mason wraps an arm around me, and I rest my cheek against his chest. He kisses the top of my head.

"My dad wanted to teach me to play the guitar," I say. "I didn't even know he played. Maybe he had a guitar he wanted to be mine one day. What if he had a whole life he intended to pass on to me and Gene just threw it all away because he hated him."

Mason tightens his hold on me. "I wish I had answers for you."

"Maybe I should learn to play."

"You'd be great at it. I know the basics. I could help you."

I groan, envisioning him behind an electric acoustic. Sleeves pushed halfway up his forearms. Hair falling in his eyes. "Of *course* you play guitar, too. Of course you do." I cackle, then sigh. "Heaven help me."

"What's the joke here?" he asks. "What am I missing?"

I push off his chest. "You're just perfect," I say, then kiss him intently. As we part and I relax back against his chest, my eyes find the laptop again. "I'd like to watch it again. You know, now that I *know* what's coming."

He grabs the edge of the table, pulls it close enough to reach the keypad, and opens the video.

"They seem very well paired, your parents." Mason observes. They do. When the screen shows my mother in labor, he makes another observation. "Your mom has on a pretty fancy dress, given the circumstances."

"They were probably at a party when she went into labor."

"Why would you assume that?"

"I was born on New Year's Eve." I cringe as soon as the words leave my lips. *Whoops*. Mason immediately pauses the video.

"Wait. Hold up. Stevie!" Gentle fingers tug at my chin until I'm looking at him. "You were going to let me take you out and not even tell me it was your *birthday?*"

I lift a shoulder. "It didn't seem important."

"It's important to me. *You're* important to me."

My cheeks burn, my heart races.

"What do you want for your birthday?" Now *that* is a ridiculous question. "What? Why are you looking at me like that?"

"Mason. Look at where we are right now. Happy birthday to me."

"You're cute. But seriously, I want to get you something. Please. I'm asking nicely."

I sigh, wedging myself between him and the couch, my head on his chest, my arm draped across his stomach. He uses his free hand to trace up and down my back, then my arm.

"You gave me my parents. You gave me that song. You're taking me out for my birthday—a first, by the way. There's nothing more I could possibly want, need, or *deserve*."

He tenses when I use that word, then whispers, "You deserve the world Stevie."

It's silent a few moments before he speaks again. "Would you at least like to make any requests as to where we go or what we do?"

I think on it a minute, my resolve waning. I know for him, this is settling. "I guess, if I have to make one request..."

"And you do," he says, low and sultry.

"December thirty-first has never really felt like my birthday. At least not since my childhood. It's always just been..."

"New Year's Eve."

"My birthday always felt like an afterthought."

He holds me tighter, and I know I'm not an afterthought anymore.

"Alright," he sighs. "Challenge accepted. I will do my best to make the fun non-New Year's Eve related."

"Are you sure we can even do this? I mean, who's gonna watch Danny?" He laughs. "What?"

"I just love how quickly your mind goes to him. At the cabin, your first thought when I said the power had gone out was whether he was warm enough. When you came inside earlier, you asked where he was. We're planning our first *date* and..."

"Well, he's my favorite human. No offense."

"None taken." I feel him smile. "But, yes, we *can* do this. Rachel's family is flying in tomorrow night, so my parents are heading back into town Tuesday. They already offered to have Dan over to spend the night for New Year's. My mom has been pushing me to start dating again, and she's *hoping* I have plans."

"Won't she change her mind when you tell her your plans involve the gold-digging skank? Or are you just not telling her?"

He releases a sharp, abrupt laugh, then squeezes me. "It'll be fine," he says. "Trust me."

I adjust, craning my neck to look him in the eyes. "I trust you," I say, then kiss him once more before settling back into him.

"Stevie Rae," he whispers.

Goosebumps. He gives me goosebumps.

"Yeah?"

"You're the best thing to happen to me in a really long time."

For a moment, everything else disappears, and it's just me, Mason, and an unbearable welling in my chest. No response seems sufficient or even possible given the weight of his words. How I love this man. How I ache to tell him. But I won't risk ruining what we have in the remarkable, exhilarating now.

"Mason?"

"Yeah."

I love you.

You're the best thing to happen to me ever.

Hold me tighter.

Kiss me longer.

"Ditto," is all I can manage.

He kisses my hair once more before resuming the video, then holds me as I watch, cry, laugh, and cry again.

CHAPTER
21

"Why am I so nervous? Merrin, my fingers are shaking. Why are my fingers shaking?" I holler at my phone while I fiddle with my hair.

"You sound echo-y."

"Speaker. Bathroom. Date crisis."

"Oh. Right."

"Merrin!"

"Alright, alright. Easy, killer. You'll hyperventilate. I'm sure you look great."

"It's not that," I whine. "Well, it's a little bit that. But it's just, we've always had a buffer. Daniel has always been there, or at least close by. But now it's just the two of us. Alone. On a *date*. I'm in a dress, and my hair is all wrong." I squeal in frustration.

"Stevie!"

"What?"

"Shut up."

"Right. Deep breaths. Got it."

"Good girl. Whatever you're doing to your hair—stop it. Shake it out, and let it be."

"But..."

"Put the bobby pin down and step away from the vanity."

"She's magic," I whisper, following orders.

"Just get out of the bathroom, away from mirrors, and stop panicking."

"You say that like it's *so* easy."

"I know, I'm off my game. Sorry."

"You okay, doll?"

"Just distracted. Luke hasn't texted in two days, and he's not answering his phone."

"That bastard," I grumble, completely serious. I like him less and less the longer they're together. "If he doesn't call tonight, I'll stake out his house. Maybe burn it down."

"You promise?"

For the first time in hours, I relax enough to laugh. "Yes, my love. I promise. He will rue the day."

"Good." She pauses, sighing. "Okay, back to you. What's the next crisis."

"I don't know. All of it. It's all a crisis."

"I doubt that. Which dress are you wearing?"

"*The* dress," I say, my stomach turning. When Merrin gave me this sparkly, silver, deep, *deep* V party dress, I laughed—snorted, even—and tried to give it back. "I'll *never* have a reason to wear this," I said. But she told me I have the boobs—and the legs—for it, and she forced the garment into my hands. Now here I am, wearing an "invisible" bra and this ostentatious, ridiculous, absolutely *fabulous* dress.

"Oh dang!" Merrin gasps. "Oh dang, oh dang, oh dang."

"Yeah."

"Well, praise the Lord and pass the ammunition. I didn't think you had it in you."

"Go big or go home, right?"

"Heck yes! Get it, girl. I'm going to need approximately one hundred pictures."

"If I can ever get my hands to stop shaking and sweating long enough to hold my phone still, sure." My black-heeled booties click-clack across the linoleum floors as I search for a kitchen towel to wipe my sweaty palms. I wipe down my armpits, too.

"Ugh, Mer! I can't stop sweating. This is so gross and embarrassing."

"Babe, you've got nothing to be embarrassed about. It's going to be fine."

"What if after tonight, he decides he was wrong about me and he doesn't want me?"

"He won't decide that."

"How do you know?"

"Well, you've continued spending time together every day since he asked you out, right?"

"Yeah."

"And who initiates that? You or him?"

"He's asked me over every day this week. Except today, of course."

"To do what?"

I sigh. "Just be together."

"No expectations, right?"

"No expectations."

"He's a good guy, Stevie. You know it. I know it. He wouldn't string you along like that if he'd changed his mind."

She's right. I know she's right. But my stomach is twisting in knots, and my mind is a black hole of worst-case scenarios.

"But how do you *know*?" I whine.

"Stevie, no one *knows* these things. But the fact is, you've been irrevocably in love with this guy for months. You have to go on this date and find out if it's been a mistake. I know that scares you, but you can't back out now. So, take a breath, gird your loins, and get the heck out there. Okay?"

"Mercy, that man does things to my loins."

She says, "Gross," but laughs for a solid minute.

"Seriously, Stevie. Go. Have an amazing time, and call me about it later. Or tomorrow. Try to consider the time difference, okay?"

I clear my throat, wiping my hands on the towel once again. "It's gonna be fine," I say. "It's gonna be fine. It's gonna be fine." I take a few more deep breaths.

"Stevie, you deserve to be happy, and you'll never get there unless you take a few risks. I love you, and I know you're very brave and independent and whatever, but when it comes to Mason, you've been keeping your heart locked up instead of going for it. I mean, I get that. He was your *boss* and all that other blah blah."

"Goodness, you're so eloquent."

She carries on as if I haven't spoken. "But you've got to trust yourself and your feelings a little more. So, hang up the phone because he'll be there any minute, and go have a good time. Okay?"

I sigh. "Yes, ma'am."

"And Stevie Rae?"

"Yes, my heart?"

"I love you. And if this thing is an epic failure, I'll take you out on a hot date when I get home. You might even get lucky."

"G'bye, weirdo."

"Prude!"

I haven't finished laughing when Mason knocks on the door.

Breathe, Stevie. Breathe. Calm the hell down! But I can't. My knees are still wobbling when I answer the door. It doesn't help that he's standing on my doorstep all tall and handsome in a slim-cut navy suit with a stray curl bouncing in front of his eye. Holy hell, it's sexy.

Keep it in your pants, Stevie.

"H-hi," I finally stammer.

His jaw goes slack.

"You..." he breathes. "You're..."

His eyes scan me, lingering in places that make my skin tingle.

Lord, give me strength.

"You're stunning," Mason whispers. His voice is shaking, which calms me, if only a little. As if waking from a trance, he says, "Shall we?"

He reaches for my hand and, with a deep breath, I take it. "Yes, please," I answer.

We both relax with a brief laugh. He squeezes my hand, and we venture out for a night of uncertainty that we both know will change everything, one way or another.

A FEW MINUTES TO MIDNIGHT, we drive to a park with good views of the fireworks—so I'm told. No one else is insane enough to be out in the cold, but I'm so deliriously happy, the bitter chill may as well be a light summer breeze. Even so, Mason drapes his coat around me after helping me from his car. I slip my arms through the too-big sleeves, then pull the collar close, inhaling his fresh scent lingering on the fabric.

While Mason grabs a blanket from the back seat, I carefully navigate the frozen ground, making my way toward the swings. I perch myself on one and begin swaying. With a lopsided grin, Mason tucks the blanket around my lap, then takes the swing next to mine. The sky is clear, the constellations shining bright. The outlines of the mountains visible under the glow of the moon.

"So, what's the verdict?" he asks.

"Best friggin' birthday I've ever had."

He arches a brow. "High praise."

I pull his swing toward mine and kiss him.

"What was your favorite part?"

With a laugh, I release his swing, and we go back to swaying subtly back and forth. "How could I possibly choose? You nailed *all* of it. I still can't believe you had the staff at that bakery sing to me. Did you call ahead?"

"A magician never reveals his secrets."

"Well, it was mortifying and adorable and I loved it," I assure him. After the bakery, he'd taken me ice skating, and we'd circled the rink for hours, talking nonstop. "And sparkly pink skates? I can hear the collective cries of jealousy from women around the globe."

"Well, you need your own gear if you're going to go regularly. And I think we should. Danny would love it."

If it's even possible, I've just fallen deeper in love with him. "He would. So would I." We share a grin. "Tonight has been perfect."

"For me, too." His eyes hold mine, conveying his seriousness. "Perfect."

Suddenly, I can't seem to remember how to breathe.

Fireworks explode above us, and celebratory cheers echo through the night.

"Happy Birthday," Mason says.

"Happy New Year."

"No, these are your birthday fireworks."

"They can be New Year's fireworks. For once, I'm okay with celebrating a new year."

"Twenty-two feeling good so far, then?"

I nod. "This is the first year in a long time where things feel different. Better. Like my life is going somewhere, and I'm finally a whole person. Not just broken fragments."

Mason frowns. I pull him closer again, kissing him softly.

"Don't be sad," I whisper. "I'm not."

"I just wish I could go back and find you sooner."

I shrug. "I might not have been ready for a relationship if you had."

An amused grin spreads across Mason's face while blood rushes to my cheeks, the significance of my words sinking in.

"Oh gosh. I just threw a label out there, didn't I? Was that too soon?"

"Stevie?"

"Yes?"

"Breathe."

"Okay." I search him for signs of hesitance, regret, joy, relief... anything. He offers no words, only a kiss. Fireworks continue to light the night sky, coming from at least three different locations. As a sequence of mortars burst into patterns of red, white, and blue, I gather my courage.

"Mase?"

"Yeah?"

"I think you should know. I'm not looking for something casual with you."

He knits his brow. "Have I given the impression that this is *casual* for me?"

I shake my head. "No. But my whole life has been one uncertainty after another. And I'm not interested in letting things go unspoken between us. Or avoiding difficult conversations, like whether or not I scared you off by essentially branding myself as your girlfriend without discussing it with you first."

He halts our swings. "Stevie, you couldn't scare me off if you *tried*. If anyone here has reason to turn tail and run, it's you."

"That's ridiculous."

"You're sure you aren't freaked out by the fact that your boyfriend—that would be me—is eight years older than you? Has a kid?"

"It's only *seven* years now," I correct. He shakes his head, but there's a smile tucked in the corner of his mouth. "And you know what Daniel means to me."

"I'm just saying most twenty-somethings with their whole lives ahead of them don't want to date that guy. Don't want to date *this* guy." He gestures to himself.

"Well, I think we've established I'm not most twenty-somethings, Mason. I *only* want to date this guy." I gesture to him, and he laughs. "I know we met like three months ago. And we started dating about a minute ago. But I don't care. I can't... I don't... Crap."

With a slow, steady breath, I try again. "I love you, Mason. Okay? I *love* you." His face freezes in place. I don't know if that's good or bad, but I force myself to keep going. "I know it might be complicated. I don't care. I want this. I've spent *months* thinking this couldn't happen, for *so* many reasons, and it's been literal torture. I can't do it anymore. So, if we aren't on the same page, you should tell me now, and I should find another job. Dead serious. I might be the world's biggest, most delusional idiot, but I'm not a masochist."

I impatiently wait for Mason to find his voice. Every second he stares at me in silence, I lose my will to live a little more. I'm about to walk away when he stands, facing me. He pushes my swing backward until our eyes are level, braces himself against me, and holds my waist. I stop breathing.

"Stevie, I... I am *so* in love with you."

Cold air fills my lungs again. "Oh, thank goodness."

He breathes a quick laugh. "The moment you chased after me with that flyer, I knew I was in trouble. After you'd been watching Danny a week, I knew I'd do anything for you." I cover my mouth as a sharp chuckle escapes. "There are messy parts of my life, Stevie. I didn't want to drag you through it. It's why I fought so hard to put my feelings aside, but they're all consuming. I'm so deep in this, I can't remember what life was without you. I don't want to."

He shakes his head, laughing inwardly at something.

"You're serious?" I ask.

"Oh, one-hundred percent," he says, nodding. I keep my hand across my gaping mouth. "Stevie, you're beautiful, but this isn't a crush. You're smart and clever and you're going places, but I don't just admire you. You're sweet and adorable and you... You take care of my son, but this isn't about me finding a co-parent, I swear it isn't. And I wish I could give you a pretty speech—I do—but it's cold, and I can't feel my face, so I'm just gonna do my best to say this before we both freeze to this swing."

I uncover my mouth, gesturing for him to continue.

"I've done the whole dating thing, before Daniel and after. I've done it to death. I don't see the point in wasting any more time. Maybe it sounds completely insane, but I just know you're it for me. I don't know why you'd want to commit to a future with me when you're so young, and you have so many paths you could take. I'm sure I'm completely out of my league here. But you told me at Christmas —you've always thought when the person was right, the time would be too. Why not? Let's stop wasting time, Stevie. Life is too damn short, and I've waited too damn long for you to ignore this."

He brings a hand up and wipes a tear from my frozen cheek.

"Marry me, Stephanie Renae. Build a life with me. Let's do this. What do you say?"

I answer with repeated nods of my head before I find my voice. But finally, I stop nodding and say yes. Absolutely, I say yes.

CHAPTER
22

It's only seven a.m., and I've been ready for the day for over an hour. Essentially comprised of butterflies and disbelief, I haven't slept at all. How does one sleep if one is legitimately *buzzing*?

I've already showered, shaved, tried on four different outfits before reverting to my first choice, dried my hair, applied full makeup, changed my mind and washed it away, going with only mascara and lip gloss instead. I've tried out two different braids that Merrin taught me—four-strand and fish-tail, then settled on neither, instead pinning my hair half up, then changing my mind again and letting it all hang loose. Now here I sit, twiddling my thumbs, desperate and giddy to see the man I love, though we've been separated mere hours.

Time passes agonizingly slow when we're apart, and all this time, I've only been capable of reliving last night over and over again. It's *all* I think about. The question, the answer, the kiss, the ring. I still can't wrap my head around the fact that he had a ring ready to put on my finger. But he insisted he knew from the moment we finally kissed, so he bought the ring the next day.

A fiancé. I have a *fiancé*.

Do I question my sanity? A little. We've been together less than a week and gone on one official date. We've not done more than kiss. Yet, we're *engaged*. But the strangest part of all this is how it doesn't feel remotely strange. It just feels *right*.

I play with the ring again, admiring it. I don't know jewelry. I have no idea what cut or karat it is and frankly, I don't care. It doesn't matter. It's amazing because it's mine and because it came from him.

I described it to Merrin—she really loved her early wake-up call—as "white gold with a big diamond surrounded by little ones so it kind of looks like a flower and holy crap I'm getting married can you believe it?" All in the same breath, of course.

I pick up my phone, open my photo gallery, and scroll through the selfies Mason and I took to commemorate our first date. Then... our *engagement*.

I am *engaged*. Until recently, my only experiences with a single moment changing my life forever have been cemented in tragedy. Now?

"I'm engaged," I whisper to myself.

I'm debating which picture to make my new wallpaper when Mason's name and number light up my screen. I'm butter as I answer with shaky fingers, smiling so wide my cheeks hurt.

"Good morning," I say.

"Good morning, gorgeous." Melted. "I hope I didn't wake you."

"You have to sleep in order to be woken."

"You too? I think I slept an hour. Maybe two."

His honesty so thoroughly unravels me—in the best possible sense—I forget how to speak.

"So." Mason interrupts the silence. "Are you up for breakfast? I thought I'd pick you up."

"Breakfast sounds amazing," I lie. My stomach is so full of jitters, it won't possibly accept food. But I'd probably agree to anything right now if it meant time with Mason.

He says, "Good," and at the same time, there's rapid taps on my front door.

"Hmm. Hold on a sec," I say, "I think there's a random dude knocking on my door."

"You should absolutely go answer it then."

I'm a breathless mess when my open door reveals Mason standing on the front step. Charming smile, amazing hair.

"Hi."

Gorgeous voice.

It seems pointless to contain myself now everything is out in the open, so I drop my phone on the carpet, take two steps forward, grab his shoulders, and jump. He catches me, and I wrap my legs around his waist. "Hi," I return before kissing him.

He parts with a grin. "All this time, I could have been kissing you."

"Seems like a waste, doesn't it?"

He kisses me once more to make up for lost time.

"What sounds good?" he asks. "I thought we could talk logistics over breakfast."

I drop to the ground, frowning. "Logistics?" I pocket my phone and keys before finding my shoes.

"Like when to tell Daniel. And other people."

"Other people meaning your parents?" He responds with a nervous smile, almost a grimace. "Do you really want me to be part of that conversation?"

"Stevie, of course. It'll be fine." He waves a dismissive hand. "I promise."

"Said the liar."

"Oh, come on. What's the worst that could happen?"

I gawk at him. "You can't say stuff like that out loud."

"Yeah, you may be right. I may have jinxed us there. Oh well. I'm starvin'. Let's go."

He nudges me towards his car while I inwardly spiral over worst-case scenarios.

COMPLETELY INDIFFERENT TO the opinions of strangers, Mason and I situate ourselves like a couple of teenagers at our booth in a quiet diner. We order hastily, make out briefly, then relax into one another as he drapes an arm around my shoulder, and I slouch against his chest. He holds my left hand in his, intermittently playing with my ring.

When his phone buzzes, he checks a text, closes it out, and sets the phone on the table in front of us. Before the screen goes dark, I see his background picture—Daniel and I sleeping in the recliner at the cabin.

"I love that picture," he says, following my gaze.

I straighten, craning my neck to kiss his cheek. I feel his smile grow. Another buzz pulls my attention away, and I sink back against him. He lets out a frustrated sigh, silencing his phone and sticking it back in his pocket. Definitely his mom.

"This is killing her," I say. "She's dying for you to call and unconfirm her worst fears. Tell her last night was an epic disaster, and you've moved on."

"She's pretending to update me on Rachel. She knows very well I already talked to Logan."

"How is she? How's the baby?"

"They're out of the woods. Still in the hospital, but the baby's off oxygen and out of the NICU. He's strong, just like his mom."

I let out a small gasp. "It's a boy? How fun for them. Are you taking Danny to meet his new cousin?"

Mason squeezes me and kisses my hair. "We're heading to Coeur d'Alene tomorrow with my parents. Meet the baby. Help Rachel's parents distract the girls. Distract *Logan*. I don't think he knows which way is up right now. You should come with us."

"They don't even know me. They don't need strangers poking around their hospital room."

"You're not a stranger anymore. You're family."

Something about this statement—or maybe the way he says it—makes my chest implode.

"You know I'd love to meet them. But maybe now is not the right time. Not when it's so chaotic, and they're adjusting to their new normal."

He kisses my temple. "What if we go over the three-day weekend in a couple weeks?"

"If you think they'd be alright with that."

"Rachel's dying to meet you. She's excited at the prospect of not being the only daughter-in-law. Takes a lot of pressure off."

"Oh, well, gee. Thanks for that." He squeezes me again. "But speaking of in-laws. Um, Nancy wants us to go over there for dinner sometime. She's kind of designated herself *mother of the bride*, and I'm not sure what level of intensity we should brace for."

He laughs. "You told them already?"

"I called Merrin around seven a.m. her time. Not sure she's forgiven me yet."

"But she's happy for you?"

"They both are. Lots of excited squeals."

"They don't think you're crazy? You know, getting engaged on the first date."

"Oh, I'm sure they think I'm certifiable. But they were kind enough not to say."

Our food arrives, and Mason keeps an arm around me as he tucks into his meal. I can't even bring myself to pick up my fork. Crepes and a fresh bowl of fruit sit in front of me—foods I love, yet lack an appetite for.

Mason clears his throat, using his fork to break off bite-sized pieces from his waffle. "So. What do you want? A church wedding? Outdoors? Skydiving down to the ceremony?"

"Definitely skydiving. For sure. Unless you think snorkeling would be a better idea." He shakes, laughing as he chews his breakfast. "I'll need you to hire at least two celebrities to show up. Don't pretend you couldn't make it happen."

"Whatever you want, Stevie Rae."

"I don't know what I want yet. Let me think on it a bit."

"Whatever you want," he repeats, "whatever your heart desires. Ask, and it shall be done."

"Can we elope? Today?"

He tenses and stops chewing.

"I'm joking, Mason. Breathe."

It's another few seconds before he relaxes.

"Good job," I tease. "I mean, I hate the idea of a long engagement, but we don't have to rush this. Besides, we have people to consider, like—"

"Daniel," he says at the same time as me. "He's gonna flip. It'll basically be a second Christmas."

"You think?"

"Stevie, I *know*."

"What if I'm not cut out for the whole *mom* thing and he sees that and..."

"Okay, let's *not* get melodramatic right now." He spears a piece of waffle onto his fork and holds it to my mouth.

"Why not?" I whine. He kisses my neck, making sure it tickles. I let out a quiet but high-pitched giggle. "Okay, okay." I open my mouth to accept his waffle offering.

"So what, for you, constitutes a long engagement?"

"Hm?" I ask, my mouth still full.

"You said you hate the idea of a long engagement."

"I don't know. And I don't want to be pushy and force you to set a specific time frame before you're ready."

"Stevie, I packed a ring along to our first date. Think it's safe to say I want this."

Dammit, I love this man. I crane my neck and kiss him, a little too deeply for public. I don't care. When we part, I sink back into him.

"What about late summer?" he says. "That should be plenty of time, right? Without dragging it on forever."

"Like early August?"

"Yeah. Sound good?"

"It could work. That should be sufficient to plan a super small ceremony, right? And it gives me plenty of time to figure out what to do with my house. I'm thinking of asking Max for help navigating that whole mess."

"Merrin's dad?"

"Yeah. He's some sort of real estate investment banker. Or

something? I think he deals mostly with *commercial* real estate, but still."

"Sounds like a solid plan."

He returns to his breakfast, and I manage a small bite of my crepe. I know I *should* eat, but my stomach is still in knots. Good knots. But knots, nonetheless.

After a few minutes, Mason clears his throat. "So, between the house and school and now a wedding to think about, is it too much on your plate this semester?"

"Subtle segue," I sigh, rolling my eyes.

"What?" he asks, feigning innocence.

I turn to glower at him.

"Okay, fine. *I'm* worried you're taking on too much this semester."

"You mean you hate that I'm working two jobs."

He nudges me. "Can you blame a guy?"

I spear a strawberry with my fork and shove it in his mouth.

"You're lucky I didn't throw that in your face," I say, smirking.

He covers his mouth, struggling to chew his food as he laughs.

"I love my jobs, Mason. I love the daycare, and I love watching Daniel. I don't want to give up either of those things."

"It's not like I *want* you to stop watching Daniel."

"Then I won't. Though, now that you bring it up, taking care of my fiancé's son doesn't seem like something I should be paid to do."

"Stevie, I didn't ask you to marry me so I could have free childcare."

"The thought never even crossed my mind."

"I know. I'm just saying..."

He sighs, taking a moment to gather his thoughts, offering me another bite of his waffle as he does. I accept and chew, suppressing a laugh.

"I know it will be a transition," he says. "I'll figure out a new work schedule. I mean, I can't do anything about spring semester. My classes are filled, and it's a done deal. But next fall, it can be different.

I didn't sign a long-term contract or anything. I'll try to make it so we're not always working opposite shifts."

"Yeah, that sounds miserable," I agree.

"I miss you enough as it is."

I bite down on my lips, blushing.

"But," he says, "I could go back to network administration if I needed to. Work from home more."

"No. You love teaching."

"I love you more."

Butterflies. Goosebumps. All of it. This man does things to me I didn't know were possible.

"We'll make it work," he says.

"I know we will. For starters, *if* you're working during the day and I'm at school, don't quote me on this, but after we're married and I'm made his legal guardian, I think we can enroll Daniel at Bright Beginnings."

"I hadn't even thought about that."

"It's a great program, *on* campus. I'd be right there if he needed anything."

"Genius."

"You're welcome."

He laughs briefly but isn't deterred. "I just hate the thought of you feeling like you have to work two jobs on top of a full course load to survive. Is it wrong that I want to take care of you a little bit?"

"No, it's not. But I don't feel like I'm suffocating anymore. Things are better."

"Only because you work two jobs."

I groan. "A lot of people do it, Mason."

"A lot of people aren't my fiancée, Stevie."

"*Mason...*"

"Alright, alright."

"Look. I love you. And I love your desire to make my life easier. But you forget, you already have. Seeing you after school and work, hanging out with Daniel in the evenings—that's the *best* part of my day. I do my homework once he's asleep. Thanks to you, I have a laptop now. I'll get all my work done and sent in faster. It couldn't get much easier. At all. And I doubt you're eager to find a replacement for me."

Mason ponders, eating the last of his breakfast. "I *do* love you being there with Dan in the evenings. The more you talk about it, the more I can't imagine you not being there. But my mom could take over a few days a week and give you a little free time."

"I like our routine, Mase."

He sighs, slumping his shoulders. "You're so stubborn."

"I prefer tenacious. You know this."

He laughs. "Right. Sorry. From here on out, can you just promise me you'll let me know if you need a night off? For whatever reason. Even if you're just *tired*."

"I won't get—"

"And you're not working for free," he interrupts. "Though I can understand how it might seem...awkward."

"I wouldn't know how to take your money every week," I admit. "I think I'd feel kinda dirty." He chokes and nearly spits out his drink.

The waitress comes by our table, eyeing Mason.

"Everything okay?" she asks.

"Yeah," I say. "He's just coming to terms with some recent life decisions." Mason shoots me a smirk, conveying something between embarrassment and adoration. "Having regrets?" I ask him as the waitress slowly backs away.

"Never," he says. Then he stands, puts a fifty-dollar bill on the table, and pulls me from my seat. Before I can take a step, he hoists me over his shoulder in a fireman's carry and saunters out of the restaurant.

CHAPTER
23

"Why don't I just wait in the car?"

Mason takes my hand as we enter his parent's house. "Breathe, love," he whispers.

Ha! Sweaty hands, heart pounding, stomach turning, completely terrified. *Breathing* seems excessive. I swallow loudly, following him through to the kitchen where we find his mother working over a cutting board. The scent of onions and peppers hangs thick in the air.

"Oh, hi, Mase! I'm making omelets. Come have some..." She spots me and stares at our clasped hands. "Breakfast. Well, Stevie. This is a surprise." She means an unpleasant surprise, that much is clear. She clutches her knife a little too tight before setting it down and bracing herself against the countertop.

Words elude me, but I manage a nod.

Miranda focuses solely on Mason; even *I'm* almost convinced I'm not in the room.

"Daniel's upstairs with your father," she says. "Should I go get him?"

"No, that's okay. I'll go up and say hi. But I need to talk to you and Dad before I take Danny home." He pulls a stool out from the island and motions for me to sit, then pries my hand from his. "I'll be right back," he whispers.

I fold my clammy hands in my lap to hide my ring.

"Do you want an omelet, Stevie? Or some of Daniel's cereal, perhaps?"

Subtle. "No, thank you. I already ate."

After two minutes—an eternity—Mason appears behind me. His

father joins us, sidling up to Miranda and smiling. He's essentially a taller, broader Mason. Same square jawline. Same wavy hair, though it's gray, and he has less of it. Basically, I'm looking thirty years into my future.

"Hi, there! I'm Wes. Good to meet'cha." He extends his hand across the countertop.

I accept it after wiping my palm across my jeans. "Stevie Parker."

"Of course, you are. Who else would he bring?" He nods toward Mason. "Poor bastard hasn't been able to talk about anyone else since he met you."

"Thanks, Dad," Mason whispers.

I try to smile but cringe instead, saying nothing.

"So what's up, kids?" Wes puts his arm around Miranda and kisses her cheek, but her stern glower doesn't retreat. No doubt, she's plotting my murder.

"Well, Pop," Mason says. "Stevie and I have some news."

"Well, then! Out with it," he orders.

Mason wraps both arms around me. "Stevie and I are..." He takes one more deep breath. "I asked Stevie to marry me."

"And I said yes," I manage, grinning nervously as the room spins. I brace myself for the worst.

"Well, hell!" Wes lets go of Miranda and walks over to us. He takes Mason by his shoulders then pulls him in for a tight hug. "Congratulations! I'm so damn happy for you." He leans back, holding Mason's face in his hands. Wes stares at his son, shaking his head. "Dammit. I'm gonna cry." The men exhale brief laughs as Wes wipes his face.

After clearing his throat, Wes grabs me up from my stool, embracing me.

"Oh," I breathe, unsure whether to hug back or keep my arms at my sides. I didn't prepare myself for *this*.

"Welcome to the family, honey."

I stumble as Wes releases me, and he takes my hands in his. "He treats you right, doesn't he?"

"Yessir," I answer, still stunned.

Wes laughs heartily and raises my hand to kiss it, stopping short when he notices my ring.

"Hell's bells! Randa, get a look at this thing!" He lets out a low whistle. "Damn, Mase. You don't fool around. I hope she's worth it." Wes winks. I blush.

"Geez, Pop," Mason groans, mortified. "Be nice. I'm begging you."

"Only kidding," he says, patting my hand. "Only kidding."

"She's more than worth it, Dad. I promise."

Wes sighs, shaking his head. "Well, hell. I hope you two'll be happy." He hugs us each again and then looks at his wife. "What'aya say, Randa?"

I hold my breath, awaiting her response. She gawks, hands on hips, her lips pursed. Yup. Definitely plotting my murder.

"This is all... Well, this is all so fast." She makes motions with her hands. Opens her mouth as though to speak, but closes it and makes more hand gestures instead.

I've seen this before with Nancy. This is *Mom* for, "I have so much to say about this, but I'm so disappointed or upset that I can't even say it." This is what I've braced myself for.

"Engaged?" Miranda spits. "You two spend a couple of days playing house at the cabin, and you're ready to make lifelong promises to each other? To *Daniel?* Mason Lane Shepard, I thought you more sensible than this."

Mason clenches his fists. "Oh. My gosh. *Mom.* Are you serious right now?"

"Are *you* serious right now? How could you possibly be sure about this? So soon?"

"Miranda." Wes goes back to her side, taking her shoulders. "He wouldn't have asked her if he wasn't sure."

"I'm right here, guys," Mason says, waving. They ignore him.

"She's so young," Miranda says. "*Too* young."

"Randa, is that really fair?" Wes asks. "We were young."

"Right here!" Mason hollers. "We're *both* right here!" He puts an arm around me.

"Well, excuse me for livin', but last time didn't go so great for you, if you recall."

"Mom!" Mason yells. I flinch, and he holds me closer, taking a deep breath. "Please, Mom. This isn't last time. I know I've made some hasty decisions in my life. Believe me, I remember. But this is real. It's happening. And it wasn't a spur-of-the-moment thing. It might seem fast to you, but trust me, it hasn't been. Not for me. Not for us."

"But the *nanny?*" Miranda asks, squinting. "Mason, please. How cliché can you get?"

Wes and Mason blurt reprimands as I cower away, certain I'll throw up if I stay in this room any longer.

"I think I'll go find Daniel," I mumble.

"Stevie." Mason clings to me, but I wriggle from his grasp.

"I think I'll just... I'll be back with Danny in a minute."

When I'm around the corner, I pause.

"Mom, are you kidding me right now? *Playing house? The nanny?* What the hell?"

"Don't you 'what the hell' me! What are you doing with that poor girl? Are you just conveniently forgetting—"

"Of course, not! It's *all* I've thought about. For months. For years. It's been a plague on my life. But just because that woman tried to burn my life to the ground doesn't mean I can't have something good. It doesn't mean I can't go after something that makes me so damn happy, I didn't know it was even *possible.* Shouldn't you *want* good things for me right now? And always?"

Background arguments fade as I go in search of Daniel. *That woman* he's referring to could be a nasty ex or maybe even Daniel's mother; he never talks about her. Maybe that's the reason? A discussion for a later time.

I find Daniel upstairs, and he's so happy to see me it dampens the sting of Miranda's rejection. Not that I expected her to rejoice in the union, but I hadn't expected such blatant hostility. Wes is happy, though; a pleasant surprise. At least *one* of his parents seems to like me.

As Daniel and I reach the bottom of the stairs, I hold his hand, keeping him from barging in as Mason and his mom exchange a few more heated remarks.

"You're not being fair to her, Mom."

"*You're* not being fair to her. She doesn't know what she's signing up for."

"She's worlds ahead of where I was at twenty-two. She can handle it. *We* can handle this. Together."

"I don't just mean *Danny*, and you know it. You clean this up, Mason. So help me."

There's a long pause, then footsteps, then Mason speaks again. "Whether or not you think I'm doing the right thing, I brought Stevie here to share the first bit of *good* life-changing news either of us has had in a ridiculously long time, and you spat in her face. Dan and I will get ourselves to Coeur d'Alene tomorrow. I can't even look at you right now, Mom."

MASON and I debate waiting until spring to tell Daniel about the engagement, but he hates the idea of hiding our relationship. It hasn't seemed to faze Danny we've been spending so much time together the last week. Today is no exception. He doesn't seem to notice Mason being more affectionate with me—holding my hand, keeping his arm around me. Danny is just...blissfully four.

We sit on the playroom floor, building block towers just so Daniel can knock them over and cackle maniacally. Every laugh pulls me further out of the funk Miranda's words put me in. Still, I can't put the incident out of my head. I've barely spoken since it happened, and Mason is doing his best not to hover or prod, though I know he's worried.

As Daniel transitions to driving magnetic die-cast trains on his roads and railways rug, Mason stands, then offers me his hand. With a heavy sigh, I accept and rise to my feet. Interlacing his fingers with mine, Mason leads us down the hall to the one room in the house I've never seen.

A sheepish tickle crawls up my spine as he walks me through the double doors into the master bedroom. Were I in any other mood, I'd probably crack a joke about him trying to seduce me with Danny right down the hall, wide awake, no less. As it is, I can't speak. I simply shuffle along while my stomach wraps itself in knots, and my heart takes flight.

"Breathe," he whispers, squeezing my hand. "I just want to talk out of earshot of a certain toddler."

His room—roughly the size of my kitchen and living room combined—is painted a subtle mint with a deep blue accent wall. Not an obvious combination in my mind, but they work together. It's beautiful in here. Peaceful. Mason drops my hand as I pause to absorb the significance of this space and its correlation to the ring on my finger. Completely aware I'm three shades of pink from my neck to my forehead, I swallow loudly, my mind splitting into two trains of thought, each racing so disjointedly I can't follow along or process any of it. One side is envisioning spending nights here, next to Mason, between the sheets of the king-size bed he's now sitting on the edge of.

The other side can't get past Miranda's words. Whether they've changed anything between us or will drive a permanent wedge between Mason and his parents. What if my existence in his life ruins his relationship with his mother? I can't be responsible for that.

Is he having second thoughts? Why does he look so sexy simply *sitting* on that bed, and how long can I go without compulsively throwing myself at him? Am I really a cliché?

That's the word she used. Not even a skank anymore. Just a cliché.

Mason creases his brow, scanning me up and down. "You doin' okay over there?" he asks.

I can't unload my neuroses on him. Not now, so soon after my massive meltdown over the videos of my parents. He'll start to think all I'm capable of is breaking down and shedding tears. He'll want the ring back.

"Stevie?"

Normal. Say something normal.

"You could fit my whole house in here."

Solid choice, Stevie.

"There she is," he says, then raises both arms to entice me toward him. "Come'ere."

I wrinkle my nose and twist my lips before running full speed at him, tumbling onto the mattress. We flop and roll in a tangle of arms, legs, and laughter until he has me pinned under him.

His hair falls in his eyes as his fingers trace my cheek, my neck, my collarbone. I all but catch fire. With only a single—albeit *great* kiss, he lies beside me, pulling me into that safe haven between his arm and chest. My arm drapes across his stomach, and I meld into him. His bed is so comfortable, I could cry.

"Good talk," I tease.

"Ha!" He presses his lips into my hair. "I've missed you."

"I've been right here."

"No," he says gently. "You haven't. But I understand. Stevie, I..." He exhales. "I'm so sorry. She's completely out of line."

"Your dad is very enthusiastic," I divert. "I like him."

I feel him relax. "That enthusiasm was completely heartfelt, by the way. He wasn't just trying to be nice."

I twist my lips back and forth. "I guess one out of two isn't the absolute worst. But...damn. I mean, she *really* hates me."

"Stevie, no," he whispers, holding me tighter.

I turn into him, burying my face in his chest. "Who is *that woman*?" I ask. "The one you two were arguing about."

"Daniel's mom. She..." I sense him struggling to find the right words.

"She hurt you, didn't she? She hurt your family."

He sighs. "Yeah. She was complicated. It felt like my life was in pieces for a long time."

He's so tense against me, and I know this is painful for him. "You don't have to talk about her. Not with me. If she hurt you, that's all I need to know." He kisses my hair. "Does she—your mom—does she think I'll hurt Danny? Is that why she hates me?"

"Stevie, she doesn't hate you. There's no excuse for what she said, but I'm sure she regrets it." He rubs my back, kissing my hair again. "I'm so sorry, sweetheart."

I'm beginning to crumble. "Can we not talk about it anymore? Please?"

"Stevie—"

I lift my head to meet his gaze. "I got *engaged* last night. To this extremely smart, talented, sexy man of my dreams. I'd like to be happy about that right now. I'd like a day to just swim in it and ignore anything that makes me sad. Okay?"

He pushes my hair out of my face, tucking it behind my ear.

"Sexy, huh?" he asks through a smirk.

"You don't even know," I say, brushing my fingers over his stubble. "I find you so sexy, it's stupid."

His smile widens. "Ditto, babe. Ditto."

I'm about to kiss him when a little voice asks, "What does *ditto* mean?"

Mason and I untangle from each other and wave for Daniel to climb onto the bed. He giggles as he flops between us.

I take his chubby toddler hand in mine and kiss it.

"Why'd you do dat?" he asks.

"Because I wanted to," I answer.

"Are you gonna stay wif us forever now?"

Tears well, but for happier reasons.

Mason kisses Daniel's forehead and strokes his hair. "Well,

Danny boy," he says. "How would you feel about that? About Stevie spending more time here and someday moving in?"

Daniel's eyes widen. "To live *here*?"

I bite my lip.

"Yeah," Mason says. "To live here."

"You can share my room," Danny says, grinning at me. "We'd can get bunk beds!"

Mason and I laugh.

"We were thinking more along the lines of—" Mason starts.

"Hey, speak for yourself," I say. "I've always wanted bunk beds."

CHAPTER
24

M errin calls the moment she's home, demanding my company. Before she hugs me, before she says hello, before I'm even *inside* the house, she grabs my hand and examines my ring.

"Good glory," she cries. "Honey, that ain't white gold. That's platinum."

"Really?"

She pulls me through the door and wraps me in a hug, squeezing a little too tightly.

"Oh, Stevie. How can you be so smart and yet so, so dumb?"

"Okay, *ouch*."

She releases me, wiping her glistening eyes.

"No," I say, pointing a finger. "Don't you dare cry. If you start crying, I'll start crying. And I'm not crying today. No."

"Sorry," she says, fanning her face. "I'm just so happy."

"Tell me about it."

We settle onto the living room sectional with snacks, scrolling through Merrin's pictures of New York. Each one has a lengthy story attached, but I'm content to listen.

By the time Merrin begins narrating the flight home, Nancy wakes from her post-vacation nap and joins us on the couch. She doesn't interrupt Merrin but holds out her palm. I offer her my left hand, and she gasps.

Merrin pauses, glowering at her mother. Nancy mouths a *sorry* as she releases my fingers.

"No," Merrin sighs. "It's ok. I'm done, anyway. I'm sure we'd all much rather talk about Stevie's fairytale engagement than relive Dad snoring at O'Hare."

Nancy makes a gargling sound, burying her face in her hands. "Please, let's never discuss it again," she mutters. She eyes my hand, biting her lip. After a moment's hesitation, she asks to see it again, and I oblige.

"I've never seen anything like it. It's stunning." She shakes her head, sighing. "And you're sure about this?" There's no malice or distrust in her words. Only genuine interest.

"I know it sounds crazy, Nan, but it was the easiest decision I've ever made in my entire life."

She nods. "That's not crazy, sweetie. I was eighteen when I met Max. Even so young, I knew. If he'd asked me on the first date, I would have said yes. And the whole year-long engagement thing? That was *only* because our parents bribed us."

"Bribed you?"

"Yeah, they joined forces. Told us if we stretched the engagement out at least a year, they'd give us a down payment on a house."

"Oh, wow!" I let out a low whistle. "Hard to argue with that."

"It was the longest year of my life," she says, seemingly staring into her past. "I thought I'd wither away and die waiting for the day to arrive. But I tell you what, seeing the looks on our parents' faces when they had to pay up?" She laughs, shaking her head. "That made it all worth it. They were counting on us either eloping or breaking up. They *never* thought we'd make it."

"But here we are," Max says, entering the room, a lightness about his tone I'm not accustomed to. He kisses his wife before settling in his recliner. "Must have done something right, eh, Nance?"

They share a look that makes Merrin audibly gag.

Nancy squeezes my knee. "Look, honey. I won't sit here and tell you it's been easy. But I regret nothing."

Her words are a salve I didn't realize I needed. It's been days since the *Miranda Incident*, and though I know Mason has likely spent time with her in Coeur d'Alene, he hasn't mentioned her to me in any capacity. It's been nothing but *I miss yous* and pictures of Danny with his cousins.

As much as I know Mason loves me, I'm feeling the weight of his mother's disapproval, almost like a bad omen slowly blacking out the sun I've been basking in ever since Mason first kissed me. Having Nancy in my corner, advocating for love, even young love, and sharing her sentiment of *no regrets*, I feel a renewed faith that things *will*, in fact, be alright.

"So, have you told little Daniel yet?" Merrin asks.

"We told him a few days ago."

"How is he handling it?"

"He seems elated. He asked if he should start calling me Mommy."

Merrin and Nancy *aww* simultaneously. Max shakes his head, standing and leaving the room. Nancy smacks his butt as he walks by, and again my best friend gags.

"Anyway," she continues with her dad out of the room. "What did you tell him?"

"Mason and I told him he should call me what makes him comfortable. It was kind of a long discussion, but in the end, Daniel decided he would call me Stevie until the wedding, then afterward, 'maybe Mama Stevie.'"

Nancy rubs my arm. "How are you feeling about that?"

"Blissful. Honestly. I feel like he was meant to be mine. Which, again, probably sounds crazy. I can't explain it."

"You don't have to, honey," Nancy assures me. "For one thing, you're an adult, and you've been taking care of yourself a *long* time. Beyond that, you're smart, and you have good instincts. I trust you, Stevie. Implicitly. And I've got pretty good instincts, myself," she adds, winking. "That being said, if you start seeing any red flags, I want you to run. Do you understand me?"

I tilt my head, squinting.

"I'm serious. It's never too late to walk away from something. Okay? Promise me."

"Yeah," I agree, nodding. "Okay. I promise."

She relaxes into the couch. "Good girl. And if there's anything you need help with—wedding planning or anything else—I hope you know you can come to me."

"Well," I say, drawing the word out, "there's actually something I'm hoping Max could help—"

Nancy bolts up. "Max! Max, get in here!"

"It doesn't have to be *now*," I start.

"Don't bother," Merrin says dully. "You said the magic word. She's been activated. Parents live for their adult children asking for help."

She says it in a whisper, but it resonates like a scream, the idea I might be considered someone's *adult child*.

Max scowls as he reenters the room. "What? Who died?"

"Good grief, Maxwell. Just sit down."

He grumbles but takes a seat in a recliner.

"Stevie has requested your help," Nancy tells him.

It might be my imagination, but I swear he perks up at these words.

"Well, the thing is," I say, "I've got this house."

THE FIRST DAY of the semester has me questioning my sanity. I'm taking too many classes, and they start way too early in the morning. But the knowledge my boys are on the other side of it keeps me going. I haven't seen them since we told Daniel about our relationship. They've been busy visiting family, and I've been so busy packing up the house and cleaning, I haven't even updated Mason on the big change. I'm still coming to terms with it.

Selling the house. I am selling my house. It will officially be on the market in under forty-eight hours. I don't even live there anymore, and I never will again. I'm taking up temporary residence in a spare room in the Caraway's daylight basement. In a real bed, on a real bedframe.

Overly eager to see Mason and explain it all to him, I don't register the somewhat familiar car parked in front of the house.

Daniel runs up to me as I come through the door. I don't bother with knocking anymore—I even have a key. Mason slipped it on my keyring the last time we were together.

"Stevie's here! Stevie's here!" Daniel announces to the house.

"Hey, little man!" He lunges at me, latching onto my leg. I drop my bag and coat where I stand, placing my hands on either side of his head, stroking his soft hair. "I missed you. How was your visit with your cousins?"

"Dey have Candyland and we'd played it every day!"

"Every day, huh? That's amazing."

"Can we'd make cookies today?"

"Maybe, sweetheart," I say, stiffening as Mason and Miranda come into view. Mason wears a smile I'm not sure I should trust.

"You're early," he says, walking toward me.

"I can go. I'll come back later." I clumsily bend to pick up my things, Daniel still an extension of my leg. Mason takes my coat and bag, kissing me as he does.

"Don't even think about it," he whispers. "It's been days since I saw you."

I ready myself to stand on my toes and kiss him again before remembering our audience. "I uh, I just..." I look down at Daniel, still smiling up at me. I drum my hands against his back, then tickle his sides. He squeals, detaching himself from me and running off to play. "My class times are a little different this semester, so I nabbed a slightly earlier shift at the daycare. I came as soon as I got off. I missed you guys. And I was excited to tell you..."

"Tell me what?" He hangs up my things and puts an arm around me, leading me through the house, ruining all hope of escape. "We missed you too," he assures me in that low, smooth, steady voice that turns me to butter.

I look at Miranda. "I don't want to interrupt."

Miranda closes some distance between us. "You're not interrupting. I came here to see you. The both of you. But I understand if you're not ready to see me."

I try and fail to respond several times before I turn to Mason and blurt, "I'm selling the house. I moved in with the Caraways."

He jerks his head back. "Wait. What?"

Without answering, I break away from him, go into the kitchen, and pour myself a glass of water. Miranda's presence has caught me off guard, and I'm glitching out. I need—but lack—a reset button.

I want to rewind to five minutes ago, notice her car, and just *not* come inside.

I want to yell at her.

I want her to love me.

Keenly aware of my audience, I drink my water, then brace myself against the kitchen counter.

"I talked with Max last week," I say, staring at the floor. "Picked his brain about my options. Whether to use the house as a rental property—an income. Or to just cut it loose, use the money for school, and invest whatever's leftover, seeing as the market is absolutely insane right now. And between school and work, I wasn't sure I wanted the stress of a rental property. You know?"

Shrugging, I finally look up. Mason has taken a seat on a bar stool. Miranda stands just outside the kitchen, giving off a *woman without a country* vibe, unsure where she belongs.

I clear my throat, then continue. "Max talked me through the pros and cons, answered all my questions. I decided to sell."

Mason nods. "And the moving in with the Caraways?" he asks.

"Oh. Yeah. Max suggested clearing the house out completely or staging it. The way I have things situated..." I trail off, but Mason understands. "People like to picture themselves in the home they're buying. No one wants to picture themselves living like I do. Or *did*, rather." I mean it to come out light, joking, but it draws concern from Miranda.

"Wait," she says, walking toward me. "What's that about?"

"Oh, nothing," I sigh. "Lower, *lower* middle-class problems," I mutter. Nothing Miranda Shepard can understand. She squints but doesn't press further.

I turn my attention back to Mason. "I spent the weekend moving out and cleaning."

He frowns. "I wish I'd have known. I wish I'd been here to help."

"You needed to be right where you were," I argue. "Your brother and Rachel needed you more than I did. Besides, it's not like I did it alone. The Caraways helped."

His frown softens. "Good."

"Max has an agent coming over Wednesday to take pictures and get it listed."

Mason shakes his head. "Wow. That was fast."

I laugh. "Tell me about it. Max doubts the house will stay on the market more than a couple weeks."

"He's not wrong," Miranda says, rejoining the conversation. "I don't know if Mason's told you this, but I've got a lot of experience when it comes to money management and investments."

My lips twitch—almost a smile. "Yeah, he did say you were a bit of a wizard."

"I mean, it sounds like you've already got someone in your corner, but if you ever want or need advice in that regard, I'd be happy to help."

I nod, biting down the stream of snarky retorts lining up on my tongue.

"Stevie, I hope you know how thrilled I am for you and Mase. I want nothing more than for everything to work out."

So many snarky retorts, just aching to be unleashed. *Keep calm, Stevie. Just. Be. Cool.*

"Are you sure about that?" I snap.

Dammit, Stevie!

But even when Miranda hangs her head, seemingly embarrassed, my mouth keeps moving.

"Miranda, I don't want to burn bridges here. Ultimately, I want us to get along. And I can't say I blame you for doubting I know anything about responsibility or love or marriage or parenthood. I'm just asking—begging you to take the time to try and know me a little before you go bad-mouthing me in front of your family, especially the little boy upstairs whom I want desperately to call me 'Mom.'" My hands shake, and my eyes burn.

Don't cry, don't cry, don't cry.

"I want—" No. "I *deserve* a chance at a family that doesn't hate or resent me." The first tears fall.

Dammit.

Mason stands, reaching for me, but his mother gets between us and surprises me with a hug.

First, I freeze. Moments later, I relax into Miranda's soft but sturdy embrace.

"What I said was unconscionable," she tells me, her voice breaking. "I was scared and didn't understand. I know better, now. Mason corrected so many of my assumptions, and I've had time to digest this. I'm so sorry for ruining a precious moment for you. I only hope you can forgive me one day."

We stay in the embrace for a silent minute before she steps back, sniffling.

"I hope you'll let me spend some time with you," she says. "I promise I'm not a horrible person."

"Well," I say, wiping my face with my sleeve, "if you can bear to be seen with the skanky nanny, I guess that would be fine."

Miranda stares stone-faced, unsure how to respond, until Mason laughs so hard he snorts. She shakes her head, trying to portray agitation when she's clearly amused.

"You two really are perfect together, aren't you?" she says, wagging her fingers at us. "I'm going to find my grandson. At least when he teases me, it's adorable."

"I don't know. I think I'm pretty adorable," I say.

Miranda shakes her head and smacks Mason's shoulder on her way out of the kitchen, but does so with an ear-to-ear grin.

The moment Miranda is out of range, Mason rushes in.

"I love you," he says between kisses. "You're friggin' magnificent. You know that, right?"

I clutch his wavy hair in my fingers as he lifts me onto the countertop. His hands slide under my shirt as my ankles lock behind his thighs, binding him closer to me. If I trap him here forever, I'll never tire of the taste of him or the way he gently but deliberately explores my body, igniting tiny fires with every touch. I arch into him as his hands press against my spine, and he moans into my mouth.

He breaks away, breathless. "How the hell am I supposed to leave for work now?"

I laugh, pulling him into a hug, guiding his head onto my shoulder.

He catches his breath as I twist a curly lock around my finger.

"There's a hitch to the whole Max thing," I say. "I couldn't tell you in front of your mother."

Mason pulls back, raising a quizzical brow.

"I have to live with them until the wedding."

"Or...?"

"Or..." I shrug. "Look, I don't know what to tell you, but Max said, 'We do this proper, you hear?' and I found myself saying, 'Yessir.' If you want to try and renegotiate with him, you're welcome to, but you should know when Nancy tried to tell him he couldn't make rules for me, he said, 'The hell I can't' and then muttered something about you being a weasel. So... I mean, do what you will, but I have no desire to argue with that man."

Mason's forehead falls to my shoulder as he laughs. "He went into *dad* mode, huh?"

"It was terrifying but also somehow endearing."

He laughs harder. "I think it's amazing he cares so much. You deserve that." He stands tall, bringing his lips within an inch of mine, framing my face with his hands. "And yes, I noticed you finally allowed yourself to say you *deserved* something back there with my mom. I've never loved you more."

My fingers get lost in his hair as I pull him in for another kiss. When we part, he braces his forehead against mine.

"Well," he says. "I guess nothing about our relationship has really been...*conventional*. Not by modern standards, anyway."

"Yeah, I hear sex and living together typically come before a proposal."

He sucks in a small breath. "You *hear*? You mean...?"

"I've never had a relationship before. Not really. And after what happened with...in the music room... There hasn't been anyone I loved or trusted enough to consider intimacy. Until you."

Unable to decipher the sigh that comes from his mouth, I freeze. I'm not sure how what I've just said could possibly hurt him, but something tells me it has.

"There's a lot more to a relationship than sex," he finally says. "It can wait."

I release the breath I've been holding. "Yeah?"

"Of course. For as long as you need. Or want." He kisses me again. "Every minute with you is already perfect, with or without *that* particular connection. What we have, Stevie? It goes so far beyond that. That day I met you, some broken, buried part of me woke up. Like all this time, what I needed to be whole again was *you*. Where you live isn't going to change that."

Before I find his mouth again, I take a moment to let those words wash over me, trying to absorb them. This kiss is somehow even better than all we've shared before, and I'd love to stay here, his chest pressed to mine, our tongues dancing, our hands roaming. I want it all, forever. But when my head bumps against a cabinet, and I laugh, I open my eyes just enough to catch sight of the clock.

"Babe," I say, cringing.

"Hm?"

"You're gonna be late." I tip my head toward the clock. He whips around.

"Oh, shi—" he stops himself when he finds Daniel standing behind him. "Shoot," he revises, picking his toddler up for a hug. "Well, you're a sneaky ninja today, aren't you? Where's Gramma?"

"She coming. She say her knees old and slow."

He laughs. "I've gotta get to work, monster. I love you."

"Love you, Daddy."

I hop down from the countertop and take Danny in my arms. Mason rushes around, gathering his things.

"Stevie?" Danny asks.

"Yes, sweetie?"

"Did you like your new guitar?"

Mason stops mid-rush, deflating with a sigh.

"What guitar?" I ask.

"You got a guitar and I got a yuka lilly and we'd gonna learn to play!"

"A ukulele, huh?" I ask, looking from Daniel to Mason, who turns to me with a resigned smile.

"Surprise?" he mutters, turning his hands up.

"Surprise!" Danny calls. "Happy birfday!"

I chew on my lip, shaking my head, wondering how in the hell I got so lucky, as Mason mouths, *love you*, then runs out the door.

CHAPTER
25

We're nearly a month into our routine, and I still turn to mush every night when Mason comes home, snatches me up, and pulls me onto the couch with him.

Sometimes we cuddle and talk. Other times we kiss until I'm dizzy. Either way, it's always the best part of my day. Mason is the best part of my everything.

I sit relaxed against his chest, listening to the beating of his heart and a Lumineers song drifting from my phone, letting the stress of school, work, life—all of it—melt away.

"You're quiet tonight," he whispers.

"Happy quiet," I add, smiling.

He huffs a laugh, then wraps his arms around me, pulling me closer. "Guess you got what you wanted, huh?" Shivers run down my spine as his hot breath ghosts over my neck.

"Just about."

"But not everything?"

Shaking my head, I pull away from his embrace. As our eyes meet, my heart goes ballistic, and I have to look at my lap in order to continue. "I've been thinking..." I pause the music on my phone, trying to clear my head.

"You can tell me anything," he says, his fingers grazing my chin. "Always."

With a heavy sigh, I look right into those chocolate eyes and let it out. "I want to adopt Daniel. Legally. After we're married."

He has no initial reaction other than stunned silence. No facial twitches. No hand gestures. Is he even breathing?

"Mase?" No response. "Look, if you're not ready to talk about this, we can shelve it. But I just..." I've practiced this in the mirror a dozen times, but in this moment, all my pre-planned, eloquent remarks are scattered in broken, useless shards, floating aimlessly in my brain. I can't grasp a single one.

"I know a piece of notarized paper can't change or add to what's already in my heart. So maybe this seems silly or unnecessary. But I don't ever want that boy feeling like he and I aren't family in every sense of the word. You know?"

In the silence that follows, my heart slowly descends into my stomach, and my hands begin trembling. Next, my chin quivers. Still, Mason offers no verbal response. Embarrassed and on the verge of melting down, I stand from the couch.

"I should go," I say, my voice pinched at the back of my throat. "Sorry for springing that on you."

I make it two steps before Mason's hand curls around my wrist.

"Stay." Such a gentle demand, I can't disregard it, even if I'm about to ugly cry all over him.

He pulls me back to the couch so I'm straddling his lap.

"I didn't mean to upset you," I whisper.

"It's not that," he says, his fingers gently brushing my cheek. "It's just that I should have told you... My first wife... She..."

"What?"

"It's hard for me to talk about her. Also, I just don't *like* talking about her because I don't ever want Danny to hear me speaking negatively about his mother. Even if it's accurate."

"I respect that, really. You don't need to tell me everything."

"But I *should* have talked with you about her, so you'd know. So she isn't this unspoken barrier between us, causing awkward conversations. That's not fair to you."

He takes my chin in his thumb and forefinger, his eyes burrowing into mine.

"Stevie, of course, I'd love for you to adopt Daniel. I'd consider it a privilege."

"Yeah?" I ask, still trying to steady my emotions.

"Hell yes. I mean...Stanford, Stevie." He shakes his head as I try to work out his meaning.

"What?"

"You gave up Stanford to care for a man who never truly grasped how amazing you were and how damned lucky he was to have you. You let go of your dreams to be there for him when he needed it, like he never was for you. I can only imagine the lengths you'd go to for Danny. You love fiercely, Stevie Rae. I've never met anyone like you."

I wipe the back of my hand across my wet cheeks, sniffling.

"I love you so much," he says. Yet there's that dark look again like something's haunting him.

My phone buzzes on the coffee table. *Twice.*

"Uh-oh," Mason says. "We've angered the parents. Haven't we?"

Technically, I don't have a curfew. But anytime I'm out past eleven, Nancy texts me, *just to make sure I'm okay.*

"Come on," he says, nudging me. "I really want them to like me. It would probably help if you went home on time, so they stopped assuming I'm...you know..."

"What?" I ask, smirking. "*Defiling* me?"

He lolls his head back. "You're killing me, Stevie," he says, deep and husky.

I kiss his neck. "Right back at'cha."

He grabs me and bolts forward, pinning me under him on the couch. His tongue parting my lips, his hips lowering onto mine, the heat rising from his skin, and yet all these layers between us. It's insufferable.

My hands slide under his shirt, and he revs up the intensity as my nails dig into his back. His lips trail down my neck to my collarbone but freeze as they reach the curve of my breast. He collapses against me, exhaling.

"I'm sorry," he says, breathless, then rolls off the couch and sits on the floor.

I release an exasperated breath and blink at the ceiling before turning onto my side, propping my head on my palm. "Why? What just happened?"

He shakes his head. "I want this, Stevie. You have no idea..." His thoughts trail, and he laughs, brief and humorless. "It's just..."

With my free hand, I brush his cheek, then rake my fingers through his hair. He's been growing it back out, and it's once again long enough to stay tucked behind his ears. Not every girl's cup of tea, for sure. But for me...it *works*.

"Mase, if you *want* to keep waiting, we can. But I'm ready."

He sets his jaw.

"I'm *ready*. So if something's holding you back, just talk to me about it, okay? Because the whole will he or won't he rip my clothes off thing is a fresh form of torture, and I've told you before, I'm not a masochist."

His head bobs as he releases a barely audible laugh.

"That's fair." Silence hangs between us for a minute, maybe longer. "Stevie, I..."

He leans in, kissing my forehead.

"Your first time should be special."

"Um, it's *you*. I promise you it'll be special. I don't need some grand plan—"

"At the very least," he says, "It should be on a bed. Without a toddler sleeping down the hall. And I want you to stay with me, fall asleep next to me. I don't want some quickie on the couch where I have to watch you leave afterward."

I bite down on my lips, making them disappear.

He scans my face, awaiting my response.

"Well," I sigh, "when you put it like that..."

He plants another kiss on my forehead, then a softer one on my nose.

"But we're both adults. It feels really stupid that we're going along with Max's house rules. Unless you're trying to protect me from something...? Are you...? Are you having doubts about marrying me? About me moving in here?"

His eyes widen. "No, Stevie. Of course not."

"So why are we doing this? Why are we having this conversation instead of making love in your bed, saying to hell with the house rules because I can just move in here? You're doubting this."

"Stevie, stop. Breathe." He takes my hand in his, pressing it to his chest. "It's me, okay. This is me. And I'm not doubting us or planning on going anywhere, okay?"

I nod, taking a deep breath. Mason isn't like the other men in my life, who've all either died or hurt me. Or hurt me *then* died. This is Mason, who gave me a job and saved my life, who changed his soap and invited me to the cabin and who holds me like he needs it to breathe.

"The Caraways are your family," he says. "I know how much you love them, which means I love and respect them. Let's give Max some time to get to know me, okay? I'd hate for you to argue with him over something so insignificant in the grand scheme of things. You know? We've got time. We don't have to rush this."

"Is that why you still don't want to talk about setting a date? You're not rushing this anymore? You proposed on the first date, but now we've got all the time in the world?" I love this man, but he's confusing sometimes.

"Stevie, there's just some things I'm trying to work out. I want to give you the best life, and I don't want to drive a wedge between you and your new family."

His eyes hold mine with a feverish intensity. I can't help but kiss him. It's deep, long, and intoxicating.

"Fine," I say as we part. "We wait a little longer. But I'ma need you to tone down your sex appeal at least eighty percent."

He wriggles his brows, gesturing to himself. "I can't turn this off, babe," he says. "I'm sorry."

"Then stop showering or something," I tease. "Or I'll have to impose a six-feet-apart rule."

His mouth gapes. "You wouldn't dare."

I start singing "Don't Stand So Close to Me," and he tickles my sides. We're moments away from tangling back together when my phone buzzes again. I roll my eyes, groaning and flopping back onto the couch as he hands it to me. I love Nancy, but the woman is a mood killer.

NANCY

Just checking in.

Remind Mason about dinner next weekend.

Heading to bed. You have your key?

Yes, I have my key. On my way. Promise.

NANCY

Thank goodness. I was trying to play it cool, but you had me panicking.

Sorry I worried you. Be home soon. xoxo

"She okay?" Mason asks.

"Yeah. Just...being a mom. And reminding you about next weekend."

"Call me crazy, but I'm looking forward to it."

"I'm sure you're counting the minutes."

"Stevie, I told you. If you love them, I love them. I want this. I want the awkward meeting of the in-laws and obligatory dinners. I want it all."

He kisses me one last time, then helps gather my things and walks me to the door.

"I told you I don't have classes tomorrow night, right?" he asks.

"Right, you and Dan have an appointment. Is it the counselor again? Is everything okay? Are there behaviors I should be looking out for or—"

He puts an arm around me, kissing my temple. "Everything's okay. We're just working through some adjustments. But it's almost over, and then we can focus on you and me. Nothing but wedding stuff."

As he hugs me goodnight, his hand slides into the back pocket of my jeans.

"If you're putting money in my pants right now, I will cut you. I told you it's too weird."

"And I told *you* I'm not letting you work for free."

"It's hardly work. Stop sneaking your dirty money into my pocket every week. I don't want it."

"It's not dirty money," he teases, swaying me back and forth, touching his nose to mine. "If I were leaving it on the nightstand, *that* would be dirty money."

I snort, shoving him away. "Good*night*, Mason."

"Goodnight, Stevie Rae." That smooth baritone threatens to melt me all over again, and I already told Nancy I'm on my way. Gathering every last ounce of willpower, I force myself out the door, my heart constricting as it latches behind me.

"Soon," I breathe, pressing a hand against my stomach. "Soon."

THIS SEMI-AWKWARD DINNER serves a dual purpose. It's an excuse for Nancy and Max to meet the Shepards—all of them. Wes and Miranda included. But we're also celebrating the fact that I accepted an offer on the house, and barring any unforeseen disasters, the buyers will close in a month.

I have mixed feelings about the house selling, but the overwhelming one is relief. Relief I never have to return to that crappy mattress on the floor. Relief I'm no longer alone, but loved, by all these people sitting around a dining room table, trying to get to know one another. I love it, but it's also mildly uncomfortable as I feel like the center of attention, and that's never been my scene.

Danny slips away from the table to play with the assortment of toys Nancy set up in the living room, and a part of me *really* wants to join him. For Nancy's sake, I stay seated, though I move my chair closer to Mason's, sinking against him as he puts an arm around me.

Nancy and Miranda find common ground easily enough, while Max and Wes share occasional grunts and dull, dead-end statements.

Merrin sits across from Mason and me, visibly depressed and annoyed. It's been four weeks since she and Luke broke up, but for the constant state of melancholy she's in, it may as well have been yesterday.

"What's new, Merrin?" Mason asks, attempting to pull her from her slump. "How's cosmetology school going?"

She shrugs, twisting her lips.

"I hear you're quite the artist," he offers.

She finally lifts her eyes from her plate. "I'm not bad. You should let me tackle..." she waves her hand in a circle in front of Mason's face. "This whole situation."

"Merrin!" I shriek.

"What? I'm just not seeing anything cohesive with your wardrobe here. It's like you can't decide whether to dress like a lumberjack or a professor. And the length of your hair? It's all...*wrong.*"

Mason would probably be offended if he weren't so clearly amused.

I tip my head up, kissing his stubbly chin. "Don't let her bully you. You're perfect."

He dips his head, pressing his lips to mine.

"Of course, *she* thinks you're perfect," Merrin says.

He laughs. "Well, hers is the only opinion that matters."

She rolls her eyes. "Fine. But for the love of Jonathan Van Ness, would you at *least* invest in some curl cream for your hair? Such wasted potential."

Mason laughs. "I'm not sure who that is. But I'll look into it."

"Give me your phone," she says. Bless that man. He hands it right over without asking any follow-up questions. Her thumbs pad against the screen, and she hands it back. "You've got my number now. Call me when you're ready to address this—" She once again waves her hand in front of his face. "I'll help you."

"Will do," he says.

"Thank you," she sighs. "Now, would you please, in the name of all that is holy, tell me you've decided on a color scheme for the wedding."

Mason and I exchange blank stares.

"Oh, come on. You're joking, right?"

"I've been really busy," I argue. "You know. The house. School. Work. I haven't thought about it."

She props her elbows on the table, massaging her temples. "Okay, so what about flowers? What kind of flowers for your bouquet?"

I shrug. "Pretty ones?"

Merrin jerks her head back, wide-eyed. "Oh, my heck. Stevie. You are *killing* me."

Max clears his throat. "We have *guests*, Merrin," he sighs. "Tone it down a bit, yeah?"

"Okay, so what about music for the reception? Have you decided on a DJ vs. a band, because I think—"

"Oh, a live band would be fun!" Miranda chimes in.

"I thought I'd just hook a playlist up to a speaker system," I say.

"Clutch. My pearls. Stephanie Renae." Merrin slowly braces her hands against the table. "Stop."

"What?" I ask. "You have your gifts. Playlists are mine."

"It's true," Mason says. "You've got skills." He takes my hand and kisses it. "Wicked callouses, babe," he observes, checking my fingertips. "Someone's been practicing."

I grin, craning my neck to look at him. "I'm trying to impress my guitar teacher. He's really hot."

He winks, then kisses me.

"Ugh," Merrin groans. "I can't even with you two right now. It's like you don't care. *At all.*"

"I care," I argue. "We care. And hey, we at least know my dress will be amazing." I still can't believe Jocelyn's offer to *make* my dress.

Nancy's paying for materials. All I have to do is send my measurements. I feel a little like a princess.

"Okay," Merrin says, "but that's one detail. A great dress does not a ceremony make."

"That's a valid point," Nancy chimes in. "Have you two at least picked a date and a venue?"

All eyes turn to me, and I stutter. I can't admit that I've been so elated over being engaged to Mason, I haven't made *any* decisions about the actual wedding. I just want to marry him. I don't care where, when, how, or in what.

Mason squeezes my knee under the table.

"We're thinking early August, tentatively," I manage. "I just want something simple."

"*We* want something simple," Mason adds.

I sit up, turning to him. "Like a barbeque in the backyard?"

He smiles. "I actually love that idea."

"Yeah?"

He kisses my forehead. "Yeah."

"But whose backyard, honey?" Miranda asks. "I love you, Mase, but you've done absolutely *no* landscaping back there. It's bare bones. Hardly wedding ceremony material."

"Well, hell," Wes booms. "Have it in our yard. It's bigger, anyway. And we've got more room for parking. Rent some tables and chairs. Throw up some lights. Easy peasy."

"What kind of barbeque are we talkin' here?" Max asks.

Nancy and Miranda discuss arches and whether an outdoor wedding is sensible given the unpredictability of weather, even in August. Tents are perhaps necessary.

Wes and Max debate which cuts of meat will be better, and how big of a grill will be required to feed fifty to one hundred people.

I look to Mason, mouthing, *one hundred?*

He presses his lips to my hair.

Merrin sinks into her chair, arms crossed. Though she wears a hint of a smile. Tonight's been good for her; she's getting her snark back.

Daniel joins us back at the table, rubbing his eyes.

"I should get him home," Mason says, pulling Danny onto his lap. "Sorry, everyone. But you'll have to finish scolding us another time."

Nancy sighs. "Look, I don't want to tell anyone how to do anything. But I've overseen enough weddings to know that no matter how simple of a ceremony you want, you *do* have to put in the work and make decisions."

"I know," I say. "I promise, Nan. We will be better about this. We'll dedicate tomorrow to wedding prep."

"Agreed," Mason says. "Tomorrow, we'll make lists and difficult decisions. Put down deposits. Whatever. We'll get it done. We've both just been...you know...basking in the excitement. Ignoring the responsibility."

Miranda and Nancy mutter, "Young love," under their breath.

I look to Mason. "I'll marry you any time. Anywhere. Just don't run me over with any more doors, and we'll be fine."

Wes laughs. "What's this about?

"It's how we met," I say, eyes still on Mason. "He rammed a door right into my face."

"And you still wanna marry him?"

"Yessir, I do."

"Well, hell. I s'pose that's all you need to know right there, ain't it?"

CHAPTER
26

"Stevie's gonna get *lai-aid*," Merrin sings, bouncing on the edge of my bed.

"Shh!" I order, my eyes darting to my bedroom door. I know Nancy and Max aren't even home, but *still*. They don't need to know about my sex life...not that I even have one. *Yet*. "I don't even know for sure that's what this is."

Merrin arches a brow. "Stevie, if he wanted to *talk*, he would have just talked to you tonight after class, or invited you out for a date tomorrow or something. He wouldn't have canceled his classes, dropped Daniel off with his mother, and invited you over."

"See, all those things—to me—make it sound like he actually wants to talk about something important. I mean, he's a professional. He wouldn't cancel his classes to get lucky." I scrunch up my nose. "I don't think. Honestly, this whole thing feels far more ominous than seductive."

When I got out of my second class this morning, I had a text from Mason, asking how soon I could come over and talk. I texted back, asking what it was about, and he vaguely said *wedding stuff*. Of course, my first thought really *was* this must be about the wedding. But the more I sat with his texts and the way he chose to phrase things, the more I thought there might be a hidden message.

So, of course, I'd called Merrin to meet me at the house for a fashion emergency. Lucky for me, she had thirty minutes to spare.

I hold up a top. "Does this say *I'm not expecting anything, but I'm totally ready for it*?"

She turns the corners of her mouth down, nodding. "I'd say it gets the job done. But you need different jeans. The dark wash ones that make your booty look fantastic."

"My booty *always* looks fantastic."

We laugh, and I get changed. She helps me with my eyeliner because, despite months of practice, I still suck at it.

"You're a fox, Stevie Rae," she says, sighing. "He's an idiot if he doesn't rip your clothes off."

"You're so sweet. Thanks." We laugh again, then I release an involuntary squeal. My skin is crawling, and I'm not sure I can wait until after my shift at Bright Beginnings to see him. "Maybe I just call in sick," I say. "I already skipped a class."

"You should. Did he say when he was dropping Daniel off?"

I huff. "No. I told him I'd come over after work. It wasn't until after I replied that I started to think... You know... And if this *is* what we think it is, do I want to run over there like I'm ultra desperate?"

Again, she arches a brow.

"Yeah, I know. I've wanted this a long time."

"Well, whatever's been holding him back, let's hope it's over now." She points her crossed fingers skyward. "I've gotta get back to school. But keep me posted. Well, not like...*during*."

I laugh, shoving her out of my room. "I love you," I holler after her as she bounds up the stairs.

"Love you more," she calls down.

With a deep breath, I smooth my clothes out in front of the mirror. "Breathe, Stevie," I tell myself. "Just breathe."

I show up for my shift at Bright Beginnings, though I'm not entirely sure why. Whether Mason wants to legitimately *talk* or something else, this seems significant. I should be with him. This is dumb. But I'm already in the building, and Marge just spotted me; too late to turn back now.

As I silence my phone before putting it in my cubby and clocking in, an unknown number lights up the screen. Oregon area code, I think. I don't know anyone in Oregon. I send it to voicemail. But then it lights up again, almost immediately. Again, I click *end*, and again, they call back. I slip into the staff restroom and lock the door before I answer.

"Hello?"

"Stevie?" an unfamiliar, high-pitched voice asks.

"Who is this?"

"You don't know me, but we have a mutual connection."

"Um, okay?"

"You're Mason's Stevie, right? You're the new woman in his life."

The blood drains from my face, and the room turns cold. "What? Who *are* you?"

"I'm Amy." She says this like I should know who Amy is. Should I *know* who Amy is?

"Is that supposed to mean something to me?" I manage.

She releases a cold, humorless laugh. "Of course, he never even told you my name."

I want to disconnect and turn off my phone. I should. But I'm stuck, intrigued, despite the wave of nausea rising in my gut.

"Hello? Are you still there?"

I clear my throat. "What do you want?"

"Do you truly love them?"

"What does it matter to you? What is this?"

She's unresponsive. Pressing a hand against my stomach, closing my eyes, I ask the question I'm not sure I want an answer to.

"What's Mason to you?"

Silence.

"Who *are* you?" I ask again.

There's a heavy breath, and then my life implodes.

"This is his wife."

His wife. His *wife?* No.

"But his wife is dead," I whisper, hardly registering I've said it out loud.

"What was that?" she asks.

"Nothing."

"Look, Stevie. I just...I want to know whoever Mason's with now is going to be good for my son. I want to know they're both taken care of."

I end the call. Immediately, she calls back. I take a long, slow breath before I answer. "I don't know what the hell this is, but I am *not* having this conversation with a complete stranger."

I disconnect, block the number just to be sure, pocket my phone, run to the toilet, and throw up.

This is his wife? The words run circles in my head.

A wife. He has a *wife*. But she's dead, right? She's dead—he told me she's dead. It's common knowledge in that house that *she is dead!*

Except she called me. Amy called me. Amy? His wife? He's never even told me her name before. I've never asked because talking about her hurt him and I wanted to spare him pain. *I* wanted to spare *him!*

Tears come without warning. The hysterical sobbing follows. I can't breathe. I don't want to; I'd rather die. It hurts so much, and I'd rather drop dead in this bathroom than exist in this moment of betrayal and disbelief another second, those words shredding me from the inside out. *This is his wife.*

There's a hesitant rap at the door. "Stevie?" Marge calls. "Stevie, sweetie, are you alright?"

I swallow my choking sobs and blow my nose. "I've been sick," I answer. "Can I go home?"

"Can I do anything? Do you need some water?"

"I need to go home," I repeat.

"Oh, okay. That's fine. We're fine here without you for the day. Do I need to call you a ride?"

"No. I just need a minute."

When her footsteps fade away, I call Merrin with shaky hands.

She answers quickly. "I know I said to keep me posted, but—"

"I need someone to pick me up at Mason's in ten minutes. Can you get away?"

"Um..."

"Can you? Or could you ask Nan for me? Please?"

"What's wrong?"

"Merrin, I need someone to pick me up at Mason's in ten minutes. Can you or your mom do that?"

"Stevie, what's going on?"

"Merrin!" I snap, trembling. "Can you be there?"

"Ten minutes," she promises softly.

"Don't come inside. Just wait for me."

I march out of the building, taking deep breaths, willing my tears to dry and my throaty cries to stay suppressed until I get this next part over with.

WALKING THROUGH MASON'S HOUSE, I latch onto a silent prayer that this is all some misunderstanding. A cruel joke. Anything but that he has a secret wife—one he's told me is gone—*dead* and gone.

I find Mason perched on the edge of his bed, his eyes downcast, and that silent prayer—that tiny shred of hope—settles like a boulder in my chest. My legs are Jell-o as I enter the room that, in the last few months, has become almost as much mine as it is his. I have clothes and shoes in the closet, books on the shelves, toiletries in the bathroom. It's all ready for me to move in as soon as we're married. Or before, if Max loosens the reigns a little bit. Except now, a single phone call has threatened that future.

It can't be true, though. That all this time, I've been the other woman? Impossible.

Braced against the doorframe, I force the words out. My voice shakes but doesn't break. I wobble, but don't fall. I *refuse* to fall.

"So, this talk," I say. "It wouldn't by chance be about your wife? Would it?"

"My ex-wife," he whispers, his lips quivering.

"Do you mind explaining why your dead wife just called me? Because 'confusing' does not even *begin* to cover it."

He rakes his hands through his hair, cursing.

"Well?"

Nothing.

"Explain yourself!" I scream.

Mason stares at his hands, which he folds and refolds in his lap. "I met Amy around the time I got my master's," he says. "We were off and on again. She wasn't the most stable person. She'd break up with me on a whim. Then come to me, threatening to harm herself if I didn't take her back. It was so messed up. But I was young and stupid. Dammit, I was stupid. But I thought... I thought I loved her? I guess. And she could be *really* fun. We had adventures. You know?"

Adventures? I swallow down bile.

"It went on a couple years. She got pregnant just after I accepted a professorship in Seattle. University of Washington. Just as I decided to move on from her and grow up. By that time, we were more off than on, and I knew she wasn't the great love of my life. I knew I didn't love her at all, actually. I'd caught onto her manipulative nature by then, but none of that mattered anymore because we were having a baby. I couldn't walk away from that. I married her. I thought it was the right thing to do.

"She went completely overboard after the baby came." He sighs, clenching his fists. "Look, I'm not cruel. I know postpartum depression is real, but this was something else. I couldn't leave her alone with Daniel. She couldn't seem to remember to feed him or change him. I came home once and she'd just left him alone in the house because she 'couldn't take it anymore.' By some miracle, he was just sleeping peacefully, no harm done. She would *scream* at him. I don't know if it ever got worse than that, and I pray it never did.

"I tried—*really* tried—to get her help. She was Daniels' *mother*. I wasn't going to throw her out, though I wanted to. She was awful. Vindictive, even. I got her an appointment with this highly recommended therapist, and she went just to throw out claims that I was abusive." He pauses, shaking his head and pounding a fist against his knee. "Everywhere she went, she made scenes, got jealous, threw out false allegations, and tried to snuff out any light in the room. I wanted a divorce, but I also didn't want to lose my son. Family court almost *always* sides with the mother." He looks at me with glistening eyes. "Stevie, I was *scared*."

After a moment his gaze falls back to the floor.

"One day, I took the baby with me to run some errands. We were only gone a couple hours. When I got back, the house had been raided and there was a note saying she'd never loved me or Daniel, and that we'd never find her, so not to bother trying. She had to have been waiting for a chance with help standing by. She took almost everything, not just the small stuff. Then she vanished. And that was it. That was the end."

My head droops between my knees as I try to digest the Amy saga.

"Why?" I ask through clenched teeth. I hold my head high again, looking right at him, daring him to meet my gaze. He doesn't. "Why did you lie?"

"I moved back home. Took a job at WSU so my parents could help me out with Daniel. We were angry, and we just wanted it to be like it never happened. We started joking about it. Someone asked about Amy, and my mom said something like, 'She died in a horrible accident. Very painful and messy.' Maybe it was unnecessarily mean, but the whole 'she's dead' thing stuck. Anytime someone brought her up, we'd come up with something new. A piano fell on her head. Mauled by some innocuous animal. Taken in the rapture. Daniel wasn't meant to hear any of it, but when he did, I couldn't bring myself to correct him."

He looks back at me, sniffling and wiping his fingers across his wet cheeks. "How—" his voice cracks, and he tosses his hands up. "How do you tell your child his mother just left him? That she never even tried? That she had a hundred resources at her disposal, and instead, she burned it all down and bolted?" He takes a slow breath and clears his throat. "I figured he was better off thinking she died than that she didn't love us. Didn't love him."

Questions and accusations build in my throat but stay trapped there.

"When you came to me about Daniel's fixation with death..." His voice cracks again. "I know I should have been clear. There were so many times I wanted to tell you the whole truth. It was cowardly and shitty and stupid of me not to, and I know I can't fix that. But Stevie... I never meant... I'm so sorry."

I take several slow breaths before I speak. "So, you're divorced?" He doesn't speak. "Mason? You *are* divorced, right?"

"Almost," he whispers.

"*Almost?*"

"I never served her with papers because I feared what that would mean for Daniel. But when I met you, I knew. I knew I *had* to move on. I tracked her down almost immediately. And, as I suspected, she didn't go down without a fight. We've been dealing with family court, lawyers, child psychologists...she's made it difficult every step of the way."

My head falls into my hands. *Please, no.* "This whole time we've been together, you've been in a custody battle with your not-quite-ex-wife? And you didn't *tell me*? No. You didn't just *not* tell me, you let me assume she was *dead*."

He's shaking. He's falling apart. But I keep pushing because so am I.

"Mason, how could you?"

"I tried to wait. Stevie, I tried. I didn't want to lie to you, but anytime I *tried* to tell you, I—" He pulls at his hair, his face. "I just *couldn't*. So, I tried to wait it out and not tell you how I felt until after everything was final. But it just kept dragging *on* and *on*, and I loved you so much. I wanted one happy thing in my life. Just *one* good thing to cling to."

Pieces fall into place. All those looks of pain, all those almost-moments. All that *I can't*, and *you deserve more*.

"All those *appointments?*" I ask. He nods. "This *whole* time. As you proposed. As you talked about our future together—you, me, and

Danny. As you agreed to me *adopting* him." I drag my hands down my face. "Oh my gosh."

"I didn't know how to tell you. I didn't know how to talk about any of it because I was terrified that *talking* about it would make it too real to handle. Family courts notoriously favor the mother, even under the most asinine circumstances. Even with all her history of instability and her walking out on him as an infant. Even with my parents and other witnesses to her behavior back then. Even with the proof that I'm a *good dad* who can more than provide for him and all his interviews with that counselor, and the counselor testifying that he was a happy, healthy kid, and had a great, stable home life. Even with the police report from the day she took everything. Even with *all* of it, it could so easily have gone the other way. Especially once I asked for forfeiture of all her rights, so you could adopt Danny. It added fuel to her fire, and she just fought harder."

I shake my head. "This *whole* time," I say again. It's all I can think to say. It's all I can *think*. All this time, he's been making promises he wasn't sure he could deliver.

"I just kept telling myself it'd be over soon, and that we'd talk it through and move on. But the longer it went on, the worse I felt, and the more I needed to tell you. That's why I asked you to come over. I was going to lay it all out, tell you *everything*. But then I got a call a while ago that she'd quit fighting it. That we could sign papers as soon as tomorrow."

"What changed? And why—*how* did she call me?"

"One I know, one I can speculate. What changed is that her supervised visit over the weekend was a disaster, and she blew it. Big time. Then she followed Daniel and me afterward. We stopped at a diner for milkshakes and she came in. Sat next to us. It scared the crap out of Dan. I had to call the police. It was a whole thing. But her violating the terms for visitation worked in my favor. So, it was kind of a blessing, I guess."

"A blessing," I spit. "Great. While I thought you and Danny were out just having *guy time*, some vindictive bitch was stalking him? And I'm not even worthy of that information?"

He shakes his head, sniffling. "No, Stevie. Of course you should have known. You should have always known. I know I was stupid, but I was scared shitless of losing my son. *And* you. I didn't have room to let you in because that paralyzing fear was taking up *all* the space." I chew on the insides of my cheeks, not responding. "She must have swiped my phone in that diner—probably when I was talking with the responding officers—because when we left, I couldn't find it in my pocket. It was back in the booth. I didn't think much about it. Until she called, right after I hung up with the lawyer. She just *laughed*. This shrill sound of pure evil. And I knew. She was probably tired of fighting and knew she'd blown it up. So, she rifled through my conversations and saw a perfect opportunity to mess with my life one last time before she surrendered."

I scoff. "With *your* life?" Chewing on my lip, I try to decide which should come first: verbally or physically assaulting him. But all I do is sit there, sinking further and further into the pit Mason's dug for me.

"If I'd just *told* you, it wouldn't have caught you off guard. I hate that I put you through that. I've been such an idiot. Stevie, I never meant for you to... I never meant..."

"For me to be the other woman?" I blurt.

"No. *You* were never the other woman. And we never... I mean, we never..."

Another lightbulb moment. Another piece falling into place. My heart plummets into my stomach.

"So that's why you held back. Why you insisted we wait. You weren't waiting for *us* to be married. You were waiting to *not* be married to *her*. You had to draw the line somewhere, right? Give yourself some moral compass so you could sleep at night. 'It's okay I'm lying my *ass* off about being married because at least we aren't screwing.' *Right?*" My words carry a venom even I haven't prepared myself for.

He closes his eyes, visibly shuddering. "Stevie, that's not..."

"How, Mason?" I yell. "How could you leave me on the outside like that?" The floodgates open. "Can you imagine how I felt when she...when she..." A foreign groan escapes the back of my throat. "'This is his *wife?*'"

He clenches and unclenches his hands, opening his mouth but never offering up anything other than a few disjointed, meaningless syllables.

"I should have known it was all too perfect. *You*, with your grand gestures and smooth voice, were too perfect. Of course, it was all a lie!" I look for something to throw, but there's nothing. "You told me you loved me." A cold, crushing weight materializes on my chest. "You said I c-could trust you. That I was s-safe with you."

He drops to the floor, crawling toward me. He tries to take my hands in his, but I pull away. "Stevie, I *do* love you. That was never a lie. I swear."

"How could you?" Saliva drips down my chin as I spit out the words in a weak, squeaky voice. I wipe my mouth with my sleeve. "I trusted you. Do you even grasp what that means for me? I told you *everything*. All the ugliest parts of my life. But you kept the most important parts of yours a secret, all the while letting me fall in love with you, with Daniel." *Daniel.* I clutch at my chest. "Oh, gosh. What do I tell that sweet boy?"

Mason puts a hand on my shoulder, and I shove him off. "Don't!"

He calls out, as though my rebuff is more akin to a bullet or a knife through his heart.

"What did you think I would say?" I ask. "When you sat me down today and said, 'Oh, by the way, all this time I've been married to a woman I told you was dead, and we're duking it out in court,' what did you think I would say?"

He flinches, then looks at the floor. "I don't know."

"Did you really think it wouldn't change things?"

"I hoped it wouldn't," he admits. "I hoped you'd understand that I've been hanging on by a thread, and the only thing—Stevie, the *only* thing keeping me going has been you and Danny. And I knew if I lost one or both of you, I'd fall apart, so I kept you in the dark, but I hated myself every second of it.

"I hoped you'd at least give me credit for telling you now, for not moving forward with the wedding until you knew the truth." His eyes meet mine. "I'm so sorry you didn't hear it from me first. I never wanted you to hear it from anyone else. I never wanted you caught up in this mess at all, but I was weak. I just wanted to be with you so badly."

Another piece of the puzzle. Another moment of clarity.

"Clean this up," I say, echoing Miranda's words back in January. "Her hostility makes so much sense now."

"It was all for me. Never you. Yes, at first, my mom was scared. Of history repeating itself. Of Danny getting hurt. She saw you were young, and she saw how...how *smitten* I was... It was a lot for her to swallow. But mostly she was angry with me for not telling you the truth. I promised her I would, but the longer things went on, the more terrified I became, the harder it was to say anything."

"Instead, you just kept stringing me along in some asinine delusion."

"It was real. *This* is real." He reaches for my shoulders, but I recoil. If he touches me, I'll cave to him, and then I'll only be deeper in this pit. I can't risk it, even if it's killing me to be so close to him, yet not wrapped in his arms.

"It was *all* real," he says. "Don't pretend like it hasn't been. I love you. I want to marry you, and I want you to live here and for us to be a family—you, me, and Daniel. Look around..." He gestures to the room. "This house feels like yours already. I hate when you leave every night. It always feels wrong. You've felt it, too. You know you belong here and always have. I don't ever want you to leave."

"Then you should have given me the choice to stay."

"I'm *begging* you to stay, Stevie."

"How can I? This wasn't some little white lie. You promised me a life you couldn't even be sure was a possibility. You begged for my trust and then shattered it. I would have given you *everything*. I would have stood by your side and fought with you if you'd just let me in. But you hid it all away, like it wasn't my hopes and dreams hanging in the balance, too. You made me insignificant. You *broke* my *heart*, Mason."

He closes his eyes, flinching at the impact of my words.

With trembling hands, I remove my ring and place it in his palm. His eyes fly open.

"No. No, no, no. Stevie, don't. Please, don't."

I remove the truck and house keys from my keyring and set them on the floor.

"I'm begging you, Stevie. Don't do this. I'll do whatever you want. We can do couple's counseling. Work through this. I'll do anything. Just please don't go."

I stand from the floor, breathing a heavy sigh and wiping snot and tears from my face.

"I'm going to pull myself together, and I'll go say a quick and light goodbye to Daniel. I won't let him see me sad, but that's the best I can do. I hope you don't have any trouble finding a new babysitter."

"Dammit, Stevie, you're not the *babysitter*! How are you so cavalier right now?"

"I'm changing my number. I refuse to live in a world where *she* knows how to reach me."

I walk out of the room, but before I make it down the hall, Mason rushes ahead of me and blocks the top of the staircase.

"Stevie, wait. I love you. It kills me that I hurt you. You have to believe that. Don't go. Don't give up on us, please." He takes my face in his hands. "I am *so* sorry. God forgive me, I'm so sorry." He rests his forehead against mine, offering a final plea. "*Stay.*"

"I'm sure God will forgive you, Mason. But I'm not sure I can. Just let me go."

That breaks him. He's sobbing and shaking as he drops his hands and steps aside, but I leave without a single glance back.

MERRIN'S WAITING for me outside Mason's house. I give her directions to Wes and Miranda's, and she forces down all the questions I know she's dying to ask.

I do my best to appear calm and collected as I knock on the door. The sympathetic sigh Miranda exerts when she answers the door almost unhinges me.

"Don't take this the wrong way, Stevie, but I truly hoped I wouldn't see you today." I nod. "Come in."

I follow Miranda into the living room. "Where is he?"

"I told him. I told Mase he'd lose you if he didn't make it right. Is there anything I can do?"

"Where's my—where's Daniel?"

"I'll get him for you." She turns to leave and then turns back. "Sweetie..." She hugs me, and I struggle to breathe. "I should have *made* him come clean from the start. I failed you. I'm so sorry. This has all just been so difficult and scary. We'd think we were near the end and then she'd throw a low blow, and we'd have to start all over again. She's made it hell for all of us."

I hug her briefly before pushing her away. "Miranda, I have to keep it together. I can't lose it in front of him, and every single second, it gets harder not to break."

"I understand." She wipes a tear from her cheek before leaving the room.

Moments later, Daniel comes running in. "I didn't know you was coming to see me, Stevie! Where's Daddy? Are we going home?"

"No, baby, your daddy's not here." I sit on the couch and pull him onto my lap. "I just needed to come say a quick hello, and give you a hug, and then I have to go."

He contorts his little face and cocks his head. "Why?"

"Sweetie, I just..." What do I say? The truth seems too harsh, but lying can't be the right answer. Can it?

"Danny Boy, I have to go away for a bit. Like on a trip. I don't know how long it will be."

"Where are you going?"

"Away, Sweetie. Just away. I... I won't be coming over to watch you at nighttime anymore."

"But how will I go to sleep if you don't sing to me?"

I hug him to my chest and kiss his head. "You'll sleep just fine. I promise."

"How many days before you come back and we all get married?"

Every word a knife.

"Oh, Danny. My heart. Stevie loves you so, so much. You know that, right?"

He giggles. "Yes, silly."

"Good. Just hold onto that while I'm gone. Just remember I love you, and whenever you miss me, sing one of our favorite songs. Okay?"

"Will it be two days before you come back?"

"Baby, I can't give you a number. I wish I could."

"You have to come back, Stevie. I promise to have good behavior. I'll brush my teeth. I won't tell you no when you asks me to."

I hide a sob with a laugh and kiss his head again. "I'm not leaving because of anything you did. You hear me? You're the best boy."

"But I don't like goodbyes," he pouts.

"They're the worst, huh?" I say. He nods. "So maybe we should say, 'I'll see you later.' Would that be better?"

Daniel hugs my neck tighter. "When is later?"

"Oh, my inquisitive little man," I sigh. "I don't know. But I promise it'll all be okay." It won't be okay; he'll miss me, and I'll ache for him. But it's better to lie at this point to spare his fragile toddler heart. I'll shamefully leave Mason to deal with the rest of it. "I will see you soon, Danny."

"Okay," he whines.

"It will be fine, buddy. Everything will be fine. You will miss me for a little while. But then you won't miss me anymore."

I smile at him—the best I can muster. But the sobs start creeping back up in my throat. He rubs my arm with his tiny hand, grinning back at me, and I know it's only a matter of moments before I crumble. I call for Miranda and pass him over. He clings to me but eventually relents with a whimper.

I kiss his hair one last time, breathing him in. "Stevie loves you so much," I whisper, then I bolt from the house, leaving any remaining pieces of my shattered heart with the confused little boy I almost called my own.

CHAPTER
27

N ancy and Merrin take turns holding me while I cry, bringing me meals and drinks. When I go forty-eight hours without sleeping, Nancy forces me to drink some nasty tea concoction that knocks me out.

Sleep remedies nothing.

When I wake up, my life is still in pieces.

Between lack of sleep, lack of will to eat, and fits of hysterical crying, my body breaks down, and I get sick. *Really* sick. It's more of a relief than anything. The physical ache distracts me from the pain of broken promises. My fevered, fuzzy brain can't handle thinking about, well, anything. It's a nice bonus.

For days, I pray for it just to take me. Swallow me whole, and let me fade into my sheets. But with Merrin and Nancy at the helm, I'm not going anywhere.

They care for me at a level I wasn't aware existed, and as I start to gain back my faculties, I fill them in on the details. I talk Merrin out of confronting Mason and Nancy from confronting Wes and Miranda. I've never seen Nancy angry at anyone, for anything, but she has choice words for those two—mostly Miranda.

"It wasn't their business to tell," I argue.

"As a mother, she should never have sat back and let that happen. I get wanting to protect your child, but you're someone's child, too."

I begin to protest—I haven't been anyone's child in years. But then I notice the tears in Nancy's eyes, and I realize she's talking about her. About *us.*

"You think of me as...as yours?" I ask.

She pulls me into a constricting hug. "Darn right, I do. I'll be your Mama as long as you let me."

"I think I'd like that." My words are muffled by her shirt. "Nancy?"

"Yes, sweetie."

"Is it super weird if I call you Mom sometimes?"

She doesn't say anything for a long time.

"Dang it!" Merrin chimes in behind me. "Now *I'm* crying."

I pull back and look at Nancy. Steady streams of tears fall down her face. "I wish I could have always been there for you," she says.

"Hey, I found you guys eventually," I say. "Thank goodness I did because I can't imagine going through this alone."

Merrin joins us in a sloppy, warm group hug, and I cry more, though it seems impossible I have any tears left.

"You'll never be alone again," Merrin says. "I'll crowd you so close you'll *wish* for solitude."

"I love you guys," I slobber. "This hurts."

"I know, baby," Nancy says.

"No, I mean, I kind of can't breathe. Y'all squeezing a little too tight."

We pull apart, laughing and wiping our faces. I pull my shirt up to clear snot and spit along with the tears.

Merrin sighs, staring at me. "Frosting?" she asks.

This time, I don't turn her down.

After two weeks of missed classes and work-study shifts, I have a choice to make. Keep pushing forward, or spend the rest of my days in bed crying about the life I almost had.

The decision is harder than it should be.

In my first days back at work, every cup of spilled milk brings tears to my eyes and hugs from children often send me running to the bathroom so I can pull myself together. In school, everything seems unfamiliar and unachievable. My professors start using phrases like, "You might be forced to take an incomplete."

By spring break, though, I find some sort of rhythm, catch up on my work, and see a light at the end of the semester. I can do this. I've stopped crying at work. I closed on the house. I'm researching cars to buy and setting up an IRA. I've totally got this.

Except the thing is, I can't stay busy every second of every day. And as soon as I share a family dinner with the Caraways and retreat to my room, I fall apart. Every night I wallow, and I cry, and I watch the video of my parents on a loop until I fall asleep. Then I do it all again in the morning, forcing one foot in front of the other, pouring all my energy into school and work until there's nothing left to expend energy on except grieving.

I DON'T BELONG HERE. I love the Caraways, but I barely know Fin. Seems like this small gathering of close friends and family for a wedding reception shouldn't involve someone he's met a total of twice in his life—the second time being this morning. Granted, it's beautiful here; I definitely can't complain about the scenery. When watching all the happy people on the dance floor becomes too much for my heart to take, I remove my high heels and trek barefoot across the soft grass, away from the festivities.

Artie and Lucy have roughly five-hundred acres in all, so I'm told. I have no idea how big the actual yard is, but it's big enough that by the time I reach the wooden fence along the west side, the dance music has faded into distant thumps and vague melodies. After testing the fence's integrity, I climb onto the top rail and watch the vibrant sunset.

"Murphy," I sigh, taking it all in.

"Beautiful, isn't it?"

I startle as a voice interrupts my solitude. When I look over, I find Artie leaning against a tree near the fence line. He's not intruding on my moment of peace; I'm intruding on his.

"Sorry," I say. "I didn't see you. Do you want me to leave?"

"Nah. I was just taking a breather. Stay. Enjoy. Palouse sunsets are the best part about living out here. Even better than the fact my nearest neighbors are about a mile away."

"Oh wow," I say after a low whistle. "Is it painful to have so many people here disrupting the isolation?"

He laughs, then walks toward the fence, bracing himself against the post a few feet from me. "I can take it once in a while. For family, anyway. Honestly, I was kind of a crappy brother to Fin most of our childhood, so this feels like the least I could do, even if I spend a good chunk of time complaining about it."

"I can't imagine any of you being crappy siblings. You all seem so close now, even given the distance. Merrin shows me some of your group texts. I wish I had that many inside jokes with anyone."

He lifts a shoulder. "It took time. As we all became adults, our relationships changed. You know?"

I look back at the rolling landscape, talking to the empty air in front of me. "I've never known anyone long enough for a relationship to evolve like that. I always wondered how it would have been between my uncle and me once I went off to college. Whether we'd grow closer as I gained life experience, and he had a chance to live without me for a while. Whether it would sever our weak bond completely. I never got to find out."

It's silent between us for a beat.

"That sucks," he finally says through a heavy exhale.

"Yup."

"So what's it like being adopted into a loud, obnoxious family after such a quiet life?"

"Who you calling loud and obnoxious?" Merrin says behind us. "Stevie, you okay? You ran off."

I turn around, smiling at her. "I didn't run. I walked. Slowly." She rolls her eyes. "I'm just taking in the view," I assure her. "Nothing's wrong. You shouldn't have pulled yourself away for my sake. Go, enjoy your family time."

She glares at me. "That includes *you*."

"Well, duh. But you see me every day. You don't get to see your siblings often. Especially not Josie."

She nods, then leans against the fence, looking ahead of me. "Gosh, it's gorgeous out here. You won the jackpot with this place, Art."

He lets out a sharp laugh. "If by 'won the jackpot' you mean 'inherited a butt-load of never-ending, backbreaking work,' then yeah. Yeah, I did." He looks at me, gesturing at Merrin. "She helped me out *one* summer for wheat harvest. *One.* She never came back."

"I was thirteen!" she squeaks. "And it was *hard!*"

"Compared to building houses in Ecuador?" I ask.

She nods, wide-eyed. "I mean, I *have* matured a lot since then. I'm not proud of how much I whined that summer, Art. Sorry you had to put up with that."

He waves off her apology, and we all go back to watching the sky. Only a sliver of sun remains visible behind the rolling hills, but the colors cast across the landscape are still unreal. Somehow, the earth shimmers beneath them.

"Do you need help this summer?" I ask.

"You offering?" Artie responds through a laugh.

"Yeah, actually. All my summer classes are online."

"Stevie," Merrin groans, "you're taking the maximum credits. In a *condensed* term. The workload is going to be ridiculous. Just enjoy what little summer you'll have. You work too hard."

"I don't like free time," I say, still watching the sun disappear.

"Well, I can't pay well," Artie says. "But I always need help."

"Keep your money," I say. For the first time in my life, I don't need it. "We're family now, right? I'll do it for meals and a couch."

"We *have* a guest room," he says. "It's yours if you're serious."

"I am. Realistically I don't even need to go back to Spokane. I brought my laptop with me. There's got to be a Walmart or thrift store or something nearby, right? I can buy a few changes of clothes and start right away."

Artie lets out a low whistle. "That's hardcore, Stevie."

"I told you. I don't like free time." Free time means thinking, and lately, my mind goes immediately to the deepest, darkest, most depressing memories.

"Well, no chance you'll get much of that around here."

"Art," Merrin says, "Can you give us a minute?"

"I should go be a good host, anyway." He looks at me before he leaves. "Whatever you decide. No pressure *or* judgment from me. Do what's right for you. Okay?"

I nod. "Okay."

With Artie gone, Merrin cozies up to me, grabbing my hand.

"Stevie, are you sure? I mean, I know you're hurting and I hate it. But are you *sure* this is the right way to handle it?"

"You wanna stick it out with me?" I ask, undeterred. "Might be fun to work together."

"I don't think *fun* is the word you're looking for."

"Oh, don't be a killjoy."

"No summer break for me, remember?"

"Oh. Right. Hadn't thought of that."

"Yup."

There's no *condensed* term for Merrin this summer. Which is great for her because she's finally to the point she gets to work in the school's salon with *real* clients, and I can't wait for her to outshine everyone else there.

"Don't love that," I admit. "You are my better half."

She nudges me. I nudge her back.

"Be that as it may, you shouldn't base your decisions around me," Merrin says. "If you want to stay and work, I'll support you. Besides, I'll be back the first week in July for our family reunion."

I sigh. "A whole month without you."

"Well, if you're taking three classes and working for Art, I doubt you'll even notice my absence."

I nudge her again. "I always notice your absence, Mer. You're my person."

With a sigh, she wraps her arms around me. I almost fall, and we laugh as I steady myself.

"You're my person, too," she says. "Even if you are abandoning me to become a farmer."

"I'm not becoming anything. I'm just..." *Surviving.* Like I've always done. Except for that brief period of time when I had everything I never knew I always wanted. Before it all fell apart and left a Mason and Daniel shaped hole in my heart. "Maybe when I get to the other side of this, I'll breathe a little easier. It still hurts, you know?"

"I know."

The sun vanished a while ago, though the earth is still well illuminated by the constellations and a three-quarter moon.

"He still texts me sometimes. Just to check in."

"Merrin..."

"I let it slip when you were sick. That really worried him."

"Mer—"

"I only ever read or respond because I want to make sure he's absolutely miserable. He is, by the way. And as your best friend, that makes me feel better. But also, as your best friend, it makes me—"

"You should get back," I whisper. "Who knows the next time you and all your siblings will be together again. Unless Josie's planning on flying back out for the reunion?"

She pauses, taking a heavy, resigned breath. "No. She could only pick one, so she chose Fin's wedding."

"All the more reason to get back."

"You coming?"

I want to say, *no thanks.* I want to go inside, shut it all away, and let everyone enjoy themselves without the weight of my sadness dragging them down. Instead, I plaster a smile on my face—even though Merrin probably knows it's fake—and I walk back with her. We dance like idiots to a cliché party playlist, and her joy is so palpable, it almost feels like my own. Almost.

Josie, Merrin, and I are bunking with a couple of Artie and Lucy's kids. The sleeping bag on the floor isn't an issue, but Josie snores. At three a.m., I sneak out of the room and into the kitchen, helping myself to a glass of orange juice.

Sitting at the dining table, I pull out my phone and open my photo gallery. Something I've been avoiding for months; it hurts too much.

A picture of Daniel, Mason, and I brings instant tears that sting my tired eyes.

"Stevie?"

The soft whisper in the darkness startles me. I clear my throat and wipe my face before I look at Nancy, shuffling toward me.

"Did I wake you?" I ask.

She sits next to me before reaching over and patting my arm. "No, honey. My bladder woke me up, but then I heard you, and I wanted to make sure it wasn't one of the little ones up to trouble."

"Ah." I nod.

She dips her head toward my phone. "What's so riveting at three a.m.?" I slide my phone over to her, and she offers a sympathetic frown. "I see."

"Believe it or not, I haven't looked at pictures of either of them in months. Not that they aren't permanently tattooed on my eyelids."

She looks closer at the picture. "I forgot how gorgeous that kid is. That single dimple and those baby blues? Oof. My heart."

"He held me so tight, Nan. And I let go. Now I'm just some woman who walked into his life and right back out again. I doubt he even remembers me anymore."

Nancy shakes her head. "Don't underestimate a child's memory. Especially for the people and things they love."

The tears start up again. "It's like part of my soul is still back there with them. Like my heart grew legs and ran away from me."

Nancy squeezes my arm then slides the phone back. "I'll be right back," she says, then leaves. She returns a minute later with a long garment bag.

"Nan..." I cup my hand over my mouth. "*Mom*, is that...?"

"Josie went ahead and finished it, anyway, then brought it with her. She made it for you, honey. I'll hang onto it as long as you want. But it's yours."

I stand, getting close enough to run my hand over the protective bag. "Did you look? Is it perfect?"

"Trust me. If Jocelyn Caraway made it, it's perfect."

I pout, fiddling with the zipper. I want to look, but also, I don't. It'll hurt. Like everything else right now. Maybe it can't possibly hurt any worse than it already does?

"Think bohemian princess," Nan whispers. "Or a sophisticated woodland fairy."

"You *did* look."

She lifts a shoulder. "I couldn't help it."

I tug the zipper down enough to reveal princess lace, ruched sleeves, and a plunging neckline. With a groan, I zip it back up. Of course, it's perfect. I can tell without even seeing the rest of it.

"Look, baby," Nancy says, "I'll support your decision to stay behind and work. I will. And if at any point, you change your mind, I'll come get you and bring you home. You do what you think you need to do to process. So long as that's what you're doing."

I narrow my eyes. "What are you trying to say, Mom?" It still sounds weird any time I say it, but it's a good, wholesome weird, so I'll keep saying it.

"Honey, there's a difference between overcoming your pain and running from it. If taking a million credits and doing manual labor is going to help you grieve and move on, fantastic. But if you're just placing all your pain on the shelf and numbly going about your life, you're not doing yourself any favors. That very real and valid hurt? It'll get dusty, but it won't go away. One day you'll stumble upon it and it'll tear you wide open, putting you right back where you started."

I chew on my cheeks, twisting my lips back and forth. Isn't that exactly what I did all those years with what happened in the music room? Pretend it never happened? Shove it so far down I almost believed the lie. Until something came along and ripped me open. Until *Mason.*

"I'll hang this in the guest room closet," she says. "And when I come back in July, we can talk about what to do with it. Does that sound fair?"

Without words, but *with* tears, I nod.

She sighs. "Good. I'm gonna get some sleep. You should try and do the same. Night, sweetheart."

I offer a smile. "Night, Nan."

CHAPTER
28

Burying my pain is stupid, but I don't have the energy for healing right now. I'm too busy running myself into the ground. As suspected, between classes and working on Artie and Lucy's farm, I never have time for myself. It's perfect. Reckless? Possibly. I'll deal with that later.

The days run from dawn until dusk, and there's always a job, research, reading, or an assignment to keep me occupied.

Whatever Artie needs help with, I do. Though their biggest harvest—wheat—doesn't begin until mid-July, there are still never-ending tasks to be done. Whether to support the business side of their farming operation or help care for their animals and crops they raise for daily sustenance.

I weed the garden and work in hot, humid greenhouses. Mow the modest orchard and pick fruit. Move pipe and muck out the goat pen. I wake up at four—four in the bloody morning—every Saturday to do Farmer's Market.

I don't care what it is; I don't care if my efforts help turn a profit or simply *help*. I do everything I can possibly learn to do. At first, Artie hesitates anytime I offer to jump in and pick up a new skill, but after I easily master driving the tractor and towing a trailer, he quits questioning me.

By the time the sun sets on the vivid, rolling hills of The Palouse, I'm caked in layers of dirt, sweating from every pore, and wholly fatigued. After a shower and dinner, I watch the video of my parents until I fall asleep.

I'm able to get through the days without crying—without wallowing, even.

I hardly have time to miss anyone. Well, that's not true. When Merrin and her parents show up the weekend before the Fourth of July, I hug her for a solid two minutes before I relinquish her.

She looks me over, tilting her head from side to side, lifting my arms, and turning me around.

"Um, may I help you?"

"Just making sure you're the same person. You're about ten shades darker, and I think you've put on ten pounds of muscle."

I tug at her hair. "Look who's talking." Her once auburn locks are now bleached blond with rainbow tips. "It suits you," I say, then pull her in for another hug.

"Aw. Clearly, you couldn't breathe without me."

We separate, and I carry her bag into the house. Max brought their camper for him and Nancy, so Merrin and I are sharing the guest room. From what I'm told, by the time the sun sets tomorrow, the yard will be full of tents and campers. Caraway reunions are a big deal.

We both plop onto the guest bed and stare at the ceiling.

"I did miss you," I say. "Like, a whole bunch of a lot."

"But are you glad you stayed? Was it the right choice?"

I don't have an answer for that. I've done my best to block out Nancy's words as I've pushed myself beyond my physical and mental limits to avoid *processing*. She told me it wouldn't work, and I already knew from experience she was right. And sure enough, the longer I sit still, the more all those memories and shattered dreams crawl to the forefront of my mind. I'll likely be nothing but a pile of debris by the time this reunion is over.

"Stevie?"

"I don't think it was the *wrong* choice," I finally say. "No matter where I was, I think I would have done exactly the same as I did here."

"Stevie, nowhere else on earth would you have learned to back up a trailer. On a tractor."

I wave a dismissive hand. "What? Like it's hard?"

She glares at me. "You realize Artie has been giving Fin, Cece, and me hell because each of us, at one point, has spent part of our summer here helping him, and *none* of us did anything remotely impressive. You're a friggin' legend as far as he and Lucy are concerned. I don't know if you realize how much you've helped them."

"Well," I say, then let my lips fumble over a long exhale. "That makes me feel..."

"Proud? Accomplished?"

"Not particularly. Just glad I helped someone."

"Did it help *you*?" she asks.

I blink at the ceiling, feeling the familiar sting of salty tears.

"Stevie?"

When I can't suppress it any longer, I turn into her and sob.

No. It didn't help. It only delayed the inevitable.

BY THE TIME ARTIE, Max, and a couple other men I don't recognize fire up the outdoor grill the next evening, there are easily two hundred people loitering about. This is so foreign to me—families going out of their way and driving hundreds of miles to see each other and camp in the summer heat. I don't hate it; I just never knew it was a thing people actually *did*.

"Are your reunions always this well attended?" I ask Merrin, having just been introduced to yet another one of her cousins. I didn't even bother trying to retain a name.

"It depends. We only do it every four years, which usually gives everyone time to plan and budget for it. That helps."

"Where did you guys do this before Artie and Lucy got married?"

"We used to rent out a campground. I think one year we did it at my Grandpa Rowdy's place—my dad's dad. He doesn't have quite this much space, though. Our last reunion was the first time Artie was able to offer up his place. It works out so well here. Everyone can still camp out, but we're on private property outside city limits, so we get to do a pretty decent fireworks show. Can't do that at a campground."

I nod. "Well, I mean, you could. But Smokey the Bear would *not* be cool with that."

She laughs. "You're so weird. And I love it. Dang it, I missed you." She throws an arm around me. "Are you having a good time?"

"Of course."

"Stevie," she sighs.

"Mer, I promise. I'm enjoying myself." In reality, the sight of this happy crew makes me a little queasy and sad. Merrin's nieces and nephews keep referring to me as "Auntie Stevie" and hugging my legs, which only compounds all the grief I've been drowning in since I quit drowning myself in work to participate in this reunion.

"Well, if you need a break from all the people, you can go hide in your room. I'll tell anyone who asks you have a migraine and not to bother you. Should buy you an hour or two alone."

"Thanks, babe."

"Oh! I know!" She clutches my arm. "Let's go steal Arwin's baby. You can't be sad around a baby."

"Well, who can argue with that logic?"

She pulls me along behind her as I wonder whether this will be a welcomed distraction or just another thing that makes me long for all I've lost.

Barbeque. Bonfires. Marshmallow roasting. Sing-alongs. It all starts blending together at some point. I try to enjoy myself and make conversation, but somewhere between a slightly botched rendition of "American Pie" around the bonfire and a large group starting a game of flashlight tag, I give up and go inside.

In my pajamas, I curl up under the covers of my bed and open the video I've seen a thousand times and still treasure as much as the first time.

When my mother starts singing her signature lullaby, I turn the volume to full and sink further beneath the sheets. As the song ends, and I sniffle, I hear a quiet knock. Nancy's standing in the doorway wearing her *Concerned Mom* face.

"Hey," I say, sitting up. "Come in."

I scoot over, and she sits beside me in the bed, not saying a word. She looks at my laptop. Relaxing my head against her shoulder, I start it over, and we watch it together. Reels of my life from birth until about age two, when—I assume—the camera broke. I wonder why they never got a new one. Maybe they just endeavored to be that couple who lived in the moment rather than filming everything? Or maybe they couldn't afford it. Or maybe they just forgot.

"Wow, Stevie," Nancy sighs. "That's special. And that lullaby?"

"Right? I was such a horrible sleeper my mom had to write a song about it."

This makes her laugh. "I had some terrible sleepers in my time. I get it. She handled it far better than I did, though. What a beautiful voice."

"Yeah."

"Merrin told me back when Mason salvaged the footage for you. Such a treasure. I can't even imagine what that felt like."

"Wonderful. Horrible. Beautiful. Tragic. Repeat."

"Sounds about right."

"Overall, it's just a blessing. I could hardly remember their voices anymore. Then…"

"Mason," she finishes.

"Yeah. Then Mason."

"It's thin, you know. That line between love and hate. Sometimes you feel like you're straddling it or jumping back and forth from one side to the other multiple times a day."

I sit up. "I don't buy that."

She slides me a look, arching a brow. "Oh, honey. I've been

married thirty-five years. Trust me. You can love a person three laps around the sun and back and still feel the urge to stab them in their sleep."

A sharp laugh releases from my lips. "But isn't that usually over the small stuff? All those tiny offenses that build through the years until they seem huge. Not legitimately *huge* things. He didn't forget my birthday or say something insensitive—he fed me lie after lie. He hollowed me out, Nan."

She puts her arm around me. "Baby, I know. What he did was awful and unfair. But here's the question I've asked myself a thousand times over the years, when I'm debating whether to let things go, talk them through, or give into my rage."

"*You* give into rage?" I ask, not believing her.

"A few times. It's never a pretty look, but there are times you've gotta let yourself be angry. But I digress. The question I ask myself is this: did he do this to intentionally hurt me?"

I laugh, thinking about Max. "Has the answer to that question ever been yes?"

"Rarely. Rarely, he's acted impulsively, usually because he was angry, and I was angry, and we were both just giving into our rage rather than talking it through. I told you, it's never a pretty look."

"I know Mason never set out to hurt me," I sigh. "He was just... stupid. And scared. But also so, *so* stupid."

"I'll give you that. It was monstrously idiotic. Reckless, even. But as a parent, I can also see the validity of his fear. He's right, you know. Family court often ignores the evidence and favors the mother, regardless of whether it's right for the child."

"I know," I say. "Which I think only makes this all hurt more. That he knew there was a possibility it was all going to fall apart, and he still asked me out. Then asked me to *marry* him. When I asked about adopting Daniel, he said yes. All while the future was so fragile and uncertain."

"Maybe he was just desperately trying to grasp at hope. Maybe clinging to the dream of a future with you was all that kept him sane while his world was burning. I can't imagine keeping it together if someone was trying to take one of my babies. Especially back when they were legitimately babies."

I mull that over while Nancy keeps an arm around me, resting her head atop mine.

"Look, honey, I'm not trying to make light of what happened. I'm just doing what moms do."

That makes me smile. "And what is it that moms do?"

"Sometimes they have to say the hard things no one wants to hear."

First, I laugh, then I cry. She shushes me, rubbing my arm and pressing her lips to my hair.

"I wish I could hate him," I whisper. "This would be easier if I could just hate him." I cry harder.

"Oh, Stevie," she coos. "If feelings were simple, the world would be a very different and boring place. All joy. No pain. If you want to hate him, or if you want to let go and walk away for *good*, that's totally your call. And no one can tell you it's wrong. But you need to really examine your heart before you take next steps."

"What next steps? I don't know where to go from here. I'm so lost."

"That's understandable, honey. It is. But you can't live where you are now. You can't unpack or hang curtains. Personally, I see why you walked away. I truly do. But now, you have a choice to make: pick yourself up, keep walking, and try again..."

"Or?" I ask, my voice weak.

"*Or*, figure out how to mend it. I can't tell you which way to go— no one can do that but you—but I can promise you that working yourself to death and hoping all your problems will just go away is not an option. That might have worked in the past, but you forget, you've got a mama now. You've got a whole family that loves you, and we won't sit by and watch you waste away. You hear me?"

I laugh, sniffling and bringing my shirt up to wipe my face. "Yes, ma'am," I say. "I hear you."

THE EXTENDED FAMILY packs up and leaves after a few nights, but Max and Nancy's crew hang around through the weekend. Between there being a new baby to dote on—Isabel, Arwin and Noah's latest— and the fact that there are six summer birthdays between all the kids and grandkids, Nancy wants to throw a collective birthday bash on Saturday before everyone parts ways Sunday morning.

I welcome the opportunity to help bake and decorate. Frosting cupcakes in the kitchen with Merrin while Cece and Lucy work on what they call a *fruit pizza*—a massive, frosted sugar cookie covered in glazed fruit—I hum absent-mindedly as family banter floats around me.

It's hard to believe, but I'm making *happy* memories in the kitchen again. Not just happy memories. *Family* memories. Not only is this an experience I'd once thought beyond my reach, it's also the first time I've felt content since my conversation with Nancy a few days ago.

Well, *almost* content.

Try as I might, I can't quit replaying my last moment with Mason over and again in my head. Sifting through each detail, trying to figure out if there was anything I could or should have done differently.

Was I too harsh? Maybe, but he was too careless.

I gave him my heart on a silver platter, and he shredded it. How can I ever trust anyone ever again?

And yet, there'd been no malice behind his actions. Only fear. I know as well as anyone, fear is a ruthless motivator.

All these questions and more take up permanent residence in my brain, always leading to something bigger.

Did I give him up too quickly?

I honestly don't know the answer.

"So," Merrin whispers, leaning in close. "You should know something."

"What's that?" I whisper back, smirking.

"I heard you talking to Mom the other night."

My jaw goes slack. "Oh."

"Yeah."

"And? Questions? Comments? Concerns?"

"Um, all of the above?" She nudges my shoulder with hers. "You just... It seems to me... You just sounded like maybe..."

"What is it, Merrin?"

"It sounds like maybe your feelings have changed. Or rather reverted to what they were before. Like maybe, if Mason were to try and reach out to you *now*, you might actually be willing to talk. Unlike a few months ago."

Pretty sure I've just swallowed a volcano because my stomach is lava.

"I don't..." I clear my throat, shaking my head. "I don't know. *Maybe.* But why do I get the feeling this isn't a hypothetical situation?"

She lifts a shoulder, scrunching her nose. "I was just thinking...I don't know. I was just thinking maybe you wouldn't hate me if I gave him your new number."

"I'll think about it, Merrin," I offer with a grin. She smiles back, then we resume frosting cupcakes.

A knock on the door sends Cece's oldest daughter Casey running through the house screaming, "I got it! I got it! I got it!"

Every mom in the house hushes her in unison.

Max's voice drifts into the room.

"The hell you doin' here?"

There's mumbling. Footsteps. Merrin's brothers all talking at once.

Max speaks again, "Yeah, that might be for the best."

We're all staring at each other with shrugged shoulders when Casey comes bounding into the kitchen.

"Auntie Stevie! Auntie Stevie!" Everyone stares at the little girl calling my name and holding a bottle of something in each hand.

"There's a man at the door who said these belong to you, but Papa definitely doesn't like him. I think he's gone now."

I freeze, a crushing weight on my chest. Cece takes a few hesitant steps toward Casey.

"Umm," she says. "Is that...shampoo?"

CHAPTER
29

My eyes narrow in on the bottles in Casey's hand. Shampoo in one, conditioner in the other. *My* shampoo and conditioner.

"Mason," I breathe.

A somber stillness falls on the kitchen, with the exception of Merrin, who gasps and claps her hands, bouncing on the balls of her feet.

My eyes dart to hers. "I thought you were just toying with the idea of giving him my number!"

Her smile turns into a grimace. "Okay, but what if after I heard you talking with Mom, I went a little crazy and reached out to him and said you *might* be willing to hear him out if he still wanted a chance? And then I gave him your number *and* the address here?"

I try to speak, but no words come out. I turn toward the front of the house, then back to Merrin, then back to the door. "I..."

"Well?" Merrin urges. "What's your choice here, Stevie?"

I rush in for a quick hug and kiss her temple. "I love my meddling little sister."

She bounces, pushing me away, then clapping again. "Go, go, *go!*"

Max stands near the front door, his sons and sons-in-law grouped behind him, a sea of crossed arms and sour faces.

"No liars allowed," Max says.

My heart swells. "You're such a good dad, Max. I think my parents would be so grateful to you. To *all* of you. But this is a conversation I need to have."

Max grunts.

"Please. I need you to trust me on this."

He uncrosses his arms. "Fine, but if he leaves you crying, we're burying a body today."

All the men nod.

I run to Max for a quick hug before I fling the door open, stepping onto the front porch in time to see Mason turning his car around. He's *leaving?* My heart sinks.

"Little storm rollin' in," Lucy hollers behind me. "Grab a jacket, *please.*"

I find a pair of irrigation boots to step into and call it good. Despite the heaviness of the too-big boots, I run after Mason's car yelling, "Wait!" and flailing my arms.

Much like the day I met him, I'm not sure what I'll say if he stops. I just know with absolute certainty I want him to.

The mud-caked Outback comes to a halt as Mason spots me in the rearview mirror. The wind is picking up as he steps out to face me.

Just the sight of him takes my breath away; that much hasn't changed. I scan him up and down, letting this image sink in. His dark-washed jeans and fitted tee, which he's paired with a blazer—an odd choice in this heat. His hair reaches past his chin now, but his beard is gone. He *shaved.* I haven't seen him without at least stubble since November. There's a heavy exhaustion behind his chocolate eyes one doesn't attain from mere lack of sleep, and his normally tan complexion is lighter, as though he's been hiding from the sun. Still, to my eyes, he's perfect.

"Hi," I manage.

"Hi," he returns, and his deep voice still lights a fire inside me I can't extinguish. Not even with all the animosity I've hoarded for him these last few months.

A heavy raindrop hits my head, followed by another on my bare shoulder.

"So. My shampoo?"

No response.

"Do you expect me to believe that you drove an hour and a half to drop off some toiletries and be on your merry way?"

"You look..." The wind begins to howl. "You look good. Great. Amazing, actually. That dress..." he says, gesturing to me. "It's... You're beautiful."

I look down at my floral print sundress Merrin insisted I wear this morning. *We should dress up for the party,* she said. *It'll be fun!* Now that I think of it, she's chosen my wardrobe and styled my hair these last several days. She said it was to make up for a month of wearing nothing but dirty work clothes and pajamas—a *fashion cleanse,* she called it. Really, she's been hoping Mason would show. His blazer and freshly shaven face take on a whole new meaning. That sneaky little minx. She didn't just get him here. She made sure he came *groomed.*

"You're so *tan,*" he says, studying me with an expression somewhere between amused and bewildered.

"Why'd you really come, Mason?"

"Would you rather come sit in the car?" he asks. "It's starting to rain."

"So? It's a thousand degrees. It'll be fine." Rain starts pit-patting around me. I ignore it, along with the wind, now howling with more determination.

"Stevie, you're getting soaked."

"Your point?" A small branch flies off a tree only a few feet away. "It won't last."

"Look, your tenacity is noted. Would you just get out of the wind and the rain? Then we'll talk."

"Fine!" I throw up my hands, then motion for him to follow as I run under the carport for cover. Heavy rain pelts the sheet metal above us. "Happy now?"

He gestures to me again, shaking his head. "You look so...strong. Before now, I wouldn't have pictured you on a farm. But it makes sense. You can do anything. Why not this?"

"I handle it alright," I say. "I can drive a tractor. And back up a trailer without killing anyone. I'm basically a professional now."

He laughs. How I've missed that laugh.

I start to smile, then quit. "Stop distracting me! Did you honestly come here to give me shampoo, or did you have something you wanted to say?"

He stares at the ground, scuffing his shoe back and forth in the dirt.

"Well?" I demand.

"Yes, alright!" He throws his hands in the air, meeting my gaze. "Yes, I came here to bring you that stupid shampoo. It's just sitting in my shower. I forgot to give it to Merrin when she came for your stuff. At first, it was nice having it there. It was a reminder. It smelled like you. It gave me hope that you might come back. But now? Now it just *reminds* me of you. All the time. I can't take it. I see it every day, and every day it just makes me miss you. It just makes me think of the whole reason it's there in the first place. Remember?"

Of course, I do, but I can't do anything but swallow the knife in my throat.

"Valentine's Day," he continues. "I had this epic date planned. Instead, Daniel threw up all over you."

"I remember," I mumble, barely audible.

"Anyone else would have gagged or run away. You just...*handled* it. You stuck around, got cleaned up. You smelled like my soap, and my pajamas about swallowed you whole, and the three of us watched cartoons in bed. Danny fell asleep between us. It was a perfect picture."

"I remember," I say again, a little louder.

"The next time you came over, you brought that shampoo, some clothes."

"Just in case," I finish.

He nods. "Just in case."

"You think I've just forgotten it all?"

"I don't know. Maybe. The point is I look at those bottles in my shower each day, and it's starting to make it really hard to function. So, if you're not coming back to me, then *please* take it back." He pauses, taking a deep breath and raking his hands through his hair.

The rain thrums steadily against the roof. I listen to it a moment, attempting to find my own rhythm. "You could have tossed it," I offer.

He shrugs, a boyish grin on his lips. "I know how you hate waste."

I cough a laugh, then roll my eyes. "Okay. So, you came here to what? Drop it off and run away? Without a word? Without even *looking* at me?"

His eyes soften, and he takes a small step toward me. "No. That wasn't the plan. But I panicked. I didn't realize the whole family was here. Merrin conveniently left that part out. Max looked at me like I was Satan, and I felt ashamed. Embarrassed. I planned to go for a drive, practice what I might say to you for the thousandth time, and come back."

I crease my brow, nodding. "So, this was your *prepared* speech?"

"Ha! No. Not even close. I forgot every word the second I saw you."

My chest grows warm, and I fight to suppress a smile.

"I have no right to ask your forgiveness, but I came here to ask it anyway. In the worst, most roundabout way possible, I guess."

A gust of wind blows debris against the carport, and we both flinch.

After a long lull, Mason asks, "Do we get a second act here, Stevie?"

I don't know how to respond. Instead, I ask, "What was so epic about it?"

He squints. "What?"

"The Valentine's Day date? What did you have planned?"

He shakes his head. "You don't want to know. You'll be crushed."

I roll my eyes. "Now you *have* to tell me."

He winces. "You remember how Hadestown was in town that week?"

I gasp. "Shut the front door. *No.*"

"I swear, I had tickets. *Great* tickets."

"Ugh. You're right. I didn't want to know that."

"It'll come back," he says. After a beat, he takes another step closer. "I did a horrible thing and I'm sorry. After all you'd already been through, I added to that heaping pile of disappointment. You trusted me, and I betrayed you. I hate myself for it."

When my eyes swim, I hang my head, staring at the dirt.

"Would it make you feel better to hear what a miserable, useless mess I am? That I can't sleep or make the simplest decisions? It's all true. I'm pathetic without you, and I miss you so damn much." He pauses momentarily. "We both do."

I jerk my head up. "Don't you *dare* bring him into this."

My breath hitches in my throat as my first tears fall. The rain lightens into a subtle dribble. The wind mellows. I keep my volume, though there's no longer a storm to yell over.

"You know it nearly killed me to walk away from him. I was ready to be his mother, dammit! Leaving him hurt like hell and it *still* does. So don't you come here and throw shampoo bottles at me and try to make me feel guilty! There's nothing you could say that could possibly make me feel any worse. We were supposed to be a *family,* Mason. He trusted me and loved me and I had to let him go." I pause, covering my mouth, reeling myself back from the ledge. "Every day, I think about him and how I failed him. He must hate me."

"He doesn't hate you at all. He hates me."

"What?"

"He's a smart kid," Mason says. "He knows it's all my fault. You'd think that a kid his age would be a little more resilient, but he's stuck in that place where he misses you, and he's mad at me. He's actually been with my parents for the last week and has no desire to come home. I offered him a puppy. A *puppy*. He didn't even flinch."

"And I'm supposed to feel at fault for this?"

"No!" Then softer, "No. I guess I just came here to see if it was really over. If we have a shot at making it work again or if you despise me and my chances are indefinitely blown."

I chew on my lip, unresponsive. I've been asking myself the same question for days and haven't been able to come up with an answer.

"Looks like you were right," he says. "The storm did pass."

He glances at the sun peeking through the clouds, then back to me, closing more distance between us. Hints of shaving cream and pine breeze toward me, and my knees shake at the flood of memories accompanying them. Kisses after dark. Saturdays cuddled on the couch, listening to music and reading while Daniel colored. Guitar lessons where I couldn't focus on anything other than the way Mason's hair fell over his face when he played. Singing harmony to his smooth, pitch-perfect melody.

"So, there's no chance we could just," he takes a deep breath, "start over? Is there?"

I shake my head, sniffling. "No." I attempt to wipe my face with my hands; I have no sleeves. *Stupid dress.* "No, I don't think we should do that."

"Oh," he whispers. As his eyes glisten, he hangs his head and takes a step backward. "Wow..."

"I said I didn't want to start over," I yell. "Not that I didn't want to start *somewhere*."

His head snaps up. "So? You're saying?"

"I don't hate you, Mason. I've tried. I've tried so hard."

The tension visibly leaving his body, he wipes his eyes. "You don't?"

"Of course not, you idiot!" I pause, collecting myself. "I love you, dammit. And I miss you so much it...it *aches*. It's like I haven't been breathing all this time. Not really. And this..." I gesture between us. "You being so close and not holding me? It's hell, and I hate it." He reaches for me, but I hold up my hand. "Is she gone? I mean, completely gone and out of your life forever?"

He nods, holding a palm to his chest. "I swear. Everything is final. The divorce. The termination of her parental rights. She won't bother us anymore. I changed my number, and as far as I know, she doesn't have our address. But if you're uncomfortable risking it, I'll sell the house, and we'll move. Not even kidding."

"You can't hurt me like that again, Mase," I say, my voice faltering.

"Never."

"I mean, you're bound to say or do something stupid and hurt my feelings. And I'll likely drive you insane with my *tenacious* willpower." He smirks. "That's normal. That's life. But there can't be any giant secrets or underground plots, alright? You can't ever hide things like that from me. We can't be a team if you shut me out."

He closes the distance between us; this time, I let him. "Stevie, if I could go back, I'd do it all so differently. I'd tell you from the beginning how I felt about you, but that my life was a mess, and I needed time. I'd let you be part of that fight. But..."

"But you can say that now because you know how it plays out," I say. "You have Danny, and he's safe with you. I know you were scared. I know. I hate that you went through that."

"It doesn't excuse what I did," he whispers. "I screwed up *so* bad, and I can't go back and change it. But if you let me..." His hand cups my cheek, leaving me an unsteady mess of butterflies and knots. "If you let me, I swear I'll spend the rest of my life making it up to you."

I reach up, grabbing his wrist. "No, you won't. Basing this relationship on the notion that you're indebted to me would be a disaster neither of us deserves. I don't want that."

He drops his forehead against mine. "Then what do you want, Stevie Rae?"

With a slow inhale, I place both hands against his chest. "I want to put it behind me and move on. With you. I want you to tell me you still love me. That we're going to be alright. I want to put on that dress that's been mocking me from the closet and marry the hell out of you."

We both laugh, and Mason gathers his hands at the base of my spine.

"I want to pick up Danny from your parents' house, go home

with you, and never leave. Let's be a family. Let's *make* a family. I don't want to waste any more time." My voice breaks.

"We won't," he promises, pulling me close. "Never again."

"I'm sorry I ran away. I just…"

He hushes me and holds me tighter. "We're gonna be alright, Stevie. I love you." He clutches the fabric of my dress. "I love you so much, it's ridiculous."

I laugh through a sob.

"Come back to me," he pleads. "Marry me."

"Yeah," I breathe, nodding. "Absolutely."

I melt as his familiar lips find mine. He adjusts his grip, lifting me up. I wrap my legs around his waist.

"One more thing," I say, pausing the kiss. "I'd like my ring back. You know, when you have a chance."

"Left pocket," he whispers.

"You're kidding?"

"You think I'd come all this way to try and win you back without it? Give me *some* credit, babe."

He shifts my weight around, both of us awkwardly trying to get the ring from his pocket. We nearly collapse in a heap of juvenile laughter. After a lengthy struggle, he slips the ring onto my finger.

"That's better," I tease and kiss him again. When the oversized boots fall off, I lock my ankles around him, and we hold each other closer.

The pitter-patter of little feet threatens our privacy.

"Auntie Stevie! Auntie Stevie!"

Angry moms threaten pain of death upon their children if they don't return to the house immediately.

I sigh, turning to watch for intruders. Mason kisses my cheek, then my neck. It sends an involuntary shudder down my spine, and I arch into him.

"Okay," I whisper, "So maybe we pick up Danny *tomorrow*."

He sputters a laugh as Casey and Julia—Arwin's oldest—come into view, skipping through fresh mud puddles. "We want to open presents!" they call, closing in. When they reach the carport, they freeze.

"Can I help you?" I ask.

Julia contorts her face. "Aunt Stevie? What are you doing?"

"You're the man from the door!" Casey says. "Who are you? And why are you holding my Aunt Stevie like she's a baby?"

I glance at Mason, pondering a moment. "This is your Uncle Mason."

"How come we don't know him?"

"Casey! Julia! You get your behinds back here now or I will throw your presents into the fireplace, you hear?" It's typically timid Arwin screaming into the wind, which gets the girls' attention. They sprint back toward the house.

"Uncle Mason, huh?" he asks, smirking.

"Soon enough," I say. "Besides. Just listen." I hold my finger towards the sky, biting my lip. After a moment, cheers erupt from the house. "*Aaaaaand* scene."

"Are they happy or gathering the mob?"

"Max might have mixed feelings. But on the whole, I'm sure they're happy. They're beyond sick of my wallowing." I kiss him briefly, then pull back. "You realize you're going to have to get Danny a puppy now, don't you?"

Mason cringes. "Yeah. I know. You think we're up for that? Training a dog?"

"Nu-uh. This one's all on you, babe. You played that card, you clean up the poop."

"That's fair," he sighs.

"Oh, lighten up. I'll help. We'll figure it out."

"Yeah?"

"Sure. For every Broadway production you take me to, I'll do..." I twist my lips, tilting my head back and forth. "One week of dog duty."

"How generous," he says through a laugh.

"Two, if it's the original cast."

"She's a *saint*, ladies and gentlemen," he chides. "What about other live music?"

"Hmm, that depends on how highly I rank the musicians. And whether it's general admission or balcony."

He laughs, planting kisses on my neck until I squeal and call for a truce.

"Let's go home, Mason," I say gently, brushing his hair back, resting my forehead against his. "Please. Take me home."

"Anything you want, Stevie Rae. As always... Anything."

EPILOGUE

Spring

"One more?"

"Sweetheart, you're so sleepy. *I'm* so sleepy. It's been a long day."

"Please, Mama?" Daniel's hopeful blue eyes blink up at me as I brush a curl from his forehead.

"One more, baby," I say, caving. I think he's learned his *please, Mamas* are my weakness. Regardless, I'll always give him one more song. "*The sun is playing hide and seek. The man in the moon is sleeping...*"

I think my mother is happy knowing I'm passing on her song to the next generation. That those words she used for me so long ago, I now sing to my son. A bittersweet reminder of how precious and uncertain our lives are. That's why I'll always give him *one more.* One more hug. One more kiss. One more song. I'll always oblige because I never know which time might be the last time.

"*...but Daniel's still not sleeping.*"

He smiles at the sound of his name, as always.

I kiss his cheek, then his forehead, gently twirling his curly locks around my finger.

"This was the best day ever," he says.

"It was pretty great," I agree through a yawn. "You have fun with your cousins?"

"Can they come back again tomorrow?"

I laugh. "Not tomorrow, pumpkin. They're leaving from

Gramma and Grampa's first thing in the morning. They've got a long ride home. But we'll see them again next month at the cabin."

"How many days is that?"

"About thirty."

"How many weeks is that?"

"About four."

"How many hours?"

"*Daniel*," I intone. He grins. "Get some sleep, bug. I love you."

"I love you, Mom," he whispers, settling further into his sheets and closing his eyes. I'd been *Mama Stevie* for approximately five minutes before he dropped the *Stevie*. Even after all these months, every whisper, giggle, or cry of *Mama* or *Mom* fills my cup.

I'm almost out the door when his sleepy voice floats across the room.

"Roscoe loves you, too. He just told me."

Our rescue retriever mutt, curled at the foot of Daniel's mattress, lifts his head at the sound of his name.

"I love Roscoe, too," I assure them both. The dog sighs as his head relaxes back into place. We adopted Roscoe back in November, and he is absolutely not allowed on the furniture. Except when he follows Daniel to bed and situates himself at Daniel's feet and looks at me with a promise in his eyes that no harm will ever befall *his* boy. Not while he's around.

It's the equivalent of Daniel's *Please, Mama*. You just can't argue with it.

"Goodnight, boys," I whisper, touching my fingers to my lips. I leave the door open just a crack, just the way Daniel likes it, and make my way downstairs.

I find Mason in the kitchen, his sleeves rolled up to his elbows, loading the dishwasher. Most of the evidence from today's festivities have vanished, save the bouquet on the counter and a *Congrats, Grad* balloon floating along the ceiling.

"You're so sexy when you do that," I say as I come up behind him, slipping my arms around his waist.

"Yeah?"

"Hell yeah."

He presses *start* and turns around. "What's sexier?" he asks, reaching up to tuck my hair behind my ears. "Dishes, or home renovation?"

I wince at his allusion to our current basement remodel, which isn't going according to plan. I keep Daniel upstairs when Wes comes over to help Mason with wiring or plumbing, ensuring little ears don't learn colorful new words. Sometimes *Murphy* just doesn't cut it.

"All the things, my love," I answer. "All the things are sexy on you."

"Called it." He flashes a brief smirk before kissing me. "So, Miss Summa Cum Laude, how's it feel?"

"Like I still have two years left," I whine. "Probably longer. I doubt I'll be able to keep a full course load next year."

"You don't *have* to take the job, you know."

"But I *want* the job," I say. With my associate's degree, I meet the requirements for lead teacher at Bright Beginnings, and the toddler room teacher just retired. While they probably would've preferred someone who already had their bachelor's, I think helping Marge apply for the grant allowing the center to purchase new classroom instruments gave me a leg up. It's possible she might have hired me either way, but I guess I'll never know. I just know fall semester is going to be an exhausting learning experience.

"I'm so friggin' proud of you," Mason says, his hands sliding under my shirt.

"Well, I'm proud of you, Mr. Five-Year Contract." Is it weird that he's a professor at EWC now? No, but only because I'm not in any I.T. classes. Thank goodness.

"Look at us. Kicking all sorts of ass."

I smile as my fingers hook the belt loops of his jeans, pulling him closer.

"You must be wiped," he says. "Ready for bed?"

I wrinkle my nose, my lips inching toward his. "Not quite."

"Excellent."

Clothes scattered across the floor, a mess of blankets enveloping us, Mason and I lie tangled together on the couch. My head rests on his chest as he gently strokes my back. Wherever I look, I'm home. This is where I belong. Not just in Mason's arms, but *here*. This is my place.

From the shoes by the doorway, to the laundry piles in the hall, to the crayons on the coffee table, to the massive canvas above the fireplace—our favorite family photo taken at the wedding merely three weeks after we reconciled. Our backyard ceremony was simple, quiet, and absolutely perfect.

The portrait reflects every ounce of joy and beauty from that day. Mason and me, side by side, Daniel sitting on a stool in front of us, an adorable bowtie around his collar. We'd wrapped him in a hug, all of us laughing at one of his clever quips. A perfect picture of an imperfect family.

The transition hasn't been seamless, but I wouldn't change any of it. Not even this new life growing inside of me.

We never expected it to happen so soon. We'd taken precautions to make *sure* it didn't happen. The doctor nearly had to drag us both up off the floor when she assured me blood tests didn't lie; this is definitely *not* just a nasty, never ending stomach bug.

Once we'd processed the news that someone has a plan for us that transcends *the pill*, we cried with equal parts elation and terror.

"You feeling alright?" he asks, his lips pressed to the top of my head.

"It's not so bad right now. Just tired." The anti-nausea meds always make me drowsy, compounding the constant exhaustion of the first trimester. Twelve weeks along, and I've been rundown and nauseated every single minute of it. Still, no regrets.

"I'm sorry." He kisses my forehead. "Maybe the couch was a bad idea."

"Living dangerously," I murmur, and he laughs.

"It was a risk," he admits.

"It paid off. Danny's still asleep. You got lucky. Everyone wins."

I yawn, adjusting myself so I'm sandwiched between Mason and the couch, my arm draped across his chest, our legs woven together.

"This is never a bad idea," I assure him. "Though I might have to crawl up the stairs."

"Sexy."

Another involuntary yawn escapes. "If I'm this wiped now, how will I manage the stairs in six months?" How will I manage *anything* in six months? *One day at a time, Stevie. One day at a time.*

"We'll get a sled for you and a harness for Roscoe. He can pull you around."

"Flawless plan, professor." My words begin to slur together. My eyelids grow heavy.

"Come on," Mason says. "Let's get you to bed."

I tighten my grip on him as he begins to adjust.

"Don't," I protest. "I'm comfy. Besides, I'll wake up in an hour to pee anyway. I can go to bed then."

He laughs, then kisses my forehead again. "Fair point."

"Night, Mase," I mumble. "Love you."

And I do. I love this man.

This man, who's turning the basement into a next-level music room that'll double as a legitimate recording studio, and indulges me anytime I suggest we learn a new instrument. This man, who's had my back every step of the way as I've navigated school and work. This incredible man, who forgoes any plans he had for the evening, carefully reaching for the remote and lounging on the couch because *I'm* comfortable.

This man, who every night waits until I'm right on the cusp of slumber to whisper, "I love you, Stevie Rae," so it's the last thing I hear before falling asleep.

ACKNOWLEDGMENTS

At the risk of sounding vain, I'd like to first acknowledge my younger self. Season One Me, as I like to call her. She took risks, made horrible mistakes, endured traumatic letdowns, and lived to tell the tale. Eventually.

In its original form, A SONG I USED TO KNOW was an entirely different story. I honestly never intended to share it with anyone. It was simply an outlet. I examined life experience, spun it, embellished the heck out of it, and created fiction.

After *many* years tucked away on the shelf, I felt I'd gained enough life experience and perspective to resurrect this story, re-write it, and pursue publication. There have been many times throughout this process where I questioned my abilities (and my sanity), and I wanted to tuck this story away and forget about it.

To those of you who didn't let me quit: Jenny, Kate, Karinna, Carissa, Rachel, Linda, & Melissa. Ladies, whenever I began spiraling about this story, you gave me hope. You were my hype women, my early readers, my sounding boards, my dose of reality, my shoulders to cry on, my everything. I wouldn't be here without you. Thank you. I love you.

A huge thanks to Julia. You held me accountable, pushed me to do better, and helped me transform this book into what it is now.

My love, my cheerleader, Brett. Thank you for always listening and reminding me of all the good things when all I could see were the bad ones. You are the *best* hype man, and I'm so lucky to have you.

To my four little loves: Thank you for teaching me patience and grace. Thank you for being feisty and fiery and forcing me to do better in all the things, always. You give Mommy all the anxiety but you also give me all the joy.

I wasn't prepared for how difficult it was going to be to edit and publish my second novel, and I am so grateful to everyone who helped cheer me on and get me through this process. I couldn't have done it without you.

ABOUT THE AUTHOR

Genalea is a sleep-deprived mom and —somehow—the author of three books: *Life After, A Song I Used to Know,* and *Lovehurts* (2024). Her work has appeared with *Broad River Review, WOW! Women on Writing, Watershed Review, Gemini Magazine, The Bookends Review,* and more. She resides in Southern Idaho with her husband, four children, and two judgmental dogs. Should you ever need to find Genalea in a crowd, simply shout a line from an early 2000s emo song and she'll be sure to answer back.

This has been an
Immortal Production

Printed in the USA
CPSIA information can be obtained
at www.ICGtesting.com
LVHW051840020124
767808LV00038B/379